WELSH PEARS

By Joel Robbins

Welsh Pears
By Joel Robbins

No portion of this publication may be reproduced, stored in any electric system, or transmitted in any form or by any means, electronic, mechanical, photocopy, recording or otherwise, without the written permission of the publisher.

ISBN # 978-0-9824703-4-3
Copyright 2011, 2013
Joel H Robbins

Publisher
Robbins Books
Nokomis, Florida 34275

Printed in the United States by Morris Publishing®
3212 East Highway 30
Kearney, NE 68847
1-800-650-7888

Acknowledgments

Thanks go to:
- My wife Sara for inspiring my writing and helping me edit.
- Alice Stollenmeyer for providing much-appreciated grammar and editing advice.
- Daughter Kristin Steffen for giving me some perspective about writing about a younger generation.
- Son Mason Robbins for discussions about writing as he began a book of his own.
- Nancy Nelson for providing feedback concerning character development and plot.
- Karl Keiper of Wayseekers for providing the ISBN number.

Author's Note

No person living or dead is portrayed as a character in *Welsh Pears*. My wife read a first draft and immediately thought she identified a character based on a friend of ours. It's hard for me to believe too, but I didn't have any individuals I know in mind when I created my characters. If you think I have based one of the characters on you, Dear Reader, you may suffer from a guilty conscious or excessive-extrapolation-syndrome, as I do. During sermons I feel the minister is addressing me and my sins personally. When I took Psych 101, every chapter was about me. I guess I'm an accomplished sinner and a complete lunatic.

Don't assume that all the opinions expressed in *Welsh Pears* are my opinions. I love to discuss an issue from one point of view just to test a theory. That way I learn a lot from hearing people defend their beliefs. Plus, playing devil's advocate can be more fun than simply agreeing with the majority, the fastest talker or the loudest. I have to continue to remind myself that being politically correct does not mean correct.

Book I

Chapter 1. Blind-Man's Puzzle

It looked like someone had glued a black box to the side of his skull. His head was turned to the left and slightly tilted upward. His eyes were glazed and focused on an invisible yet moving spider on the ceiling.

"What are you doing?" Sam Jones asked of Duke Preston as Sam walked right through the outside doorway and into the kitchen. The room was sparse. The floors throughout Duke's house were all real wood, but not fussily kept. There were gouges where an ax had slipped out of his hand and hit the floor, spots of grease near the stove, wine stains beneath a wooden chair and below benches in the living room, and other indications of the bachelor life of an outdoorsman.

There were curtains only in the bathroom and the bedrooms, and no colorful pillows on beds and benches. Several pipes and ashtrays were strategically placed around the house, even in the bathroom.

Outside, the lawn wasn't mowed because Duke didn't own a lawn mower. He liked the way nature decorated and didn't want to give the natural plants in the yard a military crew cut. Therefore a variety of wildflowers took turns blooming all summer, and the bees and hummingbirds were always in evidence. It was early September, so the weather in Wyandotte, Kentucky, was still hot.

"What?"

"*What's* what I asked you, Duke."

"Uh, sorry. I was concentrating."

"Obviously. You look like a safe cracker practicing on a kid's 'piggy' bank—a macabre piggybank."

"It's a blind man's puzzle."

The box was approximately 8 inches on each edge and flat black. The box maker likened its size to a square softball. He was one of Duke's best friends and didn't mind using *square* and *ball* in the same description of a single object. Duke liked him just because his mind worked that way.

"Okay, are you going to tell me why you have a box growing out of your ear?"

"It's a puzzle. You put a ball bearing into this green start hole and try to work it through a three-dimensional maze so that it comes out of the farthest hole, which is white."

"You're taking notes?"

"Just trying to solve the mystery of the blind-man's box."

"Sounds like a suspense novel. *The Mystery of the Blind Man's Box.*"

"Yeah, it does. My friend makes them for fun and lets me try solving them before they go into a dark closet forever?"

"He doesn't sell them? They're kind of nicely done." Sam seemed surprised.

"No, he says since nothing explodes, you don't get to beat someone up or shoot them, and there's no scantily clad girls popping up, the puzzles wouldn't be popular with today's gamers," answered Duke.

"You're right. I can't see someone sitting quietly for hours with a tissue box to their ear."

"I love them."

"You're also a pipe smoker. I had a boss that said he'd never hire a man who smoked a pipe, because they tend to be slow and deliberate. You know; think before they act. Not easy to boss because they will question and be curious about everything."

"Who said that?"

"See. Like you. I'm sure he would also say not to hire people who spend hours with a blind-man's puzzle against their temple."

"You have to listen to the bearing roll, drop onto different baffles, bounce off walls and pivot."

"And where's the fun?"

"I think this one has a half-spiral stairs going one direction while a half spiral ramp on the other side goes the opposite direction. Listen. Maybe it's a double helix."

"That's okay. You go ahead. I'm not really interested."

"Really? It's a challenge and I have to give the ball back to my friend by next week. We always bet. I'm 2 for 7. I need this one."

"Just pour it out of the green hole and tell him it came out of the white one."

"Can't. The first thing I noticed about the box was it has a one-way spring door, like a check valve in plumbing. I have to go on."

Bark, Duke's dog, had been looking from one man to the other as the conversation jumped back and forth. Finally he could tell that they weren't going hiking or fishing, so he lay his head back down and went to sleep at Duke's feet.

"Got any beer? I'll drink a PBR and watch as you stick your ear into the white hole and gaze at the ceiling. My observing a person observing a bug on the ceiling has got to be at least as entertaining as what you're doing."

"Okay. Get me a beer too, and I'll finish the puzzle later. Your conversation had better be above par, though. So, how's the cell phone business?"

"Probably more exciting than being a civil engineer."

"What should we talk about?"

"Women."

Chapter 2. Back in the Game

"Why am I unmarried? I'm not over thirty, dirty, ugly or bitchy. I make a good living teaching junior and senior high school history. I pay my bills, drink in moderation, go to church, don't talk too much and volunteer summers as a TESL tutor. I'm active, slim, well, a little skinny, and fun-loving," Madison Wentworth whispered as she looked at her reflection in the sliding glass door of her second-story apartment. She wasn't smiling.

Her body *was* slim and she had a tendency to wear black, which made her look thinner. She would probably fall right on the norm on a doctor's weight chart, but, because many people were ten to fifty pounds above that, she looked skinny in comparison. Her hair was brown, complexion dark, and eyes, well, it was hard to describe her eyes. Everyone noticed and commented on them.

She tended to walk as if she had a book balanced on her head, which caused her to look a little stiff and gave the impression that her personality was severe. Nothing could have been further from reality. She loved people but hated much of human nature, especially cruelty and greed.

Having no children, almost everything she thought of doing was to prepare her for teaching her students. She traveled and took pictures to show her students. She read books that she thought would give her more background on civilization. For the same reason, she watched the History and Discovery channels when she really wanted to watch a sitcom or movie on TV.

Walking to her desk, Madison flipped up the lid of her laptop and checked to see if anyone had responded to her profile on backinthegame.com. The site was for those out of the game because of breakups of marriages or affairs that wanted to start dating again. Madison had tried all the other dating services without luck, so she was trying this one.

Her profile read: "*Attractive female under thirty seeks long-term relationship and/or marriage. Loves to hike, camp, fish, picnic, take long walks and spend lazy afternoons on the beach. No debt, no kids. Plays tennis, reads mysteries and loves to cook. Good sense of humor and even tempered. – Teacher Madison*"

She had tried honesty, but was now claiming to love the outdoors as most of her online competitors did. She looked at her email IN box, which had five responses: Duke, Elmo, Alonzo, Dallas and William.

Duke wrote: "Hey, sweetheart, let's go fishing. What kind a pole you got? Tell me what and I'll bring your favorite live bait and beer."

Oops. Madison felt trapped already. She didn't own and never had owned fishing equipment and couldn't image herself running a sharp object into or through a slimy, squirmy and lively bait.

Elmo: "Hey, babe, let's get it on Friday. Like to party? Send me your cell no."

Alonzo: "Can you cook Tex-Mex? If so, invite me over some night. I'll show you a good time."

William: "How about a walk on the beach, followed by a picnic, reading aloud from a book of poems, popping a cork of bubbly, and getting to know each other? I'm a good listener."

Dallas: "I won't lie. I'm lookin' to hook up with someone this weekend. You free? Your house or mine?"

Her experience from corresponding with those giving similar responses clued her in on what they were like:

Duke--Nice but boring good-ole-boy in Nascar T-shirt.

Elmo--Stalker all in black.

Alonzo--Leach in chinos and skin-tight pastel long-sleeved knit shirt.

William--Liar with Dockers and polo shirt.

Dallas--Bully wearing a wife-beater shirt.

While Madison was on the computer she decided that she would finish and send another letter to the editor of the *Wyandotte Times*. She had been writing anonymous letters regularly to purge herself of the disappointment she felt about how schools were run.

Schools, Please Get Out of the Educational 'Snake Oil' Business

I can think of few things that waste teachers' time and school funds more than "new" teaching techniques, strategies and initiatives. People who for some reason didn't want to continue teaching students in the classroom often come up with WOW, BAM, SNAP, CRACKLE and POP to make a living.

The programs often utilize acronyms, such as POP (Pupils On Point or something like that), to make some old idea sound new. Jargon works too. "Collaborative and holistic methodologies for integration of performance-based modular benchmark assessment." If there were such a program, it would probably simply mean that teachers test kids' knowledge.

Administrators often embrace these "new" programs thanks to a colleague, "You're not using POP!"

For more than a hundred years, expensive educational snake oil claims, just like modern claims on infomercials, have promised to cure educational woes and make students angels and scholars. Sorry, teachers know otherwise, but administrators keep hoping there's an easy answer. There's not. To mix a few metaphors, the snap, crackle and pop of an old program dressed in new clothes turns out to be a big FIZZLE after a couple of years and is dropped.

Desk Weary

The Times must have liked her periodic ranting because it let her exceed its 150 word limit. After slipping the letter into an envelope and addressing it, she decided to crawl under her afghan and read some more of Stendhal's *The Red and the Black*. She loved the boy-meets-girl-boy-loses-girl subplots, which were numerous. She couldn't keep her mind on the plot, though. She kept thinking about the emails from backinthegame.com.

She made a rash decision. She would go out with one of these five men. In the past she would pick one at a time and trade emails with him until she found something that let her respectfully eliminate him. This time, she decided, she would pick one, email, and then meet.

But which one? She wrote their names on five orange Post-Its, folded and sealed each, and mixed them up on the table before her. She held her hand over the papers for a second and then picked the one in the middle.

Chapter 3. Wyandotte

The town of Wyandotte boasted on the signs at main entrances to the city limits that it was: "Progressive, Industrious and Friendly." The town sat in the Wyandotte Valley, with the Kananee River running precisely through the middle. The old part of town had attractive tree-lined streets and two-story houses. The subdivisions at the edge of town tended to feature single-story, smaller and more modest houses because Wyandotte hadn't been as progressive and industrious as *form/from, costumer/customer* and *access/assess*. Semordnilaps, such as *nab/ban* and *pad/dap*, were also problems

The spell checker on Word didn't help her solve the problem, so she found a list of homonyms on the Internet, printed it and then double checked for errors at home. She added other trouble words to the list as she discovered them. She never let anyone in the office see her do this.

One time Franklin's wife read a Cali-typed flyer and called Franklin immediately. Cali had typed: "You can expect the best form The Wright Insurance, because hour agents are prose. That's Wright, their's no ifs, ands or butts about it, where the best in the business." Luckily most people who read the flyer thought since the company's name was a pun, all of the "errors" were intentional and clever attention-getters.

Cali was working furiously, because Franklin was on his way over, and she wanted the letters in hiding and ready to take to the office tomorrow.

The sweat was beading on her upper lip, but her bare feet felt cold. "Do you really love me, Franklin? Then when are you going to get a divorce and ask me to marry you?" is what she planned to ask tonight. She dabbed the perspiration from her lip and continued finishing the letters. If he gave the right answer, he was going to get the best romp in the sack ever.

Chapter 6. Goodie-Goodie

The person who did everything right. That was most people's description of Mrs. Ardnas Wright, often called Miss Ardnas by her college students. Most forgot that the Eurasian name Ardnas was her Christian name and not her surname. Eventually, in the style of the American South, she became Miss Ardnas to everyone she knew.

In high school a few called her a goodie-goodie, which should have been a compliment but is usually delivered as a cruel epithet. She was the class salutatorian, Speech Club president, member of Honor Society, treasurer for Volunteers for Good, and number one on the tennis team. Unlike her husband Franklin Wright, she didn't have IT, but she had everything else.

She graduated from Silverton State University *Cum Laude* with majors in Russian and political science and stayed to complete a combined Masters/Doctorate in international relations.

She married Franklin immediately after she graduated, and they produced two children, a boy, who was now 10, and a girl, now 7. Her parental duties only allowed her to teach part-time as an adjunct lecturer in the social science department at Wyandotte University.

Light brown hair, aqua eyes, shapely body and no overpowering features made her an ideal specimen of femininity. Rival Cali, on the other hand, possessed oversized lips, eyes, cups and hips, which were sexy at first glance but just short of gross upon closer scrutiny. Cali's physiognomy would have been nearly perfect for a stage actress, because her features would still be distinct from the balcony, and her hair was so light platinum it startled many who saw her for the first time.

The smooth-haired, brunette Miss Ardnas had put on a little extra weight after having two children, but she was still shapely and sexy. She was working on the weight issue. Her subtle but most attractive features were creases at both the edges of her lips and eyes that turned up. Her eyes literally smiled.

She had read that girls show more skin when they are ovulating, and she thought some girls must be ovulating continuously. Miss Ardnas intentionally dressed unsexy a lot of the time during high school and even now. Loose clothing and hair pulled into some unflattering shape kept her from being hit on like the girls and women showing bare midriffs, thighs, shoulders and cleavage. She even wore slightly tinted nonprescription glasses occasionally to hide her attractive aqua eyes.

Dressing styles seemed ridiculous to Miss Ardnas when she had watched her high school classmates seated on the stage during a school convocation. The boys had dressed in T-shirts and jeans, socks and sneakers and sat comfortably. The girls on the other hand had been squirming to pull down their hemlines, pull up their necklines, check their midriffs and adjust the straps to their colorful tops. It appeared that some fairy godmother of hormones had dressed them at home without their knowledge, and they hadn't known how uncomfortable, inappropriate and overtly sexy they were dressed until they had gotten on stage at school. And these girls had often been mad at a boy who took the exposed skin "hint" and had made a pass at them.

She had been watching a news cable network show recently and noticed that gender dressing styles hadn't changed much from her high school days even for adults of her current age and time. The female anchor was showing skin from her thighs to her ankles, plus bare arms and a low neckline. She was wearing bright red. The male had on a white shirt buttoned tight to his chin--tightened further with a tie--and a black suit. That gave his arms at least two layers of heavy material and she had none. Miss Ardnas concluded sex sells even if you're pushing news.

Miss Ardnas had a few minutes before she had to attend a counseling session with her minister, so she decided to take her mind off her troubles with her blog. She loved satire and had lots of political opinions she wanted to keep secret. She used the blog to wake up some people and to test her theories.

The idea for blogging came from one of her son's teachers, Madison Wentworth, with whom she was now good friends, thanks to weekly tennis matches at the Wyandotte Racquet Club. Madison Wentworth had told Miss Ardnas about her anonymous letters to the editor, and Miss Ardnas loved the idea. The whole concept won her over to writing and publishing some anonymous opinion pieces.

Popping open www.ersatznews.blogspot.com, Miss Ardnas added a post:

Big Business Bails Out Fed

Ersatz Business News—New Albany

Ben Johnston, CEO of Amzatech, is heading up a consortium of big business leaders to bail out the fed.

"Why would capitalists ask the government to create jobs?" said Johnston.

So far 14 companies have signed on to loosen their purse strings and see that their companies expand and that more workers are hired.

Several large chains have been asked to change their ownership policies to allow for franchises. Johnston stated: "Why should one man or his family who controls a national or international business make billions and hoard it, when so many people need employment and seek to own and run businesses?"

Johnston expressed that a franchise holder would be happy to earn $60,000 or so a year, let alone millions or billions.

Some critics say it is the government's responsibility to create jobs and maintain a low unemployment rate. Johnston believes "that is nonsense. Government trying to manage employment means big government, and big government means regulations and more national debt."

Many of those who support Johnston's project say they have seen what happens when the government tries to control everything—one economic disaster after another.

"If American capitalism cannot support America's economy and provide citizens an honest wage that can maintain an adequate

standard of living without government intervention, then America's form of Capitalism is a failure. And I don't think it is," concluded Johnston.

Pressing the PUBLISH and then SAVE symbols made her feel a little light-headed. She made the entries look as much like newspaper clippings as possible, just to add a little more authority to a news item that was completely satirical.

She had had a discussion with a colleague about Capitalists' role during a downturn in the economy, and he had asked what incentive there was to invest his millions with so much uncertainty in the marketplace. She had responded: "Morality." She had quickly realized that investing in people wasn't part of his investment equation.

"Now, to prepare myself for telling Mark my most secret fears," thought Miss Ardnas. She washed her face again, brushed her teeth, applied a tiny spritz of perfume and reapplied her make up. A tug to straighten out the left leg of her pants and a few strokes with her hairbrush through her brown hair and she was physically ready. Psychologically, though, she felt like she had ping pong balls bouncing around in her stomach.

Chapter 7. No Magic

Pastor Mark Wellston's next Sunday sermon was haunting him. He had prayed, meditated, taken a ride in his velomobile, walked his dog, stared with his light blue eyes at the cross for an hour and randomly popped open his *Bible*, but no topic or passage had magically sprung to mind for this month's series. Wasn't God supposed to "speak" to him as many people in his congregation claim He did to them: "God was speaking to my heart about...' or "God told me to start...'"?

All Mark ever wanted to do from the time he was a teen and had accepted Christ as his savior was to be a minister. Now, here he was, with several years under his belt and a thriving congregation, but he wasn't happy. He knew his faith was a matter of lifelong growth, but he thought pastoring would become easier as he got experience.

His concerned face still appeared angular and rugged-looking, unlike the soft faces many people thought typified a pastor's look. He would never be considered handsome; therefore, no young lady ever gave him a second look in public. Also, he didn't own a car, so that made him suspicious in car-crazy America, but only to those who didn't know him.

He ran his fingers through his thick dark brown hair, puffed out his cheeks and let out a stream of breath heavy with concern. What dominated his thoughts was his personal theology, for which he was positive most of the congregation, if they knew, would tar and feather him and run him out of town on an altar rail.

He started cutting and pasting verses from his favorite online *Bible* source:

In the beginning was the Word, and the Word was with God, and the Word was God.

Whoever does not love does not know God, because God is love.

But be ye doers of the word, and not hearers only, deceiving your own selves.

Go, sell everything you have and give to the poor, and you will have treasure in heaven. Then come, follow me."

For God so loved the world that he gave his one and only Son, that whoever believes in him shall not perish but have eternal life.

If I have a faith that can move mountains, but do not have love, I am nothing.

But someone will say, "You have faith; I have deeds." Show me your faith without deeds, and I will show you my faith by my deeds.

Why he had picked these was clear to Mark. For him they were like an algebra equation or syllogism:
Jesus = The Word
The Word = Love
Believing in The Word = Salvation
Therefore Loving = Eternal life
God wanted us to Love in order to save the world.

Obviously, this opens salvation to loving atheists, agnostics, Muslims, Jews, Buddhists, Hindus and other religions. Mark never understood why people that claim that God is omnipotent, omniscience, and omnipresent would believe that He only loves the Jews, or Christians, or Muslims, or some other ethnic or religious group.

Mark loved Jesus but hated the hierarchies organized religions that sometimes created: youth pastors, junior pastors, senior pastors, bishops, cardinals, district superintendents, and other worldly lucrative positions. He also hated that so many churches started with a group of spiritual seekers that slowly constructed big church buildings and became "businesses" whose principal aim was raising money. While visiting churches, he was amazed how many times during announcements and sermons that "give us money" was the primary message.

He wanted to deliver a series of sermons proclaiming:
- Don't give your money to build a church; share it with someone who needs your support as they try to rise from poverty through education and hard work.
- Have "church" services in your homes, where you can search the scriptures for personal inspiration and wisdom.
- Don't spend money on evangelists on TV, Christian concerts, recording stars, religious authors, etc. who make a living from religion and therefore will not question modern dogmatic practices as Martin Luther did during his time.
- Stop following men (Luther, Menno Simons, Wesley, the Pope, Joseph Smith, and others) and start following God's model, Jesus, who walked the earth.
- Question the prosperity preachers who promise heaven on earth.

Mark realized he was being silly. No one really wanted to follow Jesus' model to live simply, love your neighbor, and share with the poor. Capitalism can't sustain itself with people who don't buy more than they need, filling their garages with items they don't use until they have to rent storage sheds for their material possessions. Earning and buying are full time, while Jesus may get one hour a week.

Looking at his watch, Mark noted that he had 45 minutes before a counseling session with Miss Ardnas Wright, who was concerned about the status of her married life. Miss Ardnas, her husband and Mark had been schoolmates growing up, so Mark was surprised that she was willing to choose him as a counselor. He looked in the mirror at his angular face and perpetual smile. He wished he could ditch the smile, but it seemed permanent, despite how he felt.

He was also delighted, because no other girl than Miss Ardnas ever fit his ideal of the girl of his dreams, as corny as that sounds. In his mind she was the one glimpsed through the trees in *Raintree County* or the heroine of *Children of the Mist*.

He felt it would be wonderful just to sit across from her a few minutes, even if it was in a professional setting. He decided to change his normal office attire, which was a dark sport jacket, jeans and Nike sneakers. They were comfortable when he had to make calls and usually were conversation starters. He loved the swoosh symbol on the side of his Nikes, which some people called a squashed drip. He slipped on a pair of black loafers and waited.

Chapter 8. Taking a Chance

Madison unstuck the Post-It. Taking a few deep breaths and blinking her gray eyes several times, she read: Elmo. NO, echoed through her head. Ok, she decided, I'll try again. William, the BSer. Ok, she thought, I'll throw each one away and keep the last one. Alonzo, then Dallas. She was stuck with Nascar Duke.

She decided to start emailing him:

"Hey, Duke. Read your profile and received your message. I lied about loving to fish, but I might learn to. Ditto with hiking. I have drunk beer, though. Is that close enough? The rest of my profile is true. I'm a history teacher. What about you? Madison"

She poked SEND.

Sometimes she wished she lived in a society similar to what Huxley described in *Brave New World*. Then she could simply be administered a "violent passion surrogate" or "pregnancy substitute" and forget all this other hormonal crazy chaos she was experiencing.

Her morning paper was lying on the table so she decided to see if anyone responded to her letter to the editor.

Yes, there were two:

I'm a school administrator in Wyandotte, and I disagree with Desk Weary. My teachers were trained by a couple for a week on SITNO (stage, ignite, thrust, navigate, orbit) and the kids and teachers love it. The kids yell out "sit no" each time they start a new unit. I just can't believe they didn't teach SITNO at university. It's a blessing.

Principal Benjamin Black, Wyandotte Middle School

You nailed it, Desk Weary. My school brought in two people making a thousand dollars a day each plus transportation and hotel expenses for a program called, can you believe it, SITNO. It's basically the old introduction, body, conclusion format teachers have used for a thousand years. A few years ago a SITNO came through called BASIC (begin, action, study, interrogate, closure or something like that). What good teacher doesn't introduce a unit, model the skill, teach the knowledge, practice, review, test and maybe celebrate? If schools have extra money for such junk as BASIC or SITNO, give it to teachers instead, so they don't have to spend their own money on supplies.

Anti-Recycled Strategies

It was time for Madison to drive to school. Today her students who were studying WW II were presenting skits or readings taken from *The Diary of Ann Frank, Band of Brothers, Flags of Our Fathers, Diary of a German Soldier, The Rising Sun* and others. The idea was to understand not only the playing out of WW II and America's role, but to also understand why Japan wanted to attack America and Germany wanted to take over Europe.

In past years, these presentations had brought about tears, raucous arguments, confusion about America's foreign policies and enlightenment. Madison hated studying through the adopted textbook that didn't really capture the feeling of being German, Polish, Chinese, Philippine, Indochinese, English or Japanese during the mass destruction and tremendous loss of family and friends.

Chapter 9. Mount of Holy Cross

The sun was just coming through Duke Preston's bedroom window, but he was on vacation for a week and didn't have to hurry out of bed. He stretched, flipped on his reading light and picked up John Muir's *The Mountains of California.* He read:

"Lakes are seen gleaming in all sorts of places round, or oval, or square, like very mirrors; others narrow and sinuous, drawn close around the peaks like silver zones, the highest reflecting only rocks, snow, and the sky."

Duke longed for another trip to the Rockies or the Appalachians for some backpacking. He hadn't backpacked since his trip with Sam to Mount Holy Cross in Colorado. He'd written a letter to his mom about the trek. He kept personal correspondence on the bookshelf built into his headboard, so he pulled his copy of the letter out and reread it.

Dear Mom,

How are you? I've been musing and miss sitting down with you and sharing my feelings.

How should we deal with the trials and tribulations that cross our paths each day? What must we learn to be able to cope and/or prevail?

As you know, Sam and I like to climb 14,000-foot mountains in Colorado. Most summers we spend several days "bagging" a "fourteener" or two. This last summer we decided to climb Mount of Holy Cross, famous because two intersecting crevasses in its granite face trap snow, making a lofty year-round cross.

The night before our ascent, we hiked into a canyon near the base of the mountain and pitched our tents. The sun set early because Holy Cross cast its shadow on us even before supper.

As we crawled into our tents, a downdraft began sweeping through the canyon, creating a sound that reminded me of the sea. The scent of the pines filled the air--it was ideal for sleeping. An hour later, I woke up to pip, pip, pip. I didn't want rain, but the steady beat lulled me back to sleep. Then a half-hour after that I awakened again. A rumbling was coming from the other side of the mountains. I yelled to Sam, "Jet or thunder?" He responded as I knew he would but hoped he wouldn't, "Thunder!"

Soon flashes were illuminating the inside of my tent. I tried to count the time between lightning and thunder--they were simultaneous. The booming reverberated off the mountains and echoed down the canyon. It started raining so hard I couldn't hear individual drops. I lay worrying about being struck by lightning. Would a tree fall from a gust of wind and crush me? Would the runoff from a cloudburst create a flood then wash us from the canyon?

My senses were on high alert to any noise, change of temperature, or movement. Then I heard a different, lower rumbling. As it grew louder, I lifted my head until it touched the nylon roof. I got ready to unzip my tent and prepare for the worst. I knew that sound! What was it? Snoring? It was snoring! Through all of this, Sam in the next tent was snoring.

A few lines from "Desiderata" came to mind: "Do not distress yourself with imaginings. You are a child of the universe, no less than the trees and the stars; you have a right to be here. And, whether or not it is clear to you, no doubt the universe is unfolding as it should . . . in the noisy confusion of life, keep peace with your soul."

Soon I was asleep. The next day dawned clear, and we added another fourteener to our list of triumphs.

Love ya, Mom, miss ya, Mom,
Your devoted son
Duke

After reopening Muir's book and reading more of his luring words, Duke got up, pushed some of last night's potato peels off the counter into the wastebasket and turned on a burner of his stove. He threw some bacon into his cast iron skillet, broke two eggs and dropped them in too, dusted the whole contents with pepper and parmesan cheese, then topped it all with some whole wheat bread.

There was coffee in the pot left over from yesterday, so he plopped a glob of Koolwhip in the cup and stuck it in the microwave. It came out a minute later steaming and in motion. The Koolwhip looked like a giant white amoeba chasing a dark coffee-colored one around the rim of the cup. It sure didn't look like the flat white coffee he enjoyed so much while visiting Australia. A quick stir of the spoon produced nondescript beige. It didn't taste good but it had caffeine in it.

While the bacon and eggs were frying, he brushed his teeth and combed his grizzled hair. He decided to check his email. Since his wife had run off with a younger man two years ago, Duke had been lonely. He had gone into marriage and made a binding contract, while Sylvia had gone into it because she wanted to leave a bad home life. Now she was endeavoring to live as if she could be a sixteen-year-old forever. The betrayal obviously still didn't sit right with Duke. He tried to be philosophical: "Tis the only way to make life endurable," thought Duke, misapplying Voltaire's words.

Friend Sam had found a mate on backinthegame.com and suggested Duke try it too. He did. For him it turned out to be six months of agonizing about how to date electronically. It just didn't seem very romantic, despite the movie *You've Got Mail*. "Was he and his life at 41 so pitiful that he had to resort to this?" he asked himself.

He hit the Explorer key and went to his Gmail. He had a hit. It was a girl named Madison. She wanted to know more about him. He took shredded tobacco from two metal cans and mixed them in his palm. He gently packed his pipe bowl. The pipe consisted of a dark wood bowl attached to a metal stem. The mouthpiece was plastic. It was advertised that the metal, spiral stem cooled the smoke before it reached the lips or tongue.

He lit the pipe with an Ohio kitchen match, the same kind he used to shoot out of his Daisy BB gun when he was eleven. When the matches bounced off the sidewalk, they burst into flames. He sucked slowly on the pipe and watched a tiny tornado of smoke rise from the bowl. The fragrance of the tobacco was like a mixture of sorghum and mesquite. He puffed for a few minutes, enjoying the taste and smell.

He started to type:

I'm just a country boy at heart--cowboy boots and hat. My favorite movie is Pure Country *with George Strait and Leslie Warren. Tell you something? My wife ran away with a younger man, the old story in reverse, I guess, and I'm lonely. Sounds like the lyrics of the songs I like to listen to. Just go to work, come home and read. Nothing much to tell but that I want company. Your turn. –Duke*

Chapter 10. Facing the Facts

Playing Minesweeper on his computer helped kill the time as Pastor Mark waited for the coming counseling session. He seldom got nervous, but the idea of Miss Ardnas being in his office was making his hair tingle, and he could feel a little sweat collecting on his brow. Flashes on his monitor told him that the landmines had exploded, producing a domino effect all over the grid. He'd obviously put a red flag in the wrong place. In a few minutes he would be listening, or looking, for red flags in Miss Ardnas' narrative.

Finally there was a knock on Pastor Mark's door and he rushed to open it. He told himself to slow down, which he did, and opened the door. Miss Ardnas looked great. Even though the edges of her mouth were turned upward and her eyes seemed to smile just as usual, her overall look was serious.

"Come in, Miss Ardnas."

"Hi, Pastor Wellston."

"Make that Mark. We're high school friends, remember?"

"Sorry."

"How have you been?"

"Fine, fine, but..." Miss Ardnas' throat tightened.

"Well, you're looking great." Mark hoped this didn't sound like he was hitting on her, but he wasn't prepared with any other words to give her time to recover her composure. His permanent smile was on his face. He switched the subject.

"Remember the time in high school when we were trying to prepare a cut of *Othello*? We were going to compete as a duet in the drama category of the next speech contest. You as Desdemona and I as Othello. We were freshmen, and I pulled my chin back to make my voice deeper and you were trying not to laugh. Then we got to the part where you said, 'By heaven, you do me wrong,' and I was supposed to say, 'Are you not a strumpet?' But I read it: 'Are you not a trumpet?' instead."

"Oh, yeah, I remember," Miss Ardnas said with a smile.

"We both broke down and everything was funny after that. I had to call Desdemona a whore several times, which made me blush and my voice broke. We both had to sit down because we were in hysterics."

"Yes, the good ole days when insignificant things were super important."

Mark asked Miss Ardnas why she had come.

"Well, I don't think Franklin loves me anymore. I think maybe he's having an affair."

"Miss Ardnas, I have to ask certain personal questions. Have either of you had affairs in the past?"

"I haven't, but I've often wondered about him."

In Mark's experience, if wondering didn't disappear after a few months, then there was probably some good reason. A little depression and bouts of feeling worthless often made partners suspicious, but that went away when the depression subsided.

"So, what do you want to tell me about that?"

There's no way Miss Ardnas felt like specifically explaining this to Pastor Mark. Franklin and she had always had a quirky way of making love. Miss Ardnas didn't especially like Franklin on top thumping away, so over the years she had found ways to shorten the part she disliked yet satisfy him and herself.

She'd dress up in a short nightie with no bra or panties and, when the kids were asleep, run out of the master bath past him reading in bed and then descend the stairs. He never failed to notice and take off after her. They had to sprint on their toes around the house to keep from waking the kids, so the chase through the dining room, through the kitchen, through the living room and back through the dining room in dim light got the physical and psychological juices flowing. The glimpses Franklin got of Miss Ardnas dashing in her silky sleepwear raised more than just his libido.

She would usually end up back in the bedroom and crawl under the bed. He would grab her by a leg and start to pull her out, which did enticing things to the nightie. She would pull away and jump into bed and cover up. Then his trick was to uncover her feet and run his hands slowly up the insides of her legs, deftly taking care of her climax midway up, then slide on top and bury his face in her neck. She would have worked her foreplay magic so well that a few thumps and he was done. He'd roll off and go to sleep, and she'd wrap one arm and one leg over him and enjoy her continuing rhythms in peace and comfort.

"He doesn't seem to want to make love anymore, even when I make overtures, and he makes lots of home insurance calls at night--

many more that a few years ago. He says evenings are the only time both husband and wife are at home. I don't know. What's wrong with me?"

She lifted a Puff from his tissue box and dried her eyes. He wanted to grab one himself and blot the perspiration on his forehead.

"So, how long have you felt this way?"

"More than a year."

"Have you talked to him about this?"

"Yes, but he just says I'm silly and that he loves me and still likes to, well, you know."

"Do you have any physical evidence?"

"Kind of, but it's not concrete. Smells, mostly."

"Do you have any idea who it is?"

"Yes. His secretary. Her name is Cali."

Miss Ardnas lifted a second tissue and held it to her eyes with her thumb and forefinger, trying not to smear her makeup. Mark waited until she uncovered her eyes.

"What do you want to happen?"

"I want this to go away."

"Should I talk to him, do you want to set up joint marriage counseling with me or someone else, or we could set up separate counseling with two counselors?"

"What do you recommend?"

"If he admits an affair, can you forgive him?"

"I think so."

The tissue went back to her eyes.

"Let's start with you telling him you saw me and you'd like for him to set up a session with me. Then we'll go from there."

"Thank you, Mark."

"Remember, 'All things work together for good to those who love the Lord.'"

"I hope so."

They talked about each other's lives since high school for half an hour before the conversation ran out.

"Have Franklin give me a call."

"I'll try."

"It was nice seeing you again, Miss Ardnas."

Mark thought he would love to be able to look into those aqua eyes across a breakfast table for the rest of his life.

Chapter 11. Anticipation

When the door chimes sounded, Cali was still making last minute touches to her makeup--a little too much eye shadow and lipstick that was way too dark. Her platinum blond hair was cut short but it framed her face nicely. Although she had stiffened herself for the confrontation about Franklin's divorce, she gave her shoulders a shake to try to be relaxed when greeting him.

On the way up to Cali's third-floor apartment, Franklin thought over his company's big accounts. There were several new businesses that needed employee insurance programs, and the school district was taking bids again for their personnel group package. Families moving into town were also calling his agents for quotes. Car insurance was as steady as always.

He thought over his schedule and was determined to set up tee times with the school superintendent, a few key board members and the CEO's of the new companies. "Good ole boy" networking was as good a method of selling insurance now as it had been in the old days for selling everything from horse flesh to swampland.

When Cali opened the door Franklin bundled her and her limbs into his arms and gave her a long kiss. They were going out to her favorite bar, which she liked for its Buffalo wings and celery dips. He didn't care where they ate, he was just looking forward to giving her a gift and then hopping into the sack. This all had to be done in as short of a time as possible so that Miss Ardnas wouldn't suspect anything, but long enough so that Cali wouldn't feel slighted and shut him off.

Miss Ardnas never used sex as currency as Cali did. Miss Ardnas never agreed or refused to have sex just because she did or didn't get her way on some aspect of their joint decisions. Cali, on the other hand, had to be carried along as on an emotional spider web that could break any second, and, if it did, there wouldn't be any sexual release for Franklin that night.

Cali was dressed to allure, with lots of smooth thigh and firm breast showing. She was always fluffing or tossing her startling platinum hair for effect. The intentions of her combined efforts were not lost on Franklin, which caused him to want dinner over more quickly than ever.

At the Your Bud's Bar—Franklin hated puns like that despite the name of his business—Cali had her normal shot of vodka and a Bud Lite. Franklin went to the bar and had the bartender make him a shandy, which for Franklin was half dark beer and half soda. He didn't want to smell like booze when he went home after his "home insurance meeting." He also ordered some peanuts to cover any residual beer breath.

Cali greeted a few people who were Your Bud's regulars, and Franklin tried to keep his head low and sit in a dark booth to keep his billboard-famous face from being recognized.

The shot and beer did its work on Cali and she was prepared to confront Franklin.

"Honey, I have something I want to talk about."

"Me too," said Franklin, pulling the small black box from his pocket.

"You go first, Franklin," said Cali, much relieved as her heart rate doubled. Her eyes didn't blink.

"You know how much I love you and well, uh, well, here."

As she looked at the box her lungs stopped working and her tongue became dry. She took off the wrapper, flipped open the black box. Inside were two brilliant diamond earrings. Cali could have screamed and cried at the same time. She didn't throw them at him as she wanted to, after all they were diamonds.

"How do you like them, Honey?"

"Beautiful," she choked out. She closed the box and put it in her purse.

"Now your news, Dear."

"Oh, it can wait."

The meal passed quickly. The spider web had broken and Franklin left Cali's an hour and a half later unsatisfied. She said it was because it was her time of the month. That night Miss Ardnas had to endure a lot of thumping before Franklin's libido was sated. She hadn't even asked Franklin to go see Pastor Mark yet.

Chapter 12. Surprise at the Door

Madison felt good after school because the students had worked hard on their presentations and had delivered them well. They had "taught" class, relieving her for the day, and probably had learned a lot more than on a traditional day. She always felt that kids remembered more of what they said in a class than what the teacher said, so making them do the research, write reports, prepare A/V and give presentations fit her philosophy. Slipping off her black dress and a silver necklace with one opal, she pulled on a sweatshirt and jogging shorts and stepped into her slippers. She put her brown hair into a scrunchie, then poured herself a glass of moscato.

Madison's apartment was tidy and small. It had a living room, two bedrooms, a small study, a kitchen/dining area and one bath. It had a green view looking over a park instead of the typical apartment view of a parking lot.

Only after taking a few sips of wine did she walk to her desk and the computer.

After reading dozens of emails from Duke, Madison decided to take her profile off backinthegame.com. She couldn't see herself walking into a Wyandotte, Kentucky, restaurant with a man wearing boots, big buckle and cowboy hat. Nor did she believe she could listen to twangy music with sappy lyrics as she and a boyfriend drove places in a car. She especially didn't want to spend Saturday nights watching movies with titles like *Pure Country*. She may live in a small city with lots of country music on its radio stations, but she imagined herself to be somewhat cosmopolitan.

She decided she wouldn't try the Post-It method of choosing a date again.

As Madison was filling her glass for the third time, the doorbell rang. She put her eye to the peephole and about dropped her wineglass. Even though the image of the man standing at her door was warped like a figure in a funhouse mirror, she could tell he was a hunk.

Her mind put his exaggerated stature aright, and she thought this was the most handsome man she had ever seen. Maybe it was the wine or maybe it was that he was well tanned and was obviously in great physical shape. He stood with his hat in his hand. She glanced at the oval mirror just inside the door, fluffed up her hair and opened the door.

"Hi, Madison. You look gorgeous." He bent down and pulled her to him so closely that more parts of his body were pressed against hers than she had ever remembered happening before during a hug. She felt like a feather on a string had just been pulled through her from a point between her legs, through her stomach, chest and ending in her throat.

She stepped back and looked at his intense dark eyes and lovely smile, trying to remember where she had met him and why she hadn't remembered. He saw her confusion and said:

"When you emailed that you were a teacher named Madison, I checked all the schools' websites for staff members, saw that your last name was Wentworth, looked up your address on yellowpages.com and here I am."

"But who are you?"

"I'm William, William Marshall," he stated as he ran his hand backward over his reddish-brown hair and, with the same motion, slipped the Cincinnati Reds baseball hat in his hand onto his head. "I just got finished playing softball with a community league team. Hope you don't mind my stopping by."

"William, the liar," thought Madison, then added, "Maybe I was wrong about his profile and my assessment." Her gray eyes gave away her curiosity. She had never felt anything like the feather-on-a-string sensation before, but she really liked it.

Chapter 13. Making the Rounds

Mrs. Grassley was eighty-five and pretty much housebound. She could talk, though. Boy could she talk! Pastor Mark was making a house call because a friend of Mrs. Grassley had told him she was sick and needed his prayers.

Turns out she had had a cold Saturday, fought it off Sunday and was right as rain today. She was happy for the company, though. She was also happy to see Pastor Mark's trademark smile.

"Laws, Pastor, you don't have to only visit me when I'm ill."

"You're right there, Mrs. Grassley."

"Call me Maude. Well, I was real down Saturday morning, coughing up things you don't want to hear about; sneezing, and blow'n my nose to beat the band. Didn't know a person could have so much snot in them. Laws! Oh, I probably shouldn't be saying laws."

"Well, I'm glad you're well now."

"Laws, not me. My right knee keeps going out of joint, and my left leg goes to sleep when I sit on the La-Z-Boy. Back hurts all the time, and can't see much out of my left eye, let alone my right one. Laws, my arthritic fingers twist every which way, which is only good at Halloween because it makes kids run from the door when I give them candy with my knurled hands. Laws, I get a kick out of that. Sometimes I even shake my cane at them. Is that sinful, do you think?"

"No, you're just having a little fun, Mrs. Grassley, I mean Maude."

"Where's your shoes? Don't the church pay you enough to buy decent pants?"

"I just wear what's comfortable. I know the sport coat with jeans is a dated look, but I'm retro eighties. The sneakers are comfortable"

"Where's your boots? It's almost winter."

"Yeah, but it's not that cold and there's no snow."

"Why don't you stop in more? Laws, you know I'm always home. All my friends have been listed on the obituary page years ago, and my kids live all over the country and my grandkids probably wouldn't recognize me if they ever visited."

Mark thought about how hard it was to make drop-in visits in the town of Wyandotte. He walked every day through his neighborhood. It was a lonely walk, and he wished he could stop to see some of the people he knew.

The problem was the houses seemed so forbidding. Since people set their thermostats at 72 and left them there year round, all windows and doors were kept closed. He disliked walking up to a house where the door was closed. People didn't seem to use their screen doors for ventilation anymore. He had been with people that spent so much time in controlled store, office, church and home environments that if the temperature went above 74 or below 68 they were miserable and complaining.

He'd even knocked at doors and rung doorbells with no one answering, then told the residents at church the next Sunday that he'd stopped. They'd say something like: *"Oh, I must have been watching TV in the den, and Sandi is always, what do they call it?, tweettering, facelooking and Skyping—something like that. Oh, yes, we were home. You should have knocked or rung the bell."*

People didn't hear him when he drove, or rode, up to their house, because he didn't have a motorized vehicle. Instead he rode a velomobile. It was a recumbent tricycle with two front wheels, one back one and a safety blue light-weight body. Reflective silver stripes and a head lamp were for night driving and a flashing taillight was used for both day and night safety. It was streamlined, low to the ground and kind of racy looking, but it wouldn't top 20 miles an hour. A flag flew above the trike as an extra safety precaution.

"You married, Pastor? No? Why not? How old are you anyway? I got a couple of nieces might be your age who need a good husband. Laws, I don't mean you'd marry both, but pick one or the other. I'll call you the next time they visit, if they visit. You don't even have enough money to buy decent shoes, but, lucky for you, they're not choosey."

The conversation continued to wander around through more ailments, past nosy neighbors, the fact that she was born in Wales, her two deceased husbands and ended with how awful the current President was. Mark finally got away, but vowed to visit again next week.

Chapter 14. Calling it Quits

When Franklin left, Cali did a soft trashing of her apartment. She threw pillows, lap blankets, books, magazines, and other nonlethal items at sofas, the walls and beds. She accidentally knocked over a lamp, intentionally kicked over a chair and one swipe of a pillow tore a loose piece of wallpaper border from above a mirror. After 10 minutes of venting, she opened the black box and tried the earrings on. They looked great, but would have looked better on a face not crimson. The fact that her eyeliner was making Sharpie streaks down her face and her platinum hair was quite askew didn't improve the earrings' look either.

"I'm done with that creep," she decided out loud. "He's never going to leave that woman and I'm tired of working in his office and then taking work home. Buying me presents so he can have sex makes me no better than a prostitute."

One of her undergraduate professors had told her to go on to get her Master's or a combined Master'/Doctorate degree and become a research scientist. She was a math genius who was wasting her talents in an office. That she wore dresses that were too short, sleeveless and backless and had excessively low necklines, kept most men from noticing she had a brain.

Maybe this was a signal to change the path of her life. She had taken her job at Wright Insurance because Franklin had met her at a New Year's Eve bash. He and Miss Ardnas had sat at the same table as the party Cali was with. When they struck up a conversation, she had told him she was looking for a job, and he had mentioned a job opening that was just right for her in his office.

His charm had carried her away, she applied, was hired and the whole process was over before she knew what had happened. By the time she realized she was all wrong for the work he wanted, he had already begun to take her to business dinners out of town and to the bedroom. Promises were made that lured her to stick it out. Taking the position was right for his libido but not for her future.

She vowed to give her professor a call to see if she thought financial aid would be available if she went back to university.

A problem was what to do about going to work. How could she face Franklin every day when she was harboring such anger toward him? Fourteen months of dating, sneaking around, promises, sex, more promises, and expensive gifts had been a waste. She wanted a life, a husband, public outings in town, companionship and children. Sex was not the first thing on her list as it was on Franklin's.

She poured herself a shot of Svedka, tossed it back and poured another. The second shot's sting made her cough and the inside of her nose tickle. She sneezed. Then she popped the tab top on a can of Bud Lite, curled her legs under her on the sofa and tried to concentrate on her level 5 Sudoku book.

Nothing she tried to do prevented her from feeling cheap, or worse, worthless, or worse yet, a prostitute. Why were so many secretaries so desperate and gullible, she wondered? Then she thought, "What's wrong with me that I could fall for a womanizer like him?" Her tears didn't remove her negative feelings, but they did, along with great sobs, relieve some of the feeling of being wrapped up tight like a mummy.

Chapter 15. Moving On

That Cali gave him the straight-ahead stare every time they passed in the office troubled Franklin. Although his mind was on wrapping up some of the pending accounts, he finally realized that Cali had been angry since the night he had given her the earrings.

"What did she expect," he thought. "Why can't she just 'hook up' the way the teens today have casual sex, or develop 'friends with benefits?' She knows I have a family with Miss Ardnas, so why can't it just be about fun, a fling? I don't get it. I never quite understood what actions make her happy or mad."

Franklin felt ashamed about cheating on Miss Ardnas. The image of her sweet face, framed by that silky light-brown hair, plus the edges of her mouth and aqua eyes turned up in that quirky way no other women had, passed across his mind. He did love her and didn't want to lose her, but he couldn't help himself. He couldn't see how he was different from those people who said, "Tomorrow I will start my diet?" Or, the smoker who promised himself he'd quit after the current pack was empty. Or, the drinker who told everyone he was going on the wagon for a month. Or, a gambler who swore off gambling after a big loss.

He couldn't think of one friend or acquaintances that made those kinds of resolutions who ever followed through. Maybe they'd diet for a few months and then blow back up, or quit smoking for a week, or not drink one night.

His guilt had often made him angry at himself, then he'd speed recklessly down narrow side streets with cars parked on each side or along serpentine country roads lined with trees as if suicidal. Self-effacing curses would fly out of his mouth and tears would stream down his face. He'd yell out appeals addressed to an absent Miss Ardnas and swear that he would never cheat on her again.

This time his bruised conscience and depth of despair led him to drive slowly to a deserted gravel pit with a new case of quart glass canning jars just bought at the local supermarket. He sat the jars on a cardboard box, which he started perforating with .45 ACP holes and occasionally sharding a jar or two. He reloaded his Kimberly several times and continued shooting point blank into the cardboard long after the glass was sparkling where it lay all around the box. His ears were ringing and his hand felt shaky as he put the .45 back into its case. He took a deep breath through his nose and let it out gradually from his mouth.

Justification and excuses followed his outbursts: "I'm just the same as the smoker, drinker, overeater and gambler. I can't help it. I can't help it."

He guessed it would be a good time to drop Cali, since she was acting like she was no longer attracted to him. He wouldn't have to make up an excuse, just say he had returned to Miss Ardnas because he could tell Cali no longer wanted to have a relationship. Franklin hoped Cali wouldn't make a mess out of the end of their affair with threats to tell Miss Ardnas or cause an outburst at work. He sure wasn't planning to fire her and risk getting sued for sexual harassment.

Since the greens were still open due to unusually warm winter weather, a golf match with three potential clients was only an hour away; therefore, Franklin had to end his musing and finish business at the office to make the tee time. His handicap was low, because he played a lot and took periodic lessons, but he never beat a client unless the client had tried to cheat him during a past deal. Franklin hated cheaters.

With four 15-dollar cigars in his pocket and a role of bills for betting on each hole, Franklin slid into his BMW, lowered the top and scudded off toward the Hill and Dale Country Club. Nothing was on his mind but plans for two big businesses and a policy for a school on his mind. He was going to try for a par 3 in insurance sales, even if he bogeyed every hole.

Chapter 16. Fly Fishing

It was Saturday, and Duke was standing on the banks of his favorite pond. He had on a Tony Stewart T-shirt and camouflage shorts, wool socks and boots. The property, which was only a mile from the city limits, was owned by Sam, who made sure it was kept stocked with bass and pan fish. It consisted of 155 acres of woods with a 14-acre pond in the middle. The trees were cleared back fifty feet from the water and kept mowed by four sheep, two goats and two horses. It was perfect for fly fishing.

Duke had tied a dozen assorted flies at home Friday night and wanted to see which one met the water test. He attached a dry fly and gave it a spritz of silicone. His favored 10 o'clock to 2 o'clock to 10 o'clock motion with the handle of the rod sent the line out onto the mirrored surface and the fly followed. Bark started to give chase but looked at Duke and seemed to remember his training to stay.

Pulling his Nascar cap further down on his head, he squinted his eyes and used a finger over finger pull on the line to slowly make the artificial mayfly look like it was drifting. A few ripples around the bait gave Duke some hope. Then he saw something hit the water across the pond and a fish jumped. Wrong bait, he decided. He pushed the automatic rewind, then changed the bait to a caddis. He never knew what fly would be most attractive at what time of the year. If he caught a fish, he'd slit it open and check its belly for evidence of the insects it was feeding on. Then he'd pick the fly from his assortment that mimicked those insects.

Duke snapped a PBR from its ring on a cold six-pack sitting in a plastic five-gallon bucket of ice, opened it and took a swallow. Why was the first taste always the best, bringing back memories of friends, dates and special occasions?

"Hey, you old son of a bachelor," yelled someone from the woods. "You stealing my fish?"

"They're no fish in this mud hole, just snakes and frogs."

"You sharing that beer or are you drinking to forget no one wants to date you?"

Duke grabbed Sam a beer and made sure he shook it up out of sight of Sam before turning around and tossing it to him.

When Sam stuck his finger under the tab and lifted, the spray blew his sunglasses off and sent his light hair straight up, sticking a few strands to the bill of his ball cap.

"Whoa. I guess I hit a sore spot, Pal. Seriously, you having any luck on backinthegame?"

"Nope and you just happened to hit a Saturday when all the other onliners were taken and Jenni was desperate."

"Ouch. That hurt."

"Well, I'm tired of spending evenings and weekends alone with my stinky socks and my dog Bark. Bark's tired of it too." Bark perked up his ears at the sound of his name, and his tail made a perfect circle with long hairs of two shades filling in the middle.

"I thought you had someone named Madison you opened up to. What happened?"

"Haven't heard a word from her, and she's not even listed on backinthegame anymore. She probably wasn't the right one anyway. I did like her picture, though."

"Nice flies, Duke."

"Tied them last night."

"Any luck?"

"Just got here."

"Want me to ask Jenni to fix you up with one of her friends?"

"Why not. It'd be better than sitting talking to a computer."

Chapter 17. Making a Move

William stepped back and unabashedly looked at Madison slowly from top to bottom and back to the top. No part of her slim body was missed by his eyes. Madison blushed and stepped back. She wasn't sure what to do, tell him to sit down and offer him a drink or make an excuse and say she had an appointment.

He stepped closer and Madison was against the wall and couldn't retreat.

Stretching his neck and leaning his head forward he said, "You have the most amazing silver eyes, Honey."

"I bet you say that to all the girls," was the trite answer that came to mind, so she gave it to fill the space.

Madison did have amazing eyes. They were the gray typical of a wolf or huskie but more compelling. Comparing someone's eyes to those of a dog didn't sound very flattering, so William hadn't said that. Those meeting her for the first time and looking into her eyes didn't know whether she was some kind of benevolent demon or all-seeing angel. They weren't piercing or limpid pools that made you want to dive in. The dark gray and the light gray of her irises seemed to orbit as she moved her eyes when she looked from one object to another. It reminded William of Op Art. To him they were indescribable.

"No I don't. Your eyes are special."

"Well, thanks. I wish I could ask you to stay for a drink, but I have to meet a friend across town in about 15 minutes. She's having relationship problems," Madison lied.

"Okay. Too bad. Here's my card. Give me a call. We'll go for dinner or something and I'll admire your silver eyes some more. All kidding aside."

"Okay."

William pressed forward again. Madison was well aware of each part of their bodies that were touching and the pressure exerted by his hands as he hugged her. Sure enough, the feather on the string floated through her again.

"Bye," she choked out.

"See ya, Honey."

She peeked through her window to make sure he drove away, then tried to figure out where she could go in case he watched to see if she was just trying to get rid of him. Then she thought, why would he expect that?

"I'll call Breta and tell her I'm coming over," she said aloud.

Madison looked at William's card. "William Marshall, Wines and Spirits, 1212 E. Dalton Blvd, Wyandotte, KY. 555-3829."

"What's this mean? Does he work at a liquor store or does he wholesale wines?" she asked this aloud too. She realized she had been spending too much time alone and was starting to talk to herself. "Should I keep this or toss it away? Are you crazy? YES."

Surprised, Madison realized that she had finally met one of her email "dates" face to face. She hoped this was an unexpected step toward a real date. She called Breta, told her a lie, grabbed her keys and driver's license, started her car and took off toward her house. She didn't see William.

Chapter 18. The Unbeliever

Mark was hungry after making velomobile rounds to the hospital, two nursing homes and Mrs. Grassley's. He decided to eat at the Whistle Stop Café that occupied the old railway station a block from the town square.

"Hey, Pastor," called Jake from a table half-way back. "I've got an empty seat here, a pot of coffee and an extra cup. Want to join me?"

"Hi, Jake. How are you?"

"Do'n fine."

Jake was the owner of and pharmacist at "pd drugs," in downtown Wyandotte. The original owner was Powers and the original store sign read: "Powers Drugs." After many years it got to be known as PD. People would go to PD's for soup and sandwiches or take the family for sodas and shakes at its lunch counter. When Jake had to change the faded and rusting sign, he had the painter print "pd drugs" in lower case. The message was redundant, Powers Drugs Drugs, but he liked the look. It was one of the few Wyandotte landmarks still on the town square and a favorite of out-of-town shoppers.

"Saw your 'space pod' parked at the hospital when I made a delivery today."

"I have a couple of members of my congregation recovering from surgeries."

"Why don't you drive a car?"

"Don't like them."

"Really? Why?"

"They go too fast and are too heavy to control. All those road kills make me sad. Squirrels and other animals probably don't think there's anything in nature that's so awkward or stupid that it can't avoid hitting helpless animals."

"You have a point there."

"Plus, between 30,000 and 40,000 people are killed in automobile accidents a year. And that's only in America. That's unacceptable."

"I didn't know that it was that many. Are you sure that's correct?"

"Yes. I think about 5,000 of those are teens, 16, 17, 18, and 19 year olds."

"You've got to be kidding."

"I'm also a Ray Bradbury fan. He never drove. Believed cars had no place in a world of pedestrians."

Pastor Mark's conviction about cars had been bolstered a few days earlier by an NPR interview. The guest said that people had a genetic fear of snakes, because they had had to live on the ground with them for thousands of years. He went on to say that only a few people a year died of snake bites but still jumped and screamed when they saw one. Then he added data about traffic fatalities and mentioned that people haven't been around cars long enough to have developed a genetic fear of them. He finished with: "Forget about being afraid of snakes; modern people, when they see a car, should be jumping back and screaming."

"Do you like your bike, trike, pod thing or whatever you call it?"

"Velomobile. Oh, yeah. It's exercise, and the Lord knows Americans need exercise. It doesn't pollute, waste natural resources, take up much space, and it's fairly harmless. It gets great mileage. I think the squirrels are safe from me. Enough about my wheels. I haven't seen you around for a while."

"If you'd get sick and come in, you'd find me behind the PD pharmacy counter from 8 to 4 weekdays and every third Saturday."

"I see your wife and kids at church every Sunday."

"Yep."

"I'm off duty during the noon hour so I won't preach."

"Oh, go ahead. You're wasting your breath on me."

"Not a believer?"

"Nope."

"Any reason?"

Lana, the waitress, greeted the pastor and Jake and took their orders. Both got the special, which was a fried chicken breast, mashed potatoes and gravy and California blend.

After Lana left, Jake asked, "Where were we?

"Reasons you're not a believer."

"Lots. Modern Christianity is too soft."

"Really?"

"Jonathan Edwards preached a sermon entitled, 'Sinners in the Hands of an Angry God.' Don't hear that much anymore from the pulpit."

"So you're a fire-and-brimstone advocate? Scare them into heaven."

"Not really, but Christianity is too easy."

"Why?"

"All you have to do is believe in Christ and you go to heaven. It's too easy."

"What do you propose?"

"Don't know. But a golfing friend of mine, well, you know him, so why beat around the bush, Franklin Wright, says he's saved. From what I can tell he breaks all the commandments. He's vulgar, profane, and a cheater. He cheats at golf, cheats on his wife, laughs about cheating his salespersons out of commissions, cheats on his taxes, never volunteers or joins service clubs unless it's to meet new clients, and I could go on."

"We're all sinners in the eyes of God, so you or I can't judge him or question his salvation. Plus, Franklin may be surprised when he meets his maker."

"Not according to him. He says he asks forgiveness each week at your church, believes the Apostles' Creed, and is truly sorry for his sins. He says you preach that we're all sinners, but salvation doesn't come through works or anything we do except believe in Christ."

"But believing in Jesus is supposed to change your heart and your behavior."

"He says he prays for God to help him be a better person, but God hasn't made it happen yet. He told me you preach that if you look in lust on a person it's just the same as committing adultery. Then Franklin told me with a chuckle that he might as well just go ahead and satisfy his lust if they're both the same to God."

"That's quite a corruption of the scriptures," commented Pastor Mark.

"Sounds like it to me too, but I hear a lot of my Christian friends saying that it's not how you behave, it's what you believe. Live however you want and then go to heaven."

Lana put the specials in front of Pastor Mark and Jake and asked if they wanted anything else. Neither did, and the conversation switched to lighter subjects—Jake's kids, Pastor Mark's rounds, their recent golf scores, Kiwanis Club events, Pastor Mark's church's attendance and the level of business at the pharmacy.

Mark was left second guessing his sermons' contents and his own religious beliefs. How could he continue preaching on scripture he didn't agree with, or was it that he just didn't understand the scripture? Either way, he had to do some more study and was considering calling his friend from seminary days who always seemed grounded in the scripture and his faith.

Chapter 19. No Escape

How to confront Franklin was dominating Miss Ardnas' every second. Franklin seemed to know just how strong she was at any moment and could play the pit bull and blow right past her concerns or fall into the cuddly puppy-dog ruse to make her feel guilty for something he had done. She understood these encounters and tactics but had trouble controlling and dealing with them.

She tossed her light brown hair back and forth a few times as if to clear her mind with the shaking of her head.

Pastor Mark was right, she realized, Franklin needed to go for counseling to open up the subject. "Could he manipulate Pastor Mark the way he does me?" she asked herself.

She decided that the best thing for her to do was to finish another article for Ersatz News. Writing for her was pure pleasure and she often lost herself in the endeavor.

Defense Department Seeks to Expand Reach
Ersatz Daily News—Washington

The Defense Department proposed last week to expand its influence around the world. The US already has bases or troops in 150 countries, so expanding to cover 180 of the 191 countries of the world would not be difficult.

Obviously, stated a DOF spokesperson who wants to remain anonymous, it would be advantageous to have troops in all countries, but Russia, China and a few others would resist that.

Most countries appreciate America's world-policing policy, and even some don't have standing armies because of America's protective treaties.

The nations who depend on America's superior military might, save billions, or at least millions, of dollars a year by not having to own and maintain an air force, military bases or troops.

Adding another 30 countries to the 150 America already helps protect would require a minor increase in the defense budget, claims the DOF spokesperson.

Opponents to this expansion include James Farthing, member of Farthing-Banton Institute, a Washington-based think tank, who claims America needs to bring its troops back home to protect American soil.

He states: "Expanding the CIA world-wide operations substantially would serve the same purpose as all those bases and troops and would be less costly."

Miss Ardnas was concerned about the increasing accusations that the USA had become an imperialist nation. The claims did not say that the US annexes countries around the world but uses hegemony instead. She would print her article out as if it were a real piece of news. Most of her students would never double check her material because she was the professor, and she didn't expect any of them to look up *ersatz* to see what it meant.

A good discussion was guaranteed. Then she would call a stop to the debate while the interchanges were at their most contentious and assign each student to write an opinion piece to send to the *Ersatz News* editor's desk. Few students ever complained about writing their thoughts about a subject they debated in class. She added to their instructions that there had to be data and quotations from authoritative sources to back up their point of view. Ironically she emphasized not using spurious printed or internet material.

Miss Ardnas was hoping one of her students would discover that she was the source of the articles she used in class and challenge her. That would open up another topic she wanted her students to investigate and understand—who can you believe. With talking heads on Fox, CNN and MSNBC and hundreds of newspaper editorialists spinning the same news facts, 24/7, where was the truth?

Ersatz News didn't take Miss Ardnas' mind off of her concern about Franklin for long. "Am I ugly, stupid, lazy, and unattractive all of a sudden?" she asked herself. "Obviously! When did I get to be that way and what caused it?" She pulled her head back and reached for a Kleenex when she realized that teardrops were falling onto the computer keyboard—one was black from eyeliner and the other clear. They mixed together on the spacebar. Dabbing them with her Kleenex, she told herself she had to confront Franklin today. Her tissue came away with a pattern like those on a Rorschach ink blot test.

Chapter 20. A Near Perfect Day

It was a near perfect day, thought Franklin, as he drove from work with his top down. It was a little chilly but felt good. The winter had been mild. He had on a ball cap to keep his hair from getting messed up. He was starting to forget Cali and thought she wouldn't cause any trouble because she was initiating the separation. It did trouble him a little that she mumbled something as he passed her in the office hallway. It sounded like, "Jackass." He thought, "Whatever--let her vent as long as she keeps it low key."

And now he felt free to test the waters with the cute little waitress who always flirted with him at the Hill and Dale Country Club bar.

When he got home, Miss Ardnas was sitting on the patio playing Balloon Lagoon with April and having a glass of Chablis. It was her second glass, although she almost never drank. Franklin didn't notice that she was tense and flushed. He asked for a glass of wine and Miss Ardnas got him one.

To calm herself and move toward initiating a conversation about the concerns on her mind, she asked, "How was work?"

"Fairly normal, but we've got to look for a new secretary."

"Who's leaving?"

"Cali. She says she wants to go back to university and earn a doctorate."

"How do you feel about that?"

"Well, as you probably know, I gave her the job as a favor, and she wasn't very good. I just didn't know how to get rid of her. This solves the problem."

Miss Ardnas was wondering if this solved her problem too.

"So what are you going to do?"

"Our bookkeeper will work out a little severance pay, then we'll start looking for someone who can spell and has a better personality."

"I thought you liked Cali."

"*Tolerated* would be a better term. I'm glad she leaving soon."

Franklin never caught on to Miss Ardnas' reason for the line of questioning because he was thinking again of the short skirt and low neckline of the cute female bartender at the club. He thought she was sassy, perky, peppy, sexy, alluring and nasty all at the same time. He was sure he could have her under the covers in a week.

Now that she didn't have to carry Cali everywhere as in a collegiate book bag, Miss Ardnas' shoulders dropped a half inch and her spine relaxed as she took another sip of wine. She saw no need to confront Franklin concerning her worries about the spin of two individuals within one marital wheel.

Chapter 21. Happy Birthday

"This is my ninth birthday," thought Mark aloud. Yes, it was February 29 and 35 years translated into nine actual birthdays--he liked to include the day he was born. He'd have a pile of cards from his congregation, friends and relatives.

His seminary best friend, Jerry, who had a pastorate in the next county, would send him a horoscope pamphlet specifically for Pisces found at the checkout of most grocery stores. Jerry knew Pastor Mark hated the whole horoscope business and especially didn't like being a Pisces.

A big drawing of the two swimming Pisces fish would be on the back of Jerry's birthday card envelope with *Pisces* intentionally misspelled *Pisses* underneath. If Jerry didn't send a pisses card, he found a card with an egg on it--the occasion mentioned on the card didn't matter--and then draw wheels on it to poke fun of Mark's "wheels."

Pastor Mark wondered when Franklin would call for an appointment. He also wondered if Miss Ardnas had found the courage to bring up Cali. He had to stop thinking about Miss Ardnas, because he didn't want to continually recall the Jimmy Carter lust-in-your-heart quotation that had appeared in a *Playboy* interview.

When he got to his office he checked his IN box, and, sure enough, his secretary had filled it with cards and letters of well-wishing and placed a double chocolate cupcake on top. It had nine miniature candles stuffed into the icing.

Pastor Mark called Jerry.

"Hey, Jerry. Thanks for the pisses card, you dork."

"Well, it's Pastor Markus. You feeling full of piss and vinegar at your advanced age?"

"Jerry, be careful with your joking. My secretary sometimes checks my line to see how close I am to ending a call in case someone is on the other line waiting."

"Hey, preachers can have a sense of humor too. That comment wasn't *pro fano*," joked Pastor Jerry, inserting Latin.

"Why I called, other than to be harassed, was to say I'm struggling with some issues. Instead of feeling like a counselor, I feel like a counselee, if there is such a word."

"What's troubling you, Old Roomy?"

"A couple of things—one personal and one professional."

"You're serious, aren't you, Pal? All kidding aside, I'm ready to listen. You name the date and time."

"How about Wednesday next week at your office at 11 am?"

"You got it, friend. I'll clear my appointment book."

"Thanks."

Mark decided to write some more of his upcoming sermon on faith versus works. He planned to perform a one-person two-character debate on the subject using paraphrases of scripture. It would be like the high school speech contest pieces where the speaker looked one direction as if talking to a person, then took a step, turned, looked back in the direction of the original speaker, changed his voice and responded. He briefly considered using props, such as head dress or robes, to distinguish the characters, but was fairly sure that would elicit laughter instead of attention to the content of the material. The two characters would be James, of the book of *James*, and Paul from his epistles.

Chapter 22. Shave and a Hair Cut

The couple was snuggling on the sofa watching a sports talk show. Sam Jones seemed to like to hear people talk about sports more than he liked sports. When Jenni Block had knocked on Sam's front door with their "secret code," based on "shave and a haircut, two bits," he had taken her hand and led her directly to his bedroom.

Small tree trunk-size floor candles had been lit in the four corners of the room and the scent of fresh evergreen boughs was present. A strings rendition of "Are You Lonesome Tonight" was playing softly. Elvis' low voice did things to Jenni's insides that were heavenly.

They always made love slowly and unselfishly, with loving words and soft moans—well, except for the high notes at the top of their mutual crescendo. Her high note was inevitably the same: "Wahoo!" Then he'd open his eyes and look down at Jenni and her blondish hair sticking out in all directions. She'd be wide eyed with a big silly grin on her face, looking back at him. Then she'd role out from under him, saying, "Put your bat away, Slugger, the ball game's over. Hit the showers." She'd punctuate her command with a loud slap on Sam's bare bottom and they'd step into the shower together. If it was an extraordinarily frisky night and the windows were open, the distant neighbors might hear a second "Wahoo," but this one muffled by the shower.

Many couples might start with dinner, a play or movie, foreplay on the sofa and then move to the bedroom. Sam and Jenni reversed that. They ended on the sofa where they ate their carryout of pizza, Chinese, Mexican, Buffalo wings, or burgers. Or they either decided to go out to a restaurant, club, movie or just stay home and watch one of the sports channels. Tonight it was Cleveland Cavalier basketball.

"Who we going to fix Mark up with, Jenni?"

Jenni Block wasn't overly educated, pretty, smart, sexy, well off, religious, political or ambitious, but she was just what the "psychologist ordered" for Sam--a little of all of these. She was always happy with the economy, the government, the weather, her financial situation, her hair, the arrangement of the furniture, her wardrobe, the current situation, the restaurant menu, the music that was playing at the moment and on and on. This made her not like any woman Sam had ever known.

She was stubborn on some points, though, for example when Sam asked her to marry him she replied, "Sure, Sammy, if you'll change your last name from Jones to Block." Sam was still considering whether he could do that

Her blondish hair was very short, just below the ears, a little fly-awayish at times, and her eyes were a nondescript green. Her hips were a little small and her boobs were a bit saggy for her age, but Sam didn't seem to mind at all. She didn't wear makeup, which made her features less distinct and paler than most 30 year olds.

"I'd date Duke."

"No, Honey, you're all mine."

"No. I didn't mean I wanted to date him, just that I would date him if I weren't dating you."

"Okay, but who could we find for him? He's lonely."

"Does he just want time in bed or someone to fish with?"

"Probably both."

"Megan would be great for him in bed, cause she's had lots of experience. Is he a 69er kind of guy or straight missionary? Has he had any lately?" Jenni was often frank.

"Well, I don't know the answer to the first question and really don't want to think about it. 'I doubt it' would answer the second question, but I think he wants more than that."

"What then?"

"Somebody to do things with. Company."

"Oh, I know, I know, I know. Not Megan, I know of another girl." Jenni loved to play matchmaker, but she was seldom successful. "I'll call her. She'll be perfect."

Chapter 23. What to Believe

"Hey, old Buddy, come in and sit down. Coffee?" offered Jerry

"Good to see you. A cup of decaf would be fine," responded Mark.

"Sorry, no decaf, high test or nothing."

"Nothing, then."

"Same old smile, Buddy."

"Yep, can't seem to get rid of it. I always look like a cross between Jimmy Carter and Alfred E. Neuman."

"You're not as goofy looking as Alfred E. Neuman. Well, anyway, let's get at it, Pal. Two problems?"

"Yes. The first is a professional one. I feel like a hypocrite. I'm not preaching what I believe."

"Go on."

"The Old Testament is my big problem."

Mark explained that he conducted an outreach class at a sandwich shop near Wyandotte State University. The attendees loved to challenge him. He told how hard it was to answer questions about Jonah and Noah, God telling the Jews to take the Canaanites' land or killing the innocent first born Egyptians.

"Noah's Ark is a great story for cartoons in elementary Sunday school class workbooks, but it's hard for an educated, questioning adult to swallow," continued Mark.

"Go on."

"I want a *Bible* that starts with the title Genesis, but includes a subtitle: 'A book about natural science and civilization according to the tiny Jewish tribe, one of hundreds of thousands in the world at that time that had their own version of the creation and the history of the world.'"

Jerry laughed and then apologized. "Go on."

"Seems like we were so busy studying Greek and Hebrew, homiletics, church finances, Old Testament, New Testament, liturgy, membership building, tithing, and so on during seminary that there was little opportunity for questioning. We were taught Christianity according to the 'truth' as written by Reverend Jacob Matthews Haverston. Then we were taught how to preach that 'truth' to our congregations. I don't know about you, Jerry, but basically I got the message that the *Bible* according to our seminary founder Haverston indicated Catholics, Jehovah's Witnesses, Mormons and several other Christian sects were headed for hell, and of course Muslims, Jews, Hindus, Buddhists, and all other world religions would join them there. There didn't seem to be any searching for the truth going on."

"Okay."

"My opinion is that nobody knows the whole truth. If they did they would be God. So we have to develop our beliefs on faith, prayer, study and personal experience. How can any preacher say he has 'the truth' when so many preachers disagree with each other? Is there one truth or many? Many people will say just read the *Bible* and, *voila*, you will have the literal truth. But then why do we need preachers, thousands of people writing Sunday school study guides, *Bible* commentaries, theologians, song lyrics, sermons and magazines telling us what's true? Some ministers spend their lives trying to convince themselves that what they've been told is true, while I want to spend my life trying to discover what is true."

The flow from Mark's heart continued for a full hour, with Jerry patiently adding comments, such as, "Go on," "Yes," "Okay," and "I see."

Pastor Mark took a deep breath and wiped the sweat from his upper lip with the thumb and forefinger of his right hand. Despite the obvious tension, Pastor Mark had that smile on his face.

"You hungry? Let's take a break, Mark, and have some lunch."

Pastor Mark stopped staring intently at Jerry and glanced outside as if the world had disappeared during the last hour and had just reappeared.

"Okay. Are we done? I haven't shared my personal problem yet?" asked Pastor Mark

"Hardly, Pal. You have more, and I haven't had my opportunity yet. What's the nature of your personal problem?"

"A woman."

"Oh, boy. We'd better make lunch short."

Chapter 24. Reaching Your Toes

When Madison got home from school she was exhausted. Besides trying to teach history and economics, she had had to break up a fight between two girls, monitor the cafeteria during what was supposed to be her lunch hour, take pills for her cramps and counsel with a girl after school that had boyfriend problems, maybe a pregnancy.

She had two messages from William on her cell phone and one email, but she didn't want any more drama in her life for an hour or two or until her glass of moscato reached her toes. The daily newspaper sat unread in front of her, so she checked to see if her latest letter to the editor was in. It was.

Make School 24/7

It's hard to think of any major business facility in any community that is more underutilized than a school building. Classrooms are empty two weeks at Christmas, all weekends, a week in the spring and a couple of months in the summer. Plus, most classrooms are only occupied 7 hours a day. I don't seriously believe that school should run 24/7 but maybe 14/6.

Schools used to run from 8 a.m. to 3 p.m. to roughly coincide with parents' daily work hours. Students got out of school late in May and started early in September because farm work used to require a lot of manual labor during the growing season.

Today, many factories run 24/6 or 7 and some major businesses are also open 24 hours a day. Why not have school days and hours reflect that!

Many students, teachers and administrators would be happy to start school at 7 a.m. and be done at 3 p.m., and others would be delighted to come in at 1 p.m. and leave at 9 p.m. That would address the morning-person/night-person phenomenon. Plus, just think how that would make room for more singletons, classes that are only taught once a day but are often dropped because student scheduling conflicts keep enrollment in them so small that they're not economical.

Expanded summer schools or a year-round school calendar would also help take advantage of empty classrooms. If school facilities were

better utilized, buildings could be smaller, and the tax bill for schools could be reduced. Plus, businesses would have access to teen laborers during the day.

Another bus run might be necessary, as is sometimes set up so that athletes have a ride home from after-schools practices, but most of early and late classes could be available only to students who could provide their own transportation.

Desk Weary

Madison had a ton of work to do but she was not going to grade papers or write a project direction sheet yet. The whole weekend was ahead of her. It had been a half hour since she had finished her second moscato, so she was feeling a little tingle in her toes. She decided she was ready to listen to her cell phone messages and read her email.

First message: "Hey, Honey, I got two cases of wine from a new vineyard and want to try it, but not alone. Call."

Second: "Honey, the wine's chilling, so let's do the same. Call me."

Email: "Honey, don't know about you, but I felt something special when we met. If you didn't, don't worry about it. I'll try to recover Anyway, I close the store at 11. Can I come over? Hey, it's Friday and I'm ready to relax and enjoy your company.—Lonely Will"

Madison looked at the keyboard for a long time and then hit REPLY. She stared at his email address for five minutes. She canceled the reply and stood up. She placed her empty glass on the coffee table and looked out her window into the dark. One star was low in the horizon above the park trees. She refilled her glass and plopped down on the sofa.

Before she would let herself change her mind, she sprang off the sofa, pushed the REPLY icon and typed. "You're on." SEND. She looked around for a cancel icon or a recall button or the word *delete* on the email toolbar. Her stomach felt shaky as she stared at the monitor. Nothing. "Maybe it didn't go. Maybe he won't get it." She sat back in her chair and tried to breathe normally. She sipped more wine.

"One or two bottles, honey?" Popped onto her screen on the SUBJECT bar.

"Rats! That was fast," she thought, then modestly typed "One," and sent it. "What am I going to do?" She was talking to herself out loud again.

Chapter 25. The Word Is Love

The discussion dealing with Pastor Mark's concerns about his beliefs continued after a short lunch with Jerry. It included a variety of doubts. Sitting on the edge of his chair and leaning awkwardly toward Jerry, he mentioned Jake's lunch discussion about how "easy" he thought Christianity was. He told Jerry about his formula for salvation: "In the beginning was the Word. The Word was Jesus, God is Love, Therefore believe in love and you're saved."

Jerry had tried not to show pleasure or displeasure during Pastor Mark's unloading, but he shook his head at what he felt was a convoluted syllogism.

After two hours Pastor Mark breathed deeply, moved back from the edge of his chair and leaned for the first time against the seat back. Jerry let the air clear by silently counting 1, 2, 3, 4, 5, 6, 7, 8, 9, 10, 11 and so on until he got to 60. It was a counseling technique that let both parties think about the situation before plunging into possible solutions. It seemed like it took forever to count up to a minute, but it gave Pastor Mark a chance to come out of his trance.

"Okay, Buddy, let's get back on the right path—one path. First of all, you've forgotten your role. Are you the shepherd or the flock? You're letting the flock lead, and, since you're doing outreach, you're running into many people that are leading you astray. I remember working with a volunteer from another congregation in my church's soup kitchen one Saturday. We chatted while he ladled out green beans and I dipped whole cornel corn. Finally, he asked if I was saved, then continued with four questions that would test my salvation. I failed the exam, according to him. He told me, 'Jerry, you're going to hell. Come join the church I belong to and we'll lead you to the truth about Jesus.' When I told him I was the pastor of the church we were in, he apologized for doubting my salvation. I don't know what happened to his beliefs in the four questions, but they disappeared, and I didn't change my approach to God as you seem to be doing when questioned."

"Secondly, what do you believe in your heart? Do you believe in Jesus Christ? Were you called to the ministry, or did you simply choose a profession that happened to be the ministry? Has God worked miracles in your life and in the lives or those you serve? Is a Christian way of life the correct path for your congregation to follow?"

Pastor Mark confirmed that he felt called to the ministry, that he believed in Jesus Christ, that there had been many occasions when he felt the hand of God or an angel had changed the course of an event for the better, and, positively, that the life Jesus led illuminated the best path to live on earth.

"Then keep those things in mind," commanded Jerry. "And don't get led astray by all the confusion about the Old and New Testaments. Jesus taught in parables, but some believers somehow have to accept everything in the Old Testament as literal to bolster their faith. I don't care whether Job, Noah and Jonah were real or not. I use these characters to teach a message, not as a history lesson. It's hard for me to accept that God let Satan kill Job's innocent family to test Job. But I don't dwell on it too much.

"Anyone who has Googled about errors in the *Bible* will know that it's not perfect and that imperfect man had a hand in writing it. Man absolutely had a hand in on which ancient religious writings to include, which would become the Apocrypha and which to completely discard. The *Bible* has so many holes in it that if you had a handful of BBs and threw them at the *Bible*, a couple dozen would fly through. That doesn't mean that God's message isn't there, though.

"I don't preach about the creation of the Canon in the Third Century. If members of my congregation want to read about that era of church development, there's plenty of opportunity for them. But, if it's not important for their understanding of the *Bible*, so be it.

"Be careful about believing that all religions are from God. Even if you believe the scripture according to John I:1 meant to show that Love was sent by God in human form to save the world, and, therefore anyone who loves will be saved, you're on shaky ground with most Christian believers. You've stretched the passage substantially, and I see your point, but that is going to be hard for many Christians to swallow. Most people don't want metaphor, they want the truth. That's why many preachers include in their books or sermons phrases such as: "The truth of the matter is…," "Let me clue you in to the truth…," and "Here's the truth about…

"We know that only God knows the truth, and 'now we see as through a glass darkly.' So we have to continue to tell people to strengthen their beliefs through *Bible* study and discussion, and, yes, sermons, songs, and books. We need to continue to stress living a Christ-like life as proof of truly believing. Christianity does seem too easy, as Jake mentioned, but my message to my congregation is that people will ultimately live the way they believe they should live. Therefore, if they believe in Christ they should live a Christian life. If they say they believe and are saved but don't change their lifestyle, they may be fooling themselves into believing they are saved.

"In summary, Mark, stick to your beliefs. If you think that taking the *Bible* literally helps a parishioner with their faith, so be it. Preach what you believe. You don't have to address a view against any other religion or denomination if you don't want to just because our seminary founder did."

Mark came back with: "My big concern is world peace. Christianity, Judaism and Islam all seem to be exclusive religions. If they constantly call others who believe in the same God heathens, infidels, nonbelievers, and so forth, how is the world ever going to find mutual love, come together, be at peace? Don't we need to make them at least consider the possibility that all religions are from God?"

"I don't think that's within your control. If you truly believe what you just said, you need to switch denominations and become a Unitarian/Universalist or Baha'i pastor. And if you want to do that, I'm completely in support of you. I don't agree, but I do believe that we need to follow a path that makes sense to us."

"That's more than I want to consider at this time," said Mark.

"Well, Friend, I've got a council meeting in 15 minutes that I can't miss. The problem with a woman will have to wait. Tell me one thing, though, is she single or married?"

"Married."

"We'd better say a prayer."

Chapter 26. Love, Love

"Love, love, first serve," called Miss Ardnas across the court to Madison. "FBI?"

"Sure."

Since neither player had taken time to warm up her serves, they agreed on *first ball in* on each of their first services. Since they were paying for court time at the racket club, they didn't want to waste time and money practicing serves.

It took Miss Ardnas three tries to get a serve in to start the point. When Madison began serving, she hit three long and two into the net before getting a serve in play.

After 45 minutes each player had five games. Miss Ardnas was aggressive and often played the net, while Madison never came to the net unless her opponent hit a drop shot. Miss Ardnas played the sharp angles close to the net and Madison utilized finesse and top-spin shots down the lines, often taken from around the baseline. Though they played different strategies, they were an even match.

After Miss Ardnas won the first set in a tiebreaker, the two met at the net and shook hands, then went into the lounge for a couple of ice teas, unsweetened.

"I've been reading your letters to the editor. What fun!"

"Yes, it is fun. You can say what you feel without the students, parents and school board calling to complain. I have a little news. I'm dating."

"Way to go! Tell me more."

"It's too early to know where this will lead, but I hope for a relationship rather than just bed time."

"Bed time would be nice. But tell me what he's like."

"He's fun, romantic, a little too aggressive for my liking, but I've not dated for so long I kind of forgot how forward men are about sex. Don't get me wrong, we're not doing anything. I need to get back on the pill if things progress, but I want some commitment beforehand. So how are things with Franklin?"

Madison knew from one colleague at school, who had to be the first to know and tell any gossip, that Franklin always had a skirt he was chasing and catching. She felt sorry for Miss Ardnas, who didn't seem to know or didn't care. She didn't know which.

"Oh, he's okay, business is good as always, but he seems to not be as romantic as before. That's why I said some bedtime would be nice."

Just last night Miss Ardnas had put on her slinkiest nightie and scampered from the bathroom past Franklin in bed and dashed downstairs. After five minutes of standing behind a door to the kitchen waiting for him to follow, she was too embarrassed to walk back into the bedroom half naked and obviously rejected. So she went to the laundry room and found a robe in the dirty clothes basket and slipped it on. After that she got a glass of water from the pitcher in the refrigerator, rattled a few pots and pans as if she were tidying the kitchen, grabbed a couple of Tylenol PMs and walked back up stairs and sneaked into bed. But she couldn't sleep, having wanted and not gotten intimacy and confirmation of their mutual love.

"Is he on some medicine that's causing this? Maybe he's just concentrating too much on work."

Madison knew the answer—Franklin was getting all the sexual release he needed somewhere else. Miss Ardnas was just the housewife; Madison felt the fact like a rock in her gut.

"I'm old news. Let's hear about your man. Tell me, tell me," Miss Ardnas whined with mock enthusiasm but a big smile.

"He's a wine merchant. Doesn't that sound romantic in itself? He's a hugger and wants to be a feeler and then move on to more, but I stop him at the feeling. Don't get me wrong; I love it. It's been so long since anyone hugged me with more than an A-frame hug." And, faking a bass viol vibrating tone with her voice, she added, "He gives a full body hug."

"Lucky you. Tell me more."

"Well, it's kind of embarrassing, but when he came over Friday night after work, he brought two bottles of wine, chilled. After giving me a, you know, full-body hugging, or should I say mugging, he made me sit down on the sofa while he popped the corks. Both of them.

"He found the wine glasses and filled two half full and gave me one with a kiss on the back of my neck. Cherry bomb time. Then he took his warm hands and ran them down my neck to my tight shoulders. It felt like his hands were shower heads spraying warm water through the veins in my shoulders and down my arms and spine.

"After a few minutes of that he knelt down in front of me as if ready to propose marriage and lifted my feet onto the hassock, removed my shoes and massaged my feet. Now currents were running from my soles, up my legs, through my stomach and out the top of my head. At first I thought I was in love right there and then, but restrained myself.

"When he started running his hands up my bare legs, I had to call a stop to it. I was nearly ready to fall into bed with him the way it was. But I've played that game before to an unpleasant relationship and breakup. Slowly, slowly, I had to remind myself."

"So?" Miss Ardnas was almost begging to live vicariously through more description of Madison's date.

"We talked, drank the two bottles of Merlot, but I only had a half bottle for fear of you know what. Then we talked some more, kissed a little, and talked again. At about 2 a.m., I led him to the door. He gave me a body hug that sent a feather on a string right through my insides and an open-mouth kiss that was outer galactic. He teased me about making him leave early, and I had to tug so hard on the door to get it out of his grasp that flashes--like comets chasing each other-- flicked in circles inside my eyes. When I closed the door I just slumped against it for about a minute before I could get my breath."

"I assume this means you'll see him again."

"Well, YEAH!"

Chapter 27. Blind Date

"You still haven't told me her name," carped Sam.

"It's Betsy, I think. No, Marian," said Jenni. "You know me with names. She's the one that sits by herself in the back pew of the church. I don't even believe Pastor Mark knows her name. Kind of pretty. Bad dresser. No color at all. Quiet one."

"If you don't know her name, then how did you ask her to go on a blind date with Duke?"

"I talk to her after church over coffee every Sunday. So I just asked her about a blind date, but I didn't add, 'By the way, what's your name?' She seemed a little shy about accepting, but since we had talked about going out to eat together several times....well. And, to be honest, I kind of bullied her into it."

"Oh, Boy! Well, you probably should have asked her name."

"Worry wart. I'm sure it's Marian. Marian Hammond."

"Oh, boy! The introductions should be fun."

Marian was told to meet Sam, Jenni and her blind date at the Antler Inn. When they arrived, Duke was already seated and having a PBR. He had his hat off, his goatee trimmed and a clean plaid Western-style shirt on. He stood up when he saw them.

"Hey, old boy, how you doing?" asked Sam.

"Madison!" exclaimed Duke.

"Duke?"

"Hey, you guys know each other. That's great."

Madison and Duke couldn't look at each other despite the fact that she mistakenly took a seat directly across from him in order not to sit next to him. Even in the dim bar light Duke noticed something unusual about her eyes.

"Where'd you guys meet?" asked Jenni.

Duke mumbled, "Well, we haven't actually met."

"Whatever. Let's get some beers," butted in Sam.

"They're doing the Boot Scoot'n Boogie, Sammy. Let's go. Come on, you guys," Jenni prodded.

"Later," said Madison

When Sam and Jenni were clicking their heels and laughing on the dance floor, Duke moved over to the seat beside Madison and said, "Awkward, huh?"

"Yep."

"Sorry, I didn't know. Jenni thought your name was Marian. Don't tell her I told you that."

"Marian!"

"Yeah, Marian Hammond." They both laughed. Duke noticed that the photo Madison had used online was fairly true to the original face.

"Well, we're here, so now what? Should I fake an illness of some kind and leave you three to enjoy the evening?"

"Not on my account. You line dance?"

"No."

"Time to learn if neither of us is leaving." Before Madison could make excuses, Duke lifted her out of the chair by one arm and swung her up and onto the raised dance floor.

The line dancers had just begun Cotton-Eyed Joe to *Neon Moon*, so Duke made a second row so that Madison could watch the steps of the dancers in front of her. He led her from the side and she was light on her feet. She wasn't making any sound with her soft-soled shoes, but the rest of the group was booming away.

The song ended and Madison was sweating from exertion and nervousness. She dabbed at her forehead and cheeks with the back of her hand but forgot to exit the stage. Duke nudged her and the whole dance floor went into the Electric Slide before she even knew what happened.

By the fourth beer and the 11th dance, Madison was yahooing with the rest of them. Everyone was smiling and dripping wet from under their arms, down their backs, and, with the women, between their breasts. No one seemed to mind that there were dark sweat patches on their clothes. Madison took a pee break between two dances and used a Kleenex to remove what was left of the smeared makeup from her face. Since Jenni didn't use makeup, she had no problem.

The line dancing kept Madison and Duke from the embarrassment of their email fiasco. Finally after the 14th dance, Madison begged off, and Duke and Jenni took the floor.

"So, how do you and Duke know each other?" asked Sam.

"We traded a few emails through an online dating website. Photos too," responded Madison

"Not backinthegame.com? That's where Jenni and I met."

"One and the same."

"Oh. I take it that it didn't go so well."

"My fault. I'm not very adventurous." She didn't want to insult everything she saw Sam wearing—giant buckle, western shirt and pants, cowboy boots and Nascar cap rather than a cowboy hat. She saw these all as hillbilly, redneck, backwoods, bumpkin and unsophisticated. Duke wore similar clothing. Plus Duke's online photo was pure corn rather than pure country.

"Duke's a good guy. I've known him for years. Too bad about tonight. Jenni just jumps into the middle of things without thinking. You're handling it well, though."

"Thanks. Don't worry about me. I've never line danced, but I also don't remember when I've lost myself so thoroughly in something."

"I could tell you're a natural when I looked back at you on the first dance. You were only an instant behind. When we did Cotton-Eyed Joe the second time, you had it memorized already. That's amazing."

"All those dance lessons my mother paid for counted for something," thought Madison.

As it got later the music slowed down and the lights became dim. Sam and Jenni looked at each other with silly grins after they had glanced at Madison in Duke's arms mid floor during the playing of *Islands in the Stream*. Madison even let her head swing back as Duke whirled her around the floor. They looked good together.

With her whole body wet and her hair seemingly trying to escape her scalp, kind of like Jenni's blondish hair always did, Madison let Duke walk her to her car.

"Well, sorry about all the embarrassment and ...."

Madison lifted herself on her tiptoes and planted a kiss right on Duke's lips.

Chapter 28. Pushing Buttons

Cam and April had been watching television, but Miss Ardnas made them stop and work on their homework. She stopped her own homework endeavors, writing *Ersatz News*, every fifteen minutes to check to see if they were still on task and doing the work correctly.

To spark some interest in her students during the next class and to create another argumentative essay assignment, Miss Ardnas finished a piece to add to *Ersatz News and Views*.

Drug Testing Coming to Music and Movie Industries
Ersatz Entertainment News—Las Nevados, California

The music and movie industries are working on a plan to reduce use and abuse of illicit drugs by their industries. That has initiated a group called Music Movie Drug Monitoring Association (MMDMA).

Kayle Williamshire, a lawyer representing both industries, is drafting the documents that will regulate the testing, fines and punishments for using illegal drugs.

Williamshire says that most professional sports and employers in manufacturing industries require their employees to be drug free.

Sports teams even have regular testing to assure that someone is not using drugs to enhance their performance, unfairly competing with other athletes. Even some high schools have random drug testing.

MMDMA committee members believe they need the same thing. Those with some music or acting talent should not unfairly enhance their abilities and stamina to play concerts or entertain the public. Those who aren't artificially stimulated can't keep up the touring pace of someone on illegal drugs.

According to preliminary reports, before a band could come into a city to perform, its members would be drug tested to make sure they are adhering to the industry regulations. Concerts would be canceled if illegal drug use were found. Actors would be periodically tested in order to keep their membership in acting guilds.

Williamshire continued with the following statement: "The music and movie industries care about their people just as much as the sports industry. Helping our talented pool of musicians and actors avoid drug abuse and its consequences are long overdue. Drugs are ruining the lives of our members in both fields."

Upon hearing the news, one music lover interviewed about the proposal commented, "What will happen to sex, drugs and rock and roll? I guess if the testing begins, there will still be two out of three."

Miss Ardnas prepared questions for her students?
1. Is the proposal constitutional?
2. Are movie and music stars performances comparable to athletic competitions?
3. Would music be better or worse if this proposal went into effect?
4. Would musicians and actors be better off if they were made to refrain from drug use?
5. Baseball, track, cycling and football organizations have had a hard time successfully stopping illegal drug use by athletes. Would the music and movie industries have the same problem?
6. What other thoughts come to mine after reading this article?

Essay topic: "Weighing all the pros and cons mentioned in today's discussion, what do you recommend the movie and music industries do? Conduct some research, then use quotations, anecdotes, and statistics to support your point of view. As always, be conscious of the authority of your sources, and provide credentials in your essay."

Miss Ardnas went back to thinking about Franklin. If he wasn't having an affair, why was he so disinterested in making love? She still had plenty of urges, and she had read that men have libidos that are active long past those of their wives'. "Should I try the nightie gambit tonight?" Miss Ardnas asked herself. "Could I stand it if he rejected me again?"

Chapter 29. The Fetal Position

Four Advil and an enormous cup of coffee didn't do much to relieve Cali's headache and achy shoulders and hips or to change her mood. Her temperature was over 102, and she wanted to keep it out of the danger zone. This was the second day she had basically lain in the fetal positions under three blankets. Every so often she had to throw off all the covers and use a towel to dry the perspiration. She went from hot to cold to hot again.

She had a call in to the doctor for an appointment, and a nurse said she would try to work Cali in sometime in the afternoon. The nurse would call.

Cali had been off work for three weeks, none of her grants had been granted, but she knew she could get a student loan that would be enough to live on if she shared an apartment with several other students. She was worried that she wouldn't be accepted at 32. A feeling of doom overcame her.

She tried not to think of Franklin, especially since a friend at the Wright office had called her about the hiring of a cute, short girl as Cali's replacement. The friend had said Franklin had been able to get in bed with the new girl after only one week.

"There he goes again," thought Cali. She felt like calling the new hiree and giving her the lowdown. But she knew it probably wouldn't work. She had had enough subtle and not so subtle red flags waved in front of her before she had leaped into bed with Franklin.

The phone rang and the nurse told Cali to be at the doctor's office in 30 minutes. Cali got dressed, half-heartedly applied some makeup and drove to the doctor's.

After he had examined her, he told her he was puzzled. So he took blood samples and told her not to worry that he'd get to the bottom of her aches and pains. He told her he'd have the tests run overnight since she felt so badly and her temperature was so high. He suggested two Tylenol every six hours and said he'd have a nurse call her tomorrow with the results.

Cali went home, took four more Advil, twisted back into the fetal position and covered up. She felt awful physically and emotionally.

"I feel like I'm dying. Maybe I should just go ahead," she said to herself, as she thought about the varied and potent prescription and over-the-counter medicines in her bathroom cabinet.

Chapter 30. At the Top of His Game

With a new secretary and bed partner, Franklin felt at the top of his game. His golf scores were even better. Policy sales were brisk, and his two kids were busy and successful at school. Miss Ardnas seemed more relaxed and focused on her university classes. It did bother him, though, that one night a month or so ago she had tried to lure him into having sex. He loved her but didn't see her as sexy anymore. Ironically, he felt that if he made love to Miss Ardnas he would be cheating on his new secretary.

Cali completely left his mind as Tiffany James' smooth, shapely little body filled its place. Tiffany wasn't much of a secretary, but she was nearly professional in the sack. She was a tiny dynamo. She didn't seem disparate to Franklin, whereas Cali had. Tiffany enjoyed Franklin's company, didn't mind sneaking around to edge-of-town bars, and happily met him at her condo, almost as if she were using Franklin instead of vice versa.

Franklin attended Pastor Mark's church each Sunday with his family. While interacting with fellow congregation members after the main service, he was oblivious to Pastor Mark's attempts to have a serious conversation with him. The reverend had asked Franklin several times to just stop by his office to have a friendly chat.

Pastor Mark knew about Tiffany and Franklin—no affairs in a town the size of Wyandotte were ever publicly hidden except from the cheated-on husband or wife. Pastor Mark never did understand the morality of keeping a secret about infidelity, so he felt guilty about being one who practiced this custom. He hated looking at his friends and parishioners while in possession of a personal, heartbreaking and potentially humiliating secret. Knowing that they walked around with everyone looking at them with pity or shame was almost more than Pastor Mark could tolerate.

Of course, since Pastor Mark was still carrying a torch, or let's say bonfire, inside that had started in high school, he especially disliked seeing Miss Ardnas so mistreated and ill thought of. Mark could hardly stand to look at Franklin. He wanted to bury his fist up to the elbow in Franklin's stomach, run an electric razor across his fashionable haircut, smudge some charcoal on his always creased and pristine shirt and pants, and scuff his daily shined shoes. Mark knew these were childish thoughts, but they gave him some temporary satisfaction.

Franklin was in his recently washed convertible heading for the country club. He hoped to kick his best golf buddy's butt, then meet a client and close a deal over Jack Daniels on ice. After that he would call Tiffany and tell her to leave work early and meet him at her condo for a little rendezvous. For him, it couldn't be a more perfect day.

Chapter 31. Juggling Men

Madison wondered how she had gone from no men in her life to two. Now the juggling would begin. William was very possessive and had been leaving personal and other items at her apartment—sandals, corkscrew, light jacket, case of wine, and work cell phone. Like a dog he was obviously marking his territory. When she told him she was dating around, he wanted to know why.

She tried to explain, but he started to call more often and stop by unannounced when he could. It made Madison uncomfortable, but she did like the physical part of their relationship. He was fun and a good kisser, yet the intellectual part of her wasn't stimulated by their discussions. She had gone ahead and put herself on the pill, just in case the god of wine and the goddess of hormones got the better of her. They still hadn't made it into bed, but not because William hadn't tried to pull, push, carry, drag, beg, whine and otherwise have his way.

Her dates with Duke were completely different. He took her on walks in the woods not far from her apartment. She couldn't believe there was a whole, real, alive world away from golf-course-smooth lawns, cement walks, mall parking lots, and paved roads. He pointed out the wonders of nature.

"There's a birch," stated Madison, while on one of their nature walks.

"No, that's a beech. Sadly, people like to carve hearts and names in beech bark."

Duke's dog perked up his ears but continued walking just ahead of them

"It's so quiet back here. Where are we going?"

"There's a heron rookery coming up soon."

"A what?"

"An apartment complex for 200 nesting pair of blue herons," Duke wryly answered.

"Don't patronize me, Buddy," Madison teased. "Are there snakes back here?" She was taking deliberately high steps.

"Not that eat young teachers. Look."

Madison looked up to see huge basket nests with herons perched on them. She accidently took a step forward to see past a limb and stepped on a dry branch. The cracking sound startled the birds and 25 or so giants flapped into the air and made lazy-looking loops.

The more she looked into the tall sycamores the more baskets she began to identify. One heron was flying to its nest with a three-foot or so snake dangling from each side of its bill. She couldn't believe this was in walking distance of her apartment.

They crossed a small rivulet that lead to the creek beneath the nests. Duke said, "Madison, stand over against that tree."

"What are you doing?"

Duke had a short but thick stick in one hand and had the other hand about three feet away, poised. "There's a turtle in the water, under a log."

"Oooh, let me see," shouted Madison, running forward.

Simultaneously both of Duke's hands went down, a splash and a snap were heard near the hand with the stick, and the other hand went into the water. Out came a snapping turtle by the tail as big around as a turkey platter. Madison stumbled backward, fell, got back up and placed her back against a tree. The turtle still had the stick in its mouth and didn't look too happy about what was happening at its tail end.

"He's a beauty, hey?"

Bark barked and ran over to smell the catch.

"Not too close, Boy."

"Get rid of him, get rid of him," Madison screamed.

"Okay. Okay. There you go, buddy."

To calm Madison down, Duke asked her if she'd seen a blue heron before today.

"Oh, yes. They come to the pond at the apartment complex."

"How about a green heron?"

"No. Are they really green?"

"Well, not much, bout as green as a blue heron is blue."

On the way to the pond where William knew green herons frequented, they saw two does and a fawn scramble up and dart through the trees, their metronome white tails flicking side to side. Then Duke and Madison reached a clearing with about a one-acre body of water.

"There! The bird with the long, reddish neck stuck out in front of it."

"Where?"

"There."

Duke moved behind her, touching her lightly, and pointed over her shoulder to a dark shape in a cottonwood tree.

"See it?" asked Duke.

Just then it flew to another tree.

"Yeah. It is a little greenish. How beautiful. Are they common around here?"

"Oh, yeah, but not in backyards or parking lots."

"What's that bird?"

"American redstart."

"I suppose they're common too."

"Yep. They like open areas near woods. Look here. It's a bird's nest." Duke had a keen eye for spotting the wonders of nature.

"It looks like the bird stole someone's spool of thread. See these bits of magenta?"

"Birds will use string, animal hair, twigs, and, obviously, thread."

"What other animals have you seen in here?"

"Gray fox, red fox, groundhogs, piney and fox squirrels, muskrats, possums, skunks, raccoons, cedar waxwings, barred owls, coyotes, red tail hawks, redwing blackbirds. There's too many to name them all. Frogs, toads, harmless snakes, spotted and red back salamanders."

Madison was enjoying the woods. Duke was enjoying watching her. He was standing on one leg with the other leg crossed in front of it and just the toe of his boot touching the ground. His left arm was stretched out so that he could lean on a mammoth oak. Madison was picking up walnuts, hickory nuts and acorns from under several trees and inspecting them. A squirrel dropped a walnut from about 50 feet onto a hollow log. The noise frightened Madison and she ran up behind Duke, ducked her head under the arm leaning on the tree and raised up so his arm was around her.

He tucked her in close, looked down at her face and raised his eyebrows. She looked up, batted her eyes like a flapper and twisted her lips into a goofy grin. To Duke it felt as if Madison's gray eyes were reaching into his soul.

"This is wonderful. It's like a zoo without bars."

"I like it. You should see it in later in the spring when the trillium, redbud, dogwood, and other plants are in bloom. Plus edible mushrooms galore."

"Please bring me back here then and show me."
"You're on."

Chapter 32. Round Two

"Okay, Buddy, round two" is how Jerry greeted Pastor Mark on their second counseling session. Jerry gave Pastor Mark a pat on the back and offered him a chair. Neither man had been looking forward to the meeting, but both knew that things had to be faced to be resolved.

Despite the importance of their meeting, they spent several minutes on small talk--the weather, local politics, golf and the stock market. Finally Pastor Mark asked: "Where do I start?"

"What's her name?"

"Miss Ardnas. She's called Miss Ardnas by her college students, family and friends, although her last name is Wright."

"And what is your relationship with her at this time?"

"She's a friend from high school days and member of my congregation."

"And...."

"I'm in love with her. I've been in love with her since high school."

"And she's married?"

"Yes."

"Do I know her?"

"No."

"Wait a minute. This isn't the same girl whose pictures were all over your wall at seminary is it?"

"No. Well, I don't think so."

"All your friends would come in and look at your pictures and ask something like, 'Who's the girl in most of the pictures? Unless that's his sister, I think Mark's in love.'"

"They said that?"

"Well, it was obvious. There were more photos with her in them with groups and other people than there were pictures with you in them."

"It was that obvious?"

"It sure was, Buddy."

"Well, I guess that was Miss Ardnas. I've never gotten over her and I have thoughts about her I wish I didn't have."

"Okay."

"Sometimes I wish her husband would get killed. Makes me kind of a David lusting for Bathsheba."

"Go on."

"She and I were friends, but never more than that, although I wanted more. Then she went to college, graduated and married a guy named Franklin Wright. Two kids later she's an unhappy wife with a philandering husband. She wants to believe he's faithful, but she's come to me with doubts. Actually, I'm pretty sure she knows."

"Well."

"I'm conflicted. My heart tells me to call him out, tell her the truth about him, and when they divorce ask her out."

"Wow!"

"Right. But am I wanting to confront him and help her only for my personal gain or for their sake? If it's for their sake, shouldn't I want reconciliation instead of divorce? Plus, I'm coveting my neighbor's wife. I'm committing adultery according to the *Bible* when I look at her as I would a girlfriend or wife."

"So, what are you thinking you'll do?"

"I don't sit down with other couples that have one partner covertly cheating and bring the affair out in the open, so I feel guilty about considering it with Franklin and Miss Ardnas. I love counseling Miss Ardnas, because I can be close to her, but I probably should refer her to another pastor. I guess I could pull a Pontius Pilate and wash my hands of the whole affair."

"Are you comfortable with that?"

"No, but it's probably the best I can do under the circumstances. I'll try to support them in their efforts outside the counseling sessions."

Jerry used the knuckles of his right hand to give one resonant tap of his desk the way a judge might gavel a verdict finalized: "Well, that settles it then. Let's enjoy our next hour together over lunch at Lucy's Diner while we complain about our church board meetings."

Chapter 33. Bottoming Out

The fever was still with her, her joints ached, the headache was worse, she was popping pills like a kid munching Skittles, and all she could think about was what a whore she had been with Franklin. He paid her salary, bought her jewelry, fed her at expensive restaurants, and took her on business trips. Now that she looked back on her life with Mr. Wright, she had to admit that she was just a paid escort, or, in her mind, a prostitute. She also had to admit she used her sexuality to get the material things she wanted but failed at finding love and commitment.

The phone rang and the nurse at the doctor's office gave her the good news: "All your blood tests were normal. Doctor just thinks you've got a bad virus that will go away in a day or two. Or sometimes it's FUO. If the fever persists, we'll do more tests. He said to keep taking Tylenol. Then call us next week if your symptoms continue."

When Cali put down the phone, she felt worse—psychologically and physically. It felt like someone had put a pin into each of her eyes.

"What did the nurse call it? F.U.D.? Well, that's what I feel like, FUD," she mumbled aloud.

When she Googled *FUD* and *fever* she got FUO, Fever of Unknown Origin. Oh, great. Some of the causes of FUO weren't pleasant to read about. She really felt like she was dying, and a nebulous diagnosis didn't help. Her heart seemed to be off beat, and she was panting part of the time as if she couldn't take a full breath. Did she have something so rare they didn't even know what it was? Cali wasn't a religious person, but she went down on her knees and said a prayer. Maybe she should call her mother.

Then she told herself that the doctor had checked her heart, lungs, blood pressure, and blood work and found nothing wrong. "Nothing is wrong!" she said aloud. The pain persisted and she went back into the fetal position and covered up her body and put a cold washcloth on her forehead. She felt like amoebas were taking a nip here and a nip there from all her joints so that soon there wouldn't be anything left of her.

She knew if she called her mother it would set a whirlwind into motion: "Go immediately to the ER, then call two or three specialists, and I'll pack right now and be on my way, Honey. Don't hang up. I'll talk you through this as I drive the five hours from Philly."

"I can just wait a day and see what happens. Surely I won't die that soon," she told herself. But the pins in her eyes caused her to wonder if she could wait. Plus she couldn't get that jerk Franklin out of her mind. She reached for the generic acetaminophen PM next to the bed and the bottle of vodka.

Chapter 34. More than a Full Moon

She was walking through the woods. The path was narrow, with branches and plants seeming to reach out to retard her progress. Suddenly the path opened up, and she saw a river about 40 feet below. Then she noticed a bridge, a swinging bridge.

Without hesitation, she started walking across the bridge with her hands on the guide wires on each side. The bridge started swaying on its own, and she started to panic. She was afraid she was going to fall off, but that seemed impossible unless the entire structure turned upside down.

A few steps further and she apparently, like a ghost, passed right through the left guide wire, dropping toward an eddy of the river. She woke before she hit the water. Miss Ardnas was sweating, her nightie was twisted around her and her pillow was a foot away on the floor. Par for the course, Franklin was sound asleep next to her.

While she was dreaming about the bridge, Pastor Mark, at the parsonage, was dreaming of his childhood. In the dream he and his family were on vacation near Lake Superior in the Upper Peninsula of Michigan. He and his brother had been left alone to explore the beach and nearby woods. The Big Two-Hearted River flowed into the lake near where the family was camped. Both Mark and his brother were intrigued by the artistic swirls of the dark tannin-stained river as it flowed out into the lake and mixed with the clear Lake Superior water. They discovered pieces of Styrofoam, wood, a net, a dead fish, and cardboard containers.

They also found a rowboat abandoned and washing back and forth in the waves ten feet off shore. They pulled the boat on shore, then pushed it back out and climbed in. They wanted to row in the lake a little. Mark took the oars. When they were out nearly a 100 yards, Mark's brother decided he wanted to row. In passing each other, Mark tipped the boat and they both fell in. Although the oars were wooden, they sunk.

Mark's brother became Jerry, and Jerry told Mark to climb back into the boat. When they tried, the boat filled with water and sunk. Jerry disappeared from the dream, and Mark was swimming to shore alone through the tannin.

The lake water was so cold he could hardly move and he felt his legs, back and arms cramping. He was still 20 yards from shore when he began to sink. Just as he was taking his last breath before going under for good, he felt a push from below that propelled him forward. Sand was under his feet, and he walked onto the beach where his brother was drying off. Then he woke up.

In a daze, Pastor Mark tried to make sense of the dream. The dream reminded him of when he almost drowned trying to swim across a gravel pit. Just as he was about to cramp up and sink, he felt propelled to firm ground--he always assumed by his guardian angel.

Jenni and Sam slept dreamlessly their first two hours in bed because they had spent an hour of exertion to please each other before turning in. Then Sam, in dreamland, took a truncated swing at a softball and bumped Jenni's arm. He had played church league softball four hours earlier and his ribs still ached from taking a Casey-at-the-Bat swing at the first off-speed pitch. Jenni awoke, misread the incident and punched him on the arm, saying, "Again? I'm too sleepy, Slugger. Wait till morning."

Jerry was sleeping fitfully. He dreamed that he had decided to go sky diving. The pilot changed from his wife to Mark while he was still in the plane. He jumped out of the plane but realized he had no parachute on his back. Halfway down a chute appeared on his chest and not his back, but the rip cord wouldn't work.

The plane disappeared, and Mark whizzed by him and yelled that he couldn't get his chute open and wanted help. Jerry threw him his chute and then realized he didn't have anything to save himself. Jerry's wife appeared in a hot air balloon and rescued him, but he couldn't locate Mark. Jerry woke up and accidently jostled his wife, who questioned, "You all right?"

Cali was unable to reach deep sleep, so she spent eight hours in nightmares. Planets crashed against each other like erratically flying colorful bowling balls. She fell through infinite spaces. Colliding orbs haunted her. Clicks and snaps echoed in her ears. She had no place in the universe to place her feet for security. There was no hope. Only darkness separated the bowling ball planets. When she awoke she was shaking. She thought, "Death means eternal nothingness."

Duke had fished after work, then split some wood for the fireplace, eaten a steak, green beans and fries, then finished the evening by reading with a glass of port in his hand one instant and his pipe the next. He and Bark slept like proverbial logs.

After closing at 11, William had called Madison but had gotten no answer. Then he drank a bottle from his latest case of Shiraz from Australia and sat moping. He was not a reader, TV seemed to be only commercials as he zipped through the stations, and he was horny. He slept fitfully, with dreams of faceless, but skin-flashing girls at a party making themselves available to him. In the dream he showed no interest in any of them.

Then he was climbing a mountain, but every time he reached the peak, it turned out to be a false summit, with another peak further on. He refused to give up although his lungs felt like they would burst. He awoke angry at Madison.

Madison had gone to bed early since it was a school night. As she headed for a deep sleep, images of her last-period class materialized in her mind. Most seventh-hour classes were rowdy simply because they were tired of sitting and also because they wanted to be free to move, talk at will, eat and drink food that was bad for them, swear, go to work and make out.

She had tried to get her students' minds on the Spanish-American War, but they kept trying to get her to ramble on about her three-week vacation last summer in Europe. Every time she had all the books open, pencils poised to take notes, visuals on the SmartBoard and her outline in her hand, one of the students would ask again about Rome, Paris, Munich, Pompeii, Venice or Innsbruck. This frustrating circular struggle only ended when Madison passed beyond the REM stage of sleep.

The night atmosphere had been filled with more than the light of a full moon.

Chapter 35. Give a Whistle

"Look, a maple seed, double-wing thing," called out Madison. "And there's the tree. We had a maple in our yard when I was a kid. I loved it when the propellers started to fall around me. I would chase them and try to catch one. Then I'd climb into the tree and shake a limb to make more fall."

Duke had taken Madison to a wooded area his grandparents used to own. It was in southern Indiana a few hours from Wyandotte, Kentucky.

"Okay, educator, now you're going to be the student, and I'll be the teacher. You've been lecturing me about Ohio, Kentucky and Indiana history the whole way her. You bring me a leaf and I will identify the tree. Try to stump me," challenged Duke.

"How will I know you're not making up the tree name?"

"Because I'm an honest, Boy Scout kind of guy."

"Oh, boy, you were a Scout?"

"Eagle Scout and scout master. I have badges on my badges."

Madison brought him a stack of leaves.

"See this mitten shape? Sassafras. Crumble the leaf and stem and smell it," suggested Duke.

"Root beer."

"Right, the roots of Sassafras were used for root beer. This one is shaped like a tulip. It's a poplar or tulip poplar."

"You making that up?" questioned Madison.

"Look it up when you get home."

"What about this one?"

Puffing slowly on his pipe, he said: "Well, it looks like it's from a compound leaf. Bring me the cluster of leaves and I may be able to identify it as a walnut or ash. This one is an oak. That's shagbark hickory. Did the tree have loose bark?"

"Yeeeessss. What about these two different pines?"

"The three-needle one is a red pine and the five is white. Count the needles and match them to the number of letters in the name."

"No. Really?"

"I'm not kidding."

Duke put the wing of a maple seed on his tongue and blew a whistling sound. Madison giggled. Then he whistled with the beret of an acorn. Madison began laughing, so he grabbed a blade of grass, stretched it between the bottom and tips of his two thumbs and made another whistle.

"Stop it," Madison huffed out with her eyes watering.

"Watch this." He shaped his two hands into a conch shape and whistled again. Madison dropped to her knees with her hands on her thighs, shaking with laughter. He loved entertaining her. When he cupped the two middle fingers of his left hand under and stuck the index and little finger of his left hand under his tongue and blew, the shrill sound caused Madison to leap up and clamp her hand over his mouth. When he pulled her hand away she kissed him on the cheek.

"I don't remember this kind of student/teacher relationship when I was in school. Tell me about the big handsome boys in your classes."

"Show me some more things."

"Aah, the piece de resistance."

"What?"

"Just wait."

They walked further for a half hour until they came to a dry creek bed.

"Sit down," commanded Duke.

"Here? On the gravel?"

"Yes, on the gravel."

"You sure?"

"Sit."

"I'm sitting, I'm sitting."

"Start looking through the gravel."

"Is this a joke?"

"Look."

Madison sifted the gravel through her hands.

"What are these funny looking rocks?"

"Crinoids, or Indian beads."
"Look, here's a long piece. It's a plant of some kind."
"Actually, it looks like a plant, but it's an animal and now a fossil. You're looking at a skeleton."
"What's this dark thing with the scarab pattern?"
"A trilobite or, you got it, a scarab. A petrified insect."
"They're all over the place."

The wash where they were sitting was a cut through an embankment. So Duke had Madison crawl over to its base. She wondered, "Now what?" Right away she picked up two muskmelon-size stones that looked like petrified brains.

"Weird."
"Geodes."

Duke placed one on a flat rock and struck it with the edge of another stone. The second strike split it open.

"Look."
"It's hollow."
"Look again."
"Diamonds?" blurted Madison.
"No, just quartz crystal."
"Shaped like a womb."
"In a way it is a womb," said Duke.
"What planet am I on? Have these things always been a few hours from where I've lived all my life? First the woods near my apartment and now this."
"Neat, hey? Wait till I take you on our next outing."
"You can top this?"
"Oh, yeah."

Chapter 36. No Compromises

Despite the tone and content of Pastor Mark's conversation with Jerry, he decided he couldn't in good conscience continue to preach easy sermons, back off from real problems in his congregation and compromise what he believed.

His heart told him to start a sermon series on the history of the *Bible*, especially the final putting together of the Christian Canon. Rumblings in the congregation began immediately. The dogma of most churches in Wyandotte followed traditional religious beliefs.

After a sermon during which Pastor Mark expressed his opinion that Jonah, Job and Noah were fictional characters, the board of Elders were bombarded with calls. Some families disappeared from the congregation. Almost everyone in Wyandotte Valley Church loved him, but his preaching had changed, and change for most Christians wasn't accepted. They wanted "truth" as it had been expressed for millenniums, even if the Church had to deny scientific or historical fact. The Church had gone on in the dark for years before admitting that the Earth was not the center of the universe, and it also was not even the center of the solar system. Galileo was one of the scientists who took a beating by the Church on that issue.

Although he had told Jerry he wouldn't, Pastor Mark decided to face the Miss Ardnas/Franklin affair head on. Having been brushed off whenever he met Franklin and suggested a meeting, Pastor Mark composed a letter and mailed it.

Dear valued Friend and Member of My Congregation,

You may remember that Miss Ardnas told you she counseled with me some weeks ago. Her concern was your marriage. It is well known that you have had multiple affairs over the past ten years. Sadly, everyone in the community but Miss Ardnas seems to be cognizant of them.

When she met with me, she expressed concerns about an affair with Cali, but was never sure. Now I assume she doesn't know about Tiffany. I know it's uncommon for pastors or friends to be as direct as this concerning delicate and private matters, but you made a commitment to Miss Ardnas and God when you married her. That commitment has been broken. Let's work together to repair it.

My recommendation is for you to meet with me to discuss this situation, during which I will ask you to beg God for forgiveness. That should be followed by your confessing to Miss Ardnas and asking her for forgiveness. Then I suggest we have a series of marriage counseling sessions to support a new path toward openness, honesty and fidelity.

As your pastor I am concerned with your spiritual health and wish only the best for you and Miss Ardnas. I hope to receive a call from you soon.

In Christian Love,
Mark Wellston, Pastor
Wyandotte Valley Church

It was no surprise that Franklin was missing from the Wright family pew the next Sunday. Only Miss Ardnas and the children were in attendance. When Mark asked about Franklin, Miss Ardnas explained--without apparent believing it--that he had gone to the hospital to visit an ill friend.

Chapter 37. Moving Forward

One thing William liked about Madison was that she enjoyed physical activity. They jogged some mornings before their respective jobs, they played tennis under the lights in the park or at the racquet club, they went on bike rides on the Wyandotte Greenway, and they bowled at least once a month.

He wasn't getting enough time with Madison, though. He knew she was seeing someone else and that caused him to be extremely jealous. He stopped by her house unexpectedly several times a week, but he seldom found her at home. That troubled him. If he did find her home, she wouldn't let him stay. She'd make excuses about having papers to grade or lessons to plan.

He persisted, because he felt she was someone he could love enough to marry and settle down with.

His business was excellent and she had a good job, so a marriage between the two of them would not be a problem financially. He would be happy for her to leave her apartment and move into his small house, but she would never even come to his house for more than just a short time to pick up something before tennis or bike riding.

William had intentionally been leaving personal items at Madison's, such as an extra set of keys, a tie, expensive pen, or cell phone. That gave him an excuse for showing up if he found her home.

One Saturday he took a whole day off and turned the shop over to his assistant so that he could spend extended time with Madison. They jogged to a corner restaurant for breakfast, then they met again after breakfast for a ride out into the country to the Barntown Flea and Farm Market.

They hiked into a field and u-picked lettuce to buy and take home. After the trek through the weeds they had to sit and pick bur after bur out of each other's socks. They met a third time for a salad supper at the local grocery soup-and-salad bar. That was followed by two hours of singles tennis.

William didn't have any big strokes or strategies—he came to the net when he should have stayed back and stayed back when he should have been at the net. He moved well and kept the ball in play. The fact that Madison could hit down-the-line shots from her baseline and top-spin lobs from any place on the court made the matches a little one-sided in her favor. Though the matches were interesting, she always won.

After tennis she changed into a light dress, and he put on slacks and they met for the fourth time that day at a club near her apartment for drinks. William disliked that they had to go to their respective residences to change clothes. He felt like they were boxers being told by the referee to return to their respective corners before beginning the next round. Of course, the slow pace had been Madison's idea.

When they went back to her apartment, they each took a glass of moscato, then William began his massage routine—kneading first her neck and shoulders. All of Madison's muscles were buzzing from the hours of physical activity.

They sat and drank. One glass was so soothing that they had several more. William resumed his massage. He took off her sandals. She loved that he would rub the pain from her tired feet. The buzzing increased as the wine caused her eyelids to go to half-mast over her silver irises. When he started to run his hands up her legs and under her dress, to his surprise she let him. He picked up her bare legs, and, as he placed them on the sofa, she swiveled onto her back, then stretched her arms over her head to let him remove her dress.

Her arms bent at the elbows and her hands hung over the end of the sofa arm. She relaxed as he slipped his hands under her pelvis, then moaned softly as their bodies worked in unison and shared the pleasure of their first physical intimacy.

After both Madison and William's breathing returned to normal, he pulled the afghan from the back of the sofa and covered her. He kneeled sideways to the sofa, and, while looking into her mystical-grey eyes, kissed her neck and mouth and told her how wonderfully smooth her skin felt, how beautiful her body was, how much he loved her for her intelligence, grace and charm, and how her eyes mesmerized him. Stroking her hair and kissing her still perspiration-covered forehead, he added that she had to be the most wonderful girl in the world.

He placed his head on her stomach and they both went to sleep.

Chapter 38. In Jeopardy

"Mark, you got time to talk?"

"Jerry?"

"Suicide is considered a mortal sin."

"What are you talking about?" Pastor Mark asked as he munched on a Fig Newton cookie. He hadn't had anything to eat except a piece of cake after church, and it was the middle of the afternoon.

"I'm not hearing good things about your preaching. You're really on the edge. I thought we had talked through how to handle your doubts and bypass scripture you have questions about."

"You know what? I don't want to be a minister if I have to be that way. I'm preaching to my congregation each week about integrity, while I hide behind half lies and avoid confronting what I see as sin."

"That's honorable, but you're not going to be able to bring salvation to many if you get fired."

"So be it."

"I've done some checking with friends in Wyandotte. Franklin Wright, I hear, has a strong campaign to get you sacked. What's the situation between Franklin and Miss Ardnas?"

"I wrote him a letter accusing him of adultery and asking him to come for counseling."

There was an audible sigh from the other end of the line.

"Jerry, I'm tired of watching people misuse other people when I could take action to stop it. I'm trying to be brave about not ignoring the obvious."

"What happened to your admitted conflict of interest because of your feelings for Miss Ardnas?"

"That might have been the tipping point, but I'm going to try to be more forthright with all members of my congregation."

"Let me be forthright with you, Old Friend. You're committing professional suicide. Let me come over and we'll sit down and work this all out."

"No way."

"You're sacrificing your career, health, financial future, reputation and I don't know what all else. Think this over."

"If I'm doing what I feel is right, there's no sacrifice. Does God only want me to live for my welfare, or must I follow his example and be prepared to give all? If I get sacked, I'll find another ministerial post elsewhere. I have to. It's my life."

"Please. Think it over. Call me when you have time. I'll come any hour or day. Ministry isn't about martyrdom. Be reasonable."

"I appreciate it. I'll keep you posted. I have a Wyandotte Valley Church council meeting tonight. I'm not looking forward to it."

"Keep smiling, Friend."

Jerry hung up the phone, kicked off his shoes and went right down on his knees. He prayed for a solid half hour. The content was not only for Mark to work out his problems, but for him to have some of the courage Mark was showing. Jerry faced situation after situation and continued to smile at members of his congregation and shake their hands after church just as if he agreed with what he knew was going on in their lives. Was his silence about people's cruel and ruinous lifestyles understood as a tacit acceptance of their behavior? Was Mark on the right path? His brain mined the scriptures for some nuggets of wisdom that would help him rise to his feet with confidence.

Pastor Mark closed his cell phone and began to write out a statement of belief to be presented in writing to the Wyandotte Valley Church Council. He felt that they would either allow him to be honest with himself and the congregation or fire him. It included the warning that he would confront those he felt were harming others, and he would accept any warning they wanted to give to him as council members or friends.

He concluded the letter with: "I am not God, and, until I join that Spirit in heaven, I will not know 'the truth.' So, I will be preaching about what I have come to believe from my studies, life experiences, prayer, meditation and discussions. I can do no more than that and I don't want to do less."

He was apprehensive about giving this to the church board, or, to be truthful, to anybody. He believed what he was saying, but he knew some would be shocked by what they would read. He realized that this might, probably would, put his job in jeopardy. If he was fired, he thought that with prayer and searching he could get another position serving a congregation somewhere, especially considering the thousands of open pastorates in the States.

Just as he typed *less*, his phone rang.

"Hello, this is Pastor Wellston. How are you today?" There was a slight impatience evident in his tone.

"Who's this?"

"This is Pastor Wellston. Who am I speaking to?"

"Don't end a sentence with a preposition."

"Who is this? I don't have time for a prank call," Mark blurted out.

"Frank called? No, you know Frank died. My nieces are here."

"What?"

"Nieces."

"I'm sorry, you must have the wrong number."

"My nieces are here. I think you ought to marry one or the other."

"Oh, Mrs. Grassley. How are you?"

"Laws, not so good and I have two nieces I need to marry off. Right, girls? What time are you coming here tonight?"

"I have a meeting tonight. Can I come tomorrow?"

"Don't want to meet them, hey? No offense, but you're not gay are you? Laws, I hear so much about gay ministers and priests, men and women, on TV these days. You gay?"

"No, I'm not. I have a meeting. I'll stop by your house tomorrow, even though you can tell your nieces I'm not looking for a wife at this moment. When would be a good time?"

"Ten a.m. sharp. See you then, Pastor."

"Okay, Mrs. Grassley."

Before Pastor Mark hung up his phone he heard her mumble to the nieces: "Too bad, girls. I'm afraid he's gay. Doesn't want a woman."

Mark hurriedly shouted, "I'm NOT gay," but she had already hung up.

He made copies of his letter to the church council and walked from his office to the restroom to straighten his tie, dusting some Fig Newton crumbs from his denim jeans and wiping off his sneakers on the way.

"Now the bitter cup."

Chapter 39. I Love You

She awoke and William had already gone to work. There was a note—"I love you."-- pinned to her afghan. She jumped up and searched all the wastebaskets. Madison dumped the trash from the living room, dining nook, and kitchen wastebaskets onto the floor next to where they stood. She found what she was looking for. A Trojan package. She knew she was not HIV positive, but she didn't know about William and hadn't had it together enough the night before to broach the subject before she was whisked away. She was on the pill, so she wasn't worried about getting pregnant.

She felt guilty about making love to William while she was in the middle of a warm relationship with Duke. But Duke seemed like an older brother, father figure, beloved male teacher or family friend. She didn't know if she was ready for this new development with William. She had tried so hard to keep the relationship on a friendly basis and to also keep covert emotional and overt physical commitments on the shelf. She wanted a slow path to a lasting and loving union. This was too fast and not under control, thought Madison, therefore, it might lead to the kind of misguided and doomed relationships she had had before.

Madison showered, put on a black dress, applied minimal makeup, brushed her hair and attended Wyandotte Valley Church. It was hard for her to concentrate on the sermon, although Pastor Mark was delivering it with more energy than she had remembered his using before. The tone of his voice was confident, whereas in the past it had sounded excessively controlled and uncertain. Instead of saying *God* or *Lord*, in the past he had used some exalted-sounding words, like *Gawd* or *Lawrd*. It was like he had been trying to make the words heavenly instead of earthly. Either way, they still came across as artificial.

After church she fixed herself a salad and gathered history books and materials for Monday's lessons. She loved preparing PowerPoint presentations and found the Internet's Google Images a great and easy source of photos of famous people, maps of geographical areas, pictures of protests and war, and snapshots of cityscapes and country landscapes. Googling was also good for quotations from politicians and philosophers. She used her e-board, which needed no wires to project whatever was on her laptop screen, as a second teacher.

She began to think of her largest class and the problems she was experiencing because of the dynamics of having hormonal boys and girls in the same class, inclusion of special education students, class sizes from 25 to 35, two hyperactive boys, four timid girls, a couple of geniuses, and some who barely spoke English. Juggling approximately 30 personalities and educational levels handicapped her success.

To blow off steam, Madison sat down to write another piece for her column. The newspaper had decided she was setting a length precedent they didn't want for letters to the editor, so they offered her a column.

She felt the irony of her title, but charged ahead anyway and wrote:

Believe It, Size Does Matter

Some administrators and ivory-tower pundits will say class size doesn't matter.

Imagine this: you're planning a party for the neighborhood kids. The day of the event it is raining, so you will hold it in your 28 x 28-foot garage, which is about the size of a regular classroom. You are starting to invite children you know to the party. Now, would it be easier to host 15 or 30 kids.

Plus, let's say you have to teach them something during the seven-hour party. You can't play games more than one of the hours, you can't serve cake and ice cream, but ham, cheese, carrots, green beans, celery and apples are fine. You can't find an adult neighbor to help.

You're probably thinking, I wouldn't invite this boy and that girl, because their parents let them talk back to them, throw snowballs at my car in the winter, run around the neighborhood until all hours, and/or steal toys from my children. Sorry, you have to host them all. Remember, teachers get everyone in their classrooms–future doctors and lawyers as well as future rapists, murderers, pedophiles and thieves. And teachers can often predict which kids will end up in jail for these crimes.

Hosting the party sounds hard with 5, harder with 10, chaotic with 15, then what do you think it is like for teachers to have 30, or even sometimes 35, in a classroom for 185 days a year.

What is the coach/player ratio for the local varsity boys' football team? Why not use that as a guide for teacher/student ratios for academic classrooms.

If board members, administrators, college education professors and taxpayers had to be in the classroom every day for five or six hours, they'd think size matters too.

She attached the article to an email and sent it to the editor. Then she lay down on the sofa and read the Sunday paper.

Chapter 40. Bridges

With pipe in hand, Duke went over the blueprints for the replacement bridge over the Kananee River near Wyandotte. He was working with the Crittendon and Granger Construction Company, in which he had a lot of confidence. They would make his part in the whole project easy. The work would start the next day.

The latest blind-man's puzzle was on the kitchen table with the bearing resting next to it. His score was now 4 for 9, so he felt he would soon be batting .500. Also on the table were his fly-tying tools. Bark was dreaming by his chair. His legs were moving and he was breathing hard, so Duke assumed he was dreaming about chasing a rabbit.

"I bet Sam's old boss would have said that he also wouldn't hire a man who tied his own flies," Duke mused. While Duke was shopping after church, Sam and Jenni had dropped off two cherry tarts and left them on his kitchen table. So he decided to take care of one immediately now that his dinner of hotdogs and canned spinach was settled in his stomach.

He began thinking about Madison, whom he hadn't seen as much of lately. He grabbed a ball cap, went outside and decided to start a more consistent approach to dating her. He sat for a while and smoked. He tossed some thistle seed onto the table next to him so he would have the company of several black-capped chickadees. He could feed them from his hand, but often he would pour the seed atop a flat area near him and let them eat. That freed his hands for a book, pipe, puzzle or schematics. Bark kept a keen eye on the birds, but he didn't growl or leap at them.

It was only one o'clock, so he decided to call Madison and set up a date schedule for every Friday night at the bar where they first line danced. She picked up on the first ring out of breath, which surprised him because that only happened when someone was running to the phone after it had rung five or six times. He wondered what she had been doing so actively on a Sunday so soon after church.

"Hello."

"Hi, Madison."

"Duke."

"Yep. How are you?"

"I'm fine. You?"

In Duke's normal style he talked to her about the weather, asked her about school, sprinkled in bits of current events and reviewed some of their hikes. He finally got to the reason he called.

"I thought, if you wanted to, we'd just go ahead and reserve a permanent table at the Antler Inn for Friday nights."

"Well, I'll have to check my calendar and see if that will work. Could we have coffee together after work sometime? There's something I want to ask you about."

"Sure, tomorrow? I'm free after six."

"Starbucks on Second and Elm, 6:30?"

"I'll be there. But I'm here right now, too."

"We'll talk then."

Duke didn't like the sound of the request nor the tone it was made in. He knew she was seeing someone else, and wondered if he had been beaten out by a younger, more handsome man. He took the cap off his head and slid it back over his grizzled hair three times in a row without realizing it. He then absentmindedly ran his hand over his mustache and goatee several times.

He picked up *Anna Karenina*, which he had read before. *War and Peace* was one of his all-time favorites. *Anna Karenina* was good, but not up to the level of *War and Peace*. He read and smoked, but the double and triple names of the Russian characters were too much to keep straight with his mind on one name—Madison.

Chapter 41. End of a Ministry

The meeting started with a prayer. Then Raymond Applegate, the president of the Wyandotte Bank and president of the Wyandotte Valley Church Council, asked for a reading of the minutes of the previous meeting and a treasurer's report. No one listened to either, but he rapidly threw out motions and received seconds to move the acceptance of them along.

Finally Ray opened the floor to the new-business part of the agenda.

"Pastor, I'm not going to beat around the bush on this. Two church board members have resigned because of you and the congregation is shrinking. It's affecting everyone and I think you know the cause. Most of the congregation has always loved you and your preaching, but lately it seems you're preaching from a text we've never heard of. You're being accused of becoming a Secular Humanist. Tell us what's going on."

Mark passed his prepared letter around the room. The five members who were still on the council read quietly for a couple of minutes, then a couple of them shook their heads in disbelief and others produced involuntary sighs.

"Thank you for preparing this, Pastor. Now, could you step into the hallway and let the board talk over your position?"

"Yes."

The discussion behind closed doors lasted more than an hour. Mark went from confidence to despair to hope to anger and back to confidence. His prayers helped. Finally Ray called him back into the conference room.

"Pastor, we haven't been elders, deacons, and church council members in the churches we've attended for no reason. We've all experienced many church and business ups and downs. This one is serious.

"First of all I want to know if you are physically healthy and emotionally stable. In other words, have you recently had a physical or a session with a psychologist or psychiatrist?"

"Both, and a fellow pastor from seminary. I've been suppressing my true feeling a long time, and, when I decided to change my whole life for integrity, I also questioned my physical and psychological wellbeing," answered Pastor Mark

"Okay. Jim, do you have something you want to say."

Jim owned a real estate firm, which had been the heart of most subdivision projects around Wyandotte.

"Pastor Mark, the two most fundamental Christians on this board are gone, or this would be a totally different discussion. I don't know if I can completely speak for all present, but we don't see things as all black and white. Therefore we realize that the Church is not just a religious institution. It's a community. We take communion and we commune in other ways—dinners, parties, Family Night, cookouts, Super Bowl watching, youth outings to parks, *Bible* schools, study groups, singles groups, Sunday school classes, church services and so on. Churches have replaced the neighborhoods that used to exist when people still sat on porches and stopped by to visit and drink lemonade. You have to remember that a congregation of more than 250 has just about the same number of varied religious beliefs. Luckily, they don't require the rest of the congregation to follow their specific beliefs as you seem to be doing now. That would be chaos. We would hate for the social part of Wyandotte Valley Church, which binds these people to each other and to some common Christian tenants, to disappear under your tenure here. Our church does a lot of good in the community."

Pastor Mark nodded his head as if indicating he understood, then the room was quiet for a full minute.

"Cal, do you have anything to add?" Calvin Whitehead owned a dealership that was patronized by car buyers from three counties. His salesmen were known as the most honest and helpful around. Unlike many car dealers, when you left Whitehead Motors, you didn't feel as if you had been railroaded into paying too much for a car you really didn't want when you first walked into the showroom.

"Pastor Mark, this is basically a Christian nation. You're right, many sects think the members of other sects are going to hell, and some religions believe that anyone who has not been baptized while alive or by proxy into their church is damned. Our church doesn't accept the word of other believers in God, Muslims and Jews, for example, because they don't think Jesus was also God. Actually, I really don't care about all that.

"I believe most members of Christian congregations don't want to think about it or hear about it from the pulpit. They want to try to live good lives, believe they are saved and not get into arguments about other Christian sects or foreign religions. We need churches to do the work Christ asked us to do--spread the Word, help the poor, love one another and push for peaceful coexistence. We wish you could stick to that message. Stirring up problems is not on the list. As you surely have noticed, your behavior associated with the church has been divisive."

"Jonathan, what do you think?"

Jonathan Blake was the librarian at the college. "Pastor, I'm not just the keeper of books, I'm also a reader of books. I've read about every book on religion, Christian and other, that has come into our library. Few people understand the importance of myth, superstition, tradition, customs and rituals—in other words, culture.

"Those who've read May's *A Cry for Myth*, Campbell's *The Power of Myth* or Fraser's *The Golden Bough*, have seen Christianity in a new light--a more knowledgeable and honest light. But, Pastor, don't take away what little light those who see dimly have. I'm reminded of the passages, 'These little ones believe in me. It would be best for the person who causes one of them to lose faith to be thrown into the sea with a large stone hung around his neck,' and also 'Be careful, however, that the exercise of your freedom does not become a stumbling block to the weak.'

"We need the church for our rituals no matter how much we want to disagree and argue about 'truth and Biblical interpretation. We need the church to be there to support those who want to publicly confess and promise to live a good life, who want to establish a lasting bond in marriage in the company of their friends and relatives, and who want comfort when they are sick. We need to give them hope as they or their loved ones face death, and we need to support those who want to add greater meaning to their existence. Consider this as you make your decisions about your approach to this ministry."

Ray thanked the three speakers and turned to Pastor Mark.

"Pastor, you have heard from the council members, who speak for the church. We have decided that we will be happy to keep you as our pastor if you can lead us in the ways we have just mentioned. If not, we'd like for you to send us a letter of resignation that we can present to the church. The normal two week notice is acceptable to us. We will respect whichever decision you make, but we hope that you can return to your former acceptable practices and continue to serve Wyandotte Valley Church as our minister."

"Thank you for your understanding and well-thought-out suggestions. I will take all your recommendations into consideration, pray and respond in a couple of days."

Chapter 42. Suspicions Confirmed

Franklin was not himself lately. He yelled at Miss Ardnas and the children. He had started watching TV incessantly. He didn't have to meet with people in the evenings anymore to discuss their family or business insurance needs. He did a lot of pacing. Miss Ardnas knew something was wrong. She decided to call Pastor Mark again.

"Hello, this is Pastor Wellston."

"Hi, it's Ardnas. How are you?"

"Fine. And how are you and your family?"

"I'm sorry to bother you again, but my family is why I called. Franklin is going through something, but I don't know what. He won't go to a doctor, or the counselor available through the company insurance, and he especially seems agitated when I mention seeing you. He yells at all of us and paces the floor."

"Miss Ardnas, how soon can you come to my office?"

"Why? What's wrong?"

"Can you come over right now?"

"Well, yes. The kids are in school and I don't have a class until this afternoon."

"Good. I'll see you in a few minutes."

Mark began praying and preparing. This was going to be a tough meeting for both of them, but this was the path he had set out on. He wondered whether or not he could keep to it, or whether it would be his ruin.

When she entered his office, Miss Ardnas looked to Pastor Mark as beautiful as usual, despite the concern on her face. Her complexion was vibrant, her hair healthy looking, and eyes as alive as ever. He noticed that even though she seemed stressed, the corners of her eyes and mouth still turned up in perpetual smiles as always. Obviously, seldom drinking, never smoking, and avoiding overeating were beneficial. Pastor Mark knew she played tennis regularly at the racquet club and also liked pickle ball and volleyball. She looked more fit than a few weeks ago.

"Miss Ardnas, I'm so glad you could come on such short notice. Please sit down. Coffee, coke, water? I have coffee cake my secretary brought in and some kind of apple and pudding desserts left over from last night's family night pitch-in."

"No thanks."

"Miss Ardnas, your suspicions were accurate. I was just afraid to tell you. Franklin has had an affair. In fact, he has had continual affairs for about ten years."

Pastor Mark moved quickly around his desk as Miss Ardnas slumped in her chair. He was afraid she would fall onto the floor, but she simply folded her hands in her lap. He noticed drops of water as they began to make dark green spots on her light green slacks. He gave her a Kleenex and let her recover a little. She lifted her head but kept her eyes on his desk.

"His secretary Cali was the one before his current secretary, Tiffany. Franklin wouldn't agree to meet me, so I wrote him a letter and named names so he would know exactly what I knew. I suggested he tell you and ask forgiveness, then come in for marriage counseling. I'm sorry that this is so abrupt, but I am tired of ignoring the serious problems in my congregation. So many people are doing hurtful things to themselves and others. Everyone knows what's going on, but we all just look the other way and don't help. I want that to stop."

Pastor Mark kept talking and Miss Ardnas kept looking at the desk. She didn't even lift her hands with the Kleenex to blot her tears. Mark was starting to believe that this all was a big mistake. How could he put stops to all the steps he had started taking with his sermons, confrontations of members of his congregations and the church board?

"What am I going to do? What am I going to do?" let out Miss Ardnas.

Mark got her a glass of water, which sat untouched on the edge of his desk nearest Miss Ardnas.

"What am I going to do? What will I tell the children?"

"Let's take one step at a time. Are you okay with my having confronted your husband?"

"No. I don't know. I guess yes. It was so much easier to face when it was just a suspicion and life could go on as usual. Now all has changed."

"No, it hasn't. You can still go home. Your kids don't have to know anything yet. Only one decision has to be made right now," Pastor Mark was trying to reduce the shock. "What do you want to do about Franklin's behavior?"

"I don't know."

"Let's make a list."

Mark pulled his chair around next to her and began writing a list in no specific order of importance. He made sure she could see the pad.

- ✓ Ignore it and live with it the way you have been.

- ✓ Separation, with him moving out of the house.
- ✓ Divorce proceedings.
- ✓ Confronting him and asking if he is willing to change.
- ✓ Begin separate marriage counseling.
- ✓ Begin joint marriage counseling.

"Do you have anything to add to the list, Miss Ardnas?"

"Yes, sell the house and move away from Wyandotte. Fire Tiffany and take a two-week vacation out of the country without the children. I don't know. What do you suggest?"

"Do you love him?"

"I guess."

"Do you want to stay married or get a divorce?"

"Probably stay married."

"I'll call him and tell him you know about his affairs and met with me today. Next I'll suggest he meet with me. You go on living as you were and see what he does. I'll keep you posted and you do the same with me."

"I don't know about all this."

"At least you aren't living a lie while those around you know the facts. The pressure is now on Franklin. That's why he's acting at home the way he is."

"That's what worries me. My beautiful life is crumbling. Nothing will be the same."

"Miss Ardnas, that beautiful life was based on a lot of ...."

"What am I going to do?"

"Prepare for your class, and give them a lesson they will never forget. Continue to love and nurture your children. Continue to love and pray for Franklin. This may seem like a black day, but it's a new day. We'll work together on Franklin to make it a brighter day." Pastor Mark thought this all sounded hollow and too rosy. He was afraid Miss Ardnas felt the same way.

Miss Ardnas drove home with mixed feelings of relief, horror, hope and despair. The positive and negative were stirring around in her like a two-colored cake mix that transformed itself from distinct shapes and hues to a neutral tan or gray. She wondered what Franklin would say or do when she met him at home.

He wasn't home when she arrived, so she paced a little herself before realizing she needed to busy herself with something. She knew she could usually lose herself in writing satire, so she started on a "newspaper" release for *Ersatz News*. She had recently seen a television-magazine program about college and pro athletes and their many sexual perks unknown to girlfriends and wives. That and a recent signing of a professional halfback for 10 million dollars for two years prompted her to write:

High NFL Draft Pick Refuses to Sign
Ersatz World Sports—Andarsen, Ohio

Sources from the world of professional football said a top player has refused to sign his five-year, eight-million dollar contract with the drafting team. That's nothing new in contract disputes throughout the league.

An anonymous executive with the unnamed team said negotiations continue, but no settlement is in sight.

She went on to report that the draft pick had asked during negotiations what local nurses, teachers and social workers' starting salaries were. When he found out they ranged from 35 to 40 thousand dollars a year, he said he would sign for twice that much, or about 80 thousand dollars a year.

The executive added that the player said it would be obscene for a 23 year old to earn millions of dollars playing a game while teachers and nurses earned 40 thousand.

The player says that the short playing and earning days of a pro athlete should be no excuse for giving him millions a year, because most have college degrees in some field that could earn them a livelihood after sports. "Everyone else has to work for 40 plus years, why not them?"

The team reportedly doesn't know what to do with the counter offer, fearing that there will be a backlash from other players if they offer a salary less than a million.

The next offer from the team could be one million dollars for one year, suggesting that the player can give all the money he wants to charity.

An agreement seems unlikely, though, say friends of the player. One related that the player doesn't believe rock stars, movie stars and professional athletes should earn any more than a well-paid professional.

The player has been known to comment that excessive salaries, royalties and celebrity just create people with drug and sex addictions. Television sports, news and reality shows featuring the rich and famous are proof of this. He has been married for two years and has one child.

After she posted it on her blog, she pulled out her notes on student comments about past blogs.

For the *Big Business Bales Out Fed*, one student, who was a fairly fundamental Christian, had said: "Communism is the most Christian system of government while Capitalism feeds the greedy and power hungry." That comment caused a blow up in class, especially by a student in his fifties. After discussions about the Cold War, the Christian student tried to explain that all systems of government are taken over by big business and the politically ambitious: "Most people hated Communism because the leaders of Russia and China used Fascism to rule. So they equate Communism with Fascism. If we didn't have egomaniacs and lazy individuals, Communism would be the most loving institution in the world."

After more discussion of how Capitalism has created the best material lifestyle for the most people, the Christian came back with, "True, but at what price? We have become the most bellicose country in the world. We have surpassed Ancient Greece and Rome, and probably the British Empire of a century ago, in imperialism or, at least, hegemony. We have lost thousands of our young men and women to maintain financial control over the world."

Other students then came on board and mentioned that, although they love their lifestyles, which are luxurious by world standards, they realize they're being carried on the backs of poorly treated and poorly paid labors in third-world countries, and their material possessions are the result of oil, metals and other natural resources taken from dozens of countries and wasted in America. It was agreed after the long discussion that very few of the students would be willing to give up their lifestyle and live the life of under-fed and poorly housed laborers in Asia who works 12 hours a day, 6 days a week to maintain their meager lifestyles.

One grad student had been a Peace Corps volunteer in Sub-Saharan Africa, and she had lived what the rest of the class only imagined. She wanted to tell her classmates to turn off their electricity, not use battery-powered technology, not ride any mechanized transportation, eat only one bowl of boiled rice flavored with a piece of fish or goat, go to the bathroom outside, wash in a bucket and so forth for one day, and then they would have an inkling of the way billions of their fellow inhabitants on earth live their entire lives.

The Christian got the last word just before the bell: "I wish we had moral capitalism. But I'm afraid the motto on Wall Street and in

Fortune 500 companies will never be: 'Sell all you have, give it to the poor, follow Jesus and you will have treasures in heaven.'"

Miss Ardnas sat down and calmly began writing questions for her students to consider after they had read the latest "news." She typed: "What is a fair yearly salary for an adult male or female in the following professions: trash collector, pro football player, surgeon, minister, store owner, teacher, janitor, cashier and nurse?" "How or by whom should fair salaries be determined?" "Are any occupations....." Just then Franklin came into the room.

Chapter 43. New Life

She wasn't going to die, Cali realized after a few weeks of recovery and several more with no symptoms. Depression and anxiety and guilt had simply overwhelmed her psychological and physical being. Her immune system had probably been altered and, therefore, she had been prone to whatever bug was going around.

She stayed away from the office after she quit Wright Insurance, even though she missed her friends there. Week after week things progressed in a positive way for Cali. Money was not a problem, because she had finally been promised a substantial scholarship, and she could supplement that with a low-interest student loan. She lived in graduate housing and worked as a waitress at a pancake house a few nights a week.

Other than university and work, she didn't get out much. Boys, restaurant customers and professors were constantly hitting on her, but she quickly gave them verbal smack-downs. One or two doses for most of them showed them she wasn't a pushover, and the harassment ended. She didn't have time for any of their foolish behavior.

The university had her apply for several research grants in her field. One of them was interdisciplinary, biophysics, and that intrigued her. She applied, explaining how her knowledge of physics and chemistry would support her research, and documented the university's excellent science department lab space and availability, high tech equipment and honored faculty. She got the grant.

That put her in good with the science department, and the research and resulting professional papers she had started outlining kept her mind off Franklin and helped her stop feeling worthless. Her research was going so well that several noted professors wanted to join her in the research so that they could help her get her papers published in a respectable journal. Of course their names on the papers wouldn't hurt their reputations any either.

Chapter 44. Dust of Snow

Making love to Madison had broken the ice, thought William. Now he was planning his next move. He wasn't ready to ask her to marry him, but he was ready to move into her apartment. He wondered what she would say to his suggestion of their living together.

With summer approaching and the weather warmer, they had returned to biking, and they still hiked, bowled, and played volleyball and tennis indoors. Madison didn't always let him come back to her apartment after their dates, and she wouldn't go to his little house. They hadn't made love a second time. He was still leaving things at her apartment: cans of new tennis balls, sweat bands, a sweat shirt, and, once even, his wallet.

William was ready to settle down and have a wife and maybe kids. He couldn't get very far with conversations of this kind with Madison. She had grown up with several younger siblings that she had practically raised, so she seemed in no hurry to go back to that life. He was trying to appear to her as a stable, loving, romantic and responsible fellow. It seemed to be working.

He even started going to church with Madison, but he couldn't quite figure out her pastor. What was the deal with the sport coat, jeans and sneakers, he wondered. His sermons seemed way out in left field, but they did make William take a few notes, then search his *Bible* back home in an attempt to understand what Pastor Wellston preached.

He had gone from reading to Madison from Frost to Wendell Berry and Jared Carter. Several of their regional poems about regular people in small towns made Madison cry. William often had tears in his eyes too.

One of their Frost favorites was *Nature's First Green Is Gold*. William wasn't a nature lover, city life suited him best, but he recited the poem to himself or anyone with him when trees first budded each spring. One of the highlights of his life was standing at Robert Frost's grave in Bennington, Vermont, one fall day a year ago. It was cold, a crow sat in an evergreen tree above the cemetery. In honor of Frost, William had recited aloud a *Dust of Snow*:

The way a crow
Shook down on me
The dust of snow
From a hemlock tree
Has given my heart
A change of mood

And saved some part
Of a day I had rued.

Of course, Madison loved for him to recite e e cumming's *Maggie, Milly, Molly and May* and Dickinson's *I Like to See It Lap the Miles*. Just the rhythm the verses sent to the ears made these enjoyable. But Madison and William often also worked out the poems' psychological symbolism.

Chapter 45. Vibrations

Sam's cell phone vibrated in his left hand front pocket. He pulled it out, flipped it open to read the text message: "At your house. Locked in. Come quick."

"How could she be locked in?" wondered Sam. "A person can't lock themselves in a house. Maybe the door to the bathroom isn't working right. Wait, what's she doing at my house in the middle of the day?"

Jenni was supposed to be at the Hair U R beauty parlor giving pedicures and manicures. Sam left his desk at Superior Cell Company anyway and jumped into his Toyota. He was anxious as he drove the two miles to his house on the edge of Wyandotte. When he got out of his car he heard a knocking. In the upstairs guest bedroom he saw Jenni's face and head, blondish hair looking even more fly away than usual—more like teased with a big balloon. She didn't need a balloon; she generated her own electricity.

Then the curtains swished shut, as at the end of an act at a theater. He walked to the front door but it was locked, and the security bolt on the inside was evidently in place. He heard knocking again. He stepped back from the door a few paces but couldn't locate the sound. Moving into the middle of the yard, he saw his bedroom curtain come open, displaying Jenni's bare back from shoulders to below the waist.

That curtain closed and Sam just stood there. This was obviously a several-act show. Sure enough, the curtain in the living room opened, and all he could see were Jenni's not-so-perky but sexy, never the less, boobs. Sam laughed. He was beginning to feel a little embarrassed standing in the middle of his own yard watching soft pornography coming through his own windows. The curtain closed.

Sam heard a honk coming from the road. He turned to see his neighbor Wendell stopped at the edge of the road. He trotted to the side of Wendell's Ford Focus, blocking the view of the house.

"How's it going, Sam?"

"Fine, you?"

"Fine."

"Listen, I have a tree down along the back line of my property. You still have my chain saw? I'm going to cut it up tomorrow."

"Oh, sorry. I forgot to return...." Knocking came from a window in Sam's house.

"What's that?" asked Wendell, leaning forward of the steering wheel and craning his neck to look around Sam's body.

"I think Jenni is hanging some curtains." The knock was louder and more urgent.

"You'd better go help before she knocks down a wall. I'll pick the saw up later."

Sam walked along beside the Focus as it pulled away, and Wendell was still hunched forward trying to see around him. Luckily, when Sam turned around, all the curtains were closed. As soon as Wendell was out of sight, the dining room curtain opened, showing one long bare leg stretched from one lower corner of the window toward the far upper edge. He wondered how she could hold that pose.

Running to the front door, Sam yelled: "Jenni, you let me in right now, before you get arrested and I get laughed out of the neighborhood." Now there was pounding from the back of the house. What else could he do but go look? The curtains opened in the spare bedroom window and Sam saw Jenni's belly button and stomach between two plastic placemats covered with prints of ripe fruit. The curtains closed again and Sam stepped back, scanning the windows. A bare foot appeared in the window above the kitchen sink and wiggled back and forth.

Poor Sam got mooned through the window in the garage door before he pounded on the back door and demanded that Jenni let him in. He not only was getting mad at her exposing herself so much, but he was also getting a little excited in other ways.

He heard knocking on the front picture widow and came back around to the front of the house to see the curtain open and a moment later Jenni's two legs with feet up visible to all who might be passing. Sam pounded on the front door again. This time the curtain of the full-length window next to the door parted and there was Jenni, grinning and in all her naked glory in Leonardo da Vinci's Vitruvian Man pose, legs and arms outstretched. Sam immediately jumped over in front of her and took the same pose so his girlfriend's nudity would not be exposed.

"Unlock this door right now!"

She finally removed the bolt, and, about 20 minutes later, a wahoo could be heard coming from Sam's upstairs bedroom window.

Sam queried her about the source of her mini-burlesque, and she admitted it was a takeoff, but much exaggerated, version of some of the ideas gleaned from the church's women's evening book study. After reading a book about how to keep your marriage vibrant, one lady (Miss Ardnas) told about a technique she had heard about involving a nightie and a chase through the house. Of course everyone knew who wore the nightie because of her evident enthusiasm while telling the story and also the flush on Miss Ardnas' face.

"Well, it worked on me," said Sam, remembering how anxious he got as Jenni teased him with flashes of flesh.

"Hey, Slugger, just wait till next week. It'll be time for another performance and a nooner."

Chapter 46. That's It

Pastor Mark walked into Ray Applegate's office at the Wyandotte Bank on Jefferson and Main. Ray scratched his bald head and pointed to one of the four chairs across from his desk. Pastor Mark sat down. Ray liked Pastor Mark but never understood the jeans-and-sneaker look. Ray was surprised how comfortable and confident Pastor Mark appeared considering the circumstances.

"You know why I'm here. I appreciated the suggestions and wisdom of the board members. I don't know how I could have been so blind," began Pastor Mark.

"Glad to hear it. It was our pleasure. We're here to help."

"I know that. After I reviewed all the comments and prayed, I realized that most everything said in the meeting was correct. I could hardly find anything to disagree with. So I didn't want to waste anyone's time by asking for another board meeting since this entire problems was my fault."

"We appreciate that."

"I want to apologize for the harm I have done Wyandotte Valley Church, and I also want to help rectify whatever I can. My first step toward that will be resigning my position as pastor. I will write a letter of resignation for the board. I will stay on for the standard two weeks, unless the board deems it advisable for me to leave earlier or stay a few weeks longer."

"This is not what we wanted or hoped for, Mark. Are you sure of this?"

"I see no other way. I don't know what my future ministerial position will be, but it won't be preaching or doing something I can't completely believe in. I hope to find another church where I can be of service."

"You sure you won't change your mind? We'd like for you to stay, and the board members are willing to work hard to build the church back up."

"Ray, my hope is that my leaving will bring back those who left because of me. At least that's what I pray for. No, I won't change my mind. Thanks for your help and leadership. I feel I grew a lot while trying to serve this church."

Pastor Mark left the office relieved, while Ray knew his problems were just starting. He decided to call a meeting of the church council for that evening. They had to do damage control. First of all they had to decide how and when to make the announcement. Many members wouldn't want Pastor Mark to go and would protest and accuse the board of pushing him out. Then they needed to set up a committee to begin searching for a new pastor.

It would be better to let Pastor Mark leave earlier than two weeks and call in visiting or lay pastors to preach the sermons. The elders could share the visitation duties. Ray hoped Pastor Mark's letter of resignation would include some noncontroversial reason for leaving. There was a lot to do. Ray felt sorry for Pastor Mark. Ray had no hope that Pastor Mark would ever get another position as a Christian minister.

Pastor Mark went directly from Ray's office to Mrs. Grassley's. Although he shouldn't have been, he was surprised that they were all sitting on the porch in their Sunday best drinking ice tea and soaking up the sun. Every strand of hair was in place, makeup had been applied expertly, legs were all crossed modestly, and hands were folded properly in their laps. It seemed as if he had traveled in a time warp back to the 1940s.

"You're late, preacher," called Mrs. Grassley.

Pastor Mark instinctively looked at his watch and saw it was 10:01. "Sorry. How are you pretty ladies doing this afternoon?" Each lady offered, in turn, a dainty, but limp, hand for Pastor Mark to shake.

He sat down on a metal lawn chair that had been placed conspicuously and directly across from the two Grassley nieces. One was named Naomi, a squinty-eyed brunette in paisley, and the other was Ruth, a round-faced blond in stripes. They both smiled.

"Which one do you want, Pastor? Laws, God knows, I don't have long to live."

"Auntie!" both girls gasped out with embarrassment.

Pastor Mark looked to see if Mrs. Grassley was pulling his leg or serious. He couldn't tell.

"Well, they're both so pretty it'd be impossible to choose. Maybe I'll become a polygamous and marry both. Hope you don't mind if I tease like that a little," tossed out Pastor Mark to test Mrs. Grassley's mood. The test failed.

Naomi and Ruth's rosy embarrassment showed through their makeup.

"Don't talk rubbish, Pastor. These are nice girls. My parents were proper Welsh. Laws, Reverend, these girls have Welsh starch in their veins. Are you looking for a wife? The way you talked the other day I was afraid you were gay."

"Well, I'm not gay and I'm not looking for a wife right now, but if I ever do, I'm sure courting either Naomi or Ruth would be part of the first steps."

Both girls laughed when Pastor Mark teased them, but Mrs. Grassley remained stern as she realized she was not going to get one of the girls married off before lunch, or after it either. Pastor Mark drew the girls out enough that they weren't just answering his questions and waiting for the next one, but asking questions and making comments on their own. They were really interesting, educated, unusual and delightful young ladies.

Naomi squinted her eyes tightly at Pastor Mark as she told that she was a rep for a dental supply company, and Ruth's toothy smile in her chubby face let Mark know she was proud that she was manager of a women's clothing store. Neither had a boyfriend. Both had graduated from University of Minnesota in business. Besides trips to Wyandotte, they journeyed into Canada a couple of times a year. Naomi had been on some overseas mission trips with a dental world health society.

Ruth shared that she attended a Lutheran church in a small town outside of Minneapolis, while Naomi said she was a member of a new church that was only a year old. Naomi's favorite authors were the Bronte sisters, George Eliot, William Makepeace Thackeray and Jane Austen. Ruth's favorite author was Wendy Brennan, who writes romance novels under the name Emma Darcy, and her favorite books were from Darcy's *Kings of Australia* series. Their favorite movies were *Gone with the Wind*, *The Heart Is a Lonely Hunter* and *Doctor Zhivago*, and for unknown reasons the *Friday the 13th* series. They reserved a hotel room for the two of them and had a private movie marathon every Friday the Thirteenth. Their parents wouldn't let them watch the movies in their house.

Naomi loved chocolate ice cream and Ruth vanilla. Every once in a while they would get a chocolate/vanilla twist cone, just to go way out. They played chess and Scrabble at home with each other, their parents and online with opponents from around the world. Both girls liked Pastor Mark and teased him about his Jimmy Carter grin.

Pastor Mark spent a pleasant hour with the girls only because he ignored the look on Mrs. Grassley's face. Naomi and Ruth were going back to their parents' home in Minneapolis the next day, so he wished them safe travel. He ended the visit with a prayer for travel mercies and also asked God to heal Mrs. Grassley's swollen ankles. His final words were: "Thy will be done."

Ruth walked Pastor Mark to the door and used her eyes to give him a double barrel shot and then an extra squeeze during their parting handshake.

While Pastor Mark walked back to the parsonage, it hit him. This wouldn't be his parsonage for long, he wouldn't have a church and he probably wouldn't have all these neighbors. His step was a little heavier the rest of the way home. He was determined to continue to do what God had called him to do. He desperately wanted another pastorate.

Chapter 47. Friend or Foe

While Miss Ardnas was closing her computer, Franklin came through the door and rushed at her. In fear, she leaned sharply backward and rose as far on her legs as she could while still in the confines of the chair. She raised her left arm in self-defense, as Franklin loomed over her.

He dropped to the floor at her knees. He was crying.

"I'm so sorry. I hate myself. I don't know what to do or to say. I'm so sorry, Sweetie. You've always been my best pal and only love. Those women don't mean anything to me. You know you're the only one for me. I'm such a miserable cad. I'll buy you anything, do anything you want, counsel with Pastor Mark, just say the word. We've gone through a lot together. Forgive me, Honey. Please forgive me," was the stream of sense and nonsense coming from the guilty party.

He buried his face in her lap and sobbed.

"I love you, I've always loved you, and I will love you forever. How could I have done this to you? Please forgive me," Franklin continued.

Miss Ardnas finally gave up her defensive posture and relaxed. She bent her head down next to his and wrapped her arms around him halfheartedly. She was reluctant to give in so easily.

She couldn't help herself: "I forgive you, Franklin. I forgive you."

They stayed in this position for untold moments. While Franklin's sobbing diminished, Miss Ardnas was thinking: "Do I really forgive him? Can I ever forgive and forget as Pastor Mark has often told us to do? Will he go back to his old ways? Will all this wear me down—suspicions, excuses, lies, relief, fact, confession, forgiveness, relief—in an unending cycle until I give up and just accept his behavior?"

Miss Ardnas finally decided that before they went to bed, she was going to sit down and set some parameters. She decided to draft a post-affair agreement in the form of a prenuptial agreement. In it would be clauses requiring:

1) no evening or overnight travel business without her, or associates would handle any overnight or evening business,

2) individual counseling sessions and joint marital counseling,

3) the letting go of Tiffany as his secretary,

4) her input on the choice of any new secretaries or female employees and

5) attendance at all of Pastor Wellston's sermons.

Franklin arose from the floor and looked into his wife's eyes to check her mood. The edges of her eyes were always turned up as were the corners of her mouth. So he still wasn't sure of her emotional status. His eyes were red and the bags under them were swollen. He felt awful, and wanted to move on as quickly as possible.

"I'm going upstairs to shower, then we'll go out with the kids for a bite to eat," Franklin stated in an unnaturally constricted tone.

Miss Ardnas opened her laptop and brought up Word. She began typing the agreement which ended with two places for signatures and dates and witnesses and dates. She wondered how Franklin would take to her approach. She was still in shock by the day's events but relieved that her work, home and social life weren't turned upside down.

After a confrontation and signing and witnessing of what she termed a post-affair agreement, she was determined she could continue with her normal family and university activities as usual. She wasn't worried about Franklin signing the agreement, but she knew to get him to do it in front of witnesses would be a challenge.

Chapter 48. Bad News

When Duke entered the Starbucks at Second and Elm, Madison was already sitting in a corner with a large latte in front of her. There were a few other tables occupied, and a counter had three apparent college students surfing on their laptops. Madison gave a half wave and waited for Duke to sit down.

Duke pulled out his pipe, then realized he couldn't get comfort from it in a nonsmoking establishment. He gave Madison a silly grin and put it back into his pocket. He still had on the clothes he wore to the bridge site, but his grizzled hair was neatly combed. Madison tried to grin back.

A waiter came and Duke ordered a tall black coffee. He took a few sips and then looked at Madison, waiting.

Her gray eyes looked more silver than usual because of tears. She wished she could hide her emotions better. Duke noticed the tears and, feeling her discomfort, concentrated on stirring his coffee.

"You know I'm dating someone else. His name is William. He knows I've also been going out with you."

Duke nodded his head.

"I wanted and still want to take things slowly. I've rushed into romance too many times. Well, my relationship took a little more of an intimate aspect a week ago. I'm not trying to keep any secrets about what's going on, especially from you, because of the unfortunate situation with your ex-wife."

Duke didn't want to let his imagination linger on "intimate aspect" too long. "Say no more, Madison. I don't own you. Follow your heart. I'll miss our dates and hikes, but I'm a big boy and will move on."

"That's the problem. I don't want our relationship to end. There are things I love about you and things I love about William. But I can't say I'm in love with either of you. At least not to the point of a serious and committed relationship or marriage."

"I may be old fashioned, but I believe that intimacy is more than a physical commitment in a relationship."

"You're right. I feel the same way. That's why the other night surprised me. It only felt physical to me, and, honestly, I don't plan to repeat my mistake until whoever I am dating and I both make a commitment. I'm sure that is hard to believe."

"So, where does that leave us?" asked Duke.

"Can you accept that what I did was just physical?"

"Well, it's hard, but I'd hate to lose your companionship. I do think I'm falling in love with you. I'm not saying that to put pressure on your relationship with William."

"I understand. I feel the same way, but I'm only in the falling-in-love stage. I want to wait until I've landed in love."

Duke laughed.

Madison continued: "If the offer is still open, reserve a table for us at Antler Inn for every Friday."

"Will do. I guess that's a little bit of commitment in my favor. I'll be honest too. I don't want to have this kind of conversation again. Next time just email the bad news and we'll part friends. I'll be sad, but I'll accept that you will have made the right choice."

Madison felt a little lighter driving home from having coffee with Duke, then she realized she'd have to have a similar talk with William. "Why did I ever log on to backinthegame.com?" flicked across her mind.

Chapter 49. A Post-Affair Agreement

Franklin signed the post-affair agreement with a conciliatory posture. Just as Miss Ardnas had predicted, he refused to have witnesses. He went into his excuses.

"I love you, Miss Ardnas. What more do you want me to say, Honey?"

"From what I understand, lots of people knew about you and your secretaries. I want you to make a public commitment. Just have one friend sign this."

"Honey, there's no need for that. I promise I'm a changed man. I'll go to church, I'll fire my secretary, you can have full access to my hiring practices. I've signed your silly agreement. That should be enough."

"Please. One thing I've read about habits is that you need a powerful, constant, in-your-face reason for giving them up. I think a witness would help."

"Do you want to have a second marriage ceremony on our next anniversary? I'll do that. Yeah, let's do that. In a couple of months our anniversary comes up. We'll ask Pastor Wellston to marry us again."

"Franklin, I just want you to have one witness sign this agreement."

"You're being silly now. Let's go to sleep."

Miss Ardnas was disappointed. It felt to her that Franklin's refusal was just one step on an icy slope and that in a week or two she would be back to suspicions and worry. Franklin went on to bed, while she sat down at her computer to post another *Ersatz News* story for her political science class tomorrow. Her blog was her psychological crutch.

Congress Passes Term Limits Bill

Ersatz World News-Washington. *A surprise move on the part of the new wave of senators and representatives brought a term-limit bill to the floors of both houses and they passed it.*

After the President signs the bill, senators will only be able to serve one six-year term and house representatives two two-year terms.

Plus, past congressmen will be banned from running for the same office again. Senator Wayne Goldman stated: "This is long overdue. Being a congressman was always meant to be a service, not a life-long career."

Representative Betsy Wells added: "The parties have become so entrenched that those of us coming in with new ideas have trouble voting our conscience or truly representing our district. The ranking members of congress tell freshmen how to vote."

Tom Jones, political talk host on WZED, Omaha, says, "Congressmen are campaigning year round and during their entire terms. Every time you hear one say liberal, conservative, Republican *or* Democrat, *they're campaigning for their party and not truly focusing on issues."*

"This bill is a step in the right direction," Jones added. "The longer a congressman is in Washington the more he becomes indebted to the lobbyists and big businesses that contribute to his reelection campaigns."

The President is scheduled to sign the bill sometime next week.

Miss Ardnas was encouraged by the fact that one by one her students had been coming to her after class or in her university office to tell her they knew her secret. Some laughed, and some were embarrassed it took them so long to figure it out, especially since the blog had a description that read: "Ersatz News, Views, Sports and Finance--honest, reliable, trusted, balanced, valid, true, genuine, unadulterated, actual, fair, unimpeachable, authentic, indisputable, irrefutable, undeniable, incontrovertible and fabricated satire. How do you know? We told you."

During the next class she would confess to the rest of her students, then hold a discussion about the accuracy of any news organization's reporting; what the word "true" means; how unbiased reporters go about their interviewing, research and writing; the importance of peer review of professional journal and news magazine content; and techniques for spinning facts. She knew all the cable and network news channels would be criticized by some and defended by others, depending on her students' individual political leanings.

Miss Ardnas slipped into bed quietly, but Franklin was awake and waiting. He made love to her, but she was unable to reciprocate either physically or emotionally. Franklin didn't seem to notice and dropped off to sleep immediately after he was done. The act was gross for Miss Ardnas, because, as they had sex, she visualized Franklin having sex with Tiffany and Cali. She didn't even want him to touch her right now, let alone enter her body. Miss Ardnas lay worrying that nothing had changed. What was she going to do to quell her doubts?

Chapter 50. Why Wait

Ray Applegate called Pastor Mark and told him he could leave his position at the church as soon as he wanted. A committee had already been assembled to find his replacement. Pastor Mark was now simply Mark. Mark was asked to let Ray know as soon as he was out of the parsonage, because the church would be using it on weekends to house guest ministers giving the Sunday sermon.

Mark got the disappointing message and moved out in two days. It's not that he had anything but his clothes, books, favorite CDs and toiletries. The parsonage was furnished. He received a nice severance package from the church, but he had no other money for incidentals or to cover room and board. Mrs. Grassley had a spare room and offered it to him for 75 dollars a week if he would cook for her. "So much for room AND board," thought Mark.

Luckily, Mark's room was upstairs in the back of the house, so he could pretend he couldn't hear Mrs. Grassley yell up at him every ten or fifteen minutes. His CD player turned up helped too. He only answered her if she sounded injured or it was time for him to prepare a meal.

Mark had learned from several friends that a church council member and another person had said that they would make sure Mark never preached again in Wyandotte or any other place. They also threatened to find a way of black balling him from any kind of employment in the county. This information depressed Mark.

He felt a little better when a member of Wyandotte Valley Church offered him a job at Two Dollar Buys, a variety store on the strip. He would be stocking shelves, running the cash register, helping customers and closing a couple of nights a week. Mark took the job. He had a life again, especially since he had been quickly separated from his church and most of the congregation.

About a dozen of his former parishioners wanted to know what church was going to hire him, because they wanted to continue to hear his sermons. When they found out he had no church, they begged him to start a once-a-week, evening *Bible* study. He did, and Franklin and Miss Ardnas were the first to attend, even though Mark's first encounter with Franklin since his confrontational letter was stiff and uncomfortable.

At the first meeting, Mark laid out his religious philosophy and said he would understand if some didn't want to continue attending. They all had been present as his sermons had changed from dogmatic, Biblical history as fact and "knowing the truth" to focusing on Jesus as a model for living. He stressed they would journey together on a search for personal understanding and enlightenment. He knew this all sounded New Age, but he didn't know what to do about that. He thought how Jesus had started a New Age with the Good News, and Paul had started another New Age with the Gentiles. Both men had tried to get people to be Christ like, with little success. Mark was disappointed to think that, after 2,000 years of clergy teaching about Jesus, very few people truly followed Christ's model. Sure, they said they were Christians, but they were materialistic, selfish and clannish in hundreds of ways.

Anybody would be welcome to come to the meetings as long as they were looking for a positive spiritual way of life. He invited Jake, the pharmacist atheist he often met for lunch.

Mark settled in at Mrs. Grassley's the best he could, taking into account that the small bathroom only had a tub when he liked showers, and the room was only 10 by 10 with one window. He immediately started to work on his series of *Bible* studies. He decided that a discussion of the creation of the *Bible* Canon and the types of writings in the *Bible*—poetry, drama, parables, history, first-hand narratives and other genre—would be the best way to establish a firm base for an understanding of the development of the Christian church and, therefore, what Jesus intended his followers' lives to be like.

Mark's only problem with his new "ministry" was his feeling of guilt for anxiously waiting to see his high school sweetheart Miss Ardnas each week. He secretly wished she and Franklin had gotten a divorce instead of reconciliation, but from Miss Ardnas' description of the marriage counseling sessions she told Mark about, Franklin still appeared in denial about his addiction to affairs. Miss Ardnas was sure Franklin would stop attending counseling as soon as he could, and she told this to Mark. Mark tried to push his feeling back in a dark corner of his mind, but he couldn't keep the hope of a life with Miss Ardnas from popping back into the light.

Chapter 52. Slow Down

"We've got to slow down, William," said Madison. She didn't like this part of a relationship. She always felt so awkward discussing sexual matters.

"What do you mean?"

"I want true love, as corny as that sounds. Too many relationships are based on superficial things or physical love. I want permanent love."

"I love you, Maddie."

"It's too soon to know what that means."

"I don't understand," said William.

"People who make love often say, 'I love you,' during the act, but don't show it on a daily basis. I don't want a 'I love you during sex' relationship. I want the kind of love described in 1st Corinthians 13. I know that's not realist, but I want to get as close to that as possible with someone."

"Ok. I'll try."

"Me too."

"Does that mean we can't be intimate?"

"That's right. You okay with that?"

"I don't know if I can stand it. You know men. We're more needy in that area than most women. Plus, you're very sexy and being around you makes me...uh...I want to make love to you."

"I understand, but doing that is a commitment to a relationship I'm not ready to make."

"Are you still seeing that old guy?"

"Yes. I like him a lot. He's not an old guy. He's just a few years older than you. We have not been intimate, but he's a wonderful friend right now. We have fun together."

"You know I'm jealous, and I don't like you seeing him. I was hoping I was enough companionship for you."

"You two are so different. I didn't want to be dating two people at once, especially after having no dates for a couple of years, but that's the way it is."

"So what do you two do together?"

"Line dance and hike in the woods."

"I'll take up line dancing and we can skip tennis sometimes and go to the woods." William caused his eyebrows to rise and fall a couple of times to emphasize his idea of what taking her to the woods might mean.

"Is that all you men think about?"

"Sorry."

Madison was more confused than ever about her dual love life. She had to make a decision. It was fine for her to string them along as she made up her mind, but it wasn't fine for them. It wasn't fair. She didn't want to pressure her dates into loving her or trap them by luring them with sex or the fear of a rival winning her hand. She had to determine some way to make a choice and follow it.

Chapter 53. Shedding Skin

"What's this leaf?" asked Madison. They had traveled to their favorite nature setting.

"It's not a leaf. See the hanging seeds. It's from a basswood, sometimes called American linden tree. Drop it from head high."

"Another helicopter. A little like the maple seed."

"Correct. The design lets the seeds fly out of the shade of the parent tree, where they are able to get enough light to sprout."

"You're not going to start using this as a whistle too, are you?"

"I probably could, but, just for your sake and your ears, I won't."

"What's this skinny, jagged leaf?"

"Pin oak. Notice how much thinner they are than the black or red oak leaves we have picked up."

Madison pointed at a transparent rope-sized item on the ground.

"Shed snake skin." They moved on.

"What's next?" Madison blushed, thinking about the double meaning of the question. William, Duke and she had all seemed to be wondering, "What's next?"

"Oh, let's go to the pond and catch some frogs."

"Why?"

"We won't hurt them."

"Do we have to touch them?"

"Come on. You're a big girl. Don't take that the wrong way."

When they got to the pond, Duke sat down on a log and patted for Madison to sit beside him. Bark was in the water paddling furiously.

He brought Duke a stick, which Duke threw into the water. Off went Bark after the floating stick.

Duke lit his pipe. Madison didn't like smoking and smokers, but his pipe smoke was always sweet and had become an olfactory indicator of pleasant times. He looked down at her and asked, "What?"

"What are you thinking, Duke?"

"How nice it is sitting her with you on this especially warm summer day. You're kind of cute with the sweat running down your nose."

Madison quickly wiped off her face with her T-shirt sleeve."

"Want to go skinny dipping?" Duke asked.

"You're kidding!"

"Nope. There's nothing quite as free feeling as swimming sans clothes. Have you ever skinny dipped?"

"No, never have. Don't think I will start now."

"This is one of my favorite places to swim *au naturel*. I'm usually by myself, so I don't have to be modest. If you want to swim, I can sit here and cover my eyes while you disrobe behind a tree. Then you jump in and I will strip down and follow. Peeking is no fair, though, since you'll be hidden in the water first."

"You're serious!" exclaimed Madison.

"Of course. Okay, then, turn your head and I'll go by myself."

Madison turned her head and heard his shoes hit the ground one at a time. Then came the swishes of his shirt, pants and boxers. She was tempted to either laugh or run away, but then she heard a splash. She looked up to see Duke's wet head and grizzled hair sticking above the green water. He had a toothy smile on his face she had never seen before.

"Aaaaaaah. Refreshing."

Duke swam a dozen yards and dove completely under and came back up spouting like a whale. He whooped. Madison giggled a little because when he dove down she could see the two white cheeks of his *derriere* flash just as he turned to dive under.

"That looks like fun."

"It is," said Duke. "Come on in."

Duke turned to look at the far shore and in seconds he heard a splash, then Madison was at his side.

"It, it's, it's c-c-c-ooold!" Madison said shivering, either from the water temperature or the new experience.

"It'll feel warmer as you get used to it and swim a little."

Duke saw the black straps on Madison's bra and laughed. "You're cheating."

"I'm a modest little girl," she answered.

Madison looked at Duke with her shinny grey eyes and cocked her head.

"What?"

"There are two bugs in your hair."

Duke brushed them off and watched the two dragonflies look for another perch.

"They're dragon flies mating." Then he wished he had left off the mating part.

They swam, dived and splashed each other.

"Warm now?"

"Yes. I'm surprised."

Next thing Duke knew Madison ducked under water and came up with her black panties in her hand and threw them onto the shore. Next she did some arm and body contortions and her black bra followed the panties.

"Now you're part of nature. Nothing between you and the altogether."

"This is a little scary. I feel a little vulnerable, but I do like the feel of freedom."

They treaded water and circled an imaginary point in the middle of the pond as they talked about the birds flying overhead, the fish they felt nip at their toes and the sounds of frogs and insects they heard in the wood and marsh.

Madison couldn't believe her luck to have a friend like Duke. What could possibly top the unique-to-her experiences she was having on their dates?

Chapter 54. Swoosh

"Why don't you buy some adult pants," yelled Mrs. Grassley as Mark walked into her living room.

"Don't like them. How do you like my Nike's?" Mark poked back at Mrs. Grassley.

"Kid's shoes, they are. And what's that dirt on the side?"

"That's not dirt. It's called a swoosh"

"Swoosh moosh. Laws, what's it doing on your shoes?"

"It's the symbol of the company."

"Looks a little like plain old paisley. Laws, I wouldn't think you'd wear paisley. My niece Naomi here always wears paisley."

"Are you ready to go, Naomi?" asked Mark. Ruth and Naomi had been visiting their aunt more regularly since she had an eligible bachelor living upstairs. Only Naomi had been able to come to Kentucky from Minnesota this time, which bent Ruth's nose out of shape.

Mark forgot his manners and hurried on out the door in front of Naomi before Mrs. Grassley could trap him in a lengthy conversation. The study group met at different people's houses since Mark no longer had a set of church keys. Sam was hosting this time. Mark and Naomi walked, despite the fact that Naomi offered to drive.

Besides Sam, Mark and Naomi, those in attendance were Miss Ardnas and Franklin, Jenni, Jake and his wife Laura, Madison and William, and five other couples and two college students. The discussions were always lively.

After a chance for everyone in the group to comment about important events in their lives during the seven days since the last meeting, the topic of the night—Islam—was discussed.

"What confuses me is that the Jews, Muslims and Christians have the same god but are so far apart in belief," started Sam, the night's discussion leader.

"Yes, that is one of the mysteries of religion," comment Mark. "Has anyone studied Islam or read the *Koran*."

Naomi joined the conversation: "I spent three months on a mission trip, sponsored in part by the dental supply company I work for. We weren't proselytizing, we were there with volunteer American dentists to pull teeth and train local dentists. During that time I was offered a copy of the *Koran* many times because host country nationals were upset that I was an infidel. What I got from my reading and discussions was that the Jews prided themselves on not being animists. In other words they didn't worship animals or believe spirits were in rocks and trees and other objects. Also they didn't believe in the mythological pantheon of the Greeks and Romans they had to live with. The Jews were the tribe with only one spiritual god. No sun worship or moon worship, just one god."

"But they don't believe in Jesus," said Jenni.

"You're partially correct, if I understand their religious position. They believe in Jesus, just that he's not God, or the Savior," interjected Mark.

"That's the way I understand it too," put in Naomi. "The Trinity really gives them pause. Here the Jews were so proud of not having a god for everything--harvests, fertility, good luck and so forth—then some aspects of the Christian religion come along and proclaim there's three gods."

"Three gods in one," corrected Sam.

"I don't think they liked that new math," joked Jake. "One plus nothing equals three and three minus nothing equals one, or something like that."

"Why did they call you an infidel, Naomi?" asked Miss Ardnas.

"Because you didn't believe in the *Koran*, right, Naomi?" answered Franklin.

Naomi responded: "I told them we believe in the same God many times."

"So what was their problem?" continued Miss Ardnas.

"I had to admit that Christianity doesn't include Mohammad or the *Koran*. That's one reason I read their holy book. Then I asked them if they wanted to read the *Bible*. They said they wouldn't be allowed to read it," said Naomi.

"If they believe in Christ, what do they say he is?" asked Sam.

"A prophet," added Kaitlin, one of the college students.

Laura asked, "What do they have against our *Bible*?"

"They say it's not directly from God. According to them, Mohammad received God's word directly and wrote it down, so the *Koran* is God's exact words. What little they understand about the *Bible*, they say it's written by Moses, prophets and followers of Jesus, not God," said Naomi.

The conversation continued with Sam talking about the *Bible* as being inspired by God, Laura saying she believed the *Bible* word for word as God's voice, and others commenting on Mark's lesson on the establishment of the Canon.

After two hours of discussion, Sam and Jenni brought out plates filled with cheese, crackers, fresh fruit, salami and mixed nuts. They passed these out and then brought out beer for those who drank and soft drinks for the rest. Conversations switched to kids, work, home projects, and politics.

"Miss Ardnas, do you think we ought to ask Mark to start a new church?" asked a husband of one of the couples. "I've heard several members of our study group talking about doing that. I don't want this community to lose him."

"Well, it can't hurt. I'd like that. Now, we still go to Wyandotte Valley Church because I want spiritual guidance for my kids too," responded Miss Ardnas.

Sam called the study back to order and the discussion continued. Since Naomi had spent time in such Muslim countries as Kazakhstan, Kyrgyzstan, Azerbaijan, Turkmenistan, Uzbekistan, and Tajikistan, she was the center of the inquiries and comments. After Madison heard the list of countries Naomi had visited, she was placing each one into imaginary slots of an imaginary wood puzzle of the world. Most in attendance had no idea where any of these countries were. William sat looking at and thinking of Madison on the sofa the night they made love.

Naomi was asked if she had tried to do a little proselytizing while in Central Asia.

"Not really. They didn't want to listen, and that wasn't our purpose for going. When I got back I was listening to a primetime interviewer asking a well-known evangelist about who was saved. He said the Muslims, in so many words, would not go to heaven. Well, I found out the Muslims believe the same about Christians. That's why they wanted me to read the *Koran* and become Muslim."

"You're kidding," interjected Jenni.

"When I thought about it more, I realized that if I had been born in Tajikistan, which is almost 100% Muslim, I would now be Sunni, and, if my Tajik friend Shabnam had been born in rural Kentucky, she would probably now be Christian. My Buddhist friend Benjakalyani from Thailand, if born in the United States, would also be a Christian now."

"That's an interesting way to look at religion, as more of a tradition than a faith," said Mark. "Personally I always felt God was big enough to reveal himself to all nations, not just the tiny Jewish tribe. Why he didn't make a book, *The Bible*, just appear is an interesting topic? I dislike telling other believers in a spiritual being that they have it all wrong. After all, probably half the people who believe in Christ don't believe people of other Christian denominations are saved."

"Well, the discussions I had in Central Asia opened my eyes to my prejudices. Of course, lots of Sunni and Shia Muslims don't agree with each other any more than different Christian sects agree with each other," said Naomi.

"I Googled world religions on my iPad just now, and I found that only one third of the earth's population is Christian and about one fourth Muslim," contributed Jake. "The Jews are only about one percent. I don't think anyone owns God, and what worries me is that if all sides keep telling, or at least believing, that only their religious sect is saved, while all others are going to hell, how will we ever attain world peace? We're insulting each other's intelligence, religious beliefs, traditions and culture—all the things that give us our personal identity."

The discussion continued for another half hour. These "church services" tended to naturally run between two and three and a half hours. Few people's minds wandered from the subject as often happened during a 30-minute sermon at a traditional church.

As the "congregation" was leaving, Sam thanked everyone for coming and reminded them that the next study would be at Jake and Laura's house on West Maple, with the topic being "Is there a devil?" When Mark and Naomi stepped out onto the porch, Jenni asked Mark when he was going to build a church.

Laughing, Mark answered, "You know, that's an interesting question. But it would take me longer than Naomi wants to stand here to answer it. I'm still looking and applying for positions at several churches in state and plan to expand to other states. There has to be something out there for me. Thanks for the goodies and your hospitality. Good night."

Chapter 55. Cleaning Up

Franklin had followed all of Miss Ardnas' rules in the post-affair agreement, except one. He had been sweet talking the little Hispanic girl who cleaned around Wright Insurance for weeks. He was good at bringing a target along slowly with seemingly innocent handshakes, hugs, gifts, pats, and so forth. He made sure he met her precisely when she walked behind his desk or through his door so that their bodies squeezed together as he looked down at her.

She seemed pleased about getting compliments about her hair, clothes, looks and job performance from such an important man in town. It was something for her to brag about to friends. Once he had given her a hundred dollar bill and told her it was a bonus for the good work she had done. He had told her not to tell anyone else about the bonus. This made her a little fearful. His advances went on for weeks.

After slowly breaking down her defenses, he had had intercourse with her on the desk. Afterwards, putting his forefinger to his lips, he told her this was just between the two of them. He gave her a big hug, a kiss on the neck and a pat on the butt before she left his office.

He let know that if word got out about "what when on behind closed doors," there would be no bonuses or job. Franklin knew she was supporting her parents and a brother in college. He was sure she wouldn't tell anyone from embarrassment, her finances and her future prospects for a husband looking for a pure bride.

This time he would keep his affair a secret from everyone—no bragging about his conquests to friends on the golf course, no secret meetings in public places at night, no way for Mark to find him out. When he thought about Mark, he became angry. He didn't think his affairs, public or private, were any concerns of anyone else. He hated going to the *Bible* studies, but had to keep up a good front for the sake of his marriage.

Miss Ardnas had slowly become more pleasant with Franklin at home, but she still didn't seem to want to make love. He told himself that this was exactly why men should be allowed to have mistresses or multiple wives, legally or, at least, openly. According to him, the French had the right idea. He had heard that French politicians had a wife for appearances and a mistress for excitement and sexual release. The French populace knew about their mistresses.

Business continued to be good for Wright Insurance, and life had settled down for Franklin. He was spending more time with the two kids, which made Miss Ardnas happy, although he'd rather be playing golf than Frisbee or softball in the backyard or Wii in the family room. The summer weather was invigorating and Franklin was satisfied with his life.

Chapter 56. Plato

"Since we've been dating for months now, are you ready to sleep with me?" Duke asked Madison with a smile on his face.

"You're joking, right?" Duke had never made any sexual advances during all their dating.

"Only partially. I was thinking we should go backpacking on the Appalachian Trail. This is not a come on. It would be easier to carry one tent then two, but we would have separate sleeping bags so….. It'd be strictly a platonic adventure into the wild."

"Camping? Am I ready for that?"

"Well, we'd do some overnighters close by first. You've already learned how to do your business behind a tree in the woods, but you would have to learn how to find fresh water from a spring and live without deodorant and makeup."

"I don't think I am liking this already."

"It's okay, we'd both stink."

"And that's supposed to make it all better?"

"Do you want to try some weekend camping to see if you like it? It's just doing the same things we've been doing on our day hikes, except we'd spend the night too."

"Why the Appalachian Trail?"

"You wouldn't believe what it's like at about mid-trail in mid-summer when the through hikers are everywhere. These people have been hiking for months and they are as weird as March hares."

"So I have to sleep in the woods and hike with crazy people. Does that sum it up?"

"Exactly. Nature and interesting characters all wrapped up together. And the trail names are a hoot by themselves. I was Dude instead of Duke when I section-hiked two years ago. You'll have to come up with a trail name, because nobody uses their real name."

"Are these escapees or people on the witness protection program?"

"Many of the people who are taking a five- to six-months hike in the woods are definitely escaping from something—responsibility, bad relationships, depression, reality, whatever."

"This sounds like great fun, Duke," said Madison sarcastically. "And what should my name be?"

"How about Hatter? Mad Hatter, Madison Hatter, Hatter. Get it?"

"I'm afraid I do, Dude. When is our first camping thing taking place?"

"How about next Saturday night?"

"You know better than that. Make it our line-dancing night."

"Can't blame me for trying to get two dates into one weekend can you? So, does that mean you'll sleep with me?"

"Okay, I'll say it. I'll sleep with you. Platonically, of course. Now do you feel better?"

Chapter 57. A Block

"Should I marry Jenni, Duke?"

"Sure. But you must have too many reservations about it if you're asking a divorcee like me."

"She wants to get married, but I have to take her last name instead of her taking mine."

Laughing, Duke said, "Is she serious or just pushing your buttons? She does push your buttons a lot, you know."

"She does, but not on this one. I'd be the laugh of the locker room, so to speak, if I changed my last name to hers."

"And."

"I don't know what else."

Sam fiddled with his Cleveland Indian's cap and Duke worked to keep his pipe going. He dropped a little bit of tobacco on the floor for Bark. Duke had heard it cured worms in dogs. Bark seemed to like it.

"Would you feel less manly if you took her name?" Duke asked.

"Yes. Of course. Would people call us Mrs. and Mr. Jenni Block?"

"I wouldn't mind if I loved the person. It might even break down some cultural barriers and change people's attitude about gender equality."

"I don't care about people's attitudes. I just don't want to be the laughing stock of the town."

"You seem to care about some people's attitude about name changes. I don't know what to tell you, Sam. Hey, to change the subject, how would you like to go camping with Madison and me Friday?"

"That's Antler Inn night."

"So? I only get a date with her one night a weekend."

"I'll check with Jenni. Course she likes everything."

"Great!"

"She's kind of noisy when we make love, and, since we'll be out in nature, she'll be even more amorous, as we say. Will that be okay with you and Madison?"

"By noisy, what do you mean?"

"She yells 'wahoo' when she has an orgasm. Loudly, with enthusiasm."

"Oh, great. And I'll be over there thinking like a monk with Madison a foot away and you two panting and thrashing around in the next tent."

"I like that idea. We'll go for sure."

"Can I take my offer back, Sam?"

"No way, Jose."

Chapter 58. Still Marking Territory

William had lots of concerns about his relationship with Madison and her relationship with Duke. "Now her old boyfriend has talked her into taking her on a camping trip. He's doing everything he can to get her into bed. Wish I had thought of sharing a tent with her, except I hate camping. Didn't even like it when I went to camp one summer and we had cabins," William thought.

Madison and William continued to play tennis Saturdays on cool days and take a few walks in the park. Saturday evenings they went to a movie or ate out. The fitness center had a track, so they also jogged there one evening a week, but they each went their separate ways afterwards.

He was still leaving things at Madison's apartment, but the scheme wasn't working. When he didn't take things away with him after she reminded him to, she just designated a black and white checkered box in the closet for his possessions. Her philosophy was if he needed them he would take them home. No way was she going to beg him to take the stuff. If he was just trying to get his foot in the door, the door was to the closet.

The *Bible* studies set up around Mark interested him. He had not read his *Bible* so much since he had to read it straight through for a junior high Sunday school class. Back then he didn't understand anything. He just read the words and checked off the books and chapters in order to earn a certificate and pin. Now he read for meaning. With the introduction of Islam and other religions to explore, he was beginning to pick up books on world religions too.

Madison had mentioned 1 Corinthians 13 during one of their private conversations, so that became one of his favorite chapters in the *Bible*. That level of commitment to someone you loved that was found in those verses was a little overwhelming, though.

William wanted to get married to Madison now. He wanted to be intimate with her even sooner than now. He wanted to move in with her now too. He wanted to see her every night of the week, not just while jogging or a Saturday-night date. He hated that he had to worry about her with another man, even an older one. He wasn't making headway in any of these areas. He had to come up with a plan.

Sailing came into mind. He loved to sail when the wind was just right and every tightening of the sail and turn of the rudder took you on the course you wanted. One yaw after another seemed to typify his relationship with Madison. He had felt that many times while sailing on Lake Michigan. Now he realized, just like while sailing, he had to do something radical to take control of the situation, but what?

Chapter 59. Desk Weary

She folded the one-page piece for her education column that was to be printed in the *Wyandotte Times*. This time she took out her frustrations on administrators that isolated and protected themselves as much as possible with receptionists, secretaries, assistant administrators, deans, counselors and so forth. Dealing with one person at a time in the big intimidating office of an administrator was a lot different from facing 35 hormonal teenagers in a room approximately the same size.

Require Educators to Be Teachers

One of the biggest complaints by teachers is that administrators have forgotten what it's like in the classroom. Decisions superintendents and principals make in their offices can facilitate teaching and learning in the classroom or make them nearly impossible.

Lots of times administrators pass their work down until it reaches the level of teachers. Teachers are regularly asked to complete surveys, serve on committees, conduct conferences, write curriculum, attend in-service programs, run meetings and write or rewrite policy—all during the school year when they are overloaded with classroom work. Aren't administrators specifically trained to do these tasks themselves?

Most of their directives have little impact on education in the classroom. Some directives produce documents that end up in the circular file or are intended to impress administrative colleagues and/or the public.

Other classroom interruptions are also a hindrance to learning. Some schools have school spirit rallies at the beginning of the school year that make the students so hyper teachers suffer the rest of the day with classes that won't settle down.

Many in-service programs are a farce. They sound good to administrators who don't know what teachers in the classroom need, but they end up just taking time from teachers who have papers to grade, projects to gather material for, tests to run off and lesson plans to write.

Superintendents, curriculum coordinators, vocational directors, counselors, deans of students and other certified personnel need to teach one class for at least one semester per year. It may seem obvious to require that educators be teachers, but it's a rarity in most school districts. It wouldn't hurt school board members to substitute teach four or five times a year on different levels too. Members of the educational community need be aware of what it is like on the frontline, the classroom, and how they can increase learning.

Desk Weary

Sometimes she felt guilty about her attacks. There were many dedicated teachers and administrators, but the bad ones made other administrators and teachers' lives miserable. She had to just throw the hand grenade and let people respond if they caught some shrapnel unfairly. The *Times* liked the pieces because they caused controversy. With most of the population involved with the schools as teachers, nurses, cooks, custodians, groundskeepers, parents of children or fans of the plays and athletic events, many readers waited for Madison's columns and then debated them.

She ran down and slipped the enveloped article into the mailbox slot at the entrance to the complex. Then she ran back up stairs and began preparing spaghetti and a salad. She started to think about William. She liked him a lot but felt he was pushing hard, whereas she liked Duke about as much, and he didn't push at all. She couldn't decide which was better. Pushing showed enthusiasm and jealousy, she realized, and maybe love, but what did Duke's plodding style mean? It made her mind teem with possibilities.

She wondered if Duke would ever want to have sex. He never showed it even when they had been naked together in the pond. Even his little joke about sleeping together didn't give her any clue. She didn't believe she could have a sexless marriage even if she loved Duke.

After she ate dinner she graded essays about the necessity of war. She didn't try to decide a right answer, since war was such as fog of black and white smoke merging into gray--with greed, passion, self-preservation, cultural pride, rights, freedom and religious traditions swirling under it. She wanted her students to provide appropriate quotations from those involved, whether commanders in chief or soldiers in a trench, whether pacifists or hawks, whether noncombatants overseas or at home. She stressed including statistics to back their opinions.

Madison didn't mark the papers too heavily for grammar, typos or punctuation, as long as the content made sense despite the errors.

After a few *Bible* studies with Mark's group, Madison wished she could also talk a little religion in her classes. So many wars were fought because of illusory differences in opinion about religious beliefs. She had learned in a comparative religions course how much alike most belief systems were. She loaned her DVD of *Beyond Our Differences* to any student or friend who expressed an interest in other religions. She envied Naomi for her travel experiences and the friends she had made in other cultures. She couldn't wait for Mark's group to meet again.

Chapter 60. Behave

Sam's phone beeped in the middle of the day. Oh no, he thought. Jenni had behaved the past few months. She knew she wasn't supposed to call him in the middle of the day. He didn't want it to be, but he thought to himself that it had better be, an emergency instead of monkey business.

The message read: "Am at a motel. Follow the arrows."

Sam walked out of his office at Superior Cell Service, and there by the door was a white spray-painted arrow. He looked toward his car and noticed several more leading in that direction.

"She's crazy," he thought.

He got in his car and followed the white arrows. The last one indicated a left turn. His heart started to beat with anger and anticipation of Jenni in a motel room dressed in he didn't know what. The arrows turned green two blocks ahead and then one pointed right. He turned onto the strip, with lots of motels, used car dealers, specialty shops, gas stations and fast- and slow-food restaurants.

At the second intersection the spray paint Jenni had used was yellow. The arrows pointed straight ahead. Sam wondered how she had painted down the right lane of busy streets without being caught. The last yellow arrow pointed into the Highland Inn parking lot. Then the spray paint used was orange. These arrows led to a parking place.

Before Sam exited his car he saw the red pointers leading to a walkway. He followed them at a trot. He climbed the outside stairs and the arrows ended at door 269. A red pair of panties was hung on the outside knob. He grabbed them and stuffed them into his pocket, checking right and left to see if anyone noticed.

He tapped on the door. He heard a meow from inside.

Sam whispered, "Let me in."

"Meow. Meeeoow. Meooooow." The sound became louder with every meow, reminiscence of a cat in heat.

Sam looked around again. No one was on the walkway. This time he knocked loudly and yelled: "Unlock the door."

"Okay, okay," came the answer.

After ten minutes of yelling, mostly by Sam, he stomped out. No wahoo had been emitted from the inside of the motel room.

Chapter 61. Paisley

"Why do you wear so much paisley, Naomi?" asked Mark. Naomi's dental supply company had opened a territory that included Wyandotte. Ostensibly, she had taken a territory in Kentucky because her aunt's health was continuing to worsen. She now lived across the hall from Mark in her aunt's house. She was currently working out of Cincinnati, but she only had to go to the corporate office periodically for meetings, seminars and updates on sales materials.

"My second dental mission trip was to Kashmir and India. Some say Kashmir was the place of origin of the paisley shape. Some say it's Zoroastrian in nature and symbolizes life and eternity. The shape has been associated with the mango and a flame. Paisley in Central Asia is called *buta* or *buteh*. *Buta* in Hindi means flower."

"I thought paisley was from Europe. Maybe France."

"The buta shape became known as paisley because fabric designers in Paisley, Scotland, supposedly were the first to use the shape outside of Central Asia. It's also called the Persian pickle and the Welsh pear."

"Really!"

"Useless information, right?"

"Interesting, though."

"So, what about my original question?"

"Why I wear it?"

"Yes."

Squinting harder, Naomi said, "Some believe it's one half of the yin yang symbol. And yin yang represents all the seemingly opposing energies in the universe coming together into one beautiful and complimentary way. The round shape that tapers off makes the buta look like it's moving. Like a comet going in a circle."

"And, again, why do you wear it, young lady?" Mark teased.

"Sorry, I keep spouting history and philosophy. I like that it incorporates action and harmony. I feel that having paisley, or buta, shapes on my clothing gives me energy. The individual paisley seems to be looking for its counterpart to become whole. Like men and women seeking a mate, then establishing a union that produces new life." A flush came to her face as she spoke the last lines.

"That's beautiful, Naomi."

"Why do you wear a buta, Mark?"

"What?"

"The shape on your shoes."

"Oh yeah, your aunt told me it was paisley. I don't know. Tell me more about my swoosh."

"I saw paisley designs infused with smaller paisley designs in Azerbaijan that represented marriage, children or grandchildren. They used the buta shape for their famous Maiden's Tower, and you could find the shape in giant planters in parks, on the walls of businesses, at public water wells, on carpets and, of course, on dresses."

"Interesting."

"Now. Let me turn the tables. Why do you wear a dress shirt, jeans and sneakers?"

"I guess I want to be professional, but I also want to not appear too rich. I always wondered what Jesus would wear if he were American. He dressed like others of his time, but more simply than the Pharisees and the rich. Would he wear working men's clothing or a business suit or would he dress preppy?"

"Okay. That makes sense."

"Naomi, we've spent so much time together since you moved in, but I've never asked you for a date."

"Are you asking me for a date now?"

"Sorry. Naomi, would you like to go out for dinner and a movie?"

"I would love to."

"Could we go Dutch? I'm really short on money this week."

"Let me take you. Would it embarrass you if I paid? I have a well-paying job."

"Actually, I'd love it. I'm not exactly getting rich earning minimum-wage."

They had a fun evening together. The movie wasn't much, as most of the movies seemed to have been recently. After leaving the theater they went to an ice cream shop. Over tin roof sundaes, he told her a funny story about sliding down a reservoir dam when he was in high school. He and four buddies had crammed into one boy's dad's pickup, sitting on top of each other in the front seat, and headed for the dam with some cardboard for sleds. They had slid on the dam's angled, wet and slippery spillway until the protruding rocks had torn up their sleds.

Mark was the only one dumb enough to make another run down the spillway without cardboard. Of course it had ripped his pants, boxers and hands. He had walked back to the truck with his butt hanging out.

The driver had refused to let him sit with naked butt on his seat, and nobody for sure was going to let him sit on their lap. The back of the pickup had been full of dried chicken dung that was to be delivered to a neighbor the next day, so Mark had had to ride on the back bumper and hold onto the tailgate. The manure was so dusty that it flew out of the bed easily, so they had had to drive slowly.

Every time a car had approached the truck from the rear, Mark's posterior had become the main attraction in the car's headlights. Honking of the horn and yelling from the car's window let Mark know he was going to be the talk of his home town. He was known as BB (Bare Butt), and Mooner for the rest of the summer.

Naomi topped Mark's story with an account a man named Yusif, a Tajik, who had fallen in love with her in Tajikistan. She had been helping locals in villages with dental care on a mission trip. Yusif had traveled with the American team as a translator. After a visit to one village, Yusif had followed her everywhere she went. He had brought her drinks, positioned himself beside her when the team ate meals and tried to always sit next to her as they traveled. He had finally asked her to marry him.

This behavior had so puzzled Naomi that she had a member of the team quiz Yusif about his sudden attraction to her. It turned out that he had fallen in love with her after she had used an inside restroom. Most toilets were outside in the villages, open pits and stinky. At one location they were able to use an inside restroom.

Naomi had used the facilities inside and then freshened the air afterward with a travel-size container of Summer Blossom. Yusif had entered the toilet right after her. He had been shocked at the smell. He had told the team member that he could see that Naomi was beautiful, but he was surprised that even her poo poo smelled like fresh flowers. He had wanted to marry this angel in human form.

Chapter 62. Back to Normal

Thankfully, Miss Ardnas' life was fairly settled. April and Cam were doing well in school, her college classes were progressing satisfactorily. She loved to teach and that made most of her students love to learn. Interactions had settled down between Franklin and her, and they were more intimate in bed. She loved Mark's weekly *Bible* studies. They seemed much more enlightening than standard sermons.

She sat down to send her latest news article to her blog. The fake news didn't have the impact it had had before her students knew her blog was a hoax, but the students were fascinated with her technique of using satire to promote discussion. She had them read a little of *Gulliver's Travels* and *A Modest Proposal*, so that they could see that the method was old and well accepted. They especially loved the two groups in *Gulliver's Travels* who squabbled over silly matters, such as whether to break their soft-boiled eggs on the big end or the little end. It reminded the students of the current battle between the Republicans and Democrats, and it made Miss Ardnas think about all the religious sects that argued with other sects about baptism, translations of the *Bible*, music in the church, and things like card playing or dancing.

She opened her blog and copied her article into it:

College Girls Plan to Sue Television Evangelists
Ersatz News--Las Angelos, New Mexico

Three college girls are compiling a list of television evangelists they think should be sued.

"We're fed up with TV preachers laying guilt trips on the elderly, especially lonely widows, so that they will send money to them," says Bethann Baxter, one of the college girls who established WSWD, What Should Widows Do.

The name is a take-off of WWJD, What Would Jesus Do. Baxter, Kasanya Jones, and Mere Douglas say they believe that Jesus wouldn't be soliciting money from lonely women who have fixed incomes.

Douglas adds, "We've done research on the income of the top ten most popular TV evangelists and found some are driving expensive cars, own multi-million-dollar vacation homes, hire family members at exorbitant salaries, own or rent private jets to travel from one event to another and pursue a luxurious lifestyle."

"Meanwhile, many of their contributors have to apply for free meals, can't repair their leaky roofs and don't have money for new shoes," reports Jones. "It's criminal that TV preachers use all kinds of psychological techniques to get their viewers to send them money."

One popular technique that was reported on www.preacherbums.com is to say prayers for the viewing audience. The evangelist will act as if God is revealing to him that someone specific has back problems, is in agony with pain in her feet, or is suffering from poor vision. Then he will say a prayer as if it were meant for a single viewer. Baxter muses, "Most people over 65 have all of these complaints. The preachers are just fishing, and they can't miss. They're really fishing for a donation. We believe there's fraud, misleading advertising, and deceptive and unethical business practices going on. If the preacher really got a message from God, then why not just say, 'Joe Smith in Tucson, Arizona, has back problems.'"

The Website went on to mention healings. Audiences watch while people in wheel chairs get up and walk, and the deaf and dumb start hearing and speaking. "You never see a faith healer restore an arm or miraculously heal a person whose head was cut off in an industrial accident," laughs Baxter. "Anyone can say they were deaf and now they are healed."

Another favorite, the site reports, is pictures of hungry children in the arms of the evangelist. One national investigative report showed *that only five percent of donations to a well-known anti-hunger campaign went for food, while the rest went into paying for airtime, building expensive corporate offices and lining the pockets of those running the so-called ministry.*

"Gifts" are also a popular motivation for viewers. Some of the rewards for contributing are plaques, CDs, DVDs, statues, certificates, cross necklaces and books. "The more you send in, the bigger the material reward. Most of the rewards are junk," says Jones.

Baxter, Jones and Douglas plan to find a pro bono lawyer to file a class-action suit against some of the worst offenders. Plus they're not against taking donations from fellow students and others who think the TV evangelists are charlatans. They said they will not use any of the money to cover their expenses for managing the charity, but instead use it to defray legal costs.

The three college students already have 125 stories of fraudulent practices from elderly women. They think they will get about 500 before filing a suit.

When asked about those who believe that TV religious shows bring comfort to many, Douglas said, "Sure, there are a few good shows, and the lonely get some psychological benefit from the fake promises and feel like they are giving to a worthy cause, but an evangelist's jet is not a worthy cause. The lonely would be better served at their local church or community service organization."

Baxter is a sociology major at Georgia East Technical College, Jones is a criminal science major at Barcelona University in Brazil and Douglas is a recent graduate of Bingington University. They met a couple of years ago at a revival in Texas, then kept in touch through email before deciding to do something about the questionable practices of many television evangelists.

"We three try to follow WWJD, and WSWD is one way to do that," concluded Baxter. "We're trying to throw the money changers out of the temple."

When Miss Ardnas finished, she checked her email. Two students had written pieces of satire and wanted to know if they were good enough for them to start their own "news" blogs. She made a few suggestions and encouraged them to "go for it." Other emails were ads, Facebook notifications, and funny pictures or political comments forwarded from friends.

Cam had yelled for her to come out and play basketball with him in the driveway, but she decided to check one more email first. The subject line intrigued her. It read: "I'm Sorry."

She opened and read:

"This is a coward's way of notifying you, but at least I'm doing it. I heard of your contract with your husband, and I also heard about Pastor Wellston deciding to take action when people he knows are being harmed.

"Here goes. Franklin is having an affair with the cleaning girl at work. I know, because I work in the office. His past affairs have infuriated me, but I never before had the guts to tell you about them. I'm sorry. I hope this makes up a little for my past silence.

"I know this is hard news to take, but it's true. It's not fair for you to be left in the dark. The girl involved is being pressured, I believe. She needs the job and money. I may tell her to sue him for sexual harassment, but I don't want to expose myself to firing. I need the job and I don't want Wright Insurance to close.

"My husband cheated on me and no one told me. After I found out that everyone else knew, I felt like a fool. I hope we can all work together and share information our friends need in their lives.

"Again, I'm sorry. God bless you."

Miss Ardnas slumped in her chair. Then she called Pastor Mark.

After she told Pastor Mark about the email, she asked, "What should I do?" Again, Pastor Mark was torn. He would love for her to get a divorce and be available for him to date. But he had to push that out of his mind.

"I was afraid of this. Franklin's participation in counseling and the *Bible* studies was halfhearted. I'm afraid he has a psychological problem that he can't overcome. He needs more help than I can give him."

"I think you're right. But what do I do now?"

"If you could have him diagnosed by a psychiatrist, that would be perfect. But would he ever go? He has broken his marriage pledge about 'forsaking all others' and his signed agreement with you, so morally you have every right to end the marriage. Now you're going to have to decide whether you can live with him and his behavior, and whether it affects your children's psychological stability, your work and your social life in a harmful way. I always preach 'love the person but hate the behavior.' Do you think you have the power to get him back on a moral and socially acceptable path?"

"Not really. I'm at my wit's end. This past year has been a nightmare ride on a marriage rollercoaster. I can't take it anymore."

"Sleep on it, Miss Ardnas. I'll pray. You pray. Then call me tomorrow after I get off work and we'll discuss your options."

"Okay."

Miss Ardnas went out and played HORSE with Cam, acting as natural as she could under the circumstances.

Chapter 63. A Long Road

Getting friends to take him to interviews in other towns bothered him. Mark didn't want to put people out, but he didn't have a car and there was no public transportation between towns. Taxis were out of the questions, and his velomobile just took too long to get anywhere and back in a day.

The interviews all went well, and the ministerial search committees loved Mark until he answered the tough questions.

"Are your sermons *Bible*-based?" he was asked.

"Yes, I plan each sermon series around a topic taken from a book of the *Bible*."

"Do you believe in divine intervention?"

"Yes, but not in the traditional sense. Lots of people ask for dry weather to make their picnic a success while farmers need rain for crops. They also say that God knows what we want before we pray for it, yet they will pray for God to heal them of an illness, not realizing if God wanted them not to be ill he would have prevented the disease in the first place. Belief in excessive and/or absolute divine intervention causes people who suffer tragic losses to question the very existence of God. They prayed to God for protection, thought they had it, but suffered the losses anyway. Author Ambrose Bierce wrote something like this: *To pray means to ask God to suspend the laws of the universe on behalf of one believer that admits he's not worthy.* We need to think about our motives and the consequences before we pray."

"Do you believe the *Bible* is the Word of God and infallible?"

With each honest answer, the temperature in the room dropped until the chairman thanked Mark and said they would be in touch. Most of them did get in touch, but all of them declined to have another interview or to ask for references.

"How can I live without fulfilling my calling?" wondered Mark. "What is there in life for me without the ministry?"

He didn't give up, though, and his job searches reached out even to Alaska. It seemed like nobody wanted a maverick preacher, even if they were in the wilds of the tundra. Mark felt churches and ministers were the best things communities had, and he wanted to continue to be a part of organized religion. He wondered then, "Why am I critical of so many churches and church practices. Is it just bitter grapes?" Mark was feeling desperate.

Chapter 64. Out of the Woods

Camping supplies were spread all over state park campsite number 25, which wasn't that large, and was marked on four corners with wooden posts. Sam, Jenni and Duke's cars took up much of the available space. Jenni and Sam were assembling one tent. It looked like they were wrestling with a clothesline full of sheets. Duke and Madison made short work of their tent. It was neat and the material was tightly stretched. When Sam and Jenni were finished, their tent was crooked and saggy. No one was camping on the site next to them, so they fudged a little on the placement of their chairs and extra gear.

As the sun dropped so did the temperature. Duke made a fire in the iron ring that was supplied and sat smoking in a web chair. Bark was at his side chewing on a stick. Of course Duke had his latest "blind man's" puzzle with him. Madison sat beside him poking the fire with a stick. Jenni was sitting on the bare ground tossing hickory nuts, which had fallen from the tree that shaded the campsite, into the fire. She looked like a tow-headed child playing in a sandbox. Sam was walking around in loose circles trying to find where he belonged in this camping picture.

Sam's cellphone rang. He answered it and it was his mother. He talked with her a few minutes about an upcoming trip to see her and then closed his phone. Then Sam called a friend about going fishing the following weekend.

Duke disliked any electronic or electrical devices in the woods. He didn't bring his cellphone nor a boombox. He had asked Madison not to bring her laptop, iPod or Kindle. He believed that nature and good company was all you needed while camping and that all the electrical gadgets would interfere with the experience. He remembered going to Boundary Waters Canoe Area with an experienced guide. The guide had told the group that they were all going back to nature.

The guide had said, "Don't bring any music players, watches, or other artificial trappings of civilization. We'll work with nature and not against it, so no hacking down brush to make an area for your tent and no breaking off live limbs for a fire. No makeup, no deodorant, you go swimming to bathe. We're going to eat when we're hungry, not by the clock. We'll sleep when we're tired. We'll hike when we need exercise and fish when we like. We'll crap in the woods like bears and howl at the moon like wolves if we feel like howling at the moon. We'll sit on a stump and meditate or talk to God when it suits us. Relax, enjoy, explore, live fully. Let's go."

Duke had brought sirloins to the park campsite. He pulled out a pocket knife and started cutting then into bite-size pieces on newspaper atop a picnic table. Madison chopped up potatoes with the peels left on. Jenni worked on the carrots, again leaving the peels on but chopping them into one-inch pieces. Sam was still pacing. Madison switched to rinsing off a box of fresh button mushrooms and Jenni sliced onions and shredded cabbage.

Duke grabbed his iron pot with lid and bail. He placed it right on the hot coals of the fire. He poured about a quarter cup of olive oil into the bottom of the pot and threw in the sirloin. Salt and pepper followed. The sizzle and smell made everyone's digestive juices flow. He stirred the meat until it was brown and then tossed in the vegetables, a handful of flour and a cup of water. On went the lid and the stew didn't get touched until it was time to serve it.

After everyone had eaten their fill, Sam brought out a bottle of blackberry brandy. They passed the bottle around and took sips from its mouth. The fire now was not only in the fire pit but in their stomachs. Sam finally started to relax and enjoy sitting and looking at the flames. Jenni, on the other hand, started to get antsy.

"Let's take a walk in the dark," she suggested.

At the word *walk*, Bark jumped up, wagged his tail and watched Duke for directions.

"Okay, let me get the flashlights," said Madison.

"Without flashlights," insisted Jenni.

"There's some moonlight. Why not?" added Duke.

"Not me. I just got comfortable. You guys go," said Sam.

"I'll keep Sam company," said Madison.

Jenni and Duke headed for the trail that led to the river. Jenni stumbled over a rock and grabbed Duke for support. Every so often they got off the trail and crashed through the vines and brambles, picking up a bur or two, until they found their way back to the path. Jenni took ahold of Duke's hand and let him do the guiding. The moonlight was good, but the trees occasionally blocked some of its glow.

They found the river and splashed through it up to their knees, ignoring that they were getting their pants, shoes and socks wet. They were happy and laughing at every tripping rock, crashed-into tree, foot-tangling vine and woodsy sounds. The mating call of a hoot owl caused them to stop and listen. Then they waited for the answer. It came. To Duke's surprise, Jenni pushed him hard against a tree, then pressed herself against him, hung her arms around his neck and kissed him open-mouthed on the lips.

"Whoa, what was that?"

"I like you, Duke."

"But you and Sam…"

"We broke up last week. He only came on this trip because we had promised to, and he felt you were making a move on Madison and didn't want to mess up your plans."

"I'm sorry. I didn't know you two weren't getting along."

She pushed against him again and gave him another kiss.

"Wait a minute," he said, grabbing her by the shoulders and holding her at arms' length.

"You don't really care about Madison. You never hold hands, kiss, hug or show any sparks of attraction."

"Well…"

"I've always liked you better than Sam, once I got to know you, but I thought Sam and I could develop into a fun couple. Actually, he's no fun most of the time. I have to do all the fun stuff and then sometimes he gets stuffy about the way I am. He'd rather fish than fool around, he likes sports better than real life, he'd rather lie on the couch than walk in the woods. He's boring."

"Now that you've confessed, let me confess too. I've always liked you too. You're lively while I'm kind of meditative. You're a lot more spontaneous that I am, even though I try."

"So, Big Fellow?" He was looking at her shining white hair highlighted even more by the moonlight.

"I have to admit that you're right about my relationship with Madison. We're great pals, but there's nothing else going on between us. Never has been and probably never will be."

He felt her rub against him yet again, and this time he put his arms around her and returned the kiss. She began fiddling with the buttons on his shirt, and he began working the zipper in the front of her pants. They didn't return to the campsite for half an hour.

"What did you guys see out there?" asked Madison.

"Well, we heard an owl," replied Jenni.

"I think I heard the hoot of an owl too," said Sam, accusingly.

Even in the glow of the fire, Sam could tell Jenni's face was obviously redder than usual.

The rest of the evening around the fire was quiet, with a few crickets and frogs sending mating calls through the darkness. The flames mesmerized the four campers and seemed to put them into deep thought or thoughtlessness. None could tell. They hardly looked at each other until the moon dropped below the trees and the fire died down. They went to bed in pairs but they might as well have been in separate tents or even at home alone.

Chapter 65. Being Frank

"I got an interesting email today, Franklin," stated Miss Ardnas. Then her emotions got the best of her. "How could you? With the cleaning lady?" she yelled.

"Girl! Not lady. Girl! So what? I'm tired of ….." The rest of Franklin's comments had so many F words in it that Miss Ardnas stopped listening. She thought, "So this is the real guy I married. Foul language, foul actions and foul mind."

For Miss Ardnas, who finally just told him to get out of the house, this was the tipping point. The fact was he thought of making love as a gutter expletive. She never understood people saying, "F you" or "get screwed." She enjoyed intimacy and considered it one of the highest forms of love. Why was a beautiful, natural, loving act talked about in such a crude, violent and hateful manner?"

Miss Ardnas called Mark and then called a friend who was a divorce lawyer. She wasn't going to waste any time. She would use the signed contract, a copy Mark gave her of the letter he sent Franklin, and a printout of the employee's email to make sure she had a firm position for talking about any child custody issues.

She didn't really want to think about such things, but her anger and pain made her want to create a defense and offense. It was hard for her to have any positive thoughts about Franklin. After she put the children to bed, she sat down on the sofa and cried. She released all the emotions of the last year and felt catharsis. The house seemed empty but safe.

When she was on the phone with Mark, he consoled her and asked if she needed him to come over. He was glad when she said she was okay, and he didn't need to come. He didn't want to put himself into the position of having to hold her in his arms while she shed tears of sadness and relief. He didn't trust himself. He kept suppressing what a divorce would mean for his chances with Miss Ardnas in the distant future, after all the emotion subsided. He was glad and sad for her and immediately said a prayer. He also prayed for Franklin and April and Cam.

Chapter 66. A Different Kind of Hike

Madison was shocked the next time she danced with Duke at Antler Inn. He told her he didn't know how it happened, but Jenni and he had done more than hike that moonlit night. Of course, she did understand but was hurt.

She was able to joke, "Well, that makes us even."

"Well, not exactly," responded Duke.

"I want to date Jenni. I'm hoping she and I can make a life together."

"What about Sam?"

"They're not together anymore. She told me that while we were on the walk."

"But you're dating his ex."

"I told Sam right away. At first he was angry, but, after we had a few beers and threw some rocks at a fencepost, he said, 'Good luck, Duke. She's a frisky mare that I wasn't able to handle. I'm glad I'm shut of her.'"

"Wow. Things happen fast. Miss Ardnas and Franklin, Sam and Jenni, you and Jenni, what's next?"

"You and William?"

"I'm still working on that. I guess with you out of the picture, I won't have as many excuses for dragging my feet."

"We could pretend we're still dating. I loved our walks with you teaching me history and me teaching you about nature."

"No pretending. We've been honest with each other. I want that to continue and to also be a part of whatever relationship I have with William."

"I know this sounds corny, but can we still be friends? If William will allow it."

"We'll see."

Madison went back to her apartment, opened the laptop and banged out another article for her education column.

They Don't Know What's Going on in the Classroom

If they were honest, principals, assistant principals, curriculum directors and department heads would have to admit that they don't know what's going on in the classroom.

Many school classroom visitations or observations are so short and so infrequent, that there's no way the administrator could know what's really going on it a classroom. Plus, kids and teachers often "perk up" or "clam up" when a visitor appears.

Administrators should be such frequent visitors that the students and teachers wouldn't think anything was out of the ordinary.

Too many principals do the room "walk by" to see if learning is taking place. If the kids are very noisy, that's often considered bad, even though the class might be organized into small discussion groups arguing about a controversial subject. If a class is quiet and kids are using pencil and paper, that's often considered the perfect classroom, even though the students might be involved in the lowest level of intellectual activity, memorizing and recalling.

You almost always see administrators at football and basketball games, and they usually know more about individual players and coaching records on those teams than they do about student and teacher performance. That should be reversed. They should know what's going on in their classrooms.

Madison closed her laptop, and then opened it again. She wondered whether she should reregister with backinthegame.com. Her love life was so much easier, in a way, when she had two boyfriends. Now she would have to fend for herself, she realized. She logged on and found the bright orange button labeled: "Back in the Game Again." She checked to see if by some mistake she was still listed. She wasn't. Then she looked for William. He wasn't there either. She pushed the button and uploaded a picture and typed a new profile.

Chapter 67. Characters

In Wyandotte, Jenni was considered quite a character, but on the Appalachian Trail she was just one of many. Since Duke had planned a backpacking trip with Madison before Jenni entered the picture, he decided to follow through with his new girlfriend. Of course, Duke's trail name was Dude, while Jenni coined the name Jenerator.

Duke picked a location along the trail, so Jenni and he could encounter some of the through hikers after several months or more in the wilderness. The first night on the trail didn't disappoint them. They had picked an AT hut that was a day's hike from the trail head and arrived early with a lot of their initial adrenalin still available in their veins.

Right away they could see that all the spots in the three-sided hut were taken, and a hiker was building a fire in front of the hut. Other hikers had set up tents or placed bivy sacks behind the structure. Duke and Jenni found a good spot farther out from the crowd and enough distance from the outhouse to avoid any odor.

As soon as the tent was set up, Jenni started to make the rounds meeting the hikers. She was like a kid in a magic shop. Many of the hikers were a little wild-eyed from months away from civilization, and Jenni was always wild-eyed, so she clicked with everyone. Trail names included: Downy Feather, Bulldog, Gourmand, Sassy River, Mountain Goat, and Dodger.

A banjo with a tiny drum, a guitar with normal neck but ukulele body, and two harmonicas appeared in the hands of the campers. Country, classical and bluegrass music filled the air. Jenni was right in the middle of the musicians, pounding two sticks together, humming loudly, singing or dancing around the fire with some of the other hikers. Duke sat quietly, a smile on his face, smoking his pipe.

When they finally wore down, they crawled into their tent. With their two sleeping bags zipped together, the cool night air stopped nipping at their bodies. Sleeping in the nude, skin to skin, fit both Jenni and Duke perfectly. Of course, a few minutes of intimacy produced a loud Wahoo from Jenni. People in other tents and the hut could be heard mumbling questions like: "What was that? Did you hear that animal? Where did that come from?"

With the temperature much higher in the tent after love making, they unzipped and lay on top of the combined sleeping bags. Jenni went immediately to sleep with her head on Duke's arm. For an hour Duke lay awake listening to the snores and rustling of nylon tent fabric and sleeping bag zippers. As the cold air reentered the tent, Jenni unconsciously snuggled up to Duke's warm body. Before he decided to let himself drift off to sleep, he pulled the bag back around Jenni and himself. His relationship with Jenni was cemented.

Chapter 68. Don't Worry

Miss Ardnas received a call from her lawyer.

"Don't worry about anything. Word's out that Franklin is in deep do-do over that harassment suit filed at his office. Come to find out, the little cleaning girl wasn't the only employee there he had hooked up with. Once the girl filed the suit, all the others had the courage to pile on."

"I hate all this, but what did he think he could expect?"

"He'll settle the harassment suit, or suits, out of court."

"Sounds like him."

"Gus at Wayne Realty says he's putting the business up for sale."

"No!"

"Yes. And he made an offer on an insurance business in Chillicothe, where the owner wants to retire. The offer is contingent on his selling Wright Insurance. 'No problem there,' Gus told me. He's already received two legitimate offers from other insurance firms with excellent credit ratings."

"So I'll be able to keep Cameron and April?"

"You're home safe, Miss Ardnas."

"Thank heavens."

"I'll put together all the documents that will include custody, child support and alimony requests to give to the court along with the divorce papers. I don't expect Franklin will appear in court. He'll have his lawyer face the music for him."

Chapter 69. Wings. Ribs and PBR

The marriage of Duke Preston and Jenni Block was the talk of the town. Both parties had made it known that during the wedding Duke would change his name from Preston to Block. Nobody in Wyandotte had heard of such a thing before and, rightly so, they didn't know what to think about it now. Some laughed, some gasped, some just dwelled on it for days.

It didn't bother Duke at all. He was an outdoor, free spirit, individual, who had a mustache and goatee. Plus he smoked a pipe. He worked outside as a civil engineer. If that wasn't enough for them to accept that he was a man's man, then nothing would. He just continued to smoke his pipe and enjoy life with Jenni, who had moved in with him after the Appalachian Trail trip.

The wedding was as unique as most expected. It was outside, there was no champagne but plenty of PBR in a small horse watering tank. There were no dainty canapés, but there were lots of Buffalo wings and cheese pizzas. There were no white dresses, but everyone invited was told to break out their jeans and flannel shirts, even the women. Jenni added a wraparound square-dance skirt on top of her jeans. It floated out when she twirled around, so she twirled around a lot. In honor of the occasion, Duke wore an American Flag tie with his blue and brown flannel shirt.

Even Duke's mother was wearing a flannel shirt, blue jeans and a denim jacket. She also had on cowboy boots since Jenni had told her there'd be line, square and round dancing outside.

Mark finished the wedding ceremony and announced, "I now pronounce you man and wife. You may kiss the bride," then said, "Friends and relatives, I present to you, Mr. and Mrs. Duke Block," the women cheered more than the men. Duke had the band play and sing Simply Red's version of *You Make Me Feel Brand New*. He looked into Jenni's eyes and grabbed the microphone to add his voice. Everyone cheered again. The girls' eyes filled with tears, but they had smiles on their faces.

Of course, Jenni couldn't stand still. She twisted, did pirouettes, slide up to Duke and hugged him, then took soft but energetic steps as she circled him. Once when she gave him a hug, she let out a "wahoo," but only Sam and Duke knew what had happened. The crowd gathered closer and surrounded them, joining Duke in the singing. All the while they hugged their boyfriends and girlfriends around the waist. *You Make Me Feel Brand New* was played three times until every couple was gliding around and around Jenni and Duke.

Then the band changed to faster music. Dancing of all kinds, but especially line dancing, was something to watch since the ground was hard and dusty. Couples swirled making little whirlwinds, and line dancers tried to get a good stomping sound out of the hard-packed soil. William and Madison kicked up their heels with the rest of them. The last dance was to *You Are Everything*, the version by the Stylistics. The song was played four times as Duke and Jenni snowballed through the visitors, dancing with everyone.

Later horseshoes, corn-hole toss, ladder golf, and Jarts were played in Duke's yard even after it started drizzling. A series of tugs-of-war contests over a mud pit broke the ice with even the most staunch suburbanites. Bark, of course, grabbed the rope between the two teams and held on for dear life. He was drug back and forth through the mud and loved it.

Even Madison, who was quite a city girl despite her past hikes with Duke, slid and fell and got muddy. Everyone literally got down and dirty. No one seemed to care about looks, just having fun. Duke and Jenni Block gave prizes for the winners of each competition. They included: a gift certificate for one free draft beer at Antler Inn, an old cowboy boot with a geranium growing out of it, a hand-tied fly for fly fishing, a free pedicure at Hair U R, a fish fry at the Block's house, an empty bird's nest, a cracked pickle crock and assorted other flotsam and jetsam from around the Preston-Block property.

It was one time that Jenni's blond static-prone hair actually lay flat on her head due to rain and mud. Mark participated in all the events, but his rugged face looked happiest when he did a round dance with Miss Ardnas.

Since Duke had joined Mark's *Bible* study after he and Jenni started dating, Mark, Naomi, Jake, Laura, Miss Ardnas, William, Madison, some college students and even Sam were all in attendance. Sam had as much fun as anybody because he didn't have to lasso and hogtie Jenni every time she escaped from the sanity corral. They had had one spat after another during the last weeks of their relationship. He let Duke worry about her now.

But Duke Block didn't worry. Yes, Jenni showed up at the bridge site once in the car and told Duke she didn't have anything on under her dress. They drove down the highway a little, pulled off onto a gravel road, then steamed up the windows and rocked the car for fifteen minutes. Another time she surprised Duke by following him into the men's room at the Antler Inn. She pushed him into the handicapped stall, and, after some swishing, bumping and puffing, the guy in the next stall heard, "Wahoo."

A few taps reverberated on the stall divider, and then the fellow on the next toilet yelled loudly, "Must have been a good turd, hey, Partner?"

Chapter 70. Out of the Game

William arrived at Madison's apartment early Friday night. He had made it a regular practice for his assistant to close the shop on Saturday nights. That gave him the whole evening with Madison. Since Madison had quit dating Duke, William was also having his assistant close for him Friday nights. He had brought a couple of bottles of Madison's favorite moscato wine and also a box containing a couple of crystal wine glasses he had bought as a celebration of Duke's exit from the scene. She pulled the spacer out of the box and inspected the wine glasses. They were delicate and etched with vines and grapes. This earned William a kiss.

He didn't tell Madison the real reason for the present, because he didn't want her thinking of Duke every time she drank from them. He just said he gave them to her because he loved her.

While William was waiting for Madison to boil the spaghetti, toss a salad and warm the sauce, he decided to check his email on

Madison's laptop. As luck would have it, her profile and photo for backinthegame.com were on the screen. At first he thought it was her old website account, then he noticed it was a new photo.

"Hey. What's going on?"

"What, William?"

"Your photo and profile are back on the dating website."

"Oops."

"Yeah. Oops."

"I can explain."

"You'd better."

Madison turned both burners off and put the salads in the refrigerator. Then she moved the pans from the stove onto hot pads. That gave her time to pull herself together. William was waiting on the edge of the office chair at her desk.

She came into the living room and knelt down and put her hands on his knees. He didn't move. She shifted her hands to his face. It remained intentionally unemotional. She explained her fears of commitment. She told him she loved him but was scared to death of a failed marriage, the possible loss of her profession if she had children, and the giving up of her self-image. She told him she had seen so many of her friends go from being seen as lawyers, bankers, store owners and, yes, teachers, to being known as the wife of so and so. She wasn't ready for that.

"But why go back to internet dating. We're not married but I thought we were a couple."

"That's what I mean by making a firm commitment. It was easy to have a platonic, fun and innocent relationship that would be secondary to my professional and social life as long as I wasn't engaged or married. Dating two men made it all easy in a weird way."

"You've got to stop this kind of thinking, Madison."

"I know. I know."

"Marry me. I love you. I promise not to force you to give up any of your interests except other men."

"I can't marry now."

"Please."

They talked. He soothed her with lines of poetry, and they drank a bottle each of moscato. She was especially moved by the sound and sense of: "Beauty is truth, truth beauty, that is all ye know on earth, and all ye need to know." And "Shall I compare thee to a summer's day? Thou art more lovely and more temperate."

After an hour, with the food still uneaten in the kitchen, William lifted Madison and she let him carry her to her bedroom. That night she made a physical commitment to their relationship. He spent the night in her apartment for the first time.

The next day William moved in as a trial, and both knew they were on a slow path to a permanent union. Both now wanted marriage; it's just that William wanted it sooner than Madison. Madison was dedicated to teaching, at least for now, and to her broader goal of trying to make education a more efficient and successful institution.

It was hard for her to meet all her classes and keep her thoughts on the subject for the next few days. Typically students came to her between classes with questions about assignments, complaints about grades, personal problems and requests for passes to the library during their study halls. When she got home one evening she was shaky and confused. She was on the slippery slope to marriage. When she entered the apartment she decided she'd let William make dinner, when he got home. She had a deadline to meet for the next article for her column. She typed:

Schools Never Have Enough Money

We know why many people don't choose teaching as a profession. For the same reason schools lose excellent teachers every year to higher-paying businesses. Since schools never have enough money, and legislators are pressured to keep taxes low, what are schools to do?

One, they could make athletic departments pay their own way. Think of how much money would be available for classroom instruction if schools didn't have to pay athletic directors, secretaries, coaches, assistant coaches, trainers, ticket takers, custodians, security officers and so forth with moneys, some of which comes from the general budget.

Plus acquisition and maintenance of gyms, playing fields, uniforms, signs, scoreboards, tennis courts, etc. is enormous. Add to that the cost of electricity and heating and bus transportation and most people wouldn't believe what those fun games really cost. Sometimes athletic directors brag that gate receipts from one sport, usually football, pay for all the other athletic programs. I'd like to sit down with the school district treasurer to discuss that.

Kids need healthy outdoor exercise but not to the detriment of education. Let money budgeted for education stay in the classroom. Most countries don't have sports run by schools, instead, as with Little League and similar programs for youth football, basketball, soccer and tennis, athletic programs are organized by volunteers, overseen by national organizations and supported by volunteer contributions and individual parents.

When William came home he kissed Madison on the shoulder and, seeing her typing, asked, "Did you throw another hand grenade at the school system, Maddie?"

"I'm about to."

"Hope they never find out who's writing all those articles that the school board has to address each month in their meetings."

"I may not be right, but at least I'm bringing up issues that should be addressed publicly. Sometimes there are several hours of practices for five or six sports every weeknight during the school year and two or three matches, meets or games per sport per week. That doesn't even count intramural sports. The special talents served by academic extracurricular activities pale in comparison to the time and money spent on athletic special talents."

"Yeah, but you can't get much of an audience for a speech meet, a debate, a history bowl or a spelling bee."

"I know. And it's pitiful that these intellectual activities don't get much attention from the general public."

"Come on, Honey, lots of people won't even go to a high school play, art show or band concert. Maybe parents and grandparents. They're just not very exciting."

"You too?"

"I guess you're right. Most people aren't very intellectual in their pursuits. Look at the art on their walls—prints and posters. Original art goes begging."

"Maddie, you could be a preacher."

"A teacher is close enough for me."

"Let's drop the education subject. I'm a wine merchant, and your article is now in the public domain. Let's talk about wine for a while and eat."

"Yes. Let's relax."

"Sure. You'd better have a glass of moscato. Otherwise you'll never relax."

While snuggled together, William gave recaps of the day's events at work. He had had a little squabble with his assistant, and a customer had brought in a bottle of expensive wine that he said was spoiled. Madison then told about her day--more teen problems and missed homework.

Chapter 71. Finally

After months of searching, to Mark's surprise he got a letter from a tiny church in Inspiration, Alaska. They wanted him as a pastor. Now he had to decide whether to take the job. Inspiration wasn't on any of his maps. It only had 50 or so residences in town, no teachers, no doctor, no cell phones, no electrical grid, no roads and, obviously, no preacher. Riverboats or seaplanes delivered the mail, medicine, visitors, food, gas for generators, and a teacher once a month, depending on the time of year. Isolation from civilization dominated the lightless winter months there.

Pay was $5,000 a year, but a small house was provided, and the congregation cooked meals on a rotating basis. If he also wanted to be the teacher, his salary would be $10,000, paid for by the state. He figured his diet would change from ham to Spam, spaghetti to ramen noodles and Kellogg's Frosted Flakes to hot Red River porridge, but he relished the adventure.

Mark had sent the ministerial search committee members, three people, tons of material explaining his religious beliefs and confrontational approach to sin. They wrote back that they would accept him anyway.

He was excited about the offer and wondered where he would get the money to fly to some major city in Alaska, then hire a seaplane to take him to Inspiration. He counseled with Jerry and a few members of his *Bible* study and asked them to pray for him.

The word spread quickly through his friends and the remainder of the *Bible* study group. Everyone was happy for Mark, but disappointed for themselves and what they were building through his "ministry." Miss Ardnas made a few calls and visits, which produced a flood of checks and cash to help Mark on his new adventure. In two days there was ample funding for Mark's journey.

Miss Ardnas couldn't wrap her mind around the fact that Mark would be out of her life. He had freed her from a miserable situation. Franklin was now in another city, the kids understood what had happened, and, in a way, she felt they weren't that upset about their father being gone. When he was home he usually didn't want to play with them, and he always seemed anxious to leave the house. If he had to stay with them because Miss Ardnas was teaching and no babysitter could be found, he was irritable and yelled at them.

With Franklin gone, the atmosphere in the Wright house was serene and joyful. Miss Ardnas hadn't realized how much the kids had hidden in their rooms when they really wanted to be running around the living room, drawing pictures on the kitchen table and watching TV in the family room together. And she knew it wasn't because they were lonely, because they weren't necessarily hanging around in the same room as their mother just to be near her. They were liberated by having the jail keeper move out of the house. She could never thank Mark enough, because she was unable or unwilling to accept the truth and to take the action that had needed to be taken on her and her children's behalf.

Chapter 72. Not a Wallet

"For the first time in my life I attended a so-called church service and came away inspired instead of disappointed and disillusioned," Jake told his wife. He continued by explaining that in some churches he just felt like a wallet, with the finance committee giving weekly reports, visiting his and other members' houses to get pledges, and urging their pastor to preach on tithing as often as they could get by with it. He wondered why there wasn't a committee sent to his house to ask about his and his family's spiritual health instead of his financial wealth?

Jake continued by telling Laura that he finally felt that a pastor was making salvation difficult. He explained to her how he had told Mark that Christianity was too easy. He was tired of people showing up for church once a week, proclaiming they were saved, then spending the rest of the week cheating on their taxes, cheating on their spouses, ignoring safe speed limits, wasting money on luxury cars and homes, all while casting a blind eye on the spiritual and financial needs around the community and the world.

"Just think, Laura, how the world would change if every person would give up one expensive luxury—say a sports car or a new kitchen—and use the money instead to help a worthy but poor boy or girl in a big city like Louisville or Cincinnati get a university or vocational college degree," suggested Jake. "What are these so-called Christians thinking when they spend their money on expensive vacations, second homes, antiques, clothes and big-people's toys!

"Remember when we took the vacation to Mexico. I felt ashamed because we were spending thousands to stay in a luxurious beachfront resort and eating at restaurants for $100 a meal, while the people we saw two blocks away were living in abject poverty. Many Americans and Europeans are like royalty sitting at a long banquet table. There's chicken, steak, ham and every vegetable and dessert you can think of at their end of the table. At the far end are some of our Asian, African and South American brothers and sisters working 12 hour days 6 days a week and not making a hundred dollars in a month. They're eating one bowl of rice a day and wondering how to get some of the food they see piled up at the other end of the table, uneaten and wasted by the 'royalty.' Only a few of the royalty even try to send a chicken bone done to the Asians. They like having too much of everything."

Laura expressed to Jake that her entire understanding of Christianity had changed due to Mark. She especially liked being freed from having to repeat a responsive reading, a denominational creed, the pastor's prayer and other material. The pastor or worship leader could ask a congregation to repeat after him, but that didn't mean they believed what they were saying. She used to babble along like the rest of the herd, but lately when she attended a church service and someone commanded, "Repeat after me," she just listened to see if she agreed before speaking words she might later question.

"And he's so accepting of the preaching he hears at the other churches he attends on Sunday," commented Laura. "He may not agree with some of the things they say, but he's willing to listen and learn from them. So many churches try to be proprietary, making you feel that the only place you can hear the truth is in their church or a church of their denomination. Mark's not like that. Of course, if you don't convince people you have the best product or the only product, who's going to spend big money on you?"

Laura felt that Mark had worked hard to educate the group about the two sides of the abortion issue. The members of the group still fell into opposing camps, but they were much more knowledgeable. Laura felt the facts were clear. It was uncivilized to believe that a moving, feeling being was not a human being a second before it was born, and then a human being the second after it was born. She wondered why so many people demanded their right to choose above the life of a living fetus. Pro-choice vs. Pro-life was a nobrainer for her.

Katherine Knox, on the other hand, thought abortion was addressing the community's welfare by not having unwanted children dropped into the world. The fact that they were unplanned for ruined the children's lives, the lives of the mothers and/or often the lives of the relatives or foster parents who had to raise the children.

Chapter 73. Dotty's Donuts

"I don't want Mark to go. He can't go. I'm going to tell him that he can't go. He's the best thing that's come to Wyandotte since Dotty's Donuts," commented Jenni.

Duke thought, "Oh, boy. Here's she goes. She's right, though. He's changed us and the town." Duke didn't understand the comparison to a bakery, but there were a lot of things he didn't understand about Jenni.

What Duke did understand, though, was that Mark was a thinker, like himself, and not just an empty glass to be filled with ideas, and, once filled, never having room for other ideas. Mark was continually adjusting the contents of his glass so that most of what was in his glass was believable and not superstition and myth.

Chapter 74. Immortality

Locked in the bathroom with the shower running, the lights off, the fan whirring and Celine Dion singing *Immortality* through the buds of her iPod, Naomi let all her sorrow flood forth. She didn't want Mark to hear her crying. She thought, "I've moved away from my family to be near Mark, we've been dating, and now he's leaving me. I can't go to Alaska and live next door to him. And he doesn't seem in the mood to establish any kind of relationship with me but a friendly one."

Her happiness for Mark and his future pastorate was almost smothered by her misery. Naomi knew she could go on and continue to grow in her faith with the group Mark had started. But she wanted more. She had taken a big step to further her dream of marriage to a wonderful man and the creation of a family.

Now she was going to be left alone and away from her parents and sister. She felt that the only things she had left were her job and the nursing of Mrs. Grassley as her aunt's health continued to fail. She was glad to do that, but she wanted Mark at her side.

Chapter 75. Gabriel

Sam wondered where Mark came from. He facetiously speculated that maybe he was from outer space, as many television programs suggested God was an alien that had planted life on earth and then left it alone. Mark was almost too good to be true.

The only things that caused Sam not to believe Mark was an angel in disguise were the number of times he bulled headlong into a project only to find that he was going the wrong direction. Sam figured an angel would know the correct path the first time. But Sam felt that Mark was as near a Gabriel as any man he had met. "What would life be like in Wyandotte without him?" he wondered.

Chapter 76. Inclusion

Mark's *Bible* study had become so big it was meeting in the community center senior citizen's room. Adjoining exercise and ping pong rooms were set up with tables and chairs for a sort of Sunday school atmosphere, although the studies were on Wednesday evenings. Kids were entertained or given *Bible* lessons in other rooms.

Mark sat at the front of the room, but he tried not to dominate the conversation. More young people searching for some spiritual light and not dogma were attending. It turned out that Naomi was incorporating some of the Muslim five-times-a-day prayer practices into her spiritual life and studying Buddhism. She was still a Christian, but communing with God five times every day made more sense to her than praying only at church or quickly and without meaning before meals.

More nonbelievers and believers alike began sneaking into the back of the meeting area to see what was going on. Some thought what they said there was blasphemous and what they did was sacrilege, but the members of the study were used to that. They knew that different denominations or synods privately thought and sometimes stated to each other that members of another denomination were blasphemous and sacrilegious. Mark's group felt that they were on the right track but still calmly and thoughtfully considered the logic of their critics. If the criticisms had merit, they made adjustments to their thinking and actions.

The interesting aspect of their group was the diversity. While some churches were fairly exclusive unless you believed a specific way and accepted a strict order of worship, Mark's group was more liberal. Catholics, Mormons, Jehovah's Witnesses, Baptists, Methodists, Episcopalians, and adherents of other denominations were curious to see what all the excitement was. Some came back, most didn't. That hadn't bothered Mark. It had bothered his group some, because they had wanted a "congregation" large enough to force Mark to become an official minister again with them.

They even had one Thai Buddhist attendee, who was a visiting professor at Wyandotte State University. An Indian couple, who were Hindu and had bought a motel/restaurant in town, said this was the only place they felt comfortable in public. The reason was that Mark asked them to share their religious beliefs and practices without being judgmental. For the first time, both the Buddhist and Hindi couple considered openly the full range of Christian beliefs.

Because they knew Mark had been offered a position in Alaska, some of the college students tried to push Mark into joining one of the ultra-liberal denominations and be ordained again. They wanted a liberal church in Wyandotte. He had refused, saying that he didn't want to be part of a large church hierarchy. He felt that offerings from a congregation would have to go up the chain to support a massive infrastructure of buildings, administrators and publications. A building program was discussed every so often but most agreed that what they had was special, real, believable, comforting, enlightening and spiritual. Of course Mark felt that by not establishing a formal church organization with a building in Wyandotte he might be going back on his calling. Of course, if he accepted a job in Inspiration, that would place him again in a more traditional situation.

Seminary friend Jerry came to Mark's study, but he could not break from all he had grown up with. To him, Mark was brave but maybe misguided. He envied Mark's honesty and straight forward approach to problems within his sphere of contacts, but he couldn't give up the security of everything falling neatly into black and white slots, denominational rules, an order of worship, a standard hymnal, deacons, elders, and so forth, even if some of it was simply ritual and dogma.

Chapter 77. Black and White

Those attending the Bible studies could tell Duke Block was a happy man. He had Jenni, Bark, a shared house, a good job, quiet walks in the woods accompanied by massive amounts of excitement of several kinds. Jenni was happy too. Now she could be herself--Jenni the wild-haired, unpredictable manicurist of Wyandotte, Kentucky. They both were completely absorbed in each other, but also in their spiritual growth. The two endeavors made for a perfect life in their view. Mark's meetings were an excellent balance of intellectual and spiritual enlightenment. They would miss the services.

Mark had changed their lives. Their minds and hearts had begun to work differently. With the money they saved from not having to give to maintain the Wyandotte Valley Church building, Jenni and Duke helped an unemployed neighbor down the road. They provided money for a dentist, two classes at the local technical college and some clothing decent enough for an interview. Then they helped him with interviewing skills and followed up with weekly calls to check on his progress.

Jenni had always been a churchgoer, but she liked it more after Mark's group started. She always wanted to stand up during a funeral or sermon and ask a question. One time when a minister had been talking about how much the death of a mother and her two children tested our faith and made us stronger, she wanted to jump up and ask, "Forget about us, how did it help them—the mother, the baby and the teen who were killed?"

She didn't understand those who criticized Mark's theology. They accused him of being a rebel. At the time, she thought, "Well, yeah, so Jesus was a rebel too. He changed some of God's Old Testament rules. God went from killing Egypt's firstborn to punish the Pharaoh to turning the other cheek, then from hating and killing your enemy, the Canaanites, to loving your enemy and giving him your coat. Go, Jesus."

Jenni didn't feel embarrassed or afraid to broach these subjects with Mark or the group. When she had been in most churches' Sunday schools as a child, she was scared to ask the questions she wanted answered. She never heard anyone disagree with the traditional messages. She remembered that her dad always told her to be suspect of any "truth" people told her not to question.

Group members realized that, unlike religious leaders who made you think God spoke directly to them and then they would tell you what God told them, Mark asked people about what God put on their hearts. He refused to preach to them as if God hadn't given them intelligence and spiritual experiences too.

One visitor, Dana, who later became a member of Mark's meeting, said, "I don't believe in an afterlife. I do believe, from what I've learned from all of you, that Jesus' way of life is the best way of life whether there is a heaven and hell or not." Dana was accepted in the group just as much as those whose beliefs were more traditional.

Of course, Duke was always philosophic. He couldn't smoke his pipe in the community building, so he always brought his little black boxes to fiddle with. On one occasion, when asked what he thought was the answer to the meaning of life, the universe and everything, he stated: "Life's lived mostly in the dark. I just try to use my wits to figure out how to move through the obstacles from the green opening to the white one, so to speak. God could be just the puzzle maker. Mankind has slowly divided itself into smaller and smaller parts, but it's obviously up to us to find ways to make the world fit together again. Luckily, God sends us a few hints from above every once in a while."

Chapter 78. Biophysics

Going back to school gave a boost to Cali's ego. Working for Franklin and being a home wrecker had not been pleasant, especially when she looked back on it. She had heard about Franklin and the harassment suit, but she didn't feel like getting involved. She had tried to put all that in the past, find a positive direction for her life and step forward in confidence.

Despite how she felt, she told her former friends in the Wright Insurance office that if they really needed her to testify or to help in any way she would. They told her to not worry, they had plenty of former lover-employees and evidence. She discovered that Franklin was doing everything he could to settle out of court.

Her studies were rewarding because now she was working in physics, not language, and her self-worth had risen several octaves. Like everyone who encountered a member of Mark's "congregation," she was invited to attend a service. She declined, thinking how hard it would be to face Franklin's wife. She wasn't ready to deal with all her past failings. Maybe when she had completed her doctorate and had a steady boyfriend, fiancé or husband, she would have the foundation for confronting and rinsing away the past. For now her two pets, cats, would have to provide companionship as she healed.

Chapter 79. Getting to Know the Neighbors

Pastor Mark's group had changed each member in some way. Miss Ardnas, April and Cam had started a "Get to Know Our Neighbors" project. One weeknight a week they visited someone within a few blocks of their house that was ill, a shut-in, a widow or widower, or just seemed lonely.

Before they went they spent an hour in the kitchen making some kind of healthy snack or nearly lethal sugary-buttery treat to take to the person they were visiting. Although April and Cam were still children, they were learning to give, share, love, and help.

Jacob and Laura conducted a workshop for other group families with teenagers. They brought in a plumber, electrician, seamstress and carpenter to show the parents and high school-age boys and girls in the families some simple maintenance techniques. Then the families let it be known in the community that they would do simple repairs—unplug drains, replace light bulbs, rewire lamps, glue down a loose floor tile, put new glass in broken windows, stitch a hem—for people with fixed incomes. Without this group the elderly typically had to pay a handyman service fifty dollars for a simple repair task.

When the teens had experience they were sent on jobs on their own, and they also expanded their services. Besides repairs, some younger children raked yards and shoveled snow for free. They learned that people who cared for other people did these kinds of chores willingly.

Members of one group acted as a "Welcome Wagon" to new arrivals in town, and, sometimes, to just families who were not active in the community. They took them brochures, flyers, and promotional items—key fobs, pencils, pens, letter openers, etc.--from all the churches, service clubs, social service agencies and some businesses. They also sat and visited with the family if they were asked to.

A tool library was started by a retired carpenter. One high school student in Mark's group set up a database and printed library cards for him to hand out. Then those who made a donation of a dollar received a library membership. For a quarter donation, members could borrow a hand tool and for one dollar a power tool. The tool library didn't loan items that were available from the local tool rental shop. Volunteers manned the library that was housed in the carpenter's garage.

Others in the group provided the elderly with free transportation to the grocery, doctor's office, bank and beauty parlor or barber. Some families vowed to take a shut-in out to eat with them once a month. The Reading Choir was established to visit the visually handicapped to read the *Bible*, or a book of their choice, to them in the evenings. They also helped these people use the books on tape and tape recorders provided by libraries or associations for the blind.

A tutoring program was started at the public library. A list of teens and adults that were willing to help was put together, then parents could call the library and make an appointment for special help for their child.

Chapter 80. The Church with No Name

Mark opened the *Bible* study with the question: "Why did God place you on earth?"

"Eat, drink and be merry, for tomorrow you may die," joked John, one of the new members of the group.

"To go to all the lands and spread the good news," added Brandi, also a recent addition.

"To develop faith in Jesus so that we can have eternal life," commented Miss Ardnas.

"To learn how to love and create peace among our fellowmen," said Naomi.

"I think God put us here as single-cell beings and let us evolve into what we are today. I know the idea of evolution is a hot-button topic, but just looking at skeletons of fish, birds, mammals and man, makes you see they've evolved one from another," said Sam.

"Yeah, I always wondered why God made man with such a delicate and complicated internal system. He could have more easily made us like Ken and Barbie dolls with no internal organs," added Mark.

"And no brain either," John again added humor.

"You know what I mean. A person has to take in raw food and process it through many organs, send the nutrients through the blood stream to each part of the body and eliminate the waste. Why not just have intelligent beings without all that. Man's temperature, for example, has to remain in a very narrow range for him to stay alive. What's that all about?" Mark continued.

Then Madison commented that she had seen a program that tracked the genetic pattern of the races. It theorized from DNA data from around the world that all mankind originated in Africa with the Bushmen.

"We're getting a little off base and into creation issues. Let's go back to why you're alive. On what basis do you make everyday decisions about what is right for you, your fellow man and the earth," broke in Mark. After his refocus of the group, the comments came staccato-like from around the room.

"I don't give much credence to the pearly gates and streets of gold. That's materialism. So, we're to be spiritual on earth so that we can be super materialistic in heaven? I don't get it," Sam said.

"If our goal on earth is to earn our way to heaven, then we need a manual," Brandi put in.

"Don't say earn. Faith is all you need," corrected Madison.

"Faith without works is dead, says James," came back Brandi.

"That's about works concerning Jewish law, I believe," said Mark.

"Our manual is the New Testament," said Brandi.

"I always thought Jesus' life was our 'manual,'" countered Sam.

"Being in harmony with the spirit that created the world and whatever other exalted beings inhabit heaven must require us to reach some level of spiritual sophistication here on earth. Maybe this is just a test to see if we can become loving and pure enough to dwell with the saints," stated Miss Ardnas.

"Then why are our lives so short? Seventy or so years is a blink of an eye when you compare it to forever, eternity," stated Sam.

"I know the meaning of life, the universe and everything," bragged John.

"Okay, we're ready for your next quip," said Mark with a smile.

"42," said John.

"You've been reading *Hitchhiker's Guide to the Universe*, right?" asked Mark.

"Yep. It's all settled. Don't know what 42 means in numerological terms, but I like knowing the answer to the great mystery of the world. 42," John repeated, laughing.

"Maybe the existentialists are right," commented Bill.

"Most people want the *Bible* to be interpreted literally, word for word, so that they can make everything black and white. The only problem is that few people can agree on what's black, let alone what's white," stated Mark "I have read commentary after commentary and come away not knowing 'the truth.' That's why you'll never hear me tell a congregation while preaching: 'I'm telling you the truth.' I can only express, 'I believe that this or that is correct."

"Okay, you're our spiritual leader, so what do you believe?"

"I believe in Christ, but that doesn't mean God didn't send Buddha, Mohammad, Gandhi, Luther, Mother Theresa, Menno Simons, Lao Tzu, Martin Luther King and a whole string of others. I believe God is big enough to give all mankind hints about the way to spiritual peace. For some reason God doesn't just boom from the heavens for all to hear the same message at the same time. Of course He could do that. I haven't read any holy books that didn't have errors or weren't subject to criticism. He has also given us free will to try to fight against the laws of nature, or physics and chemistry, and we can refuse to live a spirit-filled life. I believe I've seen God at special moments while being in nature. There were times when I swear the hand of an angel physically pushed me out of harm's way or a spiritual voice placed an answer to a spiritual question in my mind.

"As I remember, the Dalai Lama passed on this wisdom, 'Our prime purpose in this life is to help others, and if you can't help them, at least don't hurt them.' Still many hateful, greedy and self-centered people in the world maim and kill; hoard millions of dollars and fill their lives with useless material possessions; and become dictators of companies or nations while suppressing those beneath them.

"Most of the religious people that I have admired were willing to sacrifice rather than possess. They were not interested in luxury or ruling, rather they wanted to live modestly and to serve. Jesus seemed to be showing us that life holds as little importance as the blink of an eye that Sam mentioned earlier. Jesus went through hell on earth for a few days to show us there's a spiritual life beyond this time we spend on earth. 'O, Death, where is thy sting?'

"What that spiritual afterlife life will be like is unknown. The beauty of life on earth is the mystery. Exploration of infinite space can occupy mankind for eternity, and my personal belief is that inner space is also infinite. Why wouldn't it be? There's no end to anything, especially our lives.

"I also don't like the Pearly Gates and streets-paved-with-gold concept of heaven. Man is created in the image of God, so, he and she are thinking beings. I can't imagine anything more boring than no challenges, no events or places to spark our curiosity, and no points and counterpoints.

"It would have been nice if God had given us a set of black and white rules, but the way things are now, we have to decide individually what to believe and what to reject. There are a lot of gray areas. When is it right to abort a fetus, if ever? Is it right to kill in self-defense? Is war ever justified? Should anyone have a right to buy a piece of the earth, or thousands of acres while others are not allowed to buy any? Is capitalism a system of greed while socialism is a system of love? Or is socialism a system that weakens people and makes them dependent, when what they need is the means of developing power, strength and self-reliance?"

After some give and take about Mark's comments, Sam changed the subject and asked the question on everyone's mind: "Why don't you stay here and we'll build a church, Mark?"

"No way. I like the way we have 'church' now. I may be more educated concerning the *Bible*, but that doesn't make me right—everyone contributes his or her wisdom and experience to our 'sermons.' I think church buildings are typically a big waste of money. They are used very few hours a week. Why can't believers meet in school classrooms and auditoriums that are not used on Sundays? The money saved could be put to use better by providing it for food banks, scholarships to needy students, Kiva international loans for the poor who want to expand their businesses, and missionary trips that are aimed not at changing people's religious beliefs, but directed toward helping them reject harmful superstitions, develop better health practices and encourage educating their children."

Sam asked, "What about paying ministers?"

"Ministers can work and be part-time pastors with the help of an entire congregation. Too many churches become businesses and hire senior pastors, assistant pastors, youth ministers, music directors, custodians, and on and on. Doing that may take away the opportunity for many talented people in a congregation to serve. It absolutely takes money away from Christian projects. I don't believe Jesus ever considered the ministry an occupation, but it has made many evangelists millionaires and some ministers have become CEO's of big ministries, presidents of Christian colleges and bishops over a large religious sect," Mark stated. "Do we seek titles and positions of wealth, or do we live as close as we can to the life of Jesus?"

"Well, that surely gives us lot to think about," said Jenni.

Miss Ardnas stood up and walked to Mark. He politely stood, wondering what she was up to. She made a short speech about what Mark meant to everyone in the group, then presented him with a check for his travels to Alaska. Then she hugged him. "You have changed our lives, given us hope, helped us search for truth, loved us, visited us in the hospital, lifted us up when we've been depressed, coached our kids, confronted us when we needed it, supported all our positive endeavors and those of the community. We don't know how we'll get along without you, but we want to support you on your way to a well-deserved pastorate." Although little tear drops were falling on Ardnas' dress, the corners of her mouth and eyes still smiled. Of course, Mark always smiled, but he had tears running down his face too.

"Thank you. You're too kind. Remember, this is not my church, or your church, or some denomination's church, or some foreign religion's temple, it's everyone's church. And I mean everyone seeking God. I'm using the word *church* loosely.

I feel like it was my true calling to be a part of a group like this. I have one more thing to add. I'm not taking the position in Alaska. I can't get myself to leave people like you who I love so much," exclaimed Mark, handing the check back to Miss Ardnas. "And, I'm not going to be your pastor. But, I'll be here for you, and I hope all of you will be there for me and each other as we continue to work on our own personal faith and also peace among nations, religions and races."

Everyone applauded and some cheered. A few cried.

"We're relieved that you're staying with us, Pastor Mark," said Miss Ardnas.

"Just call me Mark."

To break the tension, Miss Ardnas said, "Let's take a break and have some of the tasty and good-smelling snacks I saw on the table in the back."

Everyone in the room mobbed Mark, crying with him, hugging him, joking with him and thanking him.

Chapter 81. Hope

Naomi loved Mark, but she knew something, maybe several things, stood between them. At first she thought it was her looks. She seldom wore her glasses so that she wouldn't look too intellectual or secretarial. Mark had asked her one time why she always squinted, then apologized for being forward. She had taken her glasses out of her purse and put them on, thinking, "There. Take that!"

Instead of his thinking her matronly in glasses, he said: "Why you're so beautiful when you're not..." He broke off the squinting part. His cheeks became red and hers did too.

She worried about him and his tiny vehicle. She was afraid that some idiot would ram into him. He considered it safer than a bicycle because he had some protection, bright colors, a floppy two-foot flag and three wheels. She did think it shapely, though, like a Welsh pear. After a few outings with her on a bike and him in his velomobile, she gave in and bought one too. Hers, though, was fluorescent green.

They walked around making house calls to members of his *Bible* study. They visited the sick in the hospitals. They volunteered at the community center soup kitchen sponsored by two local service organizations. The Red Cross always welcomed them as volunteers and donors at their traveling blood banks. They worked one Saturday together installing windows in a Habitat for Humanity house. They participated in fund-raising walks for every organization in town. They were co-coaches of a girls' softball summer-league team and helped as referees with the high school's intramural volleyball program.

They attended every church's ice cream social, fish fry and chili supper. They tutored students at schools when both could work out time away from their jobs in the middle of the day. Members of Mark's group also began to volunteer or show up at many community-service events.

Since their "church" service was on Wednesdays, Mark and Naomi made the rounds of every denomination, one church each Sunday. Everybody knew which church they were attending each Sunday, because his and hers velomobiles would be parked side by side in the church's lot, except when it snowed. On snowy Sunday mornings Naomi would pick him up and chauffer him to church. Luckily, snow seldom fell in Wyandotte, and, if it did, it melted in hours. Everyone in town knew the 'couple' as the Twin Trikers.

Mark thought a lot about Miss Ardnas, but he made no moves. He didn't want to mar the solid and trusting relationship that had been built over the last year. She was being respectfully pursued by several bachelors, widowers or divorcees in town, but she wasn't dating any of them. Mark was sure that would eventually change, though. She was too good a catch for someone not to make a play, and she needed companionship too. She had doubled her efforts toward her college teaching and also spent more time keeping Cam and April busy, hoping they wouldn't think too much about their father and his diminished role in their lives now that he was miles away.

The life he was living was satisfactory to Mark. He didn't want great wealth, a high position in a church hierarchy, lots of material possessions or notoriety. One room and a minimum-wage job was all he needed, and it freed him from maintaining lots of toys and luxuries and being always maxing out a credit card. After all, he had Jesus, whose path he wanted to follow even if most of the country refused to. This freedom and security let him serve the community in myriad ways.

Naomi made lots of money selling dental supplies, and Mark remained a few dollars from broke most of the time. That they both had bedrooms upstairs and shared a bathroom was almost more temptation than Naomi could stand. It didn't seem to bother Mark a bit. At times she felt so down that she sat in her room with her book open but not reading, tears running down her face. Even her tears looked like little butas. Once she almost stomped across the hall to his room to yell: "What's the matter with you? Are you blind? Are you gay? We're dating. I love you. I've taken a job here to be near you. Are you deaf and dumb? Wake up!"

Other times she thought that maybe letting him "catch" her coming out of the bathroom in her sexiest panties and bra would do the trick. She couldn't get herself to say or do anything like that, though. She didn't really want to badger or trick him into marriage, she wanted to be loved. She would wait and be patient. She understood that he had His work to do. If he ever wanted her, she vowed to be there--in a paisley dress.

BOOK II

Acknowledgments
Thanks go to:
- My wife Sara for inspiring my writing and helping me edit.
- Alice Stollenmeyer for providing much-appreciated grammar checking and other editing.
- Amanda Boeding, Sacha Calagopi, Martha Lawry, Rena Musayeva, Basia Stroo and Gabi Tiessen, members of a Baku, Azerbaijan, book club for providing feedback after reading Book I of *Welsh Pears*. They have the best book club I've ever attended.

Credits
Lines were used from: Goshen College speech by Wendell Berry, *Mrs. Mike* by Mary Flannigan, *The Hounds of the Baskerville* by Sir Arthur Conan Doyle, "She Walks in Beauty" by Lord Byron, *Innocents Abroad* by Mark Twain, *Our Town* by Thornton Wilder, *You Can't Take It with You* by George S. Kaufman, *The Night of the Iguana* by Tennessee Williams and *The Cynic's Word Book* by Ambrose Bierce.

Dedication
God bless all the Peace Corps and Peace Corps Response Volunteers around the world. They often don't get the credit they deserve for living in a third-world country, under the same conditions as the locals. Millions of host country nationals have had their lives improved by those working with youth development where there are few mentors, teaching school where there are few supplies, providing advice about preventative medicine where HIV-AIDS is epidemic, and working with farmers where there sometimes are not even mules or plows. Most of their dreams are of a world where there are more people promoting world peace and fewer young men having to risk their lives as soldiers.

Welsh Pears is a work of fiction, but, of course, all writing is fiction, we just mislabel it history, autobiography, biography, journalism, and so forth.

Chapter 1. Mission Colonia

Naomi Grassley was glad she had not worn her contacts. The dust from the road 15 miles south of the Mexican/USA border was spiraling around and over the side and top of the truck cab and was like a swirling, beige, soupy fog. She looked down at her arm and saw that it was covered with fine powder. The temperature was 102, and she was lacquered with sweat. Her light blue T-Shirt with a psychedelic orange paisley design on it was dark with perspiration around the collar and beneath her armpits. The dust floated on top of her slim, tanned arms like chocolate drink mix making grainy islands in a glass of milk. She slid her forefinger through the dust and sweat, mixing the two, which produced a mud streak down her arm. She grinned, then reached over and finger painted a brown heart on Mark Wellston's forearm.

When he saw it he looked down at her green eyes and smiled. Of course it always looked like Mark was smiling. It was something that used to get him in trouble during serious events at school, home or church when he was a kid. It was especially unnerving when he had been a minister delivering a eulogy. His teeth had specks of bugs and dirt on them. He kept chewing and swallowing because it would be gross to spit. It reminded him of times when he had crunched into a bit of egg or crab shell while dining--gritty.

The heart shape was pushing the relationship between Naomi, 31, and Mark, 35. Naomi was thin and attractive and Mark, a former minister, was rugged looking when you compared him to the stereotype of soft-fleshed pastors, but a perpetual grin produced a boyish, carefree appearance. They were good friends—Naomi wanted more—but a platonic comradeship was all she got. They did say, "Love, ya," when they ended their phone calls and went to their separate rooms at night to retire. Naomi lived with her aunt and Mark rented a room in the same house. Naomi had enough money to buy a house of her own, but she lived with her aunt, Mrs. Grassley, because Mark lived there. Mark didn't have a clue about that. He just assumed she lived with the aunt because the aunt had no children and needed someone to look after her in her declining years. Mark was still in love with a girl he had had a crush on in high school, Miss Ardnas Wright, and, although she was divorced and free to date, Mark had not made a move. Naomi knew about Mark's infatuation with Miss Ardnas. Actually she was one of only two who did, but she still held out hope for herself. Mark had been a pastor until his liberal religious ways got him fired, so now he worked at Two Dollar Buys. Naomi was a representative for a dental supply company based in Cincinnati.

Mark leaned over and swiped his fingers along Naomi's forehead to push some brunette bangs out of her eyes. His action left another muddy impression on Naomi's skin. She cherished the seemingly insignificant physical contact, although he thought of it as an act of a loving sibling.

"Oops. Sorry, cutie. I got mud on your forehead," yelled Mark over the sounds of the truck they were riding in.

Mark and Naomi were sitting side-by-side on one of two, two-by-twelve planks placed in the pickup bed on opposite sides. The benches were shared with four other volunteers on a mission trip to a remote, poverty-stricken *colonia*. Between them were rolls of screen wire, boxes of vitamins, cartons of vaccination ampules, a tool chest, furring strips, and assorted food staples.

The truck was owned by Reverend Noel Temple, mid-thirties in age and mid-fifties in maturity. It had the outward appearance off a beached, derelict ship. This belied that the vehicle was only a year old. A missionary friend of his had lost his wife to a gunshot wound while riding in a truck in Mexico. The shot had come through the back window of the missionary's truck cab. It had been a target mostly because the Ford 150 had been sparklingly new and the drug runners had wanted it. Noel's friend had not allowed the thugs to stop him at a burning tire in the middle of a dirt road, so they had given chase in their truck and fired the fatal shot. The friend's wife had died during the race to safety at the Reynosa, Mexico/Mission, Texas, border crossing.

This tragedy had prompted Reverend Temple to trash the exterior of his late model Dodge Ram. First he had walked around the truck and kicked dents into the fenders and one door. Then he had taken a hammer to one of his tail lights and glued the resulting plastic shards back together, making sure the repair lines were obvious but watertight, and the glue was smeared on some of the the intact surfaces. A few ballpeen hammer whacks to the top edge and face of the tailgate were visually effective. He had used some reddish-brown primer to spray the rims of the wheel wells rust colored and had thrown sawdust and wood splinters into the wet paint. When the paint had dried, he sprayed over the wood fibers to make areas that looked like patches of flaking rust. It was reminiscent of corn flakes. He had employed the same technique around the door handles and windshield and on the wheel rims that had no hub caps.

All the chrome had received a good rubbing with steel wool and sandpaper, and the word Dodge and all emblems and trim had been pried off. Covering the entire body with a light coat of spray-on adhesive and driving down a dirt road had taken care of the high gloss shine of his fairly new truck. The shiny black rubber tires had been given a similar treatment but in splotches so that the turning wheels looked wobbly, like they were out of balance. Black thread-fine lines of fingernail polish applied to the windshield and rear cab window gave the effect of cracks in the glass. Noel never washed the truck, so there were sweeping clear fan shapes in the dust on his windshield made by the windshield wipers.

Splashing bleach onto the seats, door trim and upholstery, Brillo padding the steering column and wheel, and attaching a little duct tape to the seams of the seats took care of the interior. The total affect was very convincing, even up close.

To produce the sound of a rattle trap, Temple had punched a hole in his muffler and always had a couple of loose gallon paint cans with steel ball bearings, nuts and bolts in them. Several hinges with one half loose and the other half bolted to assorted metal sheeting were affixed under the hood. The sounds produced by the containers bouncing and rolling around in the truck bed and the flapping hinges made a person wonder if the truck wasn't going to take a squat immediately in the middle of a road.

Across from the Mark and Naomi sat a married couple, Nwakaego, a green-card Nigerian, and Pakistani Kurjurnid Nabiyev, who had Kazakh parents. Madison Wentworth was next to them. Nwakaego was called Nurse Kae and no one could pronounce her last name so they didn't even remember it. For a similar reason Kurjurnid became Kurj. Madison's fiancé William sat next to Naomi. Shirley Temple sat next to her husband in the cab. All but the Temples were part of Mark's Bible study back in Wyandotte, Kentucky. The volunteers had taken a week of their vacation to visit the Temples and to help them with ministering to a poor Mexican colonia. They weren't there to proselytize, because most of the Mexicans had grown up Catholic but had been lost in the poverty that affected much of the country. They had moved close to the border because of jobs. NAFTA had caused the border on the Mexican side to sprout dozens of enormous international factories—LG, Nokia, and Black and Decker.

Each person was to play a specific role upon arrival at the colonia. Nurse Kae was going to vaccinate children with the help of Madison, who was a teacher and used to corralling kids. They would also check people for high blood pressure and write prescriptions. The prescriptions weren't legal but drug stores usually sold prescription medicines over the counter. Kurj Nabiyev, a naturalized citizen from Pakistan, was a carpenter who was going to tack on screening in outhouses and to house windows for the sake of hygiene. Having flies visit an outhouse and then alight on a fresh-baked tortilla in the family kitchen was not very healthy.

When William first met Kurj, he asked him about his name. Kurj said, "In my language it's spelled *Kurjurnit* and means eunuch."

William's eyebrows rose and he questioned: "It means what?"

"One."

"One what?"

"It means only."

"I don't get it. Only what?"

"Only one."

"I thought eunuch meant none at all. Only one what?" asked William, frustrated.

Kurj was also frustrated. "Let me show you." He took out his Android and typed. After a few seconds he turned the screen so William could see. "Look."

"Oh, *unique*," chuckled William.

As he watched William laugh, Kurj's forehead wrinkled and he said, "Right, eunuch."

William realized that Kurj basically had the correct sounds but put the accent on the wrong syllable. Kurj was a great guy and probably would have had a good laugh about the name, but William didn't explain for fear it would embarrass him. He was leery about asking the meaning of Kae's name but he forged ahead anyway. Luckily her name, Nwakaego, meant *more valuable than money.*

William, before he had bought a wine shop, had been a high school Spanish teacher, so he planned to visit English classrooms and model interactive teaching techniques. The colonia's school was the center of community activity, so the group was going to set up there. Naomi and Mark, a former pastor, were equipped to teach classes on the Bible and personal hygiene to children. They also had two boxes, one full of toothpaste and one full of toothbrushes, the handles shaped like cartoon characters, to use as incentives to attend lessons. They would soon discover that just the presence of Americans made the incentives unnecessary. The Temples would set up a miniature food bank and require parents to sit through classes on nutrition before handing out food and vitamin pills.

Temple yelled through the sliding cab window to his passengers: "Get ready." He knew that the children would talk, touch, hug, laugh and dance around all of them upon disembarking from the truck. Shirley reached through the cab window and passed back a small plastic container of moist towels, which the passengers used to refresh their faces and clean their hands, arms and bare legs. The white towels turned brown as the sandy-colored dust turned into mud as it was wiped off. All the passengers sat up a little straighter, blinked less and felt a few sparks flicking around in their stomachs.

The group had to run a gauntlet of locals. The brown-faced children pushed right up against their legs and spoke rapidly in Spanish. A few little kids held back and hid behind their mothers' orange, green and blue skirts. A colonia leader stepped forward and shooed the children away and welcomed the missionaries. Immediately several young men grabbed all the backpacks. The group was ushered into a small room full of woven mats covered with sleeping bags. They dropped their daypacks of clothes and toiletries and walked into the second room, which had a table and 10 straight-back chairs. Maria Gonzalez came in with a basket full of tortillas, goat cheese, salsa and fried goat meat. After Noel prayed, they made tacos and ate like 10-year-olds after a full day swimming and playing at a city park.

After dinner, Mark took out his computer and read through the screenplay he was writing. Two of the members of Mark's weekly Bible study had shared that they were writers, albeit in sneaky ways. Since Pastor Mark had become just Mark, he and some of his former parishioners met weekly for Bible study. Mark had always aspired to writing a novel, play or historical book. Inspired by Madison and Miss Ardnas' work, Mark had begun writing a screenplay. With his Bible study youth group so tech savvy, he decided he would challenge them. They were a mix of high school and college students and it was hard to motivate them, keep their interest, get them involved and provide them with life changing experiences.

Mark's muse Miss Ardnas Wright's light brown hair, aqua eyes, shapely body and lack of overpowering features made her an attractive mother of two. She was 35, the same age as Mark. She had started a blog of editorial comments about society. Mark's other muse, Madison Wentworth, also wrote editorial comments, but hers went to the local newspaper and only critiqued educational policy. She also had long brown hair, but was slimmer than Miss Ardnas and had perfect posture, which looked a little severe in an America infected with casual posture and outright slouching. Both had minds of their own. Madison had grey eyes that were so unique that no one ever forgot them.

Mark knew from his high school years that playing a character in a play made you practically able to quote everybody's lines and remember the best quotations for the rest of your life—the words went to your soul. He had acted in *You Can't Take It with You* and *Our Town*. He remembered the way the main character, Grandpa, prayed in *You Can't Take It with You* and his advice: "Maybe it'll stop you trying to be so desperate about making more money than you can ever use? You can't take it with you, Mr. Kirby. So what good is it? As near as I can see, the only thing you can take with you is the love of your friends," and the line by Emily in *Our Town*: "Do any human beings ever realize life while they live it . . . every, every minute?" and the stage manager's reply, "No . . . the saints and poets maybe, they do, some."

A play would be interesting but he thought a movie would be more exciting and use more of the talents of his youth group. He figured that if he could write a screenplay, they could do the auditioning, directing, acting, taping and editing. He called it *Hey, Zeus* and started the project hoping to make the script funny but insightful. The screenplay wasn't finished, but he was editing the first part of it while working out an appropriate ending.

Being on this mission trip, his third to the same area, had served and was serving several purposes for Mark. His experiences on the border and in Texas had made him choose it as the setting of his screenplay. It was a way to fulfill his philosophy of serving others, he thought it important for Americans to learn about other cultures and it motivated him to work harder to finish his play.

HEY, ZEUS

An Original Screenplay by Mark Wellston
Wyandotte, Kentucky
2012
1-991-555-9819
      FADE IN:
EXT.--BORDER CROSSING BETWEEN MEXICO AND TEXAS--DAY

HEY ZEUS CRISTIANO DELGADO GARCIA, 33 years of age, thin and a little below average in height, crawls under a truck that is in line to cross the border to Texas.

He hangs from frame members, scraping his butt most of the time when the truck moves, despite the fact that he tries to pull his stomach up against the undercarriage.

After several car-length moves toward the border, Zeus is next to the custom's building.

    CUT TO:

BILL, a 55 year old border guard, uses a mirror on the end of a rod to check under the truck for contraband.

GENE, 41, another guard, looks on from behind Bill.

BILL

Hey, Zeus. Zat you? Get the heck out from under there. This's the third time this week I've had to send you hik'n.

ZEUS crawls out and dejectedly walks away.

ZEUS

You'll see. I makes eet yet. 'aven't you never 'eard of zee burro from Phoenix that fell in the ashes an rises? You'll see.

BILL

Yeah, you'll make it to a Mexican jail, that's if you don't get run over by a truck before that.

(to Gene)

Do you believe a stunt like that!

    GENE

Hey, Zeus. Nice try. My arthritic grandfather could have done better.

ZEUS

Si. . . Si.

ZEUS walks slowly and sadly back across the Rio Grande bridge.

    CUT TO:

EXT.--BORDER CROSSING CUSTOM HOUSE--DAY

Cars and trucks slowly move toward the guards, stop, then move on.

    CUT TO:

GENE gives BILL a poke in the ribs and points to a flat-bed truck coming to a stop in front of them.

The bed is filled with racks of dresses hanging from pipes so that their hems are about 18 inches from the bed.

The cuffs and shoes of a man can be clearly seen below the hems in the middle of the bed.

GENE walks over to the truck with a billyclub and gives the toe of one shoe a solid rap.

ZEUS
CARRUMBA!
The injured foot disappears and the other foot can be seen hopping up and down.
All of this action makes a mess of the dresses.
ZEUS then jumps off the back of the truck with a couple of dresses tangled around him as Bill and Gene laugh.
BILL and GENE work together to untangle Zeus, who is dizzy and disoriented from being spun around when the dresses are removed.
ZEUS (CONT.)
You din't have to do that. I gots ears like zee jackass and knows where they point. Carrumba! Just say go way. I go! MIOS! Which way?
BILL tries to get him walking in the correct direction and guides his elbow until he is more stable.
BILL
Hey, Zeus. If I see you again this week, I'm gonna do more than tap your little Mexican toes. Come-pran-day, aye-me-go?
ZEUS hobbles and staggers toward the bridge.
ZEUS
I'll be back. You can't keep me out of zee land of milk and 'oney. Eets unamerican. Carrumba, he ruined my zapatoes! Which ways do I go?
GENE
Turn a little right, Hey Zeus. No, not that far. OK, straight ahead. ADD-DEE-OS, Hey Zeus.
ZEUS
Whatever 'appened to zee old yankeez saying about geeves me your poor, your starving, your lonely, your traveler, your Heespanic, your jobless, your ugly. Eesn't that zee motto of zee state of Liberty, out there near Virginia?
    CUT TO:
EXT.--BACK OF MEXICAN VARIETY STORE--DAY
ZEUS is dumpster picking broken piñatas, crushed sombreros, and other tossed-out, cheap Mexican souvenirs to use as disguises for his next attempt at the border.
ZEUS
(straightening a crushed sombrero)
Perfecto!
(pulling out a piñata)
Bueno!
(grabbing two plastic shopping bags)
Mucho gusto!

CUT TO:
INT.--MEXICAN VARIETY STORE
ALFRED, middle aged, an American who is Zeus's size, comes out of a changing room in a wild, new shirt, pants, hat and shoes. He is met by two ladies, Gladys and Norma, also middle-aged, who are looking him over and pulling and straightening and fussing over the new clothes.
PAN TO:
ZEUS sneaks through a back door then behind the group into the same changing room.

ALFRED
Gladys, don't you think the shirt clashes a little with the shorts?
Alfred turns around.
GLADYS
Oh, it's just perfect, Alfred.
NORMA
It's so cute on you, Alfred.
ALFRED
Cute is not exactly what I was hoping for.

ZEUS comes out of the dressing room behind them without being noticed. He is dressed in Alfred's clothes and sneaks out the back door of the store.
ALFRED turns and goes into the changing room and almost catches ZEUS.
NORMA
The greens and blues in that shirt go perfectly with Alfred's eyes, don't you think?
GLADYS
Oh, yes. And the socks are exactly the same color as the large splashes of his shorts.
NORMA
I wish he would go ahead and try those sandals over there on with . . .
Gladys and Norma are shocked when Alfred comes out of the dressing room clothed only in his boxer undershorts.
ALFRED
Hey! What happened to my clothes?
Alfred goes back into the dressing room to look again.

Chapter 2. Major Regrets

My Dearest Beloved Miss Ardnas

I am so sorry for my past mistakes. I love you, I have always loved you, I will love you forever. I will never understand how I did what I did. I can't live without you. I miss the kids. Please let me return.

The affair with my secretary meant nothing. I was completely out of line to do that. I've never had any other affairs. I would forgive you if you strayed. I know some people are willing to cast the first stone, but I hope you're not.

A friend told me to sue for the kids, but I don't want to do that. I want you, Cam, April and me to be a family again. Forgive and forget. Love and learn.

I hope you can forgive me. I know you're a Christian and to forgive is divine. I will do anything you say. I will be a slave to you. I can't live without you and the kids. Please forgive me and take me back.

Love and kisses,
Franklin

Miss Ardnas Wright, who had been married and divorced, had been addressed with the Southern-style "Miss" title by her college students who thought that Ardnas was a last name. She read the letter from her ex-husband. She knew he had written it while drunk to his eyeballs. He was never lovey and especially not sappy by nature. Her aqua eyes stared and she lifted her light brown hair behind her ears as she reread the letter. Her normally beautiful and smiling face took on a serious demeanor. The part about being a Christian made her feel guilty even though she knew he was using it as a device to get her to take him back. She thought he gave his true personally away by using *I, me* and *my* more than twenty times. It was always all about him. She hated that he was bringing all the sadness, embarrassment, pain, worry and hardships back to her through his pleading. To mention their children, Cam and April, who were 12 and 9, was also ludicrous. He had spent as little time with them as possible when they were still together.

She did what always took her mind off her troubles by finishing another news item for the Ersatznews.blogspot.com. The blog had been started a year ago as a means for her to blow off political, social and personal steam by submitting articles. Miss Ardnas was extremely disappointed in the political corruption of the government, the lack of moral fiber in everyday citizens and the overemphasis on sex and material possession in the media. The news made violence and greed sexy. She noticed that most of the women in TV and magazine ads were beauty queens and dressed in high heels, short skirts, had bare arms and low necklines. The men wore dark suits. During a college class discussion, one college male student commented: "There's nothing less sexy than a girl walking in high heels. Their legs look stiff and their strides are short and unnatural—they look awkward. Walking in high heels takes all the motion out of their hips and shoulders. Why do women wear those things?" Miss Ardnas dressed sharply but practically.

Whether many people had found the blog didn't matter; she liked writing it anyway.

Renegade News Group Hounds Anchors
SPI NEWS, Basstown, Georgia

Anchors of major 24-hour television news organizations are getting a taste of their own medicine. And they don't like it.

Renegade News, a group that sends news items to local cable public access channels, decided that they would add a little balance to news reporting.

Reggie Banks, founder of the news agency, said that she was tired of watching people who were involved in tragic situations hounded by news organizations wanting to make money from their tragic story. She related that the news agencies put mobile TV units on the streets where victims' houses are, have reporters calling all day, station reporters on the walkway in front of their houses, push mikes in their faces and chase them down streets.

Banks' group is now doing the same to major anchors of 24-hour news organizations and the major television network news anchors. They have posted people on their sidewalks, interviewed their neighbors, conducted background checks, followed them in cars, snapped photos of them coming out of restaurants with friends or fellow workers, and called them numerous times during the day asking questions about their personal lives.

Lots of embarrassing personal information has resulted from all this work and Renegade News is happy to broadcast it on public access channels. Banks says that some commercial major channels have contacted her about creating a television reality show based on their work.

The anchors, on the other hand, are furious. They don't like the tactics used by Renegade, even though they are the same tactics the major news organizations themselves use every day to pry into victims' lives, emotions and tragedies.

Some of the anchors are attempting to get restraining orders, but Banks says that then they are going to have to admit that their own actions are illegal: "I'm not worried. I'll just post stories about their attempts to limit freedom of speech or the press."

Miss Ardnas was prompted to write the faux news because CCBN was broadcasting nonstop "BREAKING NEWS" stories about a kidnapping case of a young girl. The anchors and reporters were hounding the parents, neighbors and relatives, hoping to see them crying, begging the public for help and/or threatening the perpetrators. Miss Ardnas felt for the victims and questioned the ethics and hearts of the journalists.

Having posted her "article" to the blog, Miss Ardnas' thoughts returned to Franklin. She had heard that his new business in another town had not been profitable. She had been told that he was trying to buy back his former, very-profitable insurance agency in Wyandotte, Kentucky, where he and Miss Ardnas had the home where she and the children still lived. This news was one strike against him as far as she was concerned. Was he just in trouble and wanted to make up because his new business wasn't as good as his former business? The second strike was that he included the veiled threat of suing for the kids. She wanted to scream and swear aloud, which she never did, but a dozen profanities and vulgarities passed through her mind: "Only affair? How stupid does he think I am?"

Her mind went back to the blog and what impact it might have on her political science students at the university where she taught. She hadn't included anything about the way ambitious prosecutors and politicians try to get face time on television whenever a big story hits their district. Of course, after the students read the article on the blog, she could always nudge the discussion toward the politics of tragedy as well as the greed and lack of feeling shown by the networks. She had already moderated a discussion of "beauty queen" news anchors. Using the internet and her blog entries had turned out to be an excellent method of stimulating relevant discussions in her classes.

Her thoughts were interrupted by the dilemma of Franklin's letter. Should she ignore it or respond to it? Did she still have a little love for him? Although April and Cam were glad to have their dad out of their lives, wouldn't it be better if the family could be brought back together, feelings healed, fences mended and a loving spirit created for the sake of everyone?

Dear Franklin,

I've read your letter and...

Chapter 3. The Extended Honeymoon

Duke Preston Block and Jenni Block were still in their first year of marriage. Duke had been betrayed by his first wife and Jenni had just had a series of flings, but now they were a happy couple. Duke had been a Preston until Jenni refused to marry him unless he took her last name. Breaking new ground was her passion. She was sitting on Duke's lap while he was sitting on an oversized rocking chair with his pipe in his mouth. Duke was built tall and sturdy. Jenni, whose whitish-blonde hair always radiated toward outer space, was threading her fingers through his grizzled hair and nibbling on his left ear. "Mine," said Jenni, taking the pipe out of his mouth and empting the bowl by pounding it against the leg of the rocker.

"The pipe, my hair or my ear?"

"All three." She kissed him softly and moistly on the lips. Jenni's breasts weren't perky and her hips were a little narrow for the width of her shoulders, but she had straight, long, silky legs and a hormonal aura that seemed as visible as the colorful aurora borealis. In other words, men found her looks, ambience and walk sexy.

Duke could feel her body heat rising. He had the normal sex drive of a 44 year old, but Jenni, 30, was another story. Hers was more the velocity and recklessness of a sixteen-year-old—his six-cylinder Ford pickup trying to keep up with her ten-cylinder Dodge Viper. Once her invisible mating switch had been mysteriously flipped to ON, she was full speed ahead without brakes until she yelled "Wahoo," which meant she had reached the apex of her crescendo. This surprisingly unscripted and spontaneous behavior was fine with the calm, contemplative and deliberate Duke. He tried, and did a good job, keeping up.

"In the chair, in the grass, on the sofa or in bed?' asked Duke in his typical monotone.

Since Jenni's sweatshirt was already off and her jeans were coming down, he didn't need an answer. The rocker it would be, right in the middle of the back yard. It's a good thing we live in the country, thought Duke. Bark, Duke's dog, always alert to his master's unspoken signals, rose from next to the rocker and politely lay down within earshot but out of eyeshot behind a tree. Bark had witnessed their unusual behavior before and was confused by the actions and noises produced by humans in love. He tried to ignore the rhythmic creaking of the rocking chair.

Duke's house looked like a bachelor pad—a dozen hooks by the backdoor festooned with overalls, ball caps, ski poles, belts, suspenders, sweatshirts, paint-covered T-shirts and faded flannel shirts. Cowboy boots, sneakers, work boots and sandals were strewn on a long fiber mat beneath them. The floors throughout Duke's house were all real hardwood, but not fussily kept. There were gouges where an ax had slipped out of his hand and hit the floor, slices where pairing knives had stuck in the wood, spots of tallow near the stove, wine stains beneath a wooden chair and below benches in the living room, cigar burns next to easy chairs and other indications of the one-time bachelor life of an outdoorsman and civil engineer.

There were window curtains only in the bathroom and the bedrooms--usually open--and no colorful pillows on beds and benches. Several pipes and ashtrays were strategically placed around the house, even in the bathroom. Dukes favorite pastime other than hiking, fishing and smoking his pipe was figuring out blind puzzles. He had a friend who designed and crafted wooden puzzles with levers, baffles, compartments and other devices to make navigating them utilizing a small ball bearing extremely difficult. The ball was placed in one hole and could only exit another. Duke wanted those who thought a jigsaw puzzle was difficult to try a blind puzzle, which required steering the bearing by sound. None of his friends understood why he sat around with a black box to his ear.

Outside, the lawn wasn't mowed because Duke didn't believe in lawn mowers. He liked the way nature decorated and didn't want to give the natural plants a golf-course cut the way suburbanites did. Yards were often so pristine owners didn't want children to play in them, dig mud holes, ride their bikes through them or make bare spots for softball bases and a pitcher's mound. A variety of wildflowers took turns blooming all summer in Duke and Jenni's yard, and the bees, jays, cardinals, deer, squirrels, chipmunks, orioles and hummingbirds were always welcome.

Jenni wasn't fussy like most women. She didn't mark her territory by changing everything once she had moved in. She didn't repaint every room, add carpets or throw rugs, buy new furniture—or even rearrange it. There were no knickknacks, doilies, coasters, collections or flowery curtains. She had simply moved her clothes and shoes into one side of the master bedroom closet. This was a new experience for Duke, because his previous wife had taken over the house they bought together and spent thousands in every way possible to demonstrate to everyone that she was founder, owner, CEO and chairman of the house board of directors.

Jenni wasn't even hooked on makeup. If Duke suggested they hop into the pickup and go for an ice cream cone, she'd be in the truck before he could slap on a Cabela's cap and grab his keys. Again, that was so different from his first wife, who had to do something before she could do something. When invited to do anything spontaneous, Duke's first wife would say, "Be right there," but that meant going to the bathroom, freshening up her makeup, brushing her hair, changing her blouse, dabbing on some perfume, picking out a bracelet and a necklace, brushing her teeth and reapplying lipstick. By the time she was done Duke had often moved on to something else and was out of the mood. She had behaved in a similar way when he started sweet-talking her, snuggling with her on the sofa and suggesting going a little further. Off she would go to the bathroom for a long half hour or more.

The sound of "wahoo" reached Bark's ears and he came out from behind the tree. Just as the chair slowly came to a stop, Duke and Jenni heard a truck pull into their lane. They barely got themselves decent before the truck came to a stop near the barn. It was Sam Jones, Jenni's old boyfriend and Duke's best friend. There were no hard feelings, well, probably a few, but Sam hadn't been able to handle Jenni's unpredictable ways. They'd embarrassed him. Duke had had the other type of wife, uptight, predictable, controlling and boring, and much preferred Jenni, an original--natural. He could only be embarrassed if he let himself be embarrassed. He wasn't living his life to please anyone watching life go by from a street corner or through a living room window or someone who tried to follow advice about how to have a good marriage from a paperback bought at Barnes and Noble or an hour of Dr. Phil.

Sam was just an average looking guy who dressed a lot like Duke, dark T-shirt under a flannel shirt with the sleeves turned up twice, faded jeans, work boots and a ball cap featuring a Bengal Tiger or a Cleveland Indian. He was easy going, but not as much as Duke. They liked to hunt and fish together and see who could tell the biggest lie. They both were in Mark's Bible study.

Sam was there because he was depressed. He had helped Duke through a similar bout of melancholy after Duke's wife ran away with a younger man. Now Sam needed some encouragement in finding a new direction. He still was friends with Jenni and, despite their past intimacy, knew she would help him too.

"Hey, you old married goat," yelled Sam.

"Watch what you call my man," yelled Jenni back, smiling.

"Got a cold PBR?"

"As always, my friend," responded Duke, heading for the refrigerator.

"Me too, Duke," added Jenni.

"Well, how's your little love nest, Jenni?" asked Sam.

"Feathers were flying a few minutes ago," responded Jenni with an eye-grin.

"I bet."

"Here you go, bud," said Duke as he shook up Sam's beer and tossed it to him. The beer shake was an old joke between them. Duke opened two PBRs and handed one to Jenni. "Why so glum?"

"You took my woman," responded Sam as he tapped on the PBR can to settle the carbonation before opening it.

"You chased me away into Duke's arms," shot back Jenni.

Sam took a triple gulp of beer, waited 15 seconds while looking to the woods beyond the yard and said, "Ok. I'm not happy with my life."

"You can't have Jenni back, bud," joked Duke.

"No. Seriously. I'm depressed all the time. It started long before and lasted after Jenni, so I'm not blaming her or you."

"Go ahead," prompted Jenni.

"I'm 45, no wife, no children and I'm in the cell phone business, for lord's sake, the cell phone business!"

"And?"

"I'm no great philosopher, but I realize that life has to mean more than what I have done and am doing. Maybe it's just a midlife crisis—looking back and then looking forward and seeing nothing significant."

"What were your dreams as a child?" asked Duke.

Sam took another gulp and responded, "Like astronaut, fireman, train engineer, doctor, lawyer, Indian chief, conservation officer? Sounds kind of silly, heh? Seriously, forest ranger, conservation officer, national park ranger."

"Is it too late to change careers?"

"Probably. When I've Googled professions involving nature, I've found that there are few jobs and lots of applicants just out of college with degrees in forestry, biology, park management, law enforcement, and other related fields. No one's looking for a cell phone salesman."

"Don't give up, Sam, if that's what you want. Why this field?"

"I've always spent my free time outdoors. Even as a kid my parents had trouble keeping me in the yard. I'd spend all day at the creek or in the woods, even forgetting to go home for lunch. It got so bad that my mom would stuff cookies in my pants pockets before I went out of the house summers just so I wouldn't eat my T-shirt before I came home. Even in winter, I'd get off the bus, grab a slice of bread and head for the woods. You know I love the outdoors still, hunting and fishing and just hiking. You know the thrill of seeing a barred owl perched over your head, a copperhead slither out from under some leaves, a snapper on a log or the trillium and redbuds in the spring."

"Of course!" said Jenni.

"When I travel through the mountains or the plains, I want to reach out and put my arms around them. I know that sounds silly, but that's how I feel. I kind of want to be one with nature, to feel it, to smell it, roll in it, swim in it, to find some natural harmony with the earth," continued Sam. Most of my friends and the adults I know, not you guys, don't like nature. I think they hate it, are afraid of it. Oh, they go to a state park and walk a short, wide, well-traveled trail and then go to the swimming pool or sit on a park bench or even bring CD players for picnics, and TVs if they are spending the night in a camper. They've never learned the joy of simply walking in the woods or wading in a spring. They prefer walking on the road to a trail. They prefer chasing a white ball over scalped meadows while riding in an electric cart."

"Yeah, you're right. What about the cell phone business you have?" asked Duke, lighting his pipe.

"Cell phones! The alluring gadgets that interrupt thousands of important conversations so that people can say, 'What you doin'?' 'Nothin',' 'What you doin'?' 'Nothin'.' 'Love ya'.' 'Love ya' too.' It's teaching the world's children to talk with letters, 'LMAO, FYI, LOL, BTW, Where R U?' and smiley faces. And I'm part of that shit. And worse, you can attach a cord then plug the darn things into your ear so that even your thoughts are constantly interrupted, like Kurt Vonnegut's 'Harrison Bergeron.' Or 'Spectator Sport,' by John MacDonald, just to name a couple of my favorite science fiction stories," ranted Sam.

"Ouch."

"Now people are wasting their time sending pictures to each other showing a glass of wine, a snapshot of a fictional movie hero from a poster, an airbrushed sexy model, male or female, and their teacher picking his nose. Surely there's more meaning to life than what's transmitted on cell phones via Twitter and Facebook. The one saving grace was the Arab Spring." Sam finished his beer.

"Gotcha. So, man of action, what are you going to do?" asked Duke.

Chapter 4. The Bridal Path

Madison and William pulled their bikes off the bridal path in the park near her apartment. They both pulled their water bottles from the holders on the bike frames and took long drinks. William leaned both bikes against a tree and took Madison in his arms: "Ok, honey, you've been wearing an engagement ring for two months. When are we going to set a date?"

"You know when it comes to commitments I'm a snail. You've got to..,,."

"Uht, uht, uht," he uttered to stop her excuses. "You're driving me nuts. I want to get married. Are you having major doubts? If so, tell me and let's work on them. I'm head over heels in love and want to let everyone know in a permanent way."

"Yes, I know, but..." Madison looked down at her engagement ring, which had a original design. William had asked Naomi for help making the ring and his proposal special. She came up with a design that used two stylized buta shapes turned to represent a heart. A diamond in the center completed the design. It's the exact ring Naomi wished that Mark would have given to her.

"Uht, uht, uht," William broke in again, giving her a breathtaking squeeze that made it feel like someone had pulled a feather from her toes up her legs through her chest and out the top of her head. William was able to press his body so closely to Madison's—thigh to thigh, belly to belly and chest to breast--that she felt like their clothes had melted away and they were flesh to flesh.

William was a hunk, but a well-dressed and well-groomed one. She caught her breath and just looked into William's eyes. He looked back into her gray-white eyes. They were like the eyes of a wolf or husky. They seemed to have a silver shine that could be a little eerie looking at night, but captivating during the daylight.

"Well, what kind of wedding do you want, honey?"

"William, you know that I'm not...."

"Tuht, tuht, tuht, tuht. Come on! Do you want a Duke/Jenni type hoedown, get-down-and-dirty, or a gown and tux affair with sit-down and pristine dining?" He gave her another bear hug and the feather fluttered through her again. Duke and Jenni had had a wedding on Duke's country property with line dancing, beer, barbecue and a tug of war through mud, which made it a fun, wholesome but a literal get-down-and-dirty affair. Even Duke's sixty-three-year-old mother had worn jeans that day and stomped her boots with the best of them

Madison gave William a sly grin and escaped to her bike, pedaling off as fast as she could, leaving William standing with downturned mouth. He decided she needed space and pedaled off toward his house. He was lonely since their trial of living together had ended when Madison's parents had come to visit her for a week months ago. He had tried to get back into her apartment, but she had kept sidestepping his efforts.

In her second floor apartment, she pulled her wet T-shirt off over her head. Being busy wringing it out didn't keep Madison occupied enough to stop the tears. She pressed the damp shirt to her face and sat down on a nearby stool. She wondered why she was so paranoid about taking the "lover's leap." Lover's leap, thought Madison, sounds dangerous.

Tossing the shirt onto the top of the clothes hamper to let it dry, she ran to her computer and pulled up a blank Word page. Instead of facing the real "enemy," herself, she often took to attacking educational deficiencies or methods as the target of her emotional volleys. She had sent a stream of anonymous letters to the editor of the local newspaper and now had a regular column signed with her nom de plume, Desk Weary. The *Wyandotte Times* liked her column criticizing schools and their administrators.

She had heard several of her friends at a high school reunion discussing their favorite teachers. Many of the boys still idolized a coach who had yelled at them, sworn at them, pushed them around, put them through extreme physical, mental and emotional strain, making their lives a living hell during a sporting season and even beyond practices and games.

There's Not Enough Passion in Schools

Why can't there be as much passion in the high school classroom as there is on athletic playing fields and courts? I've heard coaches yell every vulgar and profane word in the book at players. I've seen coaches shove, jerk, grab and otherwise physically get the attention of players. These would not be tolerated in the classroom. Why?

Shouldn't teachers and students be passionate about learning? Shouldn't teachers use both psychological and physical means to make students stretch, grow and develop? Evidently the answer is yes on the playing field and no in the classroom Aren't academics almost as important as high school athletics?

I've heard a lot of stories about fist fights during athletic practices and seen them during sporting events, which end with the participants not punished at all or only punished by being benched for a few minutes until they cool down. Fights in a classroom are often part of a student handbook code that requires automatic suspension.

There's a double standard that is troubling. Either psychological or physical methods are good teaching/learning tools or they are not. Schools should decide. Most teachers wouldn't want vulgarity and violence in their classrooms, but they would appreciate being allowed to have some boisterous enthusiasm, cheering, celebrations and dynamic physical interaction at times without a frown from an administrator passing the classroom.

Madison attached the Word file to the email address of the editorial department of the *Wyandotte Times* and smacked the Send button on her computer. She checked to see if she had broken the key. The action didn't make her feel any better. She loved William with all her heart, but marriages in the 20th and 21st centuries were too often short and disastrous, followed by ugly, selfish divorces just as a couple's children were challenged by puberty. Added to that were family economics ruined by lawyers seeking hardass negotiator reputations or large legal fees; children having to choose from two sets of parents and four sets of grandparents when holiday visits loomed; and children tolerating step fathers, mothers, brothers and sisters. And the worst was for pubescent girls dealing with a mom's live-in boyfriend, who often believed he had bedroom rights to both the mother and the daughter, when in actuality he should have no family rights at all, not even to the mother.

Many wedding vows still contained sections about being faithful and loving no matter what until death ends the union. But in this day of selfishness and media promoted lust, the vows should be; "I promise to live and keep you, forsaking all others, till you get old, sick, fat or I get tired of you or see someone more attractive?" Couples no longer had a fifty/fifty chance of a lifelong marriage. She wondered why people confused and connected sex with love.

Madison tried to picture herself getting married. The Block/Preston marriage had been redneck fun for everybody, but every little girl reads Cinderella and dreams about magically being transformed into a princess in beautiful, completely impractical clothing, slippers and coiffure, blowing tens of thousands of dollars on one day. The aim is to wow a handsome prince and all those in attendance at a public event that is a fairytale come true. She imaged herself being the center of attention in both scenarios. Then she wondered what William would like. Weddings often seemed to be about the girl. In Mark's Bible study one evening, Naomi had told about some of the weddings she experienced in Central Asian villages. The girl was definitely a princess for a day and then the rest of her life was in the kitchen keeping tea boiling and being a slave for the men in the house. Women often were not allowed to work outside the home, drive, go to restaurants, cafés (teahouses), and many public events that men frequented daily.

Chapter 5: Endless Line

Desks at the colonia school had been placed along the walls outside of the school and every one of them was filled. Then the line of standing parents and children continued around the school in a seemingly endless line. The school had no hallways. Instead there was a covered walkway that allowed students to move from one classroom to another without the harsh sun beating down on them. Even though only one member of a family was waiting to receive help, it was traditional for the entire family to be present.

Noel Temple's team walked through the gate to the school ground and immediately ended their excited morning bantering. All eyes turned to them. Not a sound was made by the Mexicans waiting patiently in perfect order. Even the babies were still. The Temples attached signs to classroom doors to indicate where vaccinations would be given, blood pressure would be taken, Bible classes would be conducted, food would be distributed and English conversation sessions would be held for students of English. Then the Temples and William used their fluent Spanish to direct individuals to the correct rooms and form new lines.

Meanwhile, inside the rooms the volunteer missionaries set up tables, opened windows for light, since there was no electricity in the school, arranged chairs and prepared themselves for a long, hard day of work. Noel, Shirley, and William found volunteers among the crowd who spoke enough English to translate and assigned them to a room. Most rooms admitted "patients' one at a time, but the conversation club and Bible class took ten students at a time, then, after an hour, rotated in another ten each.

Giving vaccinations was legal because the Temples had received permission from the appropriate local agencies. Those bringing children were reminded to have their vaccination records. The school principal and secretary were also in their office to look up vaccination records if needed. Most schools required children to have vaccinations before they registered, but students often moved in and out of different regions of Mexico or hadn't registered for school yet.

Each room was a little chaotic until the volunteers learned the routine. Noel went from room to room giving directions and answering questions. He also made sure all the workers stayed hydrated with bottled water they had brought in the truck. The locals were used to the heat and lack of air conditioning, so they sat or stood comfortably waiting.

Mark asked Noel, "Why don't the Mexicans sweat like we gringos?"

"When they feel themselves getting too hot, they slow down the pace, whether while walking or working. They'll also take more breaks in the shade. We Americans just keep going. Remember the saying from British colonial natives in equatorial zones, 'only mad dogs and Englishmen go out in the noonday sun.' We'll take a siesta during the hottest part of the day after lunch. When it cools down we'll start again."

Mark and Naomi took the primary-age students first. Paper, glue and crayons morphed into angels with wings and/or Our Lady of Guadalupe with a halo, adorned with an aura four times as big as the one used in Western religious art. It fit perfectly, though, with the holy image (milagro) of Mary that the children viewed daily on the walls of their houses or huts.

When noon came, food appeared from everywhere, like the loaves and the fishes. There wasn't much meat, but cheese, cucumbers, tomatoes, rice and beans were plentiful. The volunteers gave the fresh vegetables a wary eye, showing they knew about Montezuma's revenge. Noel told them to go ahead because he had a course of Ciprofloxacin for everyone. The Mexican women all smiled and said, "*De nada*," when they heard the volunteers say *bueno* or *gracias* after tasting their food.

The colonia residents were still waiting patiently around the school when the volunteers returned at 2:30. Mark and Naomi's Christian art projects had progressed from paper angel wings to crosses carved from Ivory soap bars using paring knives. The shavings were pressed into balls of soap so that the students' products had double use in the children's huts and block houses.

At nightfall the lines looked the same as they had at 8 a.m. A cooler full of cold cuts, apples, oranges, and yogurt awaited them back at the house. Peanut M&Ms and Reese's Cups were the dessert. Mark again went into a corner with a chair for a desk and a chair to sit on to continue his screenplay. Grins and frowns crossed his face as he wrote and edited, and sometimes he'd chuckle. At least I think it's funny, thought Mark.

******

    CUT TO:
EXT.--BORDER CROSSING--DAY
ZEUS, in Alfred's clothes, is in the middle of a group of American tourists -- almost hidden with plastic shopping bags, piñatas and other souvenirs -- walking past the guards.
The MEN AND LADIES are chatting the entire time, hardly aware of the guards.
FIRST LADY
Did you see this? It only cost me 5 dollars. And I got this bottle of real vanilla extract for only 2 dollars. Do you know what that much artificial vanilla would . . .
BILL
Show your passport. Thanks. Anything to declare? OK. You, anything to declare? OK.
FIRST and SECOND LADIES shake their heads and keep walking and talking.
SECOND LADY
I got something for everyone. A poncho for Sally, a tooled leather belt for Andy, and two . . .
GENE
(joking)
Did you ladies leave anything for the Mexicans to wear?
Several tourists hold up packages and smile and shake their heads.
GENE (CONT.)
Have a nice day, now.
    BILL
Yeah, they left the good stuff for the Mexicans. Ja'ever see such junk, ugly junk?
GENE
Yeah, it may not be good and it may not be pretty, but it's sure a bargain.
    CUT TO:
ZEUS, while they're making their jokes, stays low behind packages and piñatas and slips by and walks toward the gas station across the road.
    CUT TO:
INT.--SERVICE STATION RESTROOM

ZEUS only has the piñata, from which he takes his regular clothes and changes, discarding the remainder in the wastebasket.
  CUT TO:
EXT.--SERVICE STATION FUEL ISLAND--DAY
ZEUS moves from one car or truck to another, talking to the driver. Each driver in turn shakes his or her head and returns to pumping gas. Pointing north and gesturing, Zeus talks to JOSE, 66, who owns an old truck into which he is pouring a quart of oil.
JOSE
Yeah, I'm goin' to Kimmel.
ZEUS
Can I heetch a ride weeth you, then?
JOSE
Hop in, that is, if you don't smoke, drink or chew or hang around those that do.
JOSE looks pleased with his trite rhyme.
ZEUS
No, I don't haves no bad habeets or smells except my feet, but I promeeses to keeps my zapatoes on zee whole way.
  FADE OUT:
  FADE IN:
EXT.--MANILA STREET IN KIMMEL--DAY
ZEUS gets out of the truck, waves, and walks north on Manila Street. He passes a variety of poor businesses and many unpainted houses and cheap apartments.
  CUT TO:
A bag lady, MARLEEN, 54, moves her two shopping carts out of his way so he can pass.
  PAN TO:
A pretty, small, young Chinese/American girl, KAREN, 17, is sweeping in front of a Chinese restaurant on the west side of Manila Street and south of Plum Street.
  PAN TO:
A large lady, DELIA, late thirties, is standing in the doorway of a laundromat on the west side of Manila Street between Plum and Apple Streets. She is giving Zeus the once-over.
  PAN TO:
Kids are roller-blading on the cracked walks.
  PAN TO:
Young men and women stagger in and out of a crack house on the east side of Manila south of Plum. Nobody pays any attention to them.

CUT TO:
EXT.--RAMSHACKLE APARTMENT BUILDING--DAY
NATE, a black boy of eight, is sitting on the steps playing with a ball. His parents, JEFFERSON and NOELA, are arguing inside, which can be heard through the open window.
ZEUS conitnues to walk north.
JEFFERSON
There's no work, there's no decent work anywhere in this town for someone like me.
NOELA
Calm down, Honey. It's OK. Wait till tomorrow . . .
JEFFERSON
I ain't got no money to even feed us. Minimum wage is all there is out there. How will I pay the rent?
NOELA
We'll get by, Honey. You'll see. It'll work . . .
JEFFERSON
Bullcrap. I can't take it any longer. I oughta go up to Chicago where my brother is. He'll get me a good job.
NOELA
Oh, Jefferson, don't even think about that. You got me and Nate here. It'll work out.
JEFFERSON
What do ya suppose Nate thinks of his dad? Bum? No father at all?
ZEUS walks past Grape and Cherry Streets.
CUT TO:
KIDS are on the streets and in the alleys, mostly dirty and destructive. Two boys are in an alley spray-painting words and faces on the side of a brick building.
CUT TO:
ZEUS walks by an old, dark, brick, deserted church, stops, turns around and goes back to it.
CUT TO:
EXT.--BACK OF ABANDONED CHURCH--DAY
ZEUS walks around to the back of the church. He HEARS TALKING inside, and finds a panel out of one of the doors and crawls inside.

Chapter 6. The Idea

"Morning, honey," greeted Jake.

"Morning," responded Laura. "Eggs, bacon and toast or pancakes?"

"Eggs and toast. No bacon please."
"Sleep well?"
"No. Awake all night."
"Something worrying you?"
"Hey, honey. Guess what?" asked Jake.
Laura turned from the stove and looked Jake in the eyes."
"I've got an idea."
This could be one of his loony ones or shear genius. Laura never knew which.
"I'm going to get some young pharmacist to manage or buy pd drugs and I'm going to start a new business."
PD Drugs had a sign that read pd drugs, lowercase. Its original name had been Powers Drugs, but everyone had called it PD Drugs for years, a little redundant, so many just said pd's.
"You know everyone talks about being green, but it's such a farce. They want to cover their grass with a deck, patio stones, bricks or concrete. But they never go outside and use them. They cut down beautiful, old trees to put in a second garage or storage shed for motorized toys. Petitions are signed by businesses for wider roads and more parking spaces. People want to pave the world."
Here we go, thought Laura. He's 54, both our girls are grown and married, so this could be the start of his midlife crisis.
"Our neighbors pride themselves on being green, so they buy a new high efficiency dishwasher, refrigerator, stove, clothes washer and dryer and throw the used appliances in a landfill. The reason I know they bought new stuff was because Janet didn't like the color of her appliances. Bill told me so, yet the appliances had at least another ten years or more of good use in them."
He's already gone, realized Laura.
"It's not only women. The men in this neighborhood do all the outside work with a motor of some kind,. Saturdays sound like a convention of beekeepers arriving on motor scooters. I know Bill has an electric hedge trimmer, power washer and air pump. Then he has a collection of internal combustion gadgets: riding mower, chain saw, leaf blower, rototiller and weed whacker. People complain about dogs barking around here, but the worst noises come from all the gas burning, blue-smoke-blowing engines. I only have a chain saw. What's wrong with using a push mower, hand clippers, a hoe and a weed whip? It's not like the men in the community come home physically worn out from sitting behind a desk drinking coffee and talking on the

phone all day. From their waist lines it looks like they could use a little non-motorized exercise."

He's in outer space this morning, thought Laura.

"People within walking distance drive their cars to pd's and then complain there's no place to park, so they drive around the block a few times and finally park in the back. Why do people who are picking up a few ounces of medicine think they have to tote along a 3,000 pound, gas-guzzling vehicle? They're not green."

Laura realized where some of the passion was coming from. Mark had started a Bible study that focused very little on memorizing verses, praying for help and going away with good vibes and a lot on doing things to make the world a better place. American Capitalism was focused on the personal benefits of materialism and its right to use up the world's resources to make and own things. Mark and his group thought American-Style Capitalism unchristian. They each had made decisions to try to stop controlling or monopolizing and, instead, focus on serving and sharing. How could he pretend to be Christ-like if he owned a garage full of things he didn't need, made more money that 90% of the citizens of the world, owned a house that would have been big enough for 10 people in most countries, drove a car that wasted energy, agreed with war, and didn't help his neighbors in other countries? Did Jesus have a house, big salary, carriage, and toys or did he spend his life in poverty and service?

"The town keeps building bypasses that in a few years go from allowing travelers to speed around the town to creating a traffic jam because of multiple stoplights and strip malls, car dealerships, fast food restaurants, movie theaters and big box stores. It kills the downtown businesses, creates thousands of acres of more pavement—turning green fields into black parking lots—and forces people who frequent the bypass businesses to burn more fossil fuels to drive to and from them.

Here it comes, so Laura prepared herself.

"I'm going to start a mass transit system in Wyandotte."

Laura sat up straight. This was way beyond loony. Wyandotte only had 17,000 citizens, and most of the men would give up their first born before giving up their car or riding an economical public transportation system. Males had such a love affair with the false power they felt cars gave them that many would build a big, permanent garage for their cars, truck, ATV and power tools and roll in a mobile home for their wives and children.

Chapter 7. Free Pizza

Of all people to get the runs from the Mexican lunch, it was Naomi. She stayed back at the house so she could be close to the outdoor toilet and hide from the neighbors. If she hadn't hidden, the ladies would have been coming in to see her, trying to be helpful but just causing embarrassment to Naomi when she would have had to jump up and make quick trips to the outhouse. The Ciprofloxacin pill she had taken in the middle of the night was hopefully doing its job

She hadn't brought a book, but she had been reading and helping edit *Hey, Zeus*, so she picked it up and started reading where she and Mark had left off. As she read she imagined different young people in their church youth group, and adults too, playing the parts if Mark was ever able to sell the idea of having them make a movie.

******

CUT TO:
INT.--CHURCH
FIVE MEXICAN-AMERICAN TEENS are smoking marijuana. There is no light in the church except what comes through the partially draped windows.
The teens look toward Zeus, but only see his silhouette through the haze from the smoke.
ZEUS
 Alright! Outta 'ere ya bums. Now!!! Gets go'n. Andale! Andale!
FIRST TEEN
Hey, man. We ain't scared of you.
SECOND TEEN
(whispers)
Ditch the stuff! It's the cops.
ZEUS picks up the inside, heavy, cross-member of a broken window frame and, holding it over his head, slowly and menacingly approaches the teens.
FIRST TEEN
Whooa, man. It's an axe.
SECOND TEEN
(whispers louder)
No, man. It's a cross.
ZEUS
(yelling)
Out! 'ow dare you defiles zee temple of zee Lord. Zee lamb weell not lies down een zee pasture weeth zee jackass. Thees ees zee same theeng. Get out!

THE TEENS see Zeus approaching in silhouette with the "cross" raised like an axe and scamper to and through the hole in the door.
ZEUS (CONT.)
Carrumba! These American keeds spooks eesly.
Zeus looks around and sees one of the teens, PEDRO, 18, dark-skinned, well built, and handsome, hiding behind an overturned pew.
ZEUS (CONT.)
Comes outta there, goat. Thees ain't zee other side of zee sheep shed.
PEDRO
What the crap does that mean? You crazy, man. I ain't afraid of you.
ZEUS
Gets up, leettle goat boy. Zee nanny never hurts zee keeds.
PEDRO
What's witha jackass and goat stuff?
ZEUS
Goat, you not understands notheen'. You're welcomes to stay 'ere weeth me, though. I'm making thees my new home here een zee land of milk and 'oney.
Zeus starts to straighten things, picking up overturned pews, pulling rags off of the windows, etc.
ZEUS (CONT.)
Whoa! Thees place has ze steenks. Does zee plumbing work?
PEDRO
(quietly while crouched in a corner)
Yeah, the toilet works and there's water to the basement sink.
ZEUS
And 'ow about zee lights?
PEDRO
(a little louder)
Don't know about the lights . . . all the bulbs were broken before we started using it.
ZEUS
Man, I'm 'ungries. Hey, goat, you 'ungries?
PEDRO
Heck, yes, I'm hungry. But I ain't got no money.
Me neithers. So I'm going out to gets sometheeng to eat. 'ow about peezza?
PEDRO
I said I ain't got no money.
ZEUS
Who needs money for food? You can't eats Pesos.

(making a face)
Me-tal-lic tasting. You likes zee beeg word, 'ey, little goat?
PEDRO
Man, you crazy!
ZEUS
Don't you likes peezza?
PEDRO
I like lots of stuff I can't afford.
ZEUS
Comes weeth me and we'll gets peezza to bring back.
PEDRO
You're crazy, man. If you can get pizza without money, why not just have it delivered?

Chapter 8. To Write or not to Write

Dear Franklin,
I've read your letter and...

Miss Ardnas hated the old "dear" salutation—It stopped her from writing the letter, at least for a few moments. How did "dear" convert from being used to address people who were actually dear to you to being used as a polite way of starting a letter to a person you hardly knew or didn't even like? "Gentlemen" or "sir or madam" seemed awkward too. Was Franklin still dear to her? Well, yes, she guessed he was, at least in some ways.

What could she write: "Dear Franklin. Sorry, Honey, I'm Christian, but I won't forgive and forget. I'm done with you and I hope prayer will solve your problem. Good luck. –Ardnas" Kind of like brushing the dust from your sandals and moving on, she thought.

Miss Ardnas wondered if she could stand to have Franklin back into her life and face the constant worry, dread, uncertainty, turmoil, sadness, fear and depression. And what about Cam and April? They didn't like their father. Would they like him if he came back changed, reformed? They were doing so well, actually a lot better, and so was I, she told herself.

No answer was better than an answer that expressed artificial forgiveness, was her decision. She remembered that she had been through the forgiveness-and-mending routine after an affair before this last one. "I don't want to put my children and me through that again," she said out loud. Then she wondered whether Franklin would take legal steps to put pressure on her—steps to change her mind, to acquire custody of the kids or stop alimony payments. There was no easy way to deal with Franklin's ego.

Miss Ardnas spent the rest of the day playing with Cam and April in the yard. The kids put out their Slip'n'slide, put on their swimsuits, attached the hose and screamed and laughed. They especially liked seeing their mom in her aqua bikini sliding backward and then trying to pull the bottom of her swimsuit back up.

After playing, they each ate two green, blue, red, yellow or purple popsicles until their lips and tongues were multicolored. Their chins, necks and chests were stained too, so they took turns spraying each other with the hose and screeching when the icy water hit their skin that was hot from the sun.

The yard was a sloppy mess, so they ran through the mud until they were brown to their knees. Using the hose again cleaned everyone and they ran to the house for beach towels. Then Cam and April put on dry clothes and wrapped up in blankets to watch a video.

Exhilarated from the exercise, youthful joy and cold water, Miss Ardnas decided to partake of her favorite pastime:

SCIENCE Forum: New/Old "Green" Breakthrough
Central Columbus Communicator

"It's time for those who treat 'green' as the latest fad to get real," stated Lionel Jackson, professor of bio-agri-tech at Central Columbus University. "Green isn't a style to brag about, discuss over cocktails and pretend to follow."

According to Professor Jackson, the university has completed studies of local suburban landscaping techniques and styles and compared them with several test sites. He said the typical suburban yard is cropped short and requires bag after bag of chemicals to keep it green. The older trees were cut down and few and shorter trees replace them.

The test plots are allowed to be natural, which Jackson explains means grasses indigenous to central Ohio are allowed to reach their normal height and to reseed automatically. Mature trees were left on the plots. Wildflowers are not dug out or killed, so they add color and variety to the landscape.

"Many people who think they're green, yet spray poisons on their yards to kill dandelions and other native plants that aren't grasses, have a completely false idea about ecosystems," added Wendy Sanders, a colleague of Professor Jackson. "Not only are dandelions beautiful, children love to pick them, blow on their umbrella-like seeds

and people used to bread and fry the flowers and cut the greens for salad."

She suggested that if people Google 'edible dandelions' they will find recipes for a French cream of dandelion soup and also dandelion wine. The site suggested harvesting the leaves before the plants flower; otherwise the dandelions will be bitter.

Professor Jackson says he loves to make dandelion wine and use the leaves in green salads: "But I can't imagine anyone eating the leaves after they have sprayed poisons on the yard and treated it with four or five other chemicals."

Bill Holbrook, who lives with his wife Jennifer on one of the test plots, said, "It's a little hard to get used to. Neighbors that build the old way don't like the looks of our yard. We only mow enough space for our kids outdoor games that require short grass. The rest is as nature intended."

"The people on both sides of us want their yards to look like their living rooms, so they foster only one kind of grass and they want it buzzed so it looks like a short-shag carpet," said Jennifer. "They sometimes ask me how I can stand all the shade from the large trees, so I tell them we love to sit under them and feel the cool breeze."

"Our neighbors don't use their mown yards or sit under trees. If they go outside they complain about how hot it is and run back to their air conditioned family room," mentioned Bill. "Some won't let their kids dig mud holes in the yard, make bases for softball, or ride their bikes through it. It's no wonder the kids sit in their rooms all day in front of an electronic screen of some kind."

Processor Jackson's studies showed that the test plots absorbed eleven times the carbon dioxide as the typical suburban yard and gave off three times as much oxygen. He added that another plus is the decreased use of electrify to run A/C in the summer because the house and, especially, the windows are shaded by leaves, and the tree direct higher air down around the house to make a cooling current.

No poisons are sprayed or applied to the yards, so there is no need for tiny signs saying to keep off the yard or don't walk in the yard barefooted. "The test plot owners saved lots of money and were far more green than neighbors who were still treating their property in the old-fashioned way," said Professor Jackson.

Jennifer said that she wished she lived in a green community because she hates sitting outside under a tree with her family having a picnic or just talking while the neighbors are mowing, trimming, sawing, and spraying, which all are done with loud motorized tools *blowing blue or black smoke. "I don't think they mind the noise the neighbors make because they don't go outside. But when we're outside sometimes we have to stop talking until the riding mowers stop. We use a push mower and hand clippers."*

"I know people who won't use a Styrofoam cup but mow acres of lawn and broadcast a ton of fertilizer and poison on it," laughed Professor Jackson. "They don't want anything about their yard to be natural."

Chapter 9. Judging.

Two weeks later, Miss Ardnas found herself beside her lawyer in a conference room in the county courthouse sitting across from Franklin and his lawyer. He had fast tracked a custody case through his lawyer and the court system.

"I'm John Fulbright, judge of the 2nd Circuit Court."

The judge heard everyone's names and welcomed them.

"I'd prefer that you, Franklin Wright, and you, Ardnas Wright, work this out between yourselves. Keep the children in mind despite the fact that there might be hard feelings between you two. I know both of your lawyers, and they're good guys, but that doesn't mean they can't be bulldogs at times. I've seen it in court. I think they will agree with me about this--listen to your heart before you listen to your lawyer. I'll be in my chambers, but I hope you won't need me."

Franklin's attorney, Mathew Grindel, started the meeting: "Has everyone read the petition for custody filed on….." Miss Ardnas' mind wandered. Is this really happening, she wondered?

"As you have read, my client asserts that Ardnas Wright is an unstable, over emotional and neglectful parent. There are documented fits of passion on her part, which has caused her to become an alcoholic, and…"

Miss Ardnas' lawyer, Jeremy Kim, interrupted with: "Come on, Matt. Are we going to start like that? We may as well call the judge back in right now if that's the way we're going to proceed."

"Ok. Let's talk about what my client wants. He is petitioning the court for full custody of Cameron and April Wright."

Kim responded with: "I read that in the petition. Obviously that's not going to happen. I can't see the court ever taking away these children from a mother with Mrs. Wright's background. Right now Mr. Wright can have the children two weeks in the summer and the second Sunday of every month. What's wrong with that? That was the opinion of the judge at the divorce proceedings. Why wasn't that ruling challenged then?"

Franklin broke in: "It's unfair. I'm a better parent than she is. During the divorce proceedings I was too distraught to think straight. I was railroaded, but now I want my rights and my children."

"Let me get some facts straight, Mr. Wright, stated Kim. "I've reread the transcript of the divorce proceedings. You have had several affairs while married to Mrs. Wright. Is that right?"

"I object," yelled Franklin.

"Mr. Wright, this is not a trial. We're not in a courtroom. There's no judge to make a ruling."

"I still object."

"Will you answer the question?"

"You're leading the witness," continued Franklin.

"Not a trial, sir. Let me repeat: You have had several affairs while married to Mrs. Wright. Is that correct?"

"You're putting words in my mouth. I didn't say that. You said it, they're your words, you're answering your own questions and you want me to say those are my words."

"Ok. Mr. Wright. Let me put it this way. Have you ever had any affairs while married to Mrs. Wright?"

"What does that have to do with anything? Lots of good fathers have extra marital relations, especially when their spouses are frigid, drunks and neglectful parents."

"Mr. Wright, none of the accusations you are making now were part of the divorce transcript. I don't understand..,."

"I was too nice to her then. I should have told the truth and then I would have custody of the children now."

Miss Ardnas had taken a facial tissue from her purse and was blotting her eyes. Grindel rolled his eyes once at Kim to communicate that he was sorry and embarrassed. He knew that Franklin was capable of going out of control at any time, and this was one of those times.

Mr. Kim warned: "Mr. Wright. We may have to call the judge back in. If we do, this little meeting is going to expand into an unpleasant spectacle. I like money, but I don't like to make it in a nasty battle over a couple of innocent children. If you take this to court and sue for custody, Mr. Grindel and I are going to make a lot of money. Your money and money that could go to your children's future education. The judge will probably assign a Guardian ad Litem or Court Appointed Special Advocate, who will look at all of the divorce court records, your criminal background—even driving offenses. He will interview you and Mrs. Wright and your and her parents and grandparents and your neighbors, bosses, former and current employees—especially your former secretaries--and colleagues, and the children's babysitters. He will also interview the children.

"So what! If you think this stuff…"

Kim held up his hand toward Franklin's face and spoke louder and with more authority: "If you've had mental health issues, he will ask for permission to interview psychologists or psychiatrists. He will also be present for short periods of time during visitations with your children. Then he will prepare a many-page case study enumerating the pros and cons of both Mrs. Wright and you as parents. He will give this to the judge. It will include his recommendations for disposition of the children. Copies will also go to you, Mrs. Wright, Mr. Grindel and myself. There's a lot of airing of dirty laundry, as they say, but…."

"Do it! You can't scare me," interrupted Franklin.

Mr. Grindel tapped on the judge's chamber door.

Chapter 10. Fruits of the Spirit

"Does God understand English?" Asked a boy in Spanish. It was translated by one of the girls who spoke English. Mark and Naomi had said some prayers in English at the end of each high school-age Bible study. The boy had grown up Catholic, but there was no church in this new colonia. He had never heard English spoken in his Catholic church.

"Oh, yeah," answered Naomi. "And a lot of other languages too."

The *Bible* study lessons had focused on teaching the Fruits of the Spirit and the Beatitudes, in that order. Mark and Naomi wanted the teens to discover their potential according to the *Bible* and to learn what rewards living up to their potential would bring. They queried the class about saints they knew of that manifested different fruits of the spirit, since they knew that icons of patron saints often adorned necklaces and were prevalent on walls of their houses.

Being sensitive to the cultural traditions of the Mexicans and their Catholic church's liturgy was important to them. So Hail Mary's and prayers beads were discussed too. When Naomi and Mark read and discussed the Apostles Creed, they made sure to use the term *catholic,* which, when in lowercase, meant wide-ranging, instead of the terms Protestants substituted.

By the third day the volunteers could see the ends of the lines, and by the end of the day they were finished. The last two days they had spent helping people work on their huts and houses, holding church services, visiting the sick, and eating at different families' houses. Noel said that breaking bread during a regular meal was far superior than the symbolic miniature version called Holy Communion or Eucharist. Communing with people in their own homes with food prepared by hand had a dozen more social layers that also included a spiritual element.

At one small block house, Naomi had two little dark-haired, dark-eyed girls begging their parents to be able to sit next to her during dinner. When they received refusals from the mother, because there was only room for adults at the rough-plank table, they stood next to or behind her chair during dinner. They'd innocently touch her brown hair, stroke her lighter-color arm, finger the enameled pendant that was paisley shaped or watch as she folded a tortilla and dipped into the dish of rice, black beans and sauce.

Then the girls would examine Naomi's bracelet and ring. After eating they showed her around the outside of the house, where a few red and orange flowers sprouted out of the seemingly dry and barren soil. A tour of the tomatoes and peppers planted in a little plot was given. Darker ground around the plants showed that they were assiduously watered morning and night. A little coop and a wire fence indicated where the chickens roosted at night. They followed the girls and Naomi on the tour because the girls carried bits of broken tortillas and crumbled and tossed them as they walked.

After they left the family, Naomi and Mark walked around the colonia one last time. It was hard to tell whether the town was being built or torn down. Partial cement block walls with blocks strewn around them were evident on every street. Pieces of corrugated metal roofing and two-by-four studs were also lying randomly between houses or in front yards. They passed several stores, which were simply houses with signs over the doors and advertisements in windows. The shops usually had a couple of large grain sacks on each side of the front door, opened and featuring a metal scoop. Rice, beans and corn meal were sold by the scoop instead of by the package or plastic bag.

One sign read: "Ice crem on Wenesdays afer 12." They were surprised that it was in English, but not that the spelling was incorrect. Most drinks were sold room temperature. Milk was from a box of white powder. When they left one store, two kids were on each side of them. They reached up and held their hands. Mark said, "Let's go back in and buy them some candy."

"No way," responded Naomi. "Kids don't need more candy. Let's buy them some crayons or colored pencils and some paper."

They purchased the items and returned to the street to present them to the kids. Then they looked down another dirt side road and saw Madison and William walking with arms around each other. Madison and William stopped and spontaneously embraced and partook of a long and passionate kiss. The children who were following them at a short distance laughed, clapped and jumped up, down and twirled round. Then a couple of the boys puckered their lips and made kissing sounds as they chased some of the girls. Madison and William didn't pay any attention but Naomi did. Naomi watched as William took both of Madison's hands. Because she had seen this many times, she knew that he was reciting Byron, Shelley, Keats, Browning, Shakespeare or the poetry of some writer of romantic verse. She was right. She could faintly hear: "She walks in beauty, like the night of cloudless climes and starry skies; and all that's best of dark and bright meet in her aspect and her eyes:"

When Mark and Naomi got back to the house, Madison and William had already returned and everyone was sitting around partially depressed because they were leaving in the morning. Noel whispered to Mark that they were going to get rowdy soon though, because the chocolate drink prepared for them by a neighbor had loads of caffeine—like quadruple shots of espresso.

The kids who received the art supplies were thrilled with their new tools and ran home to show their families and begin drawing. Later the same kids came to the house and gave each of the volunteers and the Temples a variety of Milagros to pin on their hats, wear around their necks or carry in their pockets.

"I wish Miss Ardnas could have come on this trip. She would have loved these children," said Mark.

"Yeah," responded Naomi, halfheartedly.

Mark took a couple of sips and went to his computer to continue editing *Hey, Zeus*.

******

CUT TO:
EXT.--BUSINESS DISTRICT ON MANILA STREET--DAY
ZEUS walks down the street looking into restaurants.
He finally enters Mike's Pizza Parlor where JAIME, 21, is working alone.
CUT TO:
INT.--PIZZA PARLOR

ZEUS
'ey. What's your name?
JAIME
Jaime. What can I get you today?
ZEUS
(matter of factly)
Nothing, Jaime. What'-s zee awfulest theeng you gots to do on thees job?
JAIME
What?
ZEUS
What's zee crappiest job you haves to do here?
JAIME
Hey, man, I'm the only one working here today, so let's get to it. You want a pizza or not?
ZEUS
Jaime, I'm not keedding. Thees ees a crappy job you got, all by yourself. So, whatever your worst job here ees, I'm gonna do eet for you tonight.
JAIME
Man, you are crazy, but I'm not. Follow me.
     CUT TO:
INT.--BACKROOM OF PIZZA PARLOR
ZEUS is led into the backroom, which has cluttered shelves, opened boxes filled with cans of sauce, trash all over the floor, and a filthy toilet that sits in the open but in one corner. The sign over it says: For Help Only.
JAIME is obviously disgusted with the mess, but Zeus shows no reaction.
JAIME
It's all yours, Bud.
ZEUS
Gracias, Jaime.
JAIME goes to the door, and he pauses to watch.
ZEUS happily begins picking up trash and organizing cans and boxes on shelves.
     CUT TO:
INT.--PIZZA PARLOR
JAIME'S hands are seen making pizzas, putting them in and taking them out of the oven, and ringing up sales. Zeus is obviously forgotten. Finally, ZEUS appears in the doorway to the backroom.

ZEUS
Done!
JAIME
(doubtful)
What? Well, let's see.
> CUT TO:

INT.--BACKROOM OF PIZZA PARLOR

JAIME walks into a well-organized, clean room, followed by ZEUS. The cans and boxes on the shelves are stacked in an orderly fashion and even the toilet in the corner looks fairly respectable.

JAIME (CONT.)
Wow, man, this is beautiful! When the boss sees this he'll probably give me a raise. Man, I can't pay you noth'n, this place is barely making it now, but I owe you one.

ZEUS
You gots any leftover foods or anytheeng?

JAIME
I don't know, but I'll sure find some.
> CUT TO:

INT.--PIZZA PARLOR

JAIME (CONT.)
Hey, grab those two pizzas on the top of the oven that never got picked up. They're still warm and take these bread sticks. I need to make up a fresh batch for later tonight anyway. Take this six-pack of Coke too. I know it ain't enough, but . . .

ZEUS
Gracias, Jaime, Gracias. Eet's plenty.

JAIME
Hey, it was my pleasure . . . uh, by the way, I didn't catch your name.

ZEUS
Zeus.

JAIME
Hey Zeus, come back any time.

ZEUS
Sure. Adios.
> CUT TO:

EXT.--APARTMENT BUILDING--NIGHT

ZEUS is walking past the building with pizzas, cokes and breadsticks. NATE is sitting on the steps tossing a ball up and catching it, trying to ignore the continuing argument about money and failure going on inside between JEFFERSON and NOELA, but even Zeus can hear it.

JEFFERSON
(from inside)
I might as well leave you two here and head for Chicago. There ain't nothin' good gonna happen here for us.
NOELA
(from inside)
Oh, please, Jefferson, don't even . . .
NATE
I'll give you this ball for a piece of that pizza, mister. Looksta be more than you can eat all by yourself.
ZEUS
'ow deeds you guess, keed?
Zeus looks through the window at Jefferson and Noela, back at Nate, then at the pizza boxes.
ZEUS (CONT.)
'ey, what ees your last name?
NATE
Brown.
ZEUS
Well, Meester Brown, follows me.
    CUT TO:
INT.--HALLWAY OF APARTMENT BUILDING
ZEUS is knocking loudly on the door of the Brown apartment. Arguing can still be heard from inside, but Zeus just ignores it. He sees that the apartment is 1B.

Chapter 11. Back Talking

"Noel, you got a minute?" asked Mark as they were sitting in the airport waiting for their flight back to Wyandotte, Kentucky. Noel was sitting around keeping them company.

"Sure, what's up?"

"I've got a pastor back home that's having trouble with a parishioner."

"Just one?' Noel laughed.

"Well, this one is a big one."

"What's going on?"

"He's 80, hard of hearing, cranky and mad at God. He lost his wife some time back and hasn't gotten over it."

"So how's he a problem?"

"He talks out loud during the sermon and sometimes stops the sermon to challenge the pastor."

"You're kidding!"

"You know since I lost my pastorate I attend a different church each Sunday, and I happened to be in the Followers Church and was a witness to the whole event. My friend was preaching on why Christians still have things go wrong in their lives. Pastor Bob, a great guy, was applying some puns and mnemonics so that the message would be remembered and also maybe reach the children in the congregation. He said something like "add an *O* to *God* and you get *good*, but there can also be a dab of bad in your life too." It's kind of corny, but I understand his reasoning.

Stan whispers loud enough for me to hear: "And God spelled backward is dog, but that doesn't mean anything."

"Not nice! So what happened then?"

"Well, the pastor says that he thinks God put illness in our lives to make us appreciate the good times. Stan, the man I'm talking about, turns to a friend sitting in a pew behind him and spontaneously says, 'Bullshit' loud enough for the whole congregation to hear."

"Oops."

"Then Stan, who thinks he's mumbling, yells: 'That didn't make the two-thirds of Europe that died from the bubonic plague more appreciative.'"

"Wow!"

"Then the pastor went to the Book of James and talked about how someone who is sick should call the elders for healing. You know the verses."

"Sure."

"Well, Stan turns around to his friend again and says, 'More bullshit. We did that for my Betsy. Didn't work at all.' By this time Pastor Bob is getting upset and can't find the rhythm of the sermon again because of all the interruptions."

"I bet."

"So Pastor Bob checks his notes and goes into: 'Ask and you will receive, seek and you will find, knock and the door will be open to you.' and so forth. Stan turns and says bullshit a third time. Now Stan's receiving quieting pats on the shoulder, whispers to calm down and outright shushes. 'What'd I do?' Asks Stan, louder. 'I've read those passages in the Bible and they're not true.'"

"By this time he's got Pastor Bob listening to him instead of paying attention to his sermon outline and notes. So he starts responding to Stan's comments with: 'The Bible is a divine work, the true word of God,' and Stan, standing, asks Pastor Bob, 'Who wrote the Gospels?' Unfortunately, Pastor Bob takes the bait: 'Tradition says they're the apostles with their names on the Gospel.' Stan fires back: 'If you aren't even sure who wrote the Gospels, how do you know they're from God?' Pastor Bob says, "Because the Bible indicates they are.' Stan responses with: 'So the Bible's true and from God because the Bible says so. Isn't that circular reasoning?' Finally Pastor Bob gives up, truncates his sermon and says a closing prayer."

"Wow again!"

"Yeah. It's got Pastor Bob a little gun shy about entering the pulpit. Since he knows I was a pastor, he asked me for advice. Did I tell you Stan was a retired chemistry teacher? He questions everything. His son's name is Jake, and Jake's a handful too, but with more manners. Jake is a pharmacist and questions everything about religion and politics also. We're good friends, though."

"Have you talked to Jake?"

"No, I've been on this trip since I witnessed Stan's performance."

"Well, good luck giving Pastor Bob advice. That's a tough one. They've called your loading zone number. Thanks for bringing down a group of volunteers."

"I love working with you down here."

"Well, it's not easy. Remember to pray for us. Some people don't think prayer works, like Stan, but I can tell you with confidence that it does. I can tell when I'm not receiving prayers. I'll have a hell of a week, with generators breaking, illness, border hassles, etc., and then when I think back I realize that I had not heard from anybody about being included in their church's prayers. On the other hand, some other week will bring people like you down here to help, a big donation to pay expenses, good health and great opportunities to minister, and a letter and a couple of calls about how hard a congregation, Bible study group or a family has been praying for Shirley and me."

"You got our prayers, Noel."

"Thanks. Have a safe trip back and may God bless you."

On the plane Mark took out his computer and continued reading and editing *Hey, Zeus*.

******

ZEUS (CONT.)
'ey, opens up een there. I don't haves all day, I gotta peezzas to deliver. Opens up there.
JEFFERSON
(angrily)

What the devil do you want? I ain't got no money if you're some bill collector.
ZEUS
Let's me sees here.
Zeus puts his head around the door and looks at the apartment number again.
ZEUS (CONT.)
Yep, thees ees 1B, all right.
Zeus looks at the pizza boxes and sack of breadsticks as if they have names on them.
ZEUS (CONT.)
What ees your last name? Jones? Evans? Brown?
JEFFERSON
Brown.
ZEUS
Well, Meester Brown, thees ees your lucky day. You just wons a large peezza supremes, three, fresh breadsteecks and three Coca Colas, all compliments of Mike's Peezza Parlor.
JEFFERSON just stands there looking at the boxes.
NOELA peeks around his shoulder.
ZEUS (CONT.)
Well, ees you going to take'm?
ZEUS is very business-like and seemingly in a hurry, so he shoves the food through the doorway.
JEFFERSON is unable to speak, even to say thank you at first.
NATE runs through the door with a smile on his face and grabs the box.
NATE
Thanks, mister.
JEFFERSON
Yeah, thanks.
    CUT TO:
EXT.--APARTMENT BUILDING--NIGHT
ZEUS walks away carrying the other pizza, breadsticks and Cokes.
JEFFERSON
(from inside)
Man, I ain't never won noth'n before. Did that guy say this was my lucky day! He sure wasn't with me on the street today. I ain't never had no luck but bad luck. But tomorrow's still out there.
NOELA
How'd you win this, Honey?

JEFFERSON
I don't know.
NOELA
Well, you had to do something good to win.
>   CUT TO:
EXT.--BUSY CORNER ON MANILA STREET--NIGHT
LYLA HENDRICKSON, a white, eighteen-year-old, bleached blond, in short white dress, bright red halter-top, high heels -- ugly hooker attire -- is standing near the curb.

Despite her makeup and clothes, you can tell she has a nearly perfect body and a sweet, beautiful face.

JACK HADLEY, 35, her "man," mostly in black, is keeping an eye on her from the entrance of a closed store.

As ZEUS crosses the street toward Lyla, he sees Jack and understands the scene immediately.
LYLA
Hi, cutie. You up for a little fun tonight? I can guarantee you'll have a good time.
ZEUS
Sure, lamb, I loves to haves zee fun.
LYLA
Well, I'm the one for you then, honey. Just follow me to my place.
ZEUS
No, no. I don't do likes that. You comes to my place and haves a nice deenner weeth me.
LYLA
I don't think Jack would like that.
ZEUS
(friendly)
Jack can comes, too, eef he promeeses to acts like a human bean.
LYLA
(looking back at Jack)
I don't know.
ZEUS
What's your names, lamb?
LYLA
Lyla.
ZEUS
Come on, Lyla. I'll treats you nice.
Zeus's tone of voice and manner make Lyla trust him.

LYLA starts to follow, looking back at Jack again, expecting disapproval.
JACK leaves the doorway and approaches the couple.
JACK
No need for that. We got a nice place just upstairs here, fellow, but I need to see some money first. It's just good business, ya know.
ZEUS
I'm not een that kind of buseeness, and, besides, I likes my place better, so comes on, Lyla. You're welcome, too, Jack.
JACK steps between Lyla and Zeus, and takes a pose -- eyes unblinking, feet apart, chest out, elbows bent, and fists made ready at his hips.
JACK
No money, hey, loser. Beat it. Before things get rough.

Chapter 12. No Cell Phone

Sam called Duke on the phone. "How's it going, buddy?" asked Duke.

"Fine. Haven't talked to you for three weeks. I've been busy. Guess what?"

"What?"

"I got a job at Glacier National Park."

"You're kidding. Ranger? How could that be?"

"No. They had openings as a salesperson in a gift shop, a plumber, carpenter, volunteer campground host, campground bathroom custodian and garbage truck driver."

"So, which are you?"

"The last. They told me that if I work out there and take courses online, maybe in ten years I can become a ranger."

"Is that ok with you, Sam?"

"Well, at least I will be out in nature. I figure they have volunteer positions for trail guides, nature talks and the like that I could do."

"What about your cell phone business?"

"You interested in buying it. It's for sale."

"I'll think about it. Jenni is tired of working at Hair U R. Maybe she'd like to sell and repair cell phones. Can you teach her the business?"

"Sure. I always like working close to Jenni."

"That's not the kind of work I'm talking about. She may not like the idea at all and I may not be able to afford it."

"I bet we could work things out, such as dual ownership or something. Then if hauling trash doesn't suit me, I can come back and work at the cell phone store."

"I'll talk to Jenni. But congratulations on your new job, I think."

"Well, it'll be an adventure. I've already signed up for online forestry and conservation courses, and my assistant at the shop is working more hours. I'll probably hire an assistant for my assistant, unless Jenni becomes interested."

"Well, good luck, buddy. Talk later."

"Thanks. Later."

Chapter 13. Second Thoughts

Mark was getting worried. He had heard that Sam was thinking about selling his cell phone business and moving to Montana to take a new job, and Jake was thinking about selling pd's and starting a transit company. The big fear of leading Bible studies or preaching from pulpits about ethics, life styles and following Jesus' word was that, when people did make changes in their lives, the leader or pastor felt responsible. That's the way Mark felt now. Was his giving up his pastorate to work in a discount store or thinking about becoming a pastor in Alaska causing Sam and Jake to discard stable and profitable businesses and lifestyles for a pie in the sky? What if their lives fell apart? Mark wondered if he was being a good influence or a bad one."

Mark decided to give Jake a call.

"Jake, how are you?"

"Fine, my friend. How are you?"

"Good. How's business?"

"Great. You know I've sold out and am using the money to start a trolley-like system in Wyandotte, right?"

"Yes, I heard that." Mark swallowed hard. "Is that a good idea? Are you putting all of your money into the new business?"

"Yep! I'm going for broke. I think it's the right thing to do. You inspired me with your velomobile riding and your comments during our Bible studies. I've got to thank you for helping me see the light."

Mark didn't own a car. He rode, or drove, a velomobile, which is a fancy name for an enclosed, recumbent tricycle for adults. When asked why, he replied, "If more than 30,000 citizens were killed a year by a prescription medicine sold at pd's instead of automobiles, there would be calls for a ban. I guess you've never lived on a busy country road and had a dog that slept at the foot of your bed, spent every waking moment lying at your feet while you watch TV or dogged your every footstep. Or had to put a squirrel or rabbit out of its misery as it flopped around on the road after being hit by a car. Or come upon the scene of an auto accident where someone is killed. I have."

"I understand. Man has no business operating a vehicle that is too fast and powerful for him to control adequately to keep from killing innocent animals and humans. Well, I'm trying to make the transition to safer travel by starting a transit business here."

Oh, no, Thought Mark. "Make sure you think this through, Jake."

"I have. This will work. I've prayed and I'm confident of this plan."

"Well, ok. I wish you luck."

"Luck, smuck. I'm making it work."

"Listen, Jake, I hope you don't mind if I change the subject. I need to talk to you about Stan."

"What's Dad been up to now?"

"Well, he's making comments out loud during sermons at church."

"I bet that's got Pastor Bob's undies in a wad."

"Well, I wouldn't put it exactly like that, but, yes, it's causing him concern."

"Okay. I'll talk to Dad and see what I can do. I may have to attend church with him. Kind of keep him on a short leash. I know when he's at our house for dinner and some visitors stay into supper time, he'll mumble things like: 'When they going home? It's dinner time. They waiting for a free meal?' Of course since he can't hear well, he says it too loud and our friends turn red, look at their watches and say their goodbyes. He's probably doing the same kind of thing at church."

"You've got it. I was there and no one knew what to do."

"Dad's feeling awfully guilty. He loved Mom—treated her like they were still 17 year olds and dating right up to her death. They still slept in the same bed, and she sat in the middle of the front seat buckled in as close to him as she could get. But he gave her full respect intellectually. She owned her own paint store and brought home twice what he did teaching. When she died, he'd tell friends he wished he could have done more to save her. Then they, meaning well, said that he should have gone to this hospital or this doctor or tried this prescription or this homeopathic snake oil. You know how I feel about relying only on vitamins and minerals. I make tons of money selling them, but I know most of the claims are bogus. Anyway, his friends' advice just made him feel more responsible and guilty. He threw some of the blame on God," told Jake.

"Sorry I had to bring it up."

"No problem. I'll take care of it."

"Okay. Bye. And, good luck with your endeavors."

"Thanks, Pastor Mark. Bye."

Mark sought solace in editing his screen play. He needed to bring up his script writing at the next youth group meeting and see if he could sell the movie idea. From past experiences, he knew that the young people talked about being adventurous and risk-takers, but when you proposed something new, they pooh-poohed the idea. Mark started editing. He immediately saw areas that needed expansion or more directions for the actors.

******

ZEUS puts down the food, pulls out a red bandana, and takes two steps backward and assumes the pose of a toreador, then acts out the teasing, the goading with banderillas and the final killing of a bull as he says his lines. This is pure fun and theatrics, but Jack buys it.

JACK slowly backs away, a little intimidated by Zeus's description, but trying to hold his ground. All of this is confusing to Jack.

ZEUS is very agile and keeps Jack tense.

ZEUS

You leettle bull . . . eef I hads you een the bullring back een Mejico City, I would shows you what me, zee famous Creesteeano Delgado Garceea del Ceeudad Laredo would do weeth you.

LYLA backs against the building with a hand partially covering her mouth, expecting the worst for this stranger.

ZEUS (CONT.)

First, I would tests your reflexes weeth zee red cape, like . . . thees and thees,

ZEUS flips the bandana across Jack's face twice. Jack puts up his hands too late to defend himself.

ZEUS (CONT.)

and then two bright banderillas would be stucks eento your yellow keedneys . . .

Zeus's feint makes Jack turn a little sideways, exposing the right side of his back, which Zeus slaps loudly with his hand.

ZEUS (CONT.)

HERE . . . aaaaaand . . .

To Jack's shock, Zeus is able to trick him again so that Jack's opposite side is vulnerable, and Zeus accurately strikes again.

ZEUS (CONT.)
HERE.

ZEUS pauses and turns his back to Jack to show his mastery of the "bull."

ZEUS (CONT.)
That would makes zee blood to flow, and I likes zee smell of first blood.

Zeus turns around and pauses again, chest out, composing himself for the buildup to the finale.

Lyla's hand comes down from her mouth to expose a smile. Jack looks so silly that her hand goes back up to muffle a giggle.

Then I would takes my sword, razor-blade sharp Toledo steel, and slightly bent zee last five of the thirty-one eenches . . .

ZEUS's hands outline the shape of the invisible sword and does so delicately as if the instrument were sharp.

ZEUS (CONT.)
. . .and out of your fear you would charges and I would sleeps zee sword . . .

Again, Zeus is able to completely fool Jack, who is surprised again with a solid tap from Zeus on his collar bone.

ZEUS (CONT.)
THERE . . .

ZEUS stands with right arm raised, statue like, as if waiting for the right moment.

ZEUS (CONT.)
. . . above your collar bone, plunging eet down teell I can feels a slightly stronger reseestance, your heart, then . . .

ZEUS slowly moves forward with arm upraised, then comes down quickly toward Jack's chest.

ZEUS (CONT.)
OOMPH . . .

Even Lyla has started to believe the melodrama and is caught by surprise.

JACK
OOMPH!

The air goes out of Jack's lungs when he is struck.

LYLA
(stifles a scream)
Oh!

Lyla again raises her hand to hide an embarrassed giggle.

ZEUS keeps his eyes on Jack's chest as if he can see his heart being punctured.
JACK is still being backed up and is living Zeus's drama of his death by sword.
ZEUS (CONT.)
. . . drives through your slimy heart, keeling you eenstantly, dropping you een a pool of your own blood . . . weeth the cheers of zee arena een my ears.
JACK turns and slinks around the corner as Zeus takes dramatic bows in three different directions, stopping with a long, low bow to Lyla.
JACK
Your Mexican ass is grass, loser. Like green grass, like green card green.
ZEUS
'ey, you. Zee fat bull always gets zee green grass before zee JACK-ass . . . eets the same thing 'ere.
(to Lyla)
These street rats sure spook eesly.
LYLA and ZEUS continue toward the church.
ZEUS (CONT.)
Lyla, you promeeses to not do thees kind of thing again no more? 'ey?
LYLA
(always compliant)
I promise.
Lyla walks with Zeus as if they were father and daughter.
    CUT TO:
EXT.--ALLEY WHERE POLICE CAR IS PARKED--NIGHT
JACK leans into the car and waves his hands madly.
BERT, the middle-aged, uniformed policeman in the car, leans away from Jack's face.
BERT
Shut up, Jack, and get your, uh, stinking breath away from my nose. Don't you ever, uh, floss?
JACK finally pulls his head out of the car window, but continues to wave and dance.
BERT (CONT.)
You know I've always taken good care of this, uh, neighborhood, so stop making a scene.
JACK
I mean it. You got to do something. He's a menace to our neighborhood. I bet he doesn't have a green card.

Jack waves some bills and drops them inside the car.
BERT
I'll check on it. Get out of here before, uh, someone sees us together. I've always, uh, been an honest cop. I've got a good reputation around here.
    CUT TO:
INT.--CHURCH
PEDRO is sitting beside a metal wastepaper basket, inside of which is paper and wood on fire, producing the only light and heat.
ZEUS
Hey, leettle goat. We gots guest for deenner. Sets zee table weeth our finest.
ZEUS puts down the food and lights a couple of candles from a box near the door, puddles a little wax on the folding table at each end and sticks one candle in each puddle.
PEDRO
The name's Pedro, Crazy. Why'ja bring a whore in here? You really are crazy.

Chapter 14. House and Home

The door chimes sounded and Miss Ardnas looked out of the door window to see a stranger with a briefcase in his hand. Oh, no, an insurance salesmen, or someone from Franklin's lawyer with a subpoena or a restraining order.

"Hello. May I help you?"

"Good evening, are you Ardnas Wright?"

Oho, here it comes, though Miss Ardnas. "Yes."

"My name is Edgar Dorsey. I'm the Court Appointed Special Advocate assigned by Judge Fulbright to your custody case.

"Come in."

"Do you have time to answer some questions?"

"Sure." They sat down across from each other in the living room.

"Hey, Mom. Come shoot some baskets," yelled Cam. "Oh, sorry. Later."

"Cam, this is Edgar Dorsey. He's working for the court."

"Hi, Mr. Dorsey."

"Hello, Cam."

"Later, Mom."

"Here's my CASA certification and appointment notification from the court. A CASA represents children in a custody case, because the parents or grandparents in the case usually have attorneys representing their interests, but the child is the biggest concern, so judges want to hear the opinion of an unbiased third party."

Miss Ardnas took the court order and nodded.

"We're not attorneys, but we are trained to be advocates. I will interview everyone who has close contact with your children, look at all court documents, have a criminal background check done on you and Mr. Wright, visit the children at school, see them interact with both parents and then write a case study and make recommendations to the judge concerning the disposition of the children. You will receive the case study too."

"Ok."

Mr. Dorsey began by asking questions that were personal and at times embarrassing. *Do you have children by another man, where have you worked, did you graduate from high school, do you get along with your in-laws, do you have a current boyfriend or significant other of either sex, have you ever been treated for an emotional or mental illness, have you ever used physical punishment to discipline your children, did your husband ever use physical punishment, how much money do you make a month, do you have any major debts, have you ever hit your husband or has he ever hit you, do you have any guns in the house, do you drink or have you ever used drugs, if so, how often, etc.?*

The interview went on for more than two hours, with Cam checking back to see if his mom was free and April swinging through, being introduced, and disappearing to her room. Mr. Dorsey left and Miss Ardnas felt like someone had hooked the vacuum to her chest and sucked all the energy out. She went over every question and second guessed how she should have answered. Yes, she liked a glass of wine; yes, there were some guns in the house that Franklin had forgotten to take; yes, she had smoked marijuana a couple of times with Franklin; and, yes, she had spanked Cam once after the third time he had gone against her warnings, moved a chair to an upper pantry cabinet and pulled down bottles of Draino, bleach, muriatic acid, vinegar and ammonia.

She went to the mirror and noticed there was a wine stain on her blouse. Her hair was pooched out on one side, and her slacks had some paint drops. When Mr. Dorsey arrived, she had just finished dressing to mop some dust bunnies from under all the beds. What must the CASA have thought, she wondered. Cam had had on mismatched clothing—a striped shirt and shorts with palm leaf designs and his tennis shoes were filthy. At least April had been clean and dressed nicely.

Then Miss Ardnas looked around the living room as if through the eyes of Mr. Dorsey. The pillows were tossed carelessly on the sofa, magazines were scattered on the coffee table and a Coke can was lying next to where Cam usually sat. She also noticed some popcorn remnants next to the can. Why didn't the CASA call first? thought Miss Ardnas. The answer came to her: he probably wanted to see things as they typically were.

She wondered what Mr. Dorsey would write in his report. Her throat tightened and tears came to her eyes. Had she paid enough attention to Cam and April when they came through the living room? Had the CASA seen the wine stain? What else might he have noticed that seemed ordinary to her?

She didn't hate anyone, yet she felt she was getting close to hating the person she had once most loved, Franklin. She wondered why he had to put her and the children though so much hell, especially when he was the one at fault for the breakup of the marriage.

She had to get her mind off her studies, so she called April from her room and met Cam outside with three gloves and a yellow softball. Both kids were on teams and loved to play a triangular game of pitch and catch with their mom. After an hour the kids decided they wanted to play some badminton, so Miss Ardnas went inside. She hated looking around the house for more CASA red flags so she went to her computer.

Discussions at Mark's Bible studies had broadened Miss Ardnas' view of the world and religion. She decided to add to her blog some ironic church sign messages and supposed commentary.

Religion: Three-for-One Sale

Sun-News and Times MMN

The sign in front of the Welden, Nebraska, Holiness Gospel Church, read: "Join Us. We Have the Real Truth." The next week it read: "Three-for-One Sale: Father, Son and Holy Ghost." The other five churches in Welden didn't respond formally, but the local paper, Welden Weekly, was swamped with letters to the editor.

"God's not for sale. To sell something, you have to own it. Nobody owns God," wrote Sally Jenkins.

"If Holiness Gospel has the truth? What do the rest of our churches have? The lie?" added Max Lawson, in another letter to the editor.

Nancy Falon wrote, "I take offense at the Holiness Gospel sign that made claims that they are the 'Full-Gospel Church.' What does that make my church, First Methodist? Are we preaching the one-quarter gospel or the one-half gospel? 'Pride goeth before a fall.'"

"I think it's funny that these Christians are arguing about who owns God. God's original favorite was obviously the tiny Jewish tribe. The Jews, Muslims, Catholics and Christians worship the same God, but they all claim that the God of their religion is different and the true God. With that kind of logic, can any religion attract intelligent believers?" submitted Johnny Smith.

According to the Welden Weekly, Holiness Gospel continues to change its sign weekly. With the controversy about Holiness Gospel's signs getting play in state-wide newspapers, the Welden Weekly received another letter after the posting of the latest sign: "God only wrote one book. Shouldn't you read it?"

A letter from Akmed Hussein read: "One fourth of the world's population is Muslim, and their holy book is the Quran, which is a direct recitation from God to Mohammed. Get out of Welden once in a while and discover the rest of the world."

Concerning the signs, Reverend Sandy Godfrey, pastor of the Holiness Gospel Church, was quoted as saying, "We are what we are because God is what he is and the truth is truth."

Chapter 15. Bible Study

"Science and Christianity" was the topic of the Bible study organized by Mark but led by Jake this time. This was a topic that most Bible studies wouldn't tackle, or, if they did, it would be a one-sided affair, with most people being yes-men rather than seekers of truth or at least reason. Luckily for the health of this pseudo-congregation, most of the super fundamentalists had left the group long ago. Questioning church dogma or Bible interpretations that they had learned as children was part of their makeup. It had hardened like poured concrete and was a solid foundation for all their current understanding of life on earth and their actions.

Jake started the meeting with a prayer for peace in the world and the subtle assistance provided by our personal angels. Jake wasn't much into praying for major interventions that were contrary to the laws of physics. He had experienced minor physical assistance when his life was in danger that he had no scientific explanation for. This made him accept the possibility of angels.

"So, can science and Christianity coexist?" asked Jake.

"Of course. They have to. They do now," responded Jenni.

"Yes, but there are still problems with people refusing to put evolution in science textbooks."

"Teaching evolution doesn't bother me."

"Well, it does me," interjected Briana.

"Why?" asked Jenni.

"I don't think we came from monkeys or slugs or amoebas."

"What did we come from then, Adam and Eve?"

"Yes. That's what the Bible says," stated Brianna.

"And they had Cain and **Ab**el and Cain and Abel married and had children and populated the world. Who did those two boys have children by, their mom, their sisters by Adam and Eve, other women from other tribes that were already on the earth?"

"I don't know," admitted Brianna.

The discussion went around in circles for a while, with several people reading aloud sections from Genesis. Finally Mark asked, "What is the history of the battle between scientific discoveries and a literal translation of the Bible?"

"Didn't a lot of scientists get in trouble for stating that Genesis wasn't fact?" asked Jake.

"Yes, I'd say that is still a problem," continued Mark.

"My questions is: 'Why do we have to make science and the Bible agree? Science is an empirical pursuit and religion is spiritual. It's hard to argue with science if the facts are proven," said Jake.

"Yeah. Why is the church so slow in accepting scientific breakthroughs? They tried to deny that the earth was round, that the earth wasn't the center of the universe, and now, despite lots of DNA evidence, that man is not related to the gorilla," posited Jenni.

"I read that we share 96% of our DNA with gorillas. I feel like eating a banana whenever I think about that," added Jake.

"If you don't shave closer, Jake, you'll start looking like a gorilla," quipped Duke.

"Why does it take Christians a hundred years to accept a new scientific fact? They seem to have to fight against changes in their beliefs despite evidence. It'd sure be easier if they caught up to reality instead of thinking of the Bible as their science textbook."

"I see the Bible as Jewish history, as told by the Jews. I'd suspect we'd get a different version if the Egyptians or Canaanites had written it. I can just imagine the Canaanites writing: 'The Jews invaded our land, killing our men or making them slaves, marrying our wives, and enslaving our children. They said their merciful and all-powerful god wanted the Israelites to have our land. Well, that's not what our god wanted. The Jews must have a different definition for merciful,'" added Miss Ardnas, who felt prepared to comment because of her recent blog posting.

"Much of the Old Testament is tradition, poetry, drama and short stories. It wasn't meant to represent real people in every chapter. The authors used allegories just as Jesus employed parables in the New Testament," put in Mark.

After the Bible study, Brianna cornered Mark and asked, "Why are you so hard on Christians? I thought you were a Christian."

"Brianna, I am. I love Jesus more than anything, but I dislike the lack of common sense exhibited by the Church. As you can tell by the discussion tonight, the Christian church has a long record of being stubborn. It talks about faith as the key, but then pretends that faith is fact. It can't be both ways. If you rely on faith you can continue your beliefs no matter what, but if you're pretending faith equals fact, then the Church has to defend itself against any questioning of their facts. If what they have said is true is proven false, who's going to listen to them, send them money, give them power or buy their songs or books. The Church has lost its way."

"I see what you mean."

"I have faith that God didn't want every nation, every tribe, every religion to hate each other and to want to kill those who didn't belong or believe as they did. But that's where we are today. Christians basically tell all other religions: 'You're going to hell because you don't believe Jesus was a God.'"

"Is that how the world sees Christians?"

"How else would they see them? Missionaries don't go to other countries to discuss what Christians and those of other religions have in common. They go to make converts to Christianity. If they say that the local religion is a good way to become one with God, then why would anyone of another religion change?"

"They probably wouldn't," concluded Brianna.

"We talk about diversity and inclusion, but we tend to continue with or fall back on tribalism. I'm Catholic, he's Mormon, she's Hutterite, they're Muslims, he's French, she's Buddhist, I'm Irish or they're rednecks and I'm a college grad, I live in a mansion and they live in a rental and on and on. We have an infinite number of ways to divide one man from another."

"I guess you're right."

"Christians who make a living from Christianity, that includes missionaries and evangelists, have to convince other people that they have the only truth. Which is a joke, because we don't know the truth. God holds the truth. We have to depend on faith, not fact. If we had fact, everybody would be Christian and ministers, Christian song writers, Bible study authors and others would be out of the job of convincing people to believe and reinforcing beliefs on a daily or weekly basic. Belief takes constant reinforcement; fact is a onetime thing. But most TV ministers and others know people want fact, so they pass belief on as fact. Is there a god? I believe so. Is the red stove burner hot? Of course. I'm not in the job of telling people my belief in God and admiration for Jesus is based on fact. They have to come to their own understanding through knowledge and spiritual experiences."

"Well, I do believe that too."

"Somehow we have to reduce the importance of tribalism. I heard former President Clinton say that humans of every race or gender are 99.9 % the same, so that makes our differences only 00.1%. Yet we act like being Chinese versus Mexican is a big deal, or being a Hindu rather than a Jew super important in our relationships, marriages and business deals. Clubiness in the world proves to be very divisive and causes wars. We've got to stop the fraternity/sorority mentality and think of all people as basically equal of our time and attention. We need to make decisions in business not on gender or a good-old-boy paradigm but on education, knowledge, endeavor, talent and experience. We need…"

"You're on a roll, Mark," said Brianna with a grin.

Kae contributed: "I knew a man who had to put down on federal forms that his daughter was Black. She had been born in America. The girl's mother was blonde and blue eyed of Irish and Spanish decent but born in Germany, and her father was an American of Kenyan, English and Mayan decent. One time he filled in the blank with 'Irish, Spanish, Kenyan, British, Germanic, Mayan Indian, Black, White, Hispanic person. In a word, American.' The government employee didn't have a sense of humor. I agree about not labeling and pigeonholing people for the sake of data for a bureaucracy. If they labeled this multinational, multi-racial girl Black, obviously any correlations or conclusion drawn from the data will be flawed. All this exclusiveness of races and religions led me to become a Baha'i follower when we lived in Chicago, but there's no devotional group in Wyandotte. I kind of like Unitarian-Universalist churches too, but, again, Wyandotte doesn't have one."

"All people, whatever their background, basically want the same things in life. When you ask people what kind of life they want to live, they don't say *I want to hate and kill the people in the next country. Then I want them to retaliate and kill some of my people. After that I want to blow up a few cities. Or I want to dominate everyone where I live the way the mafia or a despot does. I want to do that until I make the people so mad they throw me in jail or rise up and kill me,*" said Mark.

Kurj commented, "I've never had a Christian I've met, except Mark, say to me: 'You're Muslim? I'm Christian and I've never talked religion with a Muslim. I read that one-fourth of the world's people are Muslim. I want to know more about how you worship God and the secret to the passion I hear about your believers.'"

Mark said, "Look at any ongoing conflict in the world and, I think, tribalism is involved. Every ethnic group that was thrown together into an artificial nation after some war has been trying to cede from that nation ever since. What does that eventually cause? Civil war and ethnic cleansing!

"Ok. The sermon is over. Sorry, I get wound up. It's a sore point with me. I read history and watch news, and tribalism, whether religions, ethnic, social or economic, seems to be ruining the world. We can't live in a global society saying, 'My little patch of earth and flag are the best, my religion is the true one, my race is more intelligent and ambitious than yours, I'm more important because I own more things—I, my, me, my, mine.' Should we be insinuating, 'Your country is not the best, your religion is all wrong and you're not very intelligent and deserving of success—take that!'"

"Listen," interjected Naomi. "I talked to many Muslims when I was in Tajikistan. One, Shabnam, argued with me about which religion was the true one. I told her that I had read the Quran. She wanted to know if, now that I had read God's actual words as recited to Mohammad, I was going to become Muslim. I told her no, and she didn't understand why I wasn't going to switch religions. When I thought about it more, I realized that if I had been born in Tajikistan, which is almost 100% Muslim, I would now be Sunni Muslim, and, if my Tajik friend Shabnam had been born in rural Kentucky, she would probably now be a Christian, protestant Baptist. My Buddhist friend Benjakalyani from Thailand, if born in the United States, would also be a Christian now. I told this to Shabnam and she just looked at me puzzled. That's the lack of global understanding we have and why there's so much tension and violence between nations and religions. Man has 6,000 years of recorded history, and thousands more of oral history. It's embarrassing that we have not become wise enough to live in together."

"Ok, folks," broke in Jake. "Time's up. Mark will be in charge of the Bible study next week. Have a safe trip home. Uh, wait, Jenni's trying to get my attention. She's at the door, so I'll let her tell you what she wants. Good night."

Jenni was hugging everyone and chattering like crazy. Duke was sitting by himself with a blind puzzle to his ear. He had a pencil and paper in front of him. He was waiting patiently for Jenni, who liked to talk for hours after a meeting if she could find an ear or two. Duke on the other hand was fine with being a wallflower.

"What are you doing?" Laura asked Duke. "Oh, your puzzle. Why do you like those so much?"

"As I tell everyone, now we see through a glass darkly, or, more precisely, into a poorly silvered looking glass or mirror. Life is like this puzzle. We use our senses to make sense out of the twists and turns of this maze we live in called life."

"I see."

"I listen to the sound of the ball bearing as it meets different objects, walls, baffles, doors, flaps, hurtles, cogs, and so forth. Then I try to make a diagram of the way I want to try to turn the box, twirl the knobs or move levers next to get the steely to overcome obstacles and out of the box. That's why I come to Bible study and like the approach Mark takes. He doesn't tell me things are black and white, dogmatic, he just says let's continue to try to figure out why we're on earth and how we should live life—come out correctly on at the end like the ball bearings. Jesus is a great model, but he's not the only one."

"Do you think I could solve one of the blind puzzles?"

"Sure. You just have to follow the hints your fingers, eyes and ears give you as you look at the holes, feel vibrations and hear rolling and knocks, then image what the inside of the box looks like. It's like trying to figure the path God wants us to follow. Look at all the hints he has spread around the world to every tribe. I just wish more people would search for and take the hints instead of thinking they know the truth already without exploration and analysis."

"Am I that way?" Laura asked with a half chuckle.

"I don't think so. You're here, aren't you? You continue to learn and explore. I would never be able to solve one of these puzzles if I started by thinking I knew exactly how the labyrinth was designed and employed only one method to solve it, over and over, even if it didn't make sense. It's not a jigsaw puzzle with the completed picture on the cover of the box. I can't imagine living my life thinking I knew all the answers, the truth. Someday in another world, I will know everything, see face to face, as the Bible puts it."

"You're a different kind of guy, Duke."

"I hope so."

"So is Mark as a preacher. So many sermons I hear in church or on television are packed with logical fallacies—equivocation, post hoc ergo propter hoc, begging the question, faulty dilemma, ad hominem, non sequitur—that a decent high school debater would turn them upside down in a faceoff on stage. That's not true of Mark."

"Is that your basic philosophy?"

Duke pulled on the collar of his T-shirt and rubbed his hand through his grizzled hair. This was more talking that he was used to. "No. It's about half. What do you do with the new information is just as important. Sometimes I wonder what goes on in seminaries. Have you ever heard a minister preach about how God changed from the Old Testament to the New?"

"God doesn't change."

"I would give the seminarians homework that required them to substitute the name Jesus for God in a select handful of chapters of the Old Testament. Then they would have to come to class and discuss their opinion of God's, or Jesus's, behavior during the story of Job, David's life, the killing of the Egyptian firstborn, burnt offerings, the conquest of Canaan."

"Tough lesson."

"Ministers, who I assume have read the Bible, have to know that there's major differences between the vain and violent God of the Old Testament and the humble and merciful God of the New, but they don't talk about it. Figuring out a problem is just one step. Acting on the new knowledge is the second."

"Now you're sounding like a preacher, too."

"Sorry about that. One last thing. Some people are so insecure in their faith that they look for someone to show them one path and then keep them on it with dogma. Discussing that there might be paths, plural, in life or religion makes them very defensive about their path. That's part of the reason the world is so contentious and bellicose."

"I guess I'm one of those that would like one sure and absolute path."

"No you're not, or you wouldn't be asking questions and listening. You would be angrily defending your path, whether it was reasonable or not. Adventurous, curious, intelligent and evolving people are the ones most likely to take a road less traveled by. And, by the way, to quote my favorite poet, Wendell Berry, forgive me, Frost, 'If anything I've said sounds like I'm an authority, I apologize.'"

"Honey, let's get going," Jenni yelled to Duke.

Thanks to Jenni's prodding, Mark's Bible study group decided to continue the communion by going line dancing. As usual the Antler Inn was smoky, noisy and crowded. No smoking signs were posted on every wall and post, but smokers didn't pay any attention. Wyandotte's mayor, the chief of police, several town firemen, a couple of attorneys and the county prosecutor frequented the bar and never said a word. Of course, it hadn't been that many years earlier that the county had been dry, thanks to overt temperance campaigns by members of fundamentalist churches and the covert campaigns of the bootleggers selling whatever brand customers wanted from the trunks of cars parked on the town square. It's where the local police had received free liquor to look the other way.

William was reluctant about going, because he didn't know how to line dance, and he knew that when Duke and Madison dated they had frequented The Antler Inn with Sam and Jenni. Carrie Underwood's "Blown Away" was being sung fairly accurately by a little black-haired, bright-eyed, long-legged girl of about 18, with the band and backup singers performing behind her. She had on cutoffs, a white cowboy hat and boots. With a goodly length of leg showing, she had the attention of all the men in the room.

Duke offered to buy the first round and asked, "Is PBR ok?" and Mark, Naomi, Sam, Jenni, Miss Ardnas, Jake, Laura, Nurse Kae and Madison said, "Fine."

Kurj, a Muslim, didn't drink, so he asked for a Coke.

"I'll have a glass of merlot," said William.

Before the drinks came, Jenni was on the floor with a friend from another table. Duke just shook his head and grinned. She danced with the inhibition of a four-year-old, only she had perfect rhythm and she got every part of her body expressing the soul of the music.

People at other tables were leaning toward Mark's group to try to figure out what language Nurse Kae and Kurj were speaking to each other. It wasn't Nigerian or Pakistani; they were speaking English with Mande and Urdu accents.

The next song was "Pontoon," by Little Big Town. The floor was packed. Mark looked at Miss Ardnas but took Naomi to an open space, Duke captured Jenni, Jake and Laura joined them and Sam asked Miss Ardnas if she wanted to dance. Only Madison and William stayed seated. William looked like he thought he was too good for The Antler Inn. Kurj and Kae danced and danced well. A Black woman and an equally dark Pakistani received their share of surprised looks. With his Dockers, sandals, and polo shirt, William didn't exactly fit in with the T-shirt and boots crowd in attendance. Madison looked bored, but her feet were moving under the table to the beat of "Pontoon."

Everyone returned to the table with a lot of red on their cheeks, a little sweaty, jostling each other and smiling or laughing. Madison smiled too, but William looked gloomy.

"This band can sing," said Sam, as he clicked glasses with everyone at the table. Everyone was gulping their beers, catching their breath and listening for another good song.

"Cruise" by Florida Georgia Line got everyone up and back on the floor. Jenni, who had danced with another friend while the rest of her friends took their break, returned to the table for a quick sip of beer and went back with a third friend. Sam took Laura's hand, Jake asked Naomi to dance, so Duke swirled Madison out of her seat and headed to the dance floor. Miss Ardnas looked hopefully at William, but got no response. She scooted over two chairs so that she could be able to talk to him above the noise. He kept his eyes on Duke and Madison, who kicked and stomped in unison as partners should.

"How is the wine shop doing, William," asked Miss Ardnas.

"Fine."

"Has the economy downturn affected your business?"

"No."

"Got any vacation plans this summer?"

"No." He was still looking straight at Duke.

"Have you ever been here before? I'm not a big country fan, but Franklin and I used to come here every so often BC, before children."

"Really?"

Miss Ardnas gave up and enjoyed the music and the footwork of the dancers.

When the song was over Duke escorted Madison back to her chair. William jumped up and partially blocked Duke, who was pulling the chair out for her. As he did so William gave Duke a meaningful elbow to the ribs. Duke countered by putting all his weight against William's shoulder and kicking his feet out from under him. This was done in such a smooth manner that it made it look like William slipped on a spill.

"Oops. Watch it, pal, there's a slick spot here," said Duke loudly. As he helped William to his feet, he put his mouth close to Williams's ear and whispered with a grin to those at the table, "Do that again and I'll forget I'm a Christian." William brushed himself off and sat down with a white streak of emotion coursing down from his ear to his chin on both sides of his face.

The lead singer stepped forward and crooned into 'Over You" by Miranda Lambert. Duke corralled Jenni, Laura snuggled into Jakes arms, Sam asked Miss Ardnas to dance again and Mark took Naomi's hand. On the way to the dance floor, Duke stopped at William's chair, gave him a rabid dog stare with his eyes, but grinned with his teeth and said, "If you don't dance with this lovely, lonely girl, one of these good ole boys here is going to swoop her up and take her home with him."

Madison looked embarrassed, grabbed William's hand and led him to the floor. He held her tightly and she rested her head on his shoulders while they danced. Duke kissed Jenni on the lips, glanced over at William and Madison, caught William's eye and gave him a nod of approval.

The fun continued and William finally relaxed and tried some line dancing. William bought a round for everyone and drank a PBR himself. When he went to the restroom, Duke was at the next urinal.

"How's it going?" asked Duke.

"Better. Sorry about that out there."

"Me too."

"But thanks. Everyone needs a kick in the ass once in a while," confessed William.

"Glad to oblige."

The night ended without Mark dancing with Miss Ardnas. She had had a fantastic time and danced with everyone at the table, even William, but not Mark. He had been friendly with her all night, but she wondered why he hadn't asked her to dance.

Duke and Jenni went straight home. After a half hour of wrestling with Duke, Jenni yelled wahoo and drifted off to sleep. She discovered herself whirling in the arms of a stranger. She was wearing jeans and boots that became a jean miniskirt and high heels, which faded into a diaphanous cotton dress and dancing slippers. Her hair was long and brown instead of spikey blond and her dress stood out like the horizontal ring of a gyroscope. Then she dropped a thousand feet into wonderful deep sleep.

Worn out, Mark and Naomi also headed home to their separate rooms at Mrs. Grassley's, Naomi went to bed and Mark tried to unwind with *Hey, Zeus*.

******

ZEUS
Pedro, thees ees Lyla, my guest. Don't calls her any names and I won't calls you . . . well, you knows what. And my name ees 'ey Zeus.
The three sit down on two sides of the table on folding metal chairs.
PEDRO avoids Lyla as he would a beloved sister who has turned into a slut.
PEDRO
Where'd you get this, out of a garbage can?
ZEUS opens the box and takes a piece and begins to obviously enjoy the pizza.
LYLA takes some pizza and opens a Coke.
PEDRO finally gives in and takes a piece. They divvy up the breadsticks and Pedro and Zeus each take a can of Coke.
ZEUS
Stops! I forgots!
PEDRO
(rolling his eyes)
Now what!
ZEUS
No eat yet. Let's pray . . . Dios mio, we thanks you for thees day as . . . as weird as eet was. Thanks you for good friends Pedro and Lyla and Jaime and Nate and zee Browns. As for thees Jack hombre, please makes hees life meeserable for a few days before you forgeeves heem. Thanks for thees peezza eef eet don't geeves us sam-and-yellow and we haves to die. Ayemen
Zeus pauses, opens his eyes, looks into the dark corners around him, then continues.
P. S. Makes sure there are no hairy rats een thees place. I hates sleeping weeth zee hairy rats. Geeves me wooly goats any day or even an old stinky jackass. Ayemen . . . again.
PEDRO
No more with the goats! You're ruining my appetite. Let's eat.
    CUT TO:
EXT.--RESIDENTIAL STREET--DAY
ZEUS is seen standing next to one of many trash cans placed in driveways near the street. A garbage truck comes along and stops.
Zeus grabs the can and tosses the refuse into the compactor on the truck. He puts down the can and places the lid upside down on the can.
DAVE, 35, the driver, comes around just in time to see Zeus's actions.
DAVE
Hey, fella. What do ya think yer doin'?

ZEUS
Man, you gots a tough job here. I'll rides along weeth you and emptyies zee cans so you don't haves to keep getteeng out of zee truck.
DAVE
Beat it, Bud. I'm not looking for any help. I'm a one-man company.
DAVE gets back into the truck and drives to a position between the next two drives.
ZEUS trots like a sneak-thief along behind the truck out of sight of Dave's vision, empties the first can, then runs to the next driveway and is just emptying the second can when Dave gets out of the cab and comes around the back of the truck. Zeus is just standing there with an innocent grin on his face.
DAVE (CONT.)
You still here? I thought I told you to beat it.
ZEUS
Sometimes I'm likes zee short-eared jackass and don't 'ear too good. Besides, I'm bored and you could stand some 'elp and company.
ZEUS's manner is so non-threatening and friendly that it catches Dave off guard. So he starts talking to Zeus as if Zeus's actions make sense.
DAVE
I ain't got no money to . . . like pay you with, ya know.
ZEUS
I don't expects no pay. I'll just 'ang on back 'ere to feeneesh thees street. OK?
Dave's face shows disbelief, but he gives in. With Zeus's help the street is quickly serviced.
    CUT TO:
INT.--DAVE'S TRUCK CAB--DAY
DAVE
Hop in, buddy. We've got quite a few blocks to the next neighborhood, where . . .
(in British accent)
we're privileged to touch the trash of the rich and famous.
ZEUS
My name's 'EY ZEUS. Some just calls me Zeus. Como se llama, I means, what ees yours?
DAVE
Dave. Zeus, you're going to love this neighborhood we're going to. Even their trash cans look new and polished. And what's best, their trash doesn't stink.
ZEUS

Nor my farts, neither.
Both Zeus and Dave laugh.

******

Was I too preachy during our discussion about tribalism, thought Mark? Sometimes he felt like he was being as dogmatic as the people he criticized. He wondered whether those attending his Bible study were being fed or led by him. He wondered how Kae and Kurj, who had wider ethnic and religious experiences, thought about what was said during the meetings. Meanwhile, at their house, Kurj and Kae were continuing the discussion begun at the Bible study.

"A great example of 'tribalism' is how men treat women. In some countries the male 'tribe' believes it is better and has more rights than the female tribe," offered Kae. "Most people want to be able to brag that they're better than somebody, so some countries pass laws so that the male half the population can keep women subjugated and seemingly inferior."

"I've had guys ask me if I wanted to go to a pornographic movie. I asked them if they had a sister or daughter. Then followed that with something like, 'Would you like to see your wife, daughter or niece in a porn movie? These girls are someone's daughter or sister.'" said Kurj.

"Did that make them think? Not want to go? I bet they couldn't process that. Some customs are so ingrained that that they seem like natural laws to these men. My tribe is good and yours is bad."

"A student in a friend's university class I visited in Khartistan asked how many women I had in America. The poor girls in the class kept their heads down, but the boy was smiling and proud of his question. I told him I was married. He said that didn't matter, and went on to ask if I wanted a wife while I was in town. He said that Arabian men need lots of women. I was dumbstruck and silent. An English foreign exchange student asked the boy, 'Are you offering your mother or sister to our guest?' My teacher friend and I had to restrain the Khartistani student, but the Brit was getting subtle, favorable looks from the girls. Prostitutes that the men have sex with aren't nameless, faceless, sexual toys. As you said, they're someone's daughter, sister, mother, cousin or friend," said Kurj.

"That's sad. You have to pity the women but also the men who lack the confidence to compete fairly with women in the world."

"Later I met with a boy from the class for tea in the university canteen. I broached the subject with him. 'Do most men have sexual intercourse with women not their wives or girlfriends?' 'Of course.'

'Do women?' 'Oh, no.' 'Why not?' 'Only bad women do that.' 'Are the men who have sex with a bad woman bad?' 'No, the women are bad.' 'Do the men enjoy sex?' 'Yes.' 'Do women?' 'Women are not supposed to enjoy sex.' 'I thought Azeri men protected their women.' 'They do.' 'Then who are these bad women? Where do they come from?' 'The men aren't bad. These women are bad women.'"

"Did the boy ever understand what you were getting at?" asked Kae.

"No. The conversation just went around in circles. You know, Eve's to blame, the femme fatale. The prejudice is so ingrained that the double standard is invisible," concluded Kurj.

"Plus, the men like it the way it is. Intense fear of women motivates them. They don't want to give up power. They're like little King Davids," concluded Kae.

Kurj continued, "One girl in the class wrote a short story that described a country where women wore chadors and men, who got off easier, only had to attach blinders to their glasses or sunglasses when in the presence of women not of their family. If they were caught staring at a lady, they risked being whipped. If they yelled sexual comments to or whistled at or made lewd gestures toward ladies, they were jailed. Men were not allowed on the streets from 7pm till 9pm on Tuesdays, Wednesdays and Saturdays, so that women could take an evening walk, visit with friends, eat together at a restaurant and/or shop without fear of being harassed by men who were too weak to control their lust. During those hours, men were expected to stay home and take care of any family members. Shops and restaurants were only run by women during these hours.

"If a man was caught in a sexual act with a prostitute or someone not his wife, both were taken to jail, sentenced to serve time and fined. Plus their photos and names were published in a local newspaper. Anonymous monetary rewards were given for direct information leading to an arrest. Plus, women could be religious leaders. Well, I guess Christians aren't much better about empowering women. I went to a Khartistan church of Christian expats that didn't have a fulltime pastor. Men took turns giving the message. Not once in six months did a woman preach. Most Catholic and protestant churches still have a dominance of male priests and pastors. I'm getting away from the girl's story. She included other points about gender bias, but I don't remember them right now.

"My friend said he read it to his university students without revealing its author. Instead of feeling ashamed and realizing their bigotry, the boys just laughed. Most of the girls frowned and gripped harder on their notebooks and pens, furious. But some tried to laugh with the boys, because they didn't know what else to do.

"What amazed me in Khartistan, was that many people, including educated teachers I talked to, loved their president. If you made a list of behaviors exhibited by dictators, this man would have a check mark next to each item: exterminate or jail opposition, cheat during elections; change the constitution so that he could be president-for-life; have affairs; control newspaper and television reporting; steal money from the government and invest it in banks under his wife and children's names; fund beautification projects while not caring about education; name everything after himself and his relatives; take over the presidency after his father died as if the nation were a monarchy instead of a republic; put out propaganda on TV and billboards with his, his grandfather and his father's photo on them; not try to solve a long-standing military conflict with a neighboring country so that citizens focused on that instead of his corrupt actions. He was even named Most Corrupt Man of the Year by an international watch group," commented Kurj.

"Well, he's a smart guy. Most nations won't vote a president out of office in the middle of a war, and dictators keep education at a minimum so that the public won't become knowledgeable enough to figure out that he's a liar and a thief," said Kae. "I've read that the opposite is true, though. Educated people read more and are easier to propagandize. Look how many people were in favorite of some of America's wrongheaded, ill-fated wars."

Kurj added, "Instead of creating jobs he had walls built and trees planted to hide poor sections of town. All you see him doing on TV is meeting with an ambassador from another nation, cutting ribbons to open a new road or giving a speech at a conference about how he is going to end the war. Of course he has been giving the same speech for 14 years, but the citizens don't seem to notice. If you want to postpone taking action on any problem, the best thing to do is have a conference. Everybody leaves feeling there is hope, but all they do is have a similar conference the next year."

"Third-world countries still want a king. They say they want a democracy, but they don't understand it enough to make it work. Even in America the constitution keeps getting 'interpreted.' Look at President Carter, who basically told the public to stop being spoiled and sacrifice a little. The citizens voted him out and replaced him with

the glitz and Hollywood style of President Reagan, who, with Nancy, became America's virtual king and queen.
******

CUT TO:
INT.--CHURCH
PEDRO is stacking pews, sweeping around them, and putting pews together face-to-face with pads to make beds that will be off the floor.
LYLA, still dressed in her street clothes, tugging at different pieces to keep herself decent, comes over to help.
PEDRO
(defensively for no apparent reason)
Get away from me. I don't need no help from you.
LYLA
(kind)
Why not. I live here too. Let me sweep.
PEDRO
(pulls back broom)
Why did you do that crap? Don't you have no pride, puta? Don't you care for your family pride?
LYLA
It's a short story, Pedro.
PEDRO
What do I care.
Pedro pretends indifference, but is visibly angry or full of pity at different times during Lyla's story.
LYLA
First it was my stepfather . . . you know what . . . when I was fourteen . . . then his two sons when I was fifteen . . . so I quit school and ran away.
(begins to lose her composure)
My mom didn't really care, obviously. She was probably happy not to have competition or a comparison that proved her age. But with no education or nothing, I found the only value I had or ever have had was . . . well, I ended up on the street.
(in tears)
And, Jack Hadley, my man, looked after me for an eighty percent cut and . . . you know . . . special favors. It's better than home.
PEDRO
Ain't you got no brothers? Man, I would keel anybody that did that to my sister.

LYLA
Well, I promised Zeus I wouldn't do that no more unless I was married to someone I loved. I don't know how I can keep that promise, though. I ain't got nothin' else of value to sell or use to keep me alive.
PEDRO
Listen, man. Stay away from me. You're disgusting.
LYLA
(offended and countering)
What's your story, Pedro? What are you afraid of that makes you live here like a tramp? You've barely looked outside, let alone gone outside.
PEDRO
None of your business, perra. Now leave me alone. Besides, I ain't scared of nobody.
LYLA begins helping despite Pedro's attitude, but Pedro still avoids contact with her.
    CUT TO:
EXT.--WASHINGTON AVENUE IN WEALTHY NEIGHBORHOOD--DAY
After ZEUS empties several dozen trash cans, he comes to a can next to a nice sofa that is being discarded by the owners.
ZEUS
(yells to Dave in cab)
Man, I'd loves to 'ave thees sofa. That'd looks great where I leeves.
DAVE
(exiting cab and walking to sofa)
Well, let's get it for you. I don't want that clogging up my compactor anyway. The furniture from this neighborhood don't crush up like the stuff from mine. We'll tie it to the side here. Untie those ropes, Zeus.
    CUT TO:
INT.--DAVE'S TRUCK CAB--DAY
Zeus and Dave are driving through a residential district. Dave pulls to a stop.
DAVE (CONT.)
This is about as close as I can come to Manila Street and still make it to the landfill before it closes. You sure you can handle that sofa by yourself?
    CUT TO:
EXT.--MANILA STREET--DAY
ZEUS carries the sofa with much difficulty over his head toward the church.

BERT drives up beside him.
BERT
Hey, buddy. Your name, uh, ZEUS?
ZEUS keeps walking as fast as he can.
BERT is forced to keep up with him in the car, and to talk to a seemingly headless and bodiless pair of legs.
BERT sticks his head out the passenger's window to hear Zeus, which causes him to scrape his tires against the curb trying to get close enough to hear.
ZEUS
(muffled)
Yes, meester ossifer.
BERT
Huh?
ZEUS
(a little louder)
Yes, meester ossifer. That ees my name OK. What ees yours?
BERT
You got any personal identification, and, uh, . . . hey, you got a receipt for that, uh, brand new piece of furniture you got there?
ZEUS
(still muffled)
My identeefeecaseeon ees een my pocket, but I can't reaches eet right now, meester ossifer. Besides the sofa ees second-hand.
BERT pulls his head back into the car and stops, then he begins to get out of the car.
Just as his foot touches the grass, his radio squawks and he gets back inside the car to hear something on his police radio, then he turns it up to listen more carefully.
BERT
You're lucky this time, Zeus. I gotta go, but next time I meet you, uh, I'm going to see your identification papers. You'd better have them or you're going to, uh, take a short trip to jail or a long trip to Mexico.
ZEUS
OK, meester ossifer. I'm always leestening to zee poleece.

******

Mark hesitated and wondered how Miss Ardnas had enjoyed the evening.

Since Cam and April were staying at friends for the night, Miss Ardnas went home to a haunted house. She had so many good memories of the house and also where she and Franklin lived before they had children. Line dancing with the opposite sex and slow dancing in the arms of a man at the Antler Inn made her lonesome for male company. She remembered when she and Franklin had had evenings dancing, kissing and holding each other closely at nightclubs.

Miss Ardnas thought of herself as somewhat of a creative lover. One of her typical tricks was played after they had spent the night dancing while wrapped in each other's arms. Both she and Franklin couldn't wait to get home and into bed, but that's where Miss Ardnas' fun began. Franklin would let Miss Ardnas off at the front door and then drive to the unattached garage, get out of the car, open the garage door, get back into the car, drive it into the garage and get out and put down the door.

 Meanwhile Miss Ardnas would run up to the bedroom, hurriedly take off her coat, pull her dress off over her head and kick off her shoes. Then she would put on a camisole, followed by a short-sleeved T-shirt, a long-sleeved T-shirt, and a sweatshirt. Then she would pull on some running shorts, jeans and sweat pants. A pair of cotton socks would be covered with some long wool stocks. Then she would top all that with Franklin's heavy robe.

By the time he was done putting the car away, she would be back down stairs and sitting on the porch swing with two beers. Franklin would give her a weird look, take her hand and lead her upstairs to the bedroom. She'd play pussycat and flop on her back on the bed, arms spread wide and whisper with a silly grin, "Take me."

She refused to help as Franklin literally disrobed her, which started out with smiles and giggles but turned serious as a scattering of clothes began to cover the floor. Once in a while she would whisper again, but this time, "Hurry." Both were moist with perspiration by the time their bodies were bare and touching. Needless to say they added several years of wear and tear to the mattress, pillows, bed slats and headboard during those nights.

Of course now she was alone, looking at her clock at 2 a.m., 2:30 a.m., 3:10 a.m., and 4 a.m. before she went to sleep on a tear-stained pillow.

******

CUT TO:
INT.--CHURCH
Pedro, Lyla and Zeus proudly and playfully try out "glamourous" poses on the "new" sofa, with Pedro always keeping Zeus between himself and Lyla, even if he has to sit on one of the arms to avoid her.
Then they move it to a new spot and play "musical chairs" again.

ZEUS
'ey, what you kids wants for supper tonight? 'ow about Chinese. I've been 'ungries for Chinese.
PEDRO
I hate Chinese. Besides you're going to get caught some day stealing pizza or Chinese or sofas.
ZEUS
I don't steals notheen'. I only takes foods and stuff that ees geeven to me.
PEDRO
Sure, and when I smoke a joint, I don't inhale.
ZEUS
(angry)
You smokes a joint een 'ere and I breaks every joint een your punys body.
PEDRO
Chill, man. I was just kidding.
    CUT TO:
INT.--CHINESE RESTAURANT
ZEUS stands in front of the owner, Kim Lung, at the cash register. Kim's son, Ralph, and daughter, Karen, are standing in the kitchen looking through the opening they pass food through to the waiters.
KIM
I no understand what you want. Want carry-out or eat-in?
ZEUS
(slowly enunciating)
No, no, no, what ees zee 'ardest and dirtiest work anyone 'as to do een thees restaurante?

Chapter 16. Walk in the Woods.

Before marrying Jenni, Duke had dated Madison, but it had been a purely platonic relationship, something many thought impossible between male and female heterosexuals. They were great friends, but somehow they had never clicked enough for it to become love. They had promised each other to continue to be good friends. She taught him a lot about history and he taught her about the outdoors. Jenni was fine with this; she wasn't the jealous type, but William didn't like it at all, especially since he could not get Madison tied down with a wedding ring.

Since it was summer, Madison was out of school, but Jenni was working at Hair U R and William was at his wine shop, so Duke took a day off work to hike in the woods with Madison. They headed for their favorite spot, which included a pond where they had once gone skinny dipping. She was hoping they would go again. She liked the freedom of no clothes and the slight pressure all over her body of the water. It was probably a prenatal recollection. It was also nice to spend time with a man who didn't hit on her. She felt equal and free to just enjoy a relationship with a virile man that didn't have any tension attached to it.

"Close your eyes, Madison," commanded Duke. Then he crushed a bunch of leaves and put them to her nose.

"Yuck. What is that? Oh, I remember, skunk cabbage."

"I promise better smells to come."

They walked along and Madison told Duke about the end of school. She had had the students participate in a county-wide Model UN. It had meant a lot of preparatory work for her during school days and evenings and weekends. Her four groups were assigned Iraq, North Korea, Australia and Liberia. Her students assigned to represent North Korea especially had their work cut out for them. Trying to convince the rest of the countries—USA, England, Russia, France, Brazil, Argentina, China, etc.—that North Korea deserved nuclear weapons just as much as India, Pakistan, Israel and China produced a lot of loud debate.

"They didn't get anyone to agree with them to have nuclear weapons except for Iran."

"Was the simulation worth it?"

"Oh, yeah. It made world tensions and the negotiations that make the news come to life. I had the students do weeks of research about their countries' politics, enemies, ambitions, unique culture, religion and natural resources before going to Model UN. People who have not traveled have no idea that each country has superstitions, religions, food preferences, dating customs and taboos different from the ones in America. Without other places to intimately compare America to, many people don't consciously know of their own taboos, superstitions and prejudices. They've always been part of their lives."

"Excellent."

" One students research and ultimate opinion was insightful, He said he had read that America has 170,000 or more soldiers stationed in 150 nations, and more than 1,250,000 active duty personnel overall, while only 8,000 Peace Corps volunteers served in 74 counties. He added that he had studied American and world history by its wars. He thought it would be interesting if we labeled historical eras by periods of peace instead of wars or depressions. He said he would love a label, such as, The Second Pax Americana, like the Pax Romana during the 1st and 2nd centuries."

"I guess the simulation was worth it."

"I want to continue to build on it every year I teach."

"Close your eyes again."

"Maybe I don't want to. The last smell is still in my nose."

"Come on."

"Okay."

"Here."

"Oh, nice. Pine needles."

"Close enough, sap from a cedar. Keep them closed."

"Wow! What's that? It smells like onion."

"Very good. It's chives or wild onion."

"Are they edible?"

"Sure."

They walked on kicking acorns, walnuts and hickory nuts, most of which no longer had a hull and had been either emptied of their meat or discarded by squirrels as worthless.

"If you were Iran or North Korea and you wanted nuclear weapons because you felt threatened, what would you do?" asked Madison.

"Probably the same thing they're doing. I wish no one had the bomb, but as paranoid as a big country like the US is about enemies, you can imagine what a tiny country feels like. The US has bases, CIA, naval ships and so on all over the world. It seems like Russia, America and China try to make everyone afraid of them with constant saber-rattling, surveillance and sanctions. What if the Arab nations that produce oil put sanctions on the US because of our attacks or interferences in Libya, Pakistan, Afghanistan, Iraq, Egypt, etc.? That's not including the US's fiddling in all nations' internal politics."

"Yeah, I know. We see ourselves as having God and the world on our side. It's hubris. Boy, are we ever wrong! Naomi has traveled in that part of the world and told me they don't understand why we killed all those innocent Iraqi fathers. They didn't want to fight. They were forced into the Iraqi army and dropped their guns and ran away from America's firepower as soon as they were out of Saddam Hussein's lethal reach."

"I don't understand our own country at times," commented Duke.

"The Arabs especially didn't understand why, when the US wanted to oust Saddam Hussein, they blew up Baghdad's water and electrical system. That mostly hurt the citizens. Why were those military targets?"

"I'm tired of our country going around blowing things up. What do we expect to happen in the States if we keep going other places and bombing them or stationing troops in foreign countries?"

"They're going to bomb us too," put in Duke.

"I'm afraid so. You can't keep having aircraft carriers pointing weapons at everyone around the world and not have them eventually get pissed off," said Madison.

"And they probably would love to have military bases on American soil. Can you imagine if we had a Russian base in Florida, a Chinese base in California, an Iranian base in Nevada or an Argentinian base in Texas?"

"Where do we have bases or troops stationed? I think Cuba, Germany, South Korea, Italy, Brazil, Japan…and at least a dozen more places. Let me check on my Android. Looks like more than a 100. Unbelievable!" reported Madison.

"Enough politics. Let's have fun. People are always warning others not to discuss politics and religion with friends."

"What's more important than your soul and finding ways to live peacefully with the world? If we can't put our souls into politics, then we're doomed. I always wished there was something called Ethical Capitalism."

"Close your eyes. Deep breath," instructed Duke.

"Oh, I know this one. Root beer."

"Right, sassafras."

"We're at the pond," said Madison. "You go play hide with your face against that tree and count to ten while I disrobe--nice term this disrobe, hey? Then I'll dive in."

"Where's the seek part of hide and seek?"

"You're an old married man now. No peeking."

"Ok, and same for you when it's my turn to disrobe, as you call it."

The two friends bobbed and dived and splashed each other and spouted water from their mouths like two prepubescent playmates, oblivious to the other's sexuality. They tried to dunk each other. If there had been an Eden, this must have been how Adam and Eve lived.

Madison's problem was that she loved Duke but didn't want to make love with him, and she wanted to have sex with William but wasn't sure she loved him. She could understand why so many people just lived with someone of the opposite sex. They wanted to make love or they wanted to be loved, even though both seldom happened in the same relationship. She guessed she wanted both at the same time for a lifetime, which seemed to her like the fairytale to end all fairytales.

Chapter 17. Surprise

Mark received a call from Pastor Bob with an invitation to meet him at Denny's Restaurant. Mark was glad that he had talked to Jake about Stan's behavior at church. He was sure Jake would see that there were no more interruptions.

"Pastor Bob. How are you?"

"Ok. Mark. And you?"

"Still kicking. Hey, I think you'll be glad I talked to Stan's son about Stan's behavior at church. His actions were terrible and Jake apologies. He'll probably give you a call to tell you himself."

"Well, that's not the worst."

"Oho. What now?"

"It's about you."

"Me. What about me?"

"Well, people think you're the cause of spiritual unrest in the community, especially the churches."

"Really?"

"Yes, my church board members and elders are friends with your former church board members. They have talked about why your former church let you go."

"Oh, no."

"Yes, and they don't like you attending my, our, or, let's say, the Wyandotte Followers Church."

"Ok. I don't want to be a negative impact."

"I don't like this. It's like a mini witch hunt or the Spanish Inquisition."

"I wonder what's going on."

"I think it has a lot to do with the TV ministries. They're always preaching about false prophets, the Antichrist, etc."

"They think I'm a false prophet? The title prophet is quite an honor but I don't like the false part."

"'Beware of false prophets, which come to you in sheep's clothing, but inwardly they are ravening wolves. Ye shall know them by their fruits.' During your ministry and especially since, you have consistently done the Lord's work, produced Christian fruits, so I don't know what's bothering the elders of my church."

"But, remember, if I'm seemingly going against dogma or what they see as biblical truth, then they see me as bearing false fruit."

"Well, that's maybe it," said Bob.

"I have not tried to proclaim the 'truth' to anyone. Instead I try to facilitate understanding, growth, inclusion. Some of the TV ministers are constantly talking about false prophets, which make people assume the minister speaking is not one and has the only truth. It's a good money maker and source of power to proclaim the 'truth,' even though the Bible talks about believing, about faith, faith in things unseen."

"I'm not against you. You have done more to help all classes of people in this community than anyone. Your mission trips are awesome, and our church, up till now, has appreciated your assistance with our youth outings to Cincinnati."

"I love those block parties in rundown neighborhoods your youth group organizes. No preaching, just social communion. If I can't be a part of your church anymore, I will miss them and the kids."

"I can't seem to be able to convince them they're wrong, and I don't want to tell you not to come to our church. I don't agree with some of your beliefs, but that's also the case with the Mormons, Mennonites, Muslims, Lutherans, Catholics, Jews, Jehovah's witnesses, and other religions or denominations. You know what? I've thought about resigning over this."

"Please don't do that. That would probably add fuel to the fire that I'm disrupting religion in Wyandotte. I'll not come to church anymore, unless they start to feel differently. I don't want to be a negative influence, but I guess I already have been."

"Some leaders in my congregation aren't very open-minded. They're good people, but they can't understand your approach to accepting world religions as viable. I guess I don't understand either, but I don't see any harm in exploring God's word and seeing how the rest of the world fits in."

"Well my understanding of the Book of John is that God sent the Word to man, the Word was Love personified and He told us to follow this Love incarnate. Then 'the church' started making rules and making salvation more complicated than just following the Word (Love) which has led to selling indulgences, creating the idea of a trinity of gods, Holy Wars--there's an oxymoron--amassing treasures in the Vatican, inquisitions, creating empires that include Protestant church organizations, colleges and TV ministries, cults and so on. Simple churches grow to two churches, then to 100 and then there's a big money-hungry business to feed, along with bishops, directors, headquarters, high-maintenance churches that are empty 90% of the time, and lots of waste. What happened to taking care of the widow and orphans and loving our neighbors? 'Where your treasures are there will your heart be also.' When I'm talking political or religious corruption, Naomi always quotes Watergate's Deep Throat: 'Follow the money.' "

"You have a point."

"Plus, I know people of many Protestant religions and people of world religions who live Christian lives, who follow Jesus' ways better than many so-called Christians, yet they are told that an omniscient, omnipresent and omnipotent God is so vain that they will be damned to hell by him if they don't praise his name only. They're told that God, for some human-like reason, plays favorites and only manifests himself to a tiny Jewish tribe or to religions that sprung from the God of the Jews. I don't want the world to think that way, to think of Jesus that way or to think of Christians that way. I do go on, don't I? Sorry, I guess I miss giving sermons, but with you, most likely I'm preaching to the choir or being blasphemous."

"That's okay. I would be, well, I guess I am, upset too."

"It just seems like the lack of knowledge and experience makes people more prejudice and the world doesn't need religious excuses to be prejudging. We already have a lot of tribalism. That's another one of my pet peeves—exclusiveness—what I believe is right and what you believe is wrong. We get enough of that in America with the knee-jerk Democrats and knee-jerk Republicans. Can't people see both sides of an issue or at least a little bit of someone else's reasoning?"

"I fear not. Don't think of yourself as the enemy, but I felt like I had to talk to you about what's going on at our church," stated Bob.

"Thanks for the heads up, Bob. You keep doing what you've been doing, because the ministry needs people like you. I'll try to lay low awhile. Since I attend all the churches, synagogues, cathedrals and other religious centers in town, this is going to be hard on me if this so-called excommunication spreads."

"Well, I hope it doesn't. God bless you, Mark."

"I need all the blessing I can get. May God bless you too, and your congregation and church leaders."

When Mark got home he spent an extra-long time losing himself in his screenplay.

******

KIM
(fake smile)
I wepeat. Want carry-out or eat-in?
ZEUS
(even more slowly enunciating)
No, no. What ees zee theeng that nobodies who works 'ere likes to do?
KIM
(smile fading)
I wepeat again. Want carry-out or eat-in?
KAREN sees and hears her mother's predicament and comes out of the kitchen to help. And, again, Zeus seems so innocent and friendly that they let him have his way.
KAREN
He wants to clean the toilets, Mom. You know, my usual job. I'll be glad to show him where they are.
KIM bows to Zeus.
ZEUS bows to Kim and Kim bows back. This goes on for several seconds.
KAREN, fully Americanized and impatient, grabs Zeus by the arm and leads him away.
Karen returns and walks over to her mom.
KAREN
He's harmless, Mom. He'll probably ask for a five to go get a bottle of cheap liquor or something. I'll be happy to give him a five just to not have to clean the restrooms myself.
    CUT TO:
EXT.--MANILA STREET--NIGHT
ZEUS is walking toward the church with a large cardboard box lid full of different-sized, white, carry-out boxes.
He passes the Brown apartment and Nate, Noela and Jefferson are all sitting on the steps eating ice cream cones.
ZEUS
'ey.
NATE
Hey.
JEFFERSON
(smiling)
Hey, man. That pizza I won was a real winner. Thanks.
ZEUS
Don't thanks me, eet was your good luck.
JEFFERSON

Sure. Well, I did have luck today. I got a good job . . . with benefits. We were ready to move, we were so broke.
ZEUS
Glad to 'ear eet. Keeps up zee good work. See ya.
NOELA
Bye, and thanks again.
ZEUS walks on and sees the bag lady.
MARLEEN has two shopping carts, one full of solid objects of different descriptions and one piled high with clothing. She is in the middle of the sidewalk.
ZEUS has to maneuver to get around her. Then he turns and notices she has both seen and smelled the Chinese food in his hands.
ZEUS
What ees your names?
MARLEEN
Marleen.
ZEUS
Well, Marleen, I'm 'ey Zeus and I'm 'aving a few peoples over for deenner tonight, just a small gathering of three. Would you likes to joins us and makes eet a fourth-some, or sometheeng likes that?
MARLEEN
(meekly)
OK.
MARLEEN humbly follows Zeus, who is now the leader of a small side-walk parade, considering how Marleen deftly pushes one cart and pulls the other and he is carrying the box lid in front of him.
    CUT TO:
INT.--CHURCH
The folding table is covered by open and partially empty Chinese food cartons.
ZEUS is leaning back on a pew, PEDRO has gone to his favorite corner to sit on the floor in the dark.
MARLEEN and LYLA are fixing up an area for Marleen to sleep, trying to arrange moveable bulletin board panels to make a more private ladies' area.
MARLEEN
Pardon my forwardness, but your clothes barely fit you.
LYLA
Yeah, I know. But it's all I got.
MARLEEN
(chuckling)

Come over here and let's look in my "traveling ladies' shop."
LYLA and MARLEEN, like mother and daughter, spend some time with clothes from the shopping cart, a hair brush, and some removal of old make-up. They finally come over to sit with ZEUS.
ZEUS
Dios Mio, who 'ave we 'ere? Muy bonita, señorita. Look, Pedro, a beauty contestant 'as comes to makes a veesit.
PEDRO notices the difference and his lack of words and his inability to look at Lyla more than a few seconds tell how much of an impression she has made.
ZEUS (CONT.)
I theenk tomorrow we looks for you a job, Lyla.
LYLA
Really, Zeus, I don't know how to do anything. I've never even had a job . . . well, you know, a really, honest job.
ZEUS
You see, zee lamb and zee goat don't stays together een zee mountain pasture forever.
PEDRO
(eyes rolling)
Oh, for crap sake! You keep telling pasture stories and I'm going to have to buy some hip boots.
MARLEEN looks more open and erect in the security of her new "home," and prepares to go to bed as if she has always lived in the church.
LYLA looks at herself in a small mirror.
    CUT TO:
EXT.--WASHINGTON AVENUE--DAY
ZEUS and DAVE are shown working the ritzy street together again. Parts of a bed are strapped onto different sections of the truck.
DAVE
Hey, Zeus, people are going to think I've gone into the used furniture business.
ZEUS
Good ideal, Dave. Maybe you gots a friend somewhere needs a job.
DAVE
(surprised)
You know I do, Zeus. My brother-in-law, Carl, over on Apple Street, is out of work, but he has a chance to lease a nice store front from a friend who is holding it for him.
ZEUS

Si.
DAVE
He can't afford any inventory, so he's about ready to tell him to drop the idea. He and I could fill that place up fast on this street. I can see it now, Carl's Pre-owned Furniture. That's the way those used car lots advertise on TV.
ZEUS
(worried)
Can we waits a leettle unteel I gets my place furnished first, Dave?
DAVE
(laughing)
Sure. There'll still be plenty for Carl.

******

Mark paused and wondered: "Is my Bible ministry doing the very thing I accuse other religious leaders of doing? Am I just plowing ahead not considering whether I'm going in the right direction or causing destruction wherever I go? Did God give us an absolute truth as many Christians say? If so, why can't I find it? Why can so many ministers stand in front of their congregations or audiences and proclaim the truth with such confidence while I plod along on faith? Why do I have to question everything? What's going to happen with the lives of Madison, William, Jenni, Duke, Kae, Kurj, Jake, Laura, Sam, Brianna and others, especially the youth? Why do I feel so responsible for their physical and spiritual wellbeing?"

He knew something was going to have to change in his life and in his thinking, or he felt that he would implode. He dove back into finishing *Hey, Zeus*.

******

CUT TO:
EXT.--THE CHURCH--DAY
ZEUS and DAVE are unloading the parts of the bed and handing them through the door to PEDRO.
CUT TO:
INT.--PIZZA PARLOR
Zeus and Lyla stand in front of the counter.
JAIME
Hey, Zeus. Man, things are still looking good in the back, and the boss did give me a little raise. Business still ain't great, though.
Jaime can't help but look Lyla over carefully.
JAIME (CONT.)
What can I do for you, Zeus, and who ya got with ya today?

ZEUS
Thees ees Lyla, and she ees looking for to works free for you tonight, JAIME, so she cans do some ray-sum-mee building.
(to Lyla)
You likes zee beeg word, 'ey?
(to Jaime)
You knows, she'll needs a commendation or something for 'er own real job one of these days.
JAIME
I don't know, Zeus. What'll my boss say? What if he comes in? I can't afford to get fired. I need this job.
ZEUS
Just tells heem the truth, Jaime. I'll comes back to peecks Lyla up about 11:00, after I've gotten supper somewhere.
JAIME
(Answering the phone and trying to stop Zeus)
Hello . . .
(to Zeus)
Now, wait a minute, Zeus. Zeus . . .
(to customer)
Hello, I'm here . . .
(to Lyla)
Where'd he go? . . .
(to customer)
Sorry. Hold one second, please.
JAIME hands the phone to LYLA with an order blank.
JAIME (CONT.)
Lyla, is it? Well, you my'swell start now.
(says rapidly)
Put check marks next to the correct style, size and ingredients on this form. Add up the amounts -- they're on this chart here -- and put the total at the bottom, repeat the order back to the customer, take his name and phone number, and tell him it'll be ready in 20 minutes.
LYLA calmly takes the order, despite the rapid directions she was given.
JAIME runs to the door to see if he can still catch Zeus. He looks down the street both ways.
JAIME
ZEUS . . . ZEUS . . . how in heavens did he disappear so fast?
When he comes back shaking his head, he looks over Lyla's shoulder at the order form, then begins putting the pizza together.

LYLA
(in a sweet voice)
Could I have your name and phone number, please? Thank you. Would you like breadsticks or drinks with that?
... Thank you, your order adds up to $19.75 and it'll be ready in just 20 minutes. We'll be waiting for you, Mr. Longley.
Not knowing LYLA's past successes as a "street saleswoman," JAIME's face shows his obvious pleasure as he listens to her handle the customer.
JAMIE
Sweet job, Lyla. How did you remember all those instructions and even ask about breadsticks and drinks?
LYLA
I don't know.
JAIME
Zeus was fooling me. You've done this kind of work before.
Although she tries not to show pride, a smile makes her face seem even more beautiful.
DWAYNE and AL
walk by the parlor window and look in and see Lyla. They stand at the screen door.
DWAYNE
I don't know what the pizza's like, but this looks to me like a good place to eat.
AL
(eyeing Lyla)
She gets ... I mean, it gets my vote.
  CUT TO:
EXT.--A KOSHER DELI--NIGHT
ZEUS looks over the menu on the window, then enters.
  CUT TO:
INT.--THE KOSHER DELI
ABE Steiglitz, the Jewish owner, about 50, dark hair, dark eyebrows, strong looking, average height, with hands on hips, glares down at Zeus from behind a low counter. Typical of foreign deli owners, he's overly emotional -- seemingly angry one second, joking the next and hugging someone the next.
ABE
What this is? I never heard like this nothin' before. Well, maybe I do need some help tonight, as long as your name's not Jesus Christ.
Abe is making an innocent, religious joke, and laughs loudly.

ZEUS
(seriously)
No, señor. Eet's 'ey Zeus Creesteeano.
ABE
(still laughing)
Just kidding, Mister Hey Zeus. What religion are you, anyway?
ZEUS
(thinking fast)
Ahhhhh. Pre-pressed-bap-terian.
ABE
Is that a Baptist church?
ZEUS
Yeah. That's eet. I'm parts Baptreest, I guess.
ABE comes around the counter and, with his over-friendliness, gives Zeus a crushing hug of acceptance and guides him toward the backroom.
    CUT TO:
INT.--THE PIZZA PARLOR
ZEUS, standing inside the door, is holding a large, white paper bag with STEIGLITZ DELI and a caricature of Abe on it. There are two people standing at the order counter, all tables are full of people, mostly men but a few couples, being served by Lyla.
LYLA is so changed in appearance that no one recognizes her as the girl on the street from just a few days ago. She, the former professional, is teasing and being teased by most of the customers.
JAIME is going crazy trying to keep up with orders, and, HECTOR, his sixteen-year-old cousin, is working behind the counter with him.
CUSTOMER
(to Lyla)
Marry me, baby. I'm in love.
Lyla is nodding toward a strange man who happens to be looking at her.
LYLA
I can't. I just just promised to marry that man over at the table by the window.
As the customer looks, Lyla waves at the man and he smiles and waves back.
CUSTOMER
How about tomorrow, then?
LYLA

We'll see. Tomorrow's another day, honey. And Nevada's only a short round-trip by air.
JACK is sitting at a corner table. Lyla treats him as she would any other customer.
LYLA (CONT.)
What can I get for you, sir?
JACK
You know what I want. This acting respectable stuff makes me sick. I'll give you one more day to come to your senses, then watch yourself when you're walking alone.
LYLA turns around and takes care of the other customers.
JACK gets up and leaves the parlor.
ZEUS throws a kiss, laughs, and moves forward looking in the direction Jack turned.
JAIME
(out of breath)
Hey, Zeus, what have you done to me? I had to call Cousin Hector to help me. Once the word got around about . . .
JAIME nods his head toward Lyla, who is magnetic as she moves from table to table refilling glasses and talking to the customers.
JAIME (CONT.)
. . . this place started jumping. Put on an apron and help me.
ZEUS moves around behind the counter and reaches for an apron.
    CUT TO:
EXT.--MANILA STREET--NIGHT
ZEUS is cradling the deli sack in one arm with a six-pack of Cokes, compliments of Jaime, dangling from his fingers, and his other arm is linked into Lyla's like a father to a daughter.
LYLA
(about ready to cry)
Jaime paid me five dollars an hour for tonight, Zeus. With tips, that's almost as good as I did when I worked for Jack.
ZEUS
Thees ees good. See, he gaves us these Cokes, too.
LYLA
Jaime's got to OK it with his boss, but he's sure that'll be raised even higher once he sees the profit the parlor made tonight. We ran out of two different ingredients. Jaime said that'd never happened before tonight.
ZEUS

Eet's likes I always tolds my leettle goats . . . when you comes to zee wooden breedge over the creek, you keeps . . .

LYLA laughs, cutting him off, and Zeus puts his hand behind her back as they pick up the pace and walk toward the church.

She's so happy that she misses seeing Jack Hadley watching and listening from the shadows of a doorway.

ZEUS doesn't and, pulling out his red bandana, waves it a couple of times behind his back at him.

    CUT TO:

EXT.--MANILA STREET--DAY

ZEUS is walking with difficulty toward the church with a large easy chair over his head.

BERT pulls up in front of him and stops. He gets immediately out of his squad car and walks over beside Zeus with billyclub in hand. Zeus keeps up his stumbling pace, bumping Bert at times.

BERT

Hey, watch it, buddy.

ZEUS

Who ees eet?

BERT

(tapping the chair with his club)

OK, Zeus. This is . . . uh . . . it. Get out your identification papers.

ZEUS

(muffled)

Who ees there?

Bumps Bert again.

BERT

Hey, uh, watch what your doing with that, uh, chair.

ZEUS

Sorry, meester. What ees your name?

BERT

You know darn . . . uh . . . well who I am. Give me your I. D. . . . uh . . .

ZEUS

I can't 'ears you so good. You wants my I-D-uh. Well, I says eet's a nice day to go feeshing. Wants to?

BERT

(yelling and drawing his gun)

Give me your I. D., uh, buster, or I'm going to, uh, run you in.

ZEUS

OK. Helps me weeth thees chair. I've gots my I. D. right 'ere een my pant pockets.

ZEUS slyly gets BERT to hold the chair over his head, which frees both of Zeus's hands, although he is still under the chair with Bert.
BERT's club and gun, during the partial transfer, end up in Zeus's hands. He puts the pistol in his back pocket to free one hand.
Zeus pretends to adjust the chair on Bert's hands, head and back and slips Bert's wallet out of his pocket. Both of Bert's hands are steadying the heavy-and-getting-heavier chair, and it's dark under it.
ZEUS holds Bert's wallet with the badge under the shadow of the chair for Bert to see.
BERT
(squinting at his own I. D.)
Oh. You're kidding me, huh? I can't believe it . . . uh . . . a fellow officer, huh?
ZEUS
(smiling with eyes up at the chair)
Yes, undercovers.
BERT
(strained voice)
Sorry I, uh, bothered you. What are you investigating in this neighborhood?
ZEUS
Eet's clastafied. But I'll tells you. People are im-press-ion-ating ossifers. Top secret, though, so don't says anytheen' to nobodies.
BERT
(impressed deeper voice)
You're kidding me -- impersonating officers! I, uh, understand. Mum's the word.
ZEUS bumps BERT as a distraction and slips the wallet back into Bert's pocket.
He then gives Bert his gun and club back, one hand at a time, so he can re-take full possession of the chair.
Zeus picks up his pace as he moves away from Bert.
        CUT TO:
INT.--SQUAD CAR--DAY
BERT drives away from the church down Manila Street and turns left on Plum Street.
BERT
Think of that. An officer the, uh, whole time. Badge just like mine, uh . . . wallet just like mine, uh . . . badge number just like mine . . . uh . . .
(realizing the truth)
DANG that Zeus!

CUT TO:
INT.--CHURCH
The church interior is more organized, and, with used furniture from Dave's route, is beginning to look more like a home. The LIGHT BULBS have been changed and are lit, giving the church a respectable look.
PEDRO is sitting in a corner chair daydreaming.
MARLEEN approaches him with books.
MARLEEN
(hands books to Pedro)
I've got a couple of books in my cart that you might like to read to pass the time. Here's The Time Machine by H. G. Wells and Mrs. Mike, which is a true adventure story about the Canadian provinces.
PEDRO
(refusing the books)
I don't need no books to pass the time. I hate reading.
ZEUS comes in and drops the chair in an empty spot in their "living room."
ZEUS
Someteeng's deefferent. 'ey, lets there be light, huh? What 'appened?
MARLEEN
Lyla bought bulbs from her pay this week. Wasn't that sweet.
ZEUS
Yes, eet was. My man Pedro, when are you going to gets out and smells zee fresh air? You wants me gets you a job like I deed Lyla? You knows about zee goat who stayed een the corral . . .
PEDRO
I don't want to hear no more goat stories, and I don't need no job.
ZEUS
OK, OK, well, then, what do you wants for supper tonight?
PEDRO
Mexican.
ZEUS
No way, man. I've eat'n real Mexican food all my life, why would I wants thees fake Tex-Mex garbage? 'ow about Greek?
CUT TO:
INT.--GREEK RESTAURANT
Zeus is talking to DIMITRI, the fifty-five year old owner, who is standing next to a bar.
DIMITRI

Your name is Zeus, huh? You got a little Greek blood in you, huh Zeus? You a little puny, though, to be named after Zeus. Maybe I got a job for you anyway, compatriot.
ZEUS
Yeah, maybe, but I only wants to do your dirtiest job tonight, not full times.
DIMITRI
(laughing)
My awfulest job, huh? Well, you'll have to go home to my wife instead of me then. I just kidding. I love my wife. Now, wha's it exactly you wanna do again here, Zeus?

******

Mark took a break and prayed: "God, what do you want me to do? What is my purpose here on your earth? My church is gone, I serve a good Bible study, but do you have more for me? Church leaders are again questioning my religion. I try to include all churches and all religions and all peoples in my little ministry." His prayer went on for more than 30 minutes and then ended with: "If I'm on the wrong path give me a sign. Should I leave Wyandotte? Dear Lord, guide me, lead me, show me the way. Amen." When he finished he wondered if God had already given him plenty of signs.

******

CUT TO:
INT.--CHURCH
ZEUS comes in and finds everyone, including Dave, sitting around the table ready to eat.
ZEUS
Are you guys ready to eats some geero-scopes and some theen's I can't pronounce? Hola, Dave.
(to Pedro, teasing)
I knows there's some goat or lamb stuffed een thees pita bread, Pedro. You wanna eats anyway?
(to Lyla)
What are you doing here, Lyla?
LYLA
The parlor is doing so well, now, and I've been working so many late hours that Jaime gave me a half day off. Hector's subbing for me.
DAVE
Zeus, ya know, this neighborhood has always been a wreck, but these people around here want something better.
ZEUS

Me too.
DAVE
Several of the business owners want to have a meeting, and they thought maybe here. We could unfold the chairs and move some of the pews.
ZEUS
(smiling at Pedro)
'ey, I don't cares, anytime, I don't owns thees place. Come anytime excepts supper time. The way Pedro eats just heemself, there's hardly any theeng lefts for me, let alone a crowd.
DAVE
And, Zeus, since everybody seems to know you better than anyone, and they know how well you can organize storerooms and get things done, they want you to call the meeting and run it.
ZEUS
Carrumba, what do I knows about politeecs! But, lets them come. You knows that when a herd of goats sees an opening een zee fence, looks out. That goes for sheeps even more.
Zeus leaves, Marleen goes to the basement, leaving Lyla and Pedro alone.
LYLA
Pedro, would you like this last gyros?
PEDRO
Not if you've touched it.
LYLA
Why won't you give me a chance? Someone may have hurt you, but I never have.
PEDRO
You've turned into a goody-goody overnight with a job and money. I'm not buying it. Ya come in here and buy bulbs like we're all charity cases or something.
LYLA
Sorry that offended you. I was just trying to help, not show you up.
PEDRO
Who said anything about showing anyone up? You're nothing, perra.
LYLA
I guess those were the wrong words. My life's no bed of roses, ya know. By buying a few bulbs I was trying to make things better for me as well as the rest of you.
PEDRO

Well, I . . . WE don't need any help from you. Job or no job, you're still a puta.
LYLA
I can't change my past. I'm just trying . . .
LYLA turns her back and weeps.
PEDRO slinks into his favorite corner and covers his eyes with the bill of a baseball cap that he has been wearing backward on his head.
    CUT TO:
EXT.--GARAGE SALE ON WASHINGTON AVENUE--DAY
The driveway is filled with planters, beautiful clothes hung on a bar, tables of dishes, a workbench covered with tools, and boxes of old toys. About a dozen PEOPLE are looking over the goods.
ZEUS is taking pants off the bar and holding them up to himself.
ZEUS sees a SHOPPER who is about the size of Marleen, then, when the shopper is not looking, he holds up a dress to her back and nods with approval.
SHOPPERS begin to notice and avoid Zeus. He obviously doesn't belong in this neighborhood and, besides, they see him make suspicious movements out of the corners of their eyes.
ZEUS, without being seen, chases a YOUNG LADY about Lyla's size around and between the tables and boxes, and, when the lady is busy looking at merchandise, conducts more size testing.
ZEUS
(to homeowner)
'ey, meesses. What you do weeth theese clothes and stuffs when zee sale ees over?
    CUT TO:
EXT.--MANILA STREET--DAY
ZEUS is walking toward the church with a couple of pair of jeans, a couple of T-shirts for Pedro and himself and dresses for Marleen and Lyla draped over his head from side to side like an enormous wig.
BERT pulls up next to him on the wrong side of the street in his squad car.
BERT
Hey, Zeus, is that you in, uh, there? Stealing again, are you? Clothes this time, huh?
ZEUS
(muffled)
Who you want? Don't knows no Zeus guy. I'm Pancho Villa and I'm justs taking these clothes to Goodwill for Mom, Señora Villa, and my seester, Poca Villa, meester ossifer.

BERT has to stick his head out of the car again, and, since he is on the wrong side of the street, cars are honking and swerving to miss him. He keeps one eye on Zeus and the other on the traffic.

BERT
(yelling at honking driver)
Same to ya, buddy. What's his, uh, license number? Dang it, I can't read through a mirror, uh, backwards.

ZEUS
I don't even 'ave no meerror, meester ossifer.

BERT
I wasn't talking to, uh, you.

ZEUS
Dees ees good, so I'll just mosey along then.

BERT
No. Yes. I mean I was talking to you but I, uh, yelled at this driver but I was talking to you, uh, about . . .

BERT stops his car, grabs his billyclub and gets out and starts toward Zeus. Then he looks at where he is parked and hears more HORNS HONKING. He looks at Zeus in the "wig," and he shakes his head, makes a motion with his hand to indicate "go on" and returns to his car. Without creating a street comedy with himself as the star, Bert realizes he can't check the veracity of Zeus's claims.

    CUT TO:

INT.--CHURCH
PEDRO and MARLEEN are alone again.

MARLEEN is reading *Mrs. Mike* supposedly aloud to herself, but Pedro, in his corner, is all ears.

MARLEEN
(reading with emotion)
". . . there is something wrong with everything when a wildcat is chased by a badger. I caught my breath, for I realized now what it was that forced the wild things of the forest to take suddenly to the paths of men. Only one thing could make the badger run with the lynx, and that one thing was fire. I ran on toward the office, and three gray rabbits ran with me. The smoke was thicker now, and hot ash and cinders sifted down on the path. But the animals were running with me. That meant the fire was behind us. I wondered if it would reach the house . . . ."

MARLEEN looks at Pedro, who looks away.

MARLEEN (CONT.)
My eyes are getting tired, Pedro. Would you read aloud to me so we can find out what happens to Kathy?

PEDRO
What makes you think I was listening to that stupid story?
MARLEEN
(kindly)
Pedro, aren't you ever honest? I was a teacher for thirty years, and I know when someone is hiding. What are you hiding from?
PEDRO
I ain't afraid of nothing. Leave me alone.
MARLEEN
Pedro, everyone is afraid. Probably every day.
PEDRO
(rudely)
Oh yeah?
MARLEEN
Some wisely avoid what they fear, some face and overcome the fears they can, and some let their fears overcome them.
PEDRO
(viciously)
You sound like a stupid teacher. Talk, talk, talk. Full of B. S. but no action. Look at you. Are you better off than I am? What are you hiding from? What are you afraid of? What the devil's so normal about you? You . . . me . . . we're the same.
MARLEEN pauses to think about this.
MARLEEN
You're right, Pedro. I have been hiding for years on the street and now I'm hiding here. I'm sorry about what I said about you. I'm much older and have no excuse for living this way.
PEDRO
(more kindly)
Forget it, man. Like you said, everybody's got fears. I've learned to avoid mine since I can't do nothing about them.
MARLEEN
(motherly)
I'll make you a deal, Pedro. I'll tell you my fears, but you've got to keep them a secret. Then you tell me yours with the same stipulations.
PEDRO
If that big word means you won't tell either, then maybe. Go on.

Chapter 18. Beautiful Eyes

Miss Ardnas was beside herself. Since the interview by the CASA, which felt like an interrogation, she had seen the CASA three more times: at Mark's Bible study sitting with her children during their lessons, at home visiting with the children on the patio while she was in the living room and once at the park. When others asked who he was, Miss Ardnas took a deep breath before explaining that the court had assigned a volunteer advocate to represent her children in a custody case. Intellectually she knew they wouldn't expect child abuse, but emotionally she felt that they might.

Mark no longer had an office since he had lost his parsonage, so Miss Ardnas, who had counseled with Mark before her divorce from Franklin, called and asked to meet with him at Mrs. Grassley's. Mark and Miss Ardnas sat down at the dining room table while Mrs. Grassley watched television from her day bed in the living room.

Miss Ardnas and Mark had been good friends in high school and he still had a crush on her. She had never suspected his feelings and treated him still as a friend and pastor. He relished being with her one-on-one and wished he had the nerve to ask her out. The divorce had been final more than a year ago, so no one at this late date would suspect a prior relationship between the two might have caused the breakup.

"Your aquamarine eyes are as beautiful as ever, Miss Ardnas. I fell in love with you the first time I saw them when we were freshmen in high school," was what he wanted to say, but instead all that came out was: "How are you?"

After five minutes of such typically meaningless pleasantries, he asked how he could help her.

"It's Franklin. He's suing for custody of the children. He's calling me every name in the book. A CASA, you know what a CASA is, is making visits to see if I'm a good mother."

"CASA, sure, a court appointed advocate for children, or, it must be special advocate."

"Right. Every time I'm asked a question during his interviews or have to sit with him while the kids play Frisbee in the park, I feel like I'm on trial."

"I've had to work with CASAs before, and they're normally well trained and objective. I don't think you have anything to worry about."

"That's what I think, but I'm so used to the TV shows about court where something embarrassing that nobody knows about and the suspect had even forgotten about herself comes up under cross examination and the whole trial changes directions," Miss Ardnas said in one breath.

"Miss Ardnas," stated Mark and his voice broke with feelings for her, "there's no way you will lose those children. You have a ton of friends. Did you put me on the list of friends to talk to?"

"Well, no I didn't. I should have. I will now."

Mark then thought of his meeting with Pastor Bob. Maybe he wouldn't be a good character witness since his own character was suspect. He had thought about this meeting with Miss Ardnas as a possible opportunity to see if she would like to meet sometime for coffee or even go on a real date, but the Pastor Bob situation and the fact that she was coming to him for help ruined that idea. He still kind of felt he was her professional counselor, and a relationship seemed inappropriate. He looked at her across the table with such unabashed admiration that only a woman in emotional turmoil could have missed the love he felt for her.

Slowly Mark could see that his encouragement, calm voice and directives were having an effect. Miss Ardnas left with a smile on her face and dry eyes.

"You still wearing those sneakers? Laws', you're a grown man. And it's got that squashed drip on it," yelled Mrs. Grassley when Mark sat down in her living room for a chat.

"Hey, be nice. Have you ever noticed what Naomi, your sister's daughter, you know her," he said teasing," the one that lives upstairs…."

"Now you be nice," teased back Mrs. Grassley.

"She wears lots of squashed drips, as you call them."

"You mean you wear paisley on your shoes?" continued Mrs. Grassley with a smile. "Cute."

"Well, yes, I guess I do, but Nike doesn't call it a squashed drip."

"Laws' they should. It's pitiful."

"I've done some research on the design. Some say it's Iranian or Indian in origin. Some say it from the yin yang."

"Laws', speak up. Tin can?"

"No, yin yang." Mark took a Post-It and drew the shape. "Good and evil, love and hate."

"I've seen that. There's no such thing as hate, just love and lack of love, which is worse than hate."

"Well, anyway, the name Paisley comes from Paisley, Scotland, where the West first used the design. Others call it a Welsh pear, Persian paisley, buta or Persian pickle, because of its shape.'

"I had wallpaper with that design in my bathroom fifty years ago."

"See, the design on my shoes are classic."

"Squashed drip to me."

He felt better about his predicament but it took ten more minutes talking to Mrs. Grassley about Dr. Phil's current guest on the TV in front of them for his heartbeat to return to normal. He felt like such a sixth-grader when it came to women. He remembered all the "I like you do you like me" notes that were passed daily from boyfriend to friend to the girlfriend or from the girlfriend to a friend to the boyfriend. He still had a few from girls named Candice, Janet, Beverly and Kelly in the bottom of his sock drawer. It would be simpler if the world were just yin-yang, but he imagined it probably was more of an infinite double helix.

Mark left Mrs. Grassley and went to his room. More editing would help him take his mind off Miss Ardnas. He needed to finish the screenplay and present the idea to his youth group. In fact, he decided that he would give them a synopsis and present the idea at the next meeting. The editing went slowly.

******

MARLEEN
(looking down)
I didn't get married when girls normally marry. And after a few years I was afraid no one would want to marry me, so as a teacher the students became mine, you know, like the children I should have had and loved.
(she looks at Pedro)
 I'd do anything for those students, and they trusted me and I trusted them completely. Then one day a student slipped some LSD in my coffee cup as a joke. I'd read about that happening in another city, but . . . . Well, I was taken to the hospital, released that night, and told what had happened.
(more quiet since Pedro doesn't react)
I never went back to teaching . . . I was afraid to. In fact, I didn't trust anyone. Well, my savings didn't last long, I was too young to start collecting my teacher's pension and I had no family, so, with no money . . . you know where I ended up . . . and I haven't trusted anyone until Zeus asked me to come here. I don't even know why I followed him here. It just seemed right . . . It seemed safe . . . You, Lyla, Zeus, there's something good and right about us being together here.
MARLEEN is crying at the end of her story, and she takes out an old hankie to dry her eyes.
PEDRO
(tears running down his face)

Bull! I don't know why I said I'd do this . . . Well, first, I can't read . . . Crap, you knew that...You knew that when you asked me to read. What can you do in the world if you can't read! And...my little sister ... she was killed in uh . . . uh drive-by with me standing next to her ... why couldn't it have been me! I couldn't do nothing to stop it, to help her.

Marleen puts her hand on his shoulder and nods that she understands. It seems to calm Pedro down.

PEDRO (CONT.)

Then my folks moved somewhere, I don't care no more. Dang it, man, I'm afraid of everything and I'm trapped here . . . and Lyla reminds me of my . . . of being helpless with my sister. Everything about me is screwed up something awful.

MARLEEN

Well, Pedro. We've got different problems, but can't we help each other, all of us? Lyla needs a good brother. She never had one growing up. And you need a sister. And I need you, Pedro, and I need Lyla.

Marleen and Pedro hug like mother and son.

ZEUS stumbles through the back door with clothes covering his whole head, including his face and runs into several pieces of furniture before he spins and falls, making his own pile on the floor.

ZEUS

(peaking out from under the clothes)

New clothes for everyones.

MARLEEN and PEDRO take one look at Zeus and begin laughing. Then they go to him to help him get out from beneath the pile.

They start trying on clothes behind different portable bulletin boards.

ZEUS strides into view looking and posing like a man-of-the-world.

MARLEEN parades out and does clumsy runway turns and fake gestures.

PEDRO also comes out and does a macho routine with the flexing of his muscles and taking boxer stances.

ZEUS appears from behind a bulletin board as a toreador and makes some twisting moves with his bandana in hand.

MARLEEN comes out with her hair pinned tightly to her head and wearing an old-maid teacher dress.

MARLEEN

Zeus, did you know that I used to be a seventh grade teacher?

ZEUS

Well, eet ees a . . .

MARLEEN

Yes, and I'm going to be a teacher again some day. But to start with, I need to get back into practice. Is there a young girl or boy in this neighborhood who could use some tutoring.
Pedro, embarrassed, looks away.
ZEUS
(laughing)
Only about 150 zeellion.
MARLEEN
Well, I only need one to start with.
ZEUS
I'll haves one leettle goat 'ere tomorrow at exactly 4:00 PM.
PEDRO walks over to MARLEEN and sits down, picks up Mrs. Mike and holds it so both of them can see it.
PEDRO
(reading)
Wuh . . . wuh . . . we had-n't . . . uh, no, why had-n't I buh . . . bra . . .
MARLEEN
Brought.
PEDRO
the . . . dogs with me? But the . . . they wuh . . . wuh . . . were . . .
    CUT TO:
INT.--GROCERY STORE
WILMA Johnson owns the store. She's a pretty, slim, thirty-seven-year-old divorcee, who stands for no nonsense.
ZEUS enters with a smile.
ZEUS
Can I talks to zee manager?
WILMA
This store doesn't have a manager.
ZEUS
Can I talks to zee owner.
WILMA
(no smile)
Standing in front of you, bud. What do you want? I ain't got all day to stand here and make quaint conversation with a short, dark stranger.
ZEUS
What's zee worst kind of chore you gots to do around 'ere?
WILMA
What are you, a reporter for the Green Grocer's Gazette or something?
ZEUS
(smiling)

That ees funny. Ha, ha.
WILMA
Now that you've had your laugh, why don't you get the heck out of here.
ZEUS
(trying to smile)
You know, for a señora, muy bonita, you ees one tough cookies.
WILMA
(with straight face)
Wrong. The tough cookies are in the fourth aisle. I may sound like I'm joking, but I'm not.
WILMA puts her hand beneath the counter and Zeus stops smiling.
WILMA (CONT.)
Listen, buster, I've got my pretty little fingers wrapped around a .32 caliber Baretta and it's aimed at your guts. So if you make any funny moves, you're going to have trouble holding water, soup, and root beer for a long time.
WILMA reaches with her left hand for the phone and clamps it between her chin and shoulder. She starts to call on her cell phone.
WILMA (CONT.)
Now you just hold still there and I'll make a call to the police and my friend Bert will help you leave the neighborhood before . . .
ZEUS
No, no, señora. You makings beeg meestake. I wants to help you. Call Jaime over at Mike's Peezza Parlor. He tells you you shouldn't shoot me. Eet's 555-9182.
Without taking her eyes off Zeus, WILMA raises the automatic and points it at his belt buckle. Then she dials Mike's.
ZEUS (CONT.)
Whoaa! Careful, lady. Don't aims so low, eet makes me nervous.
WILMA
(to ZEUS)
What's your name?
ZEUS
'ey Zeus.
WILMA
(aims a little lower)
I'm not joking, buster. What is it?
ZEUS
(hands covering himself)
No, really! Eet's 'ey Zeus, Zeus for shorts.

WILMA
(into the phone)
Jaime? Wilma. Fine. And you? Good. Listen, do you happen to know a scrawny, ugly, little Mexican guy who goes by the name of Hey Zeus or Zeus?
(looks Zeus up and down)
You're crappin' me. He does what? Say that again. Oh, nothin'. I was just about to turn him in to a peg board. Ok, I won't. Bye.
ZEUS shakes his head at her insults, then he is nodding his head at her surprise to Jaime's answers.
WILMA laughs and puts the gun away.
WILMA
OK, Hey Zeus, I don't know what your real game is, but you've got folks around here fooled, according to Jaime. So here's the deal. I'll give you two loaves of day-old bread, any lunch meat that's just gone out of date and a case of mixed dented canned food. For all of that, you've got to empty the dairy cases, clean them out with bleach water, rinse them thoroughly, wipe off all the milk, yogurt, sour cream and cottage cheese cartons and put them back into the cases.
ZEUS just stands silent. He's never had so much trouble getting permission to do dirty work.
    CUT TO:
INT.--BACKROOM OF GROCERY
WILMA and Zeus come through the door into the backroom and she gives him a bucket, points to the utility sink, hands him some Chlorox, hands him a large sponge, and gets a clothes pin out of a drawer.
ZEUS
What's zee clothes peen for?
WILMA
You've never cleaned out a dairy case, have you?
    CUT TO:
INT.--STORE
Zeus's head and shoulders are hung down into an old-fashioned dairy case in an aisle near the check-out counter. Buckets and old towels are on the floor beside him.
    CUT TO:
WILMA enjoys the scene as she waits on customers up front at the check-out.
ZEUS

Whoaa-whee! Eet smell like Leemburger cheeses down 'ere. Whoaa-whee! I've smelled sheep deep that's sweeter smelling than thees stuffs. Where'd I puts that clothes peen?
    FADE OUT:
    FADE IN:
INT.--CHURCH
The lined-up pews contain about twenty neighbors who have businesses.
DELIA CARTER, 40, owns a laundromat and is very large and loud. Her husband, Tom, 42, 6' 5" and about 280, is beside her.
ZEUS
Well, thees ees a meeting, I theenks. Deed I ever tells you zee one about why zee goat lefts zee shed and then he corssed...
JEFFERSON
(laughing)
Zeus, no insult intended, but let's skip the rancho stories and go straight to business.
ZEUS
Thees ees zee first meeting of zee . . . of zee . . . who are we?
TOM
(getting up)
How about . . .
DELIA
Sit down, Tom. How bout the Manila Street Gang?
TOM nods his head in approval as everybody laughs.
DAVE
How about Manila Street Committee.
JEFFERSON
Or, Manila Street Improvement Committee.
ALL
Yeah!
TOM
(getting up again)
That's a perfect . . .
DELIA
Sit down, Tom. Make it Manila Urban Street-Improvement Committee, and I'll vote for it.
DAVE
I'll buy that, then our motto can be "Make M.U.S.I.C."
All laugh.

ZEUS has to bang a short two-by-four on the pulpit to get the audience's attention.
DON, 53, who owns a drugstore, is sitting in the front row.
ZEUS
So, what are zee improvements going to be?
DON
Don't we need a little money if we're going to make all of these improvements?
DELIA
Give'm a ten, Tom.
Tom gets a ten out of his wallet and gives it to Don.
KAREN
Here's five. Maybe I can give more later.
NATE
My dad gave me a dollar. Here.
DAVE
I've got a fiver for the cause.
CARL
I'm new around here. Name's Carl. Just opened Carl's Pre-owned Furniture over on Cherry Street, thanks to the help of Dave here. Glad to have any business you might be able to send me. Oh yeah, here's twenty-five bucks.
STRANGER
If I want to write a check here, who do I make it out to?
DON
Just make it out to M. U. S. I. C.
Amid laughter, men, women and children continue to parade forward with maybe a dollar bill, two quarters, a handful of change or a check.
DON (CONT.)
I'll hold the money at my drugstore until I can get to the bank and open a new account. Sorry, to interrupt, Zeus, go ahead . . .
    CUT TO:
INT.--CRACK HOUSE
Five boys and men are sitting around a room on beat-up furniture. Different drug paraphernalia is present.
JACK paces the floor in front of them. Only the one called DUDE seems to be able to sustain a conversation.
JACK
Now, you deadheads have got to get out there and sell more. Look at all those kids on the street. What are they good for but a little money

for us. They're not happy, we're not happy. This way we can at least be happy.
DUDE
We got all the dope we need to stay happy.
JACK
Yeah? Well, it's crack I bought for you. With Lyla playing princess of the pizza parlor, I'm short on money. That means you're out of dope.
DUDE
All right. We'll start tomorrow.
JACK
You'll start today. I want all of you hanging around the schools, movie theaters, arcades and ice cream shops with pockets full of candy and gum. Make some friends out there.
DUDE
What about you, Hadley? What're you going to do? Jack?
JACK
(deep in thought)
Huh? What am I going to do? I'm going to figure out a way to take care of Zeus. Then I'm going to get Lyla back.
   CUT TO:
INT.--PIZZA PARLOR
ZEUS is complaining to a busy LYLA and JAIME.
ZEUS
Nasty meetings! An' they mades all these suggestions -- have a parade, feex the streets, repairs and paints houses, gets reed of crack houses, gets more equeepment for the school playground, makes a neighborhood park, and they takes up money. What I needs with money?
JAIME and LYLA are leaning against each other as they laugh at Zeus.
LYLA
Relax, Zeus. We'll make you your favorite pizza and get you a red cream soda. Sit down and take it easy. It'll all work out.
ZEUS slumps into a booth in the corner.
   CUT TO:
EXT.--WASHINGTON AVENUE--DAY
ED, a city dump truck driver, 38, is backing over a newly patched pothole.
ZEUS
Hey, meester, can I help you feell some pot-holes.
ED
Huh? What'd you say?

ZEUS grabs a shovel from the truck bed, gets a blade full of gravel and tar, and places it in the next pothole.
ED takes off his hat and scratches his head.
ZEUS
Drive over that, meester. I want to see how thees works. Maybe I need to add another shovel or two to zee crater.
Zeus and ED work the street together, Zeus shoveling and Ed compacting with the truck wheels.
    CUT TO:
INT.--ED'S TRUCK CAB
ED
Here, Zeus, take this. My wife always makes me three sandwiches for lunch and I usually throw the third one away. There's a six-pack of Mountain Dew in the cooler. He'p yourself.
ZEUS
So, you leeve near Maneela Street, just down Plum, huh? Do you ever patches that street? Eet's got holes een eets 'oles.
(grinning)
I saw a boy and girl pulls about a two-pound catfeesh out of one zee other day.
ED
(laughing)
Where's my fishing pole? No, really, are you kidding! They never dispatch me to that part of town. I catch flack when I patch the block I live on.
ZEUS
Well, we sure got a lot of bad holes over there on Maneela. Eef you ever have some patch left over, I knows where to put eet.
    CUT TO:
EXT.--MANILA STREET IN FRONT OF STEIGLITZ's DELI--DAY
ED and ZEUS are patching the holes just as they did on Washington Avenue.
ABE looks on happily and points to other holes.
ZEUS and ED nod back. When they are done, they stand next to a filled pothole and look at the crackhouse.
ABE
What're we going to do about that, Zeus?
ED
I could back my truck up to the door with a load of hot tar and . . .
ZEUS

That Jack-ass Hadley leeves there, don't he. What's wrong weeth that guy anyways?
ED
He needs to loosen up. Not enough fiber in his diet at all, I'd say. Hates the world.
ABE
I no like having that house in this neighborhood. Suppose we could report a fire in there some night and call the police and have firemen chop the door down, break out all the windows, cut a hole in the roof and water everything and everybody down?
ED
You're kidding
ABE
No, I heard of another neighborhood doing that.
ED
Ya don't say.
ABE
I guess it only took four visits from the fire department at 3 a.m. for the crackpots, crackhoods, or whatever, to move to another part of town where they could smash or bash, or whatever, all night without being awakened and hosed down.
ZEUS
That's not a bad idea. Anyone een our group a fireman? I'm not een too good weeth the firemen and poleece around 'ere right now.
ED
We'll think of something.
      CUT TO:
INT.--CHURCH
It is 4:00 PM and MARLEEN is sitting with NATE as he reads his literature assignment aloud.
NATE
(reading)
All the boys and girls were hot and tired. Then the fireman put a large . . . wuh . . .
MARLEEN
Wrench.
NATE
(still reading)
. . . large . . . wuh . . . wrench on the nut and turned. A . . . suh . . . spuh . . . spray of water wet the sidewalk.
MARLEEN

(giving Nate a hug)
Good, Nate.
Karen Lung comes in to drop off her little sister, Susanne, 11.
KAREN
Hi. I'm Karen Lung, you know Lung's Chinese restaurant. I've brought my little sister Susanne for her lessons. She was sick a couple of weeks, and she's behind in her schoolwork.
MARLEEN
Nice to meet you, Karen and Susanne. This is Pedro.
KAREN looks and smiles at Pedro.
PEDRO, obviously attracted to Karen because he can't return her look, tries to smile in return, then turns back to working with Nate.
MARLEEN (CONT.)
Now, Pedro is also going to help you with your homework. Last night he read through your lesson in the extra reading book your teacher loaned us. Continue here, Pedro.
KAREN
Excuse me a second. Mom doesn't want Susanne to walk home alone. There's a weirdo, Jack Hadley, who's always hanging around Manila and Plum near the crack house about dusk. Could you give me a call when you're done and I'll come back and get her?
MARLEEN
(to Karen)
We don't have a telephone here, but I'd be happy to take Susanne home when we're done, if that's OK with you.
KAREN
Are you sure you want to? The streets are creepy at night.
MARLEEN
(laughing to herself)
Yes, I'm sure. The streets don't bother me.
KAREN
OK. Thanks. I'll see you later, Susanne. Bye, everybody.
KAREN glances again at Pedro then leaves.
PEDRO, pretending he hasn't heard, continues to slowly learn new words as he reads to the children, but when Karen turns her back to go his eyes follower her to the door.
PEDRO
(reading)
The big-gest boy . . .

MARLEEN mouths the word WALKED then HYDRANT above Nate's head. With the prompt, Pedro remembers the words from Marleen's help last night and can read.
PEDRO (CONT.)
walked to . . . the hy-drant and . . . played in the wat-er.
MARLEEN
Nate, hear how slowly and distinctly Pedro reads. Now you read the next line. Then we'll let Susanne read the line after.
    CUT TO:
INT.--HOME BUILDING CENTER
ZEUS is at the counter talking to BOB WAGNER, manager.

Chapter 19. Pisces

"Hey, Pal. What problems are you causing over in Wyandotte now? You still being a pisses?" This was Jerry's favorite pun on Mark's horoscope sign and about as dirty as he would get as a minister. "I was looking at a black and white yin yang symbol the other day that was designed with two fish swimming in different directions, and I thought of you."

"Hello to you, too, Jerry," said Mark.

"Sorry. I couldn't keep from giving you a couple of jabs. Remember all the short-sheeting you did to my bed in college, not counting all the fuzzy fake spiders under my pillow, cold and slick gummy bears in my socks, shoestrings tied in a knot when I was late getting dressed for chapel, Brylcreem squeezed into my Pepsodent tube, alarm clock set for 3 a.m. on a Saturday morning, belts and ties hidden on Sunday morning--have I left anything out?"

"That about covers it. What have you been hearing about me?"

"I remember you once getting kicked out of chapel for sailing a paper airplane from the balcony onto the stage."

"It slipped out of my hand as I was setting it on the railing."

"Sure enough. Why did you make a paper airplane during chapel, and I suppose by accident it just missed the speaker's head by a whisker? A red whisker as I remember."

"What have you heard?"

"You got kicked out of the Followers Church. I see a definite trend here."

"I hate to admit it, Jerry. But that's true. I know you like to joke, Jerry, but to me this is no joking matter."

"What are you doing down there in Wyandotte?"

"Same old stuff."

"Maybe it's time to change. We're good friends, and I hate to sound preachy, but let's rewind to seminary. Mark, do you feel you're saved? Do you feel like your sins are forgiven? Do you have a personal relationship with God? You know doctors say that 75% of illnesses are psychological—people not forgiving themselves and not asking forgiveness from others and God."

"I don't know, Jerry. Sometimes I feel like I don't even know what those phrases mean. My Bible study of former parishioners used to throw those around and I'd just look at them. They'd raise both hands and tell me that they had Jesus in their heart," said Mark with his head bent forward and his elbows on his knees.

"Do you have Jesus in your heart?"

"I think so. I know I have a conscience, I have an innate need for a spiritual life, I want to serve others, and I love Jesus."

"What's wrong with that?"

"These people who said they had this personal relationship would say and do the weirdest things."

"Like what?"

"They'd say that only Christians can be right with God in a world where only one-third of the people claim to be Christian--CLAIM. You have to be baptized as a child to be saved. The pictures or statuettes of saints on the top of a bookshelf will help you stay well. You must convert your ancestors so they will be saved. They make jokes about Mormons and Jehovah Witnesses spreading the word. They praise and idolize modern-day misers who hoard money while keeping their workers poor or uninsured, which has forced the government to get into the health insurance business. I apologize, Jerry; I'm such an analytical skeptic."

"You've got one wheel of your velomobile in the ditch and it's liable to pull the rest of the vehicle and you in too. We need to plan a weekend together and work things out."

"Good idea, Jerry. I really feel lost."

"If your world view is the same as it was the last time we talked, your problem isn't that you want to save people, it's that you want to save the world. I've got my fifth meeting of the day coming up, so I've gotta go. Take care, Pal."

"What am I supposed to do? What should be my lifestyle as a Christian? I'm disappointed that so many people don't travel and don't learn about their worldwide neighbors first hand. I'm tired of labels, Ethiopian, Kiwi, Alaskan, Lap, Hindu, etc. I saw on PBS news that two ethnic groups were killing each other. You know that smudge finger icon on Gimp, Photoshop and other graphic manipulation programs, well I'd like to put one group next to the other group and smudge them together, saying, there, now you're just earthlings or globals, whatever you want to call everyone in the world. You want to say, 'Stop being nationalists, chauvinists, patriots, tribal, jingoists, zealots, sexists, etc. Just be human beings.' Mark Twain said, 'Travel is fatal to prejudice, bigotry, and narrow-mindedness, and many of our people need it sorely on these accounts. Broad, wholesome, charitable views of men and things cannot be acquired by vegetating in one little corner of the earth all one's lifetime.'"

Jerry tried to interrupt.

Mark continued: "What can I do but try to get people to love and accept each other? What did Jesus do? He spoke to the woman at the well when that was taboo, she was a despised Samaritan, and he asked her to give him water to drink, which would have made him ceremonially unclean. He could have excluded her from his circle of acquaintances for three reasons, which would have been perfectly acceptable according to the Jewish tradition and to many Christians. Should Christians tell people of other faiths that their beliefs are false, adding that they will go to hell if they don't discard their faith? We see and hear every day how exclusiveness affects peace among nations and religions. What am I to do? Just keep quiet?"

"Sorry, Mark, I really have to go."

"My friend Kae told me that in one of her college literature classes the professor discussed the similarity among archetypes in the three books they were reading, *To Kill a Mockingbird, Catcher in the Rye* and *Siddhartha*. He said they all had Christ figures, Jem, Bo, Atticus Finch, Tom Robinson, Holden Caulfield and Siddhartha. He said they represent the life goal of most Christians, which is to sacrifice oneself to serve another or a community. All I want to do…"

"Pal, I really gotta go. This will all work out. I'll be praying for you. God bless you."

They made plans to meet, and Mark put down his cell phone and went to the kitchen for a Coke. He returned to his room and thought about Miss Ardnas for a while. He wondered why Duke and Jenni, Kurj and Kae, Noel and Shirley, Jake and Laura and William and Madison could have such good relationships and he couldn't even approach Miss Ardnas for a date. He felt that if he didn't have such good friends, such as Jerry and Naomi, he would be on Prozac right now.

He was thinking, should I go to a church this Sunday? Should I give up the weekly Bible study before I do more damage to believers? Should I have taken the job in Alaska after I was fired as pastor here? Was it a mistake when my Bible study members and my conscience talked me out of it? What about my youth group?

Hey, Zeus was lying on his desk ready for him to dig into it again. He got his red pen out and began to mark more typos, misspellings, tense problems and punctuation errors while he read.

******

ROB
Well, I don't know what your game is, but that large pile of split and warped lumber out there has to be moved to behind the last building and burned.

ZEUS
What eef I just moves eet out of your ways and off your property eenstead?

ROB
(shrugging)
Whatever.

    CUT TO:
EXT.--SIDE YARD OF CHURCH--DAY
DAVE, ED, TOM and ZEUS are unloading an enormous pile of lumber from the garbage and dump trucks and sorting the boards and plywood into stacks.

TOM
Listen, there's a lot of good wood here if we work around the bad sections. A lot more than I thought there would be.

ZEUS
Do any of zee people on Maneela knows how to makes repair?

DAVE
That's why I asked Tom here to come. He's had his own contracting firm for 15 years.

TOM
Yeah, I'll try to make a list of what we are capable of doing as far as repairs, then we'll try to get the right lumber stacked in piles and labeled for each place.

ED
Tom, why don't you go ahead and start talking to people up and down the street, and I'll stay here and sort.

TOM

Listen, we need to keep this as quiet as possible, because a job like this would require a permit for each building we touch. It'd take weeks to process the paperwork and cost thousands of dollars that we don't have. Tell everyone to keep it in the neighborhood.
ED
Man, that's going to be tough.
TOM
There's one good thing, though, I know the guys that inspect this area, and I know some other interesting things besides.
    CUT TO:
EXT.--BUILDINGS ALONG MANILA STREET--DAY
Almost every other building has several men, women and children prying off rotten boards, measuring and sawing new boards, nailing, replacing windows, etc.
They have to saw good sections from the lumber and throw away the warped and damaged segments.
LYLA, JAIME and PEDRO take down the sign saying Mike's Pizza Parlor and put up one with L & J's Pizza on it.
LYLA
(surprised)
I really appreciate your voluteering to help, Pedro. You surprised me!
PEDRO
(blushing)
Hey, family has got to stick together.
Lyla hugs Pedro. He grins, but he doesn't hug back.
    PAN TO:
THE BROWNS are replacing broken window panes.
    PAN TO:
ABE is fixing a couple of rotten boards at the doorway to his deli.
    PAN TO:
KIM, RALPH and KAREN are replacing an awning over the door to their restaurant.
    PAN TO:
DIMITRI and a helper are pouring cement to patch a hole in the sidewalk in front of his restaurant.
    PAN TO:
ZEUS is busy just carrying boards to people. Abe and Dimitri approach him.
ABE
Hey, Zeus
ZEUS

Hola, Abe.
DON, ED and Ralph join Abe, Zeus and Dimitri.
DON
Look'n good, Dimitri. Could you come down to my drugstore later'n help me pour a base for a couple of concrete benches that I want out there in front of my store? Tom's made the forms already.
DIMITRI
You betcha. Soon as we're done here, I bring my mixer down.
ZEUS
(to Dimitri)
Don't forgets to welcome the new buseeness on the block, Lyla and Jaime boughts out Mike. Now eet's L & J's Peezza. It's gots . . .
RALPH
Zeus, if you see Tom down that way, tell him we need him at the restaurant.
ED
Here he comes now. Who are those two men in suits with him?
HAROLD SMITH and BARKLEY LAYMAN, 30 and 50, respectively, are inspectors for the city. They both are looking at the massive quantity of illegal work being done all around them up and down the street.
TOM, a clipboard and stack of folders under his arm, walks with the two men.
TOM
Now, Harold, Barkley, we've worked together before. There's no wiring or plumbing being done. There are no additions being put on. No load-bearing walls are being taken out or added. There's no cement work that sticks out into the street. What do we need permits for?
BARKLEY
Tom, you know better. I can see asbestos right there where that kid just took off that board. You gotta have special permits and union crews to come in and dispose of that stuff before you can re-side that restaurant.
HAROLD
We can appreciate what an improvement all this is making to the neighborhood, Tom, but look over there. That post on that overhang has to meet code, and the overhang can only be . . .
TOM
OK, OK. Well, you got us.
BARKLEY
Sorry, but that's our job, Tom. You have to think of safety too. You go ahead and stop this work here now, then we'll see you in the morning

and help begin the paperwork. We'll ignore any infractions, penalties and fines.
HAROLD
Is that OK, Tom?
TOM
I guess, but I need some advice from the both of you about a different legal matter before you go. Come over here behind this apartment.
Tom takes Harold and Barkley past a shabby, two-story, wooden apartment house. In the back of the yard is a jungle. Grasses and weeds are growing head high.
TOM
Look at this, Barkley. Are people allowed to grow unrestricted gardens like this?
BARKLEY
It's ugly, but there's no code that I can think of against it. It's not blocking the view of drivers through the cross alley and . . .
TOM
What if I said this plot is mostly home-grown marijuana?
HAROLD
Well, that's another story, Tom. We'd have to call in Vice to investigate the owners.
TOM
Bark, step right through here into the middle of that clump there and see if I'm right about it being marijuana.
Both Harold and Barkley are flattered to be asked to investigate as "experts" a matter that is obviously out of their jurisdiction. The activity gives them a break from their normally routine jobs, and they move forward with self-importance.
BARKLEY
Ground's pretty soft in here.
HAROLD
What's that awful smell, Barkley?
BARKLEY
I don't know, but a dead skunk couldn't be worse. Tom, I can't see any marijuana in here. It's so thick I almost can't see anything at all.
TOM
I think it's just a little farther in. Look to your right there.
HAROLD
What the heck!
BARKLEY

For crap sake, I'm into mud up to my knees. Man, I can't believe this. My first day in this new suit. $400 shot.
HAROLD
That's not mud, it's sewage. The pipe must be broken from the house to the alley. For crap sake, both my shoes are full of . . .
TOM
How could that be? This section is all on city sewage, isn't it?
HAROLD
The owner is responsible for the line out to the main. This has been broken for months. Look at this mess. Why wasn't this reported?
Harold comes out of the weeds and is trying to wipe greyish-blue sewage off his shoes onto the grass.
BARKLEY
Tom, did you know about this? If you did you'll never get another permit from the city of Kimmel as long as you live.
TOM
I swear. I was told that those were marijuana plants in there. I never smoked the stuff, how would I know it wasn't. Weeds that high, they all looked strange to me.
HAROLD
Who owns this place? Whoever it is is going to get the biggest bunch of fines in history.
BARKLEY
Do you know who owns this place, Tom? I can't wait to get my hands on him.
TOM
(looking into folder)
Well, the plats of the neighborhood are in my folder here. Let's take a look. I think those are lots M17, M18 and M19. So this one must be M18.
HAROLD
Let me have that. Here it is. This wreck of a half block is owned by the same person. It's being handled by Samuelson, Dodd and Taylor. You got your flip phone with you, Bark, give'm a call so we'll know who to nail for this.
BARKLEY
Operator, could you give me the number of Samuelson, Dodd and Taylor? Thanks.
BARKLEY punches in the number.

HAROLD looks at the muck on his pants and shoes, then tries to scrape some of it off his shoes onto the grass again. He picks up a large twig and works unsuccessfully on his pant leg.

TOM continues walking around to keep his distance from the stench coming from both of them.

BARKLEY (CONT.)

This is Barkley Layman, city inspector no. 3078. I need to know the owner of lot M18 on Manila Street. That's right, three in a row. Who? Dang it. James Calhoun? Jimmy Calhoun? THE Jimmy Calhoun? Like Mayor Calhoun? Thanks.

(flips the phone closed)

Let's go, Harold. Tom, if I ever find out you set this up I'll hound you out of business, clear out of this town, maybe even out of the state.

TOM

(trying not to smile)

But, Barkley, Harold, I'm really sorry. How could I have known it was the mayor's property? Well, I guess I'll see you two in the morning to begin working on our permits.

BARKLEY

Forget permits. I didn't see anything and neither did Harold. Come on, Harold, let's get out of this skunk hole.

HAROLD and BARKLEY walk bowlegged and with arms away from their sides -- trying to keep from spreading muck all over themselves -- and head in the direction of the street.

     CUT TO:

INT.--JONES HARDWARE AND PAINT STORE

JONES, dazed, shows ZEUS and JEFFERSON a storeroom full of old cans of paint in disarray.

ZEUS and JEFFERSON look at each other, nod, give each other low fives and begin sorting and stacking.

     CUT TO:

EXT.--MANILA STREET--DAY

ZEUS and JEFFERSON are laboriously pushing large handcarts stacked with boxes of returned and mis-mixed paint towards the church.

BERT

Hey, Zeus. Now, what?

ZEUS

Hi, ossifer Bert.

BERT

You know, I got your number. You're going to be outta here soon. I'd run you in right now if that wouldn't leave a big load of paint in the middle of the sidewalk.
ZEUS
I don't knows what you means, meester Bert.
BERT just stays parked and watches the mysterious Zeus go by. He takes a bite of a donut, shakes his head, then drives away.
   CUT TO:
INT.--CHURCH
There are two groups of young boys and girls sitting on the floor. One is sitting around MARLEEN and the other is sitting around PEDRO.
A boy, 10, named BLAKE, is sitting across from Pedro. One little girl, KARI, 9, is sitting in Pedro's lap.
SUSANNE is sitting leaning against Pedro, obviously a little jealous of Kari. They are telling stories. Pedro is laughing and nodding.
PEDRO
Good story, Blake. Now you tell us a story, Kari.
CARRIE
Well, my dad and mom took me to the zoo and we saw big scary bears and the monkeys made me laugh and dad bought some peanuts from a machine near their strong cage . . .
(big breath)
. . . and we threw peanuts and the monkeys chased after them and then we went to the petting farm . . .
(breath)
. . . and fed the goats and patted the sheep and there was a little deer . . .

Members of Marleen's group are taking turns reading around the circle. Marleen is very attentive but she glances with pride at Pedro and his group.
   CUT TO:
EXT.--MANILA STREET--DAY
It's PAINTING DAY. All of the people living or working on the street seem to have ladders, paint scrapers, and brushes, and they are busy helping each other make the buildings look good. The only obvious exception is the crack house.
JEFFERSON
(laughing and pointing)
Hey, Dimitri, you missed a spot way up there.
DIMITRI
Well, Mister Brown, it's going to stay missed. I'm no bird with wings.

RALPH is painting with plain white paint beside the windows of the restaurant.
KIM is making beautiful Chinese letters where the paint is dry.
RALPH
Mom, what do the letters mean.
KIM
(proudly)
The letters mean health, wealth, joy and our last name, Lung.
  PAN TO:
LYLA is leaning against Jaime and he has his arm around her waist. They are looking at the crack house, which really stands out now that the rest of the street has been painted.
ZEUS and JONES join them looking at the crackhouse.
JAIME
Zeus, what in the world are we going to do about that crackhouse?

Chapter 20 'Give Me a Call'

  Madison heard a beep that told her she had missed a cell phone call. She checked her messages and saw that it was not from the expected William, but Mark. It read: "Give me a call."

  She was wondering whether she had forgotten to do something for the weekly youth group meeting before Mark's Bible study. She called and found out he needed help selling his high school and college students on producing a movie.

  "You're the best talker I know, Mark. What can I say that will be any better than what you tell them?"

  "I'm afraid they'll all put the movie idea down."

  "What would make you think that? You're the one that inspires us every day!" exclaimed Madison.

  "Well, I don't feel very inspiring just now."

  "What's wrong?"

  He told her a little about the criticism of his actions and beliefs and then said, "It's a long story, but I feel a little fragile right now. Would you help me?"

  "Of course. I'll make some notes about who I would suggest to do what parts in making the movie. Send me an email about what you're thinking. We'll give them the old one-two punch."

  "Thanks, Madison."

  She flipped closed her phone and thought about how hard Mark had worked during Week of Caring(WOC) the first week after school let out. It was an annual event and Mark was one of the mainstays from the community. All the junior and senior students were supposed to participate as part of their service learning program. It ticked her off that so many of the men she met at service club meetings smiled at or flirted with her before and after her WOC presentations but couldn't find time to participate.

Since she had to chaperone lots of student projects around town that week, she saw some of these businessmen. She was surprised one morning to see two of these men in suits walking leisurely into businesses and three others going to an expensive restaurant for lunch. Later she noticed some of them were on the golf courses in the afternoon.

As she was working up a good mad, Miss Ardnas called. Madison unloaded the entire story on her. The whole thing reminded Miss Ardnas of her husband Franklin, who belonged to every club he could but never volunteered for an office or participated in any major, productive way. He played golf and ate at the Wyandotte Country Club so that he could "glad hand" the well-to-do. These activities, and billboards with his photo on major highways around town, had made his insurance agency the most lucrative in the county. Only his best friends knew what a fake he was. Even Miss Ardnas thought he was being a good citizen until she discovered his affairs and some of her friends told her the truth about his apathetic attitude toward service organizations.

After Miss Ardnas got off the phone with Madison, she sat down and wrote another genuine, authentic, real, absolute, true, trusted satirical news story for ErsatzNews.blogspot.com.

Mayor 'Calls Out' Slackers

NCNC NEWS: Bainter, Illinois

"Take off your ties and get off you're sorry a--es," said Mayor John Krantz during an interview after Day of Sharing (DOS).

DOS provides volunteers an opportunity to do beautification projects for Bainter. The elderly especially need help repairing picket fences, touching up house trim, fixing broken steps or banisters and planting summer flowers. The city park also gets a facelift from DOS participants.

A student, senior Sandy Johnson, said, "I worked in Memorial Park. We painted picnic tables, cleaned the playground equipment, added more mulch around the swings and replaced the nets on the tennis courts and the basketball goals."

Clifton Adams, a sophomore, worked on a widow's house. "We replaced rotten boards on her porch, reglued her rocking chair, painted her fence and weeded around the flower beds. She brought us hot cookies and milk. It made me feel good to help her."

Mayor Krantz participated too. The controversial city mayor is known for his blunt statements and his criticism of those who only want to take advantage of a community's resources for their own financial gain.

Last year he criticized the National politicians for doing more "conspiring than inspiring. They just spend their time and our money campaigning for their reelection or the reelection of their presidential candidate."

This time he was upset by how few businessmen showed up to help their elderly or unfortunate neighbors do home repairs or work to improve parks during DOS.

"We've got too many businessmen who join Kiwanis, Lions, Optimists, Junior Chamber, Habitat for Humanity, and other organizations just to network and rub elbows with potential clients," stated Krantz, when he was phoned to comment on the success of DOS.

He went on to say that he had heard bankers, insurance agents and real estate agents brag about how many boards of directors they served on. "Not one of those slackers showed up to work during Day of Sharing."

Part of Krantz's unique positions on politics is that "public servants should only serve one term in office. They should get paid no more than the average man or woman in their community. And they should not be campaigning for a party."

He ended with: "They should vote their conscience, not vote according to the party line. In fact why do we have political parties?"

One of Krantz's first acts as mayor of Bainter was to have the city council reduce the mayor's pay and to pass a statute to limit city council members and mayors to one term. The motion passed by only one vote.

Mariam Douglas, physical education teacher at Bainter High, was the chairperson of DOS. She was pleased by the student turnout, especially because it was summer vacation. She said 317 students helped, plus 11 businessmen, 15 teachers and 28 other community members. "We especially liked the support of Mayor Krantz, who seemed to work the longest and the hardest of anyone."

This is the third year for DOS, but the first held when school was out. "In the past," related Douglas, "DOS had been a school-wide service-learning project, so all 490 high school students participated. Of course in the summer, many students work or are out of town. I want to thank all those who participated."

Miss Ardnas posted the rant on Ersatznews.blogspot.com. She felt a little less angry. That night writing and teaching dominated Miss Ardnas' sleep once she dozed off. In her dream she was at her desk typing for her blog. Then the walls disappeared and she was walking in the university hallway with only her skirt and bra on. She went to her room to get a blouse but her skirt disappeared as the students for her next class strolled in. They didn't seem to notice as she began to nonchalantly start a lesson. She immediately woke up, remembered her dream and thought, do all teachers and writers at times feel naked or that they're walking in public in their underwear? Writing with hyperbole and sarcasm could be construed by some as revealing the actual beliefs of the author..

On the other hand, after the phone conversation with Miss Ardnas, Madison continued to steam about the lack of support by businessmen. What really pissed her off was that teachers had spent weeks during off hours planning activities, searching out projects, collecting money, buying paint and other supplies and encouraging the students. Then they gave up a week of their summer vacation, which for many was not a vacation because they, unlike the businessmen, didn't earn six-figure salaries. The teachers worked second jobs, took master's classes, enrolled in state-required continuing education seminars, prepared for the next school year or taught summer school. These teachers were also the first to be asked to teach Sunday school, coach the summer youth baseball, softball and soccer leagues, lead service organizations and run the boy and girl scout troops.

Madison pictured some of the men she had done business with as they sat in their offices, wearing suit and tie, protected from the public by a secretary and a receptionist. She on the other hand arrived at school at 7:30 am, had to deal with 20 or 30 people at a time and hardly had time for a potty break. Lunch was a fast walk to a cafeteria, supervising students sitting around her, gobbling down starchy food and hustling to the restroom before another batch of teens invaded her classroom. She would love to do as the businessmen and deal with one person at time, or have a secretary say, "Students, she's out of her classroom right now. Have a seat and she will be back in an hour." Or "She's not in today, please come back tomorrow after 10 am."

She would love to be able to take a leisurely hour and a half for lunch with colleagues at a restaurant with a calming ambience, followed by a walk in a park—she didn't play golf. Most of those businessmen would wet their pants if they had to meet 25, hour-long classes of 30 hormonal teenagers a week. They were used to dealing with one customer at a time, not 30, with the secretary running interference for them.

Madison didn't start to calm down until she let William in, and he worked his magic. He kissed her on the lips, poured her a glass of Moscato, and kneeled in front of her. He slowly untied the strings on her tennis shoes and delicately rolled the socks from each foot. Her feet were always cold, so his large warm hands, one wrapped around each sole, made her shoulders untense, and she relaxed her head against the back of the sofa. Her arms fell limp at her sides.

His strong fingers kneaded the supple, silky bottoms of her feet, and he massaged toward her toes, each of which received its due attention. When he rubbed her heels, a feather ascended up through Madison's legs, paused at her pelvis, circled her heart and exited at her shoulders. William tried to talk her into letting him spend the night, but, despite the goose down flying around inside her chest, she held her ground.

After William left, Madison undressed, burrowed into bed and slipped easily into a light sleep and dreamed. She was an Indian going with tribal members to drink from the river. She put her face to the water to quench her thirst and got her hair wet, which she didn't like; so she placed her hand in the water and then licked the water from it. While her family members had their faces half in the water lapping like dogs, she began drinking out of the cup of her hand. She decided to carry water in her palm back to her grandmother at the camp, and during her walk her hand turned into a leaf, then a hollow gourd. Suddenly she was back at the river dipping the gourd into the river at a bank of clay. Where she pressed the gourd into the ground to collect water a puddle was created. She and another girl dug under the clay puddle and lifted it out with the water still in it. They were walking back to the camp when everything went dark and the tribe was sitting cooking and eating around a fire. The next morning the puddle was empty and the clay had baked hard. Then a dozen clay pots and bowls appeared by the fire. Everyone was amazed and her name was changed to River Carrier. Madison continued through the night without waking.

Chapter 21. The Plan

Madison had notified everyone about Mark's "fragile" constitution. They decided that they all would be at the youth meeting to help him sell the screenplay idea. Duke, Jenni, Jake, Laura, William, Sam, Kae, Kurj and, of course Naomi and Madison attended. They met an hour before the youth meeting so that they could create a plan of attack.

Before they got down to business, the typical personal greetings were exchanged and sharing took place. Jake told about selling pd's and starting a transit company in Wyandotte. Jenni, who was tired of giving pedicures and manicures at Hair U R, seemed interested in buying Jake's business with Duke's help, and Madison blew off about Week of Caring. Miss Ardnas was quiet. Everyone thought they knew why. And, lastly, Sam told about his new job in Glacier National Park.

After they got down to business about the movie, they each took a part of the project and decided to set up tables. At each table they would explain what they thought the job would entail and accept volunteers. They would leave casting to Mark, Naomi would take costumes, Miss Ardnas would handle props, Jake would be in charge of shooting locations, Kae and Kurj would work with scenery, Duke would handle anything to do with vehicles, Sam would handle the technical aspect of filming and editing. Jenni would be in charge of make up and Laura, who had once worked for a studio photographer, would see to interior lighting. Agnikaa and Paawan, a Hindu couple who arrived late, said they'd keep the shooting schedule and make sure there were snacks and water on the "sets."

The group figured that if they promised to support the youth volunteers in getting started they could then step back and help only as advisors when needed. A desk was set up for each job and the adults made notes about what they wanted to explain. A signup sheet was also on each desk. They decided that, although there would be specific positions, someone working at one position could assist anyone else if needed. The important thing was to acquire a good leader for each position then encourage working as an harmonious team.

Mark entered the school room that they rented for youth group meetings. He was wearing a sport coat over a blue oxford shirt, jeans and Nike sneakers. The sport jacket was threadbare at the elbows. "What are you guys doing here?"

"Divide and conquer," answered Miss Ardnas with a bigger smile than usual. Mark was amazed that Miss Ardnas could smile with all the hell Franklin was putting her through. She looked proper as usual in a smart ecru pantsuit.

"Where's the war?"

"We're ready to sell the movie idea to the wunderkind," added Jake.

They took a few minutes for the group to explain their overall plan and to give details about the individual committees. Mark's perpetual smile broadened.

The teens and young adults trickled in, not having any idea of what was on the agenda. When they were all seated, he told them about the screenplay he was writing. "It's called *Hey, Zeus*."

"Jesus, in Spanish," explained one of the girls.

"That's right. You know, you are a talented bunch and I want to propose a group project that is beyond anything most youth groups would tackle. I want you to take my screenplay and make a movie. Right here in Wyandotte, with you doing the casting, playing some of the parts, taping, editing, and everything else."

Silence.

"Crazy, right? Who's crazy enough to help?" challenged Mark.

"Count me in."

"Hey, I am."

"We are."

"Me."

"Yeah. Let's do it."

"I'm crazy enough."

"Always wanted to be in a movie."

"I will."

These were the canned comments of Duke, Jenni, Kae, Jake, Kurj, Miss Ardnas, Laura, Sam and, of course Naomi and Madison who had jumped to their feet and raised their arms before the students could even take in the concept. Before any whining and questioning could take place, Mark said: "Ok, stand up and go to a table that represents where you would like to help."

The adults turned over the signs at their tables and started calling the students over.

"Mia, follow me. I think you'd be a good actress," directed Mark.

"Over here, Josh. We need techies to do editing. Ok?" yelled Sam.

Naomi, in a violet and purple paisley blouse and dark slacks, called to Brittney, who also dressed with style, to sign up for costumes.

The adults kept their committees together as Mark recited a synopsis of the screenplay. Then the committees started brainstorming. After twenty minutes Mark asked for nominees for director, and Josh, who they all knew was a movie trivia buff and technically a phenomenon, was the only one mentioned. With the directorship settled, Mark called an end to the meeting. All those in attendance were revved up about the project and left the meeting talking about more filming ideas.

Mark went home and dug into *Hey, Zeus*. Some of the adults and youth were already asking for a copy so that they could begin annotating and memorizing. He decided that he would sit at his desk until it was finished.

******

ZEUS
Let's let Jones 'ere takes care of eet. Jones? You gots any ideas, Jones?
JONES thinks for a second, then goes into his store and comes out with three, large, aerosol cans. ABE, RALPH, DELIA, DAVE, WILMA, ED, and others gather in the middle of the street.
JONES
This ought to do it.
JONES hands ZEUS and JAIME each a can and he keeps one.
They HUDDLE for a second as if they're getting a play from a quarterback. Then Jones runs to one side of the house, Jaime to the other, and Zeus to the front.
They snap off the tops of the protective caps and THROW THE CANS through three different already-broken windows and run.
They end up together in the middle of the street again as crackheads come out of every window and door and run into and down the back alley.
JACK stumbles out the front door, sees everyone laughing at him and heads for the alley, too. Odd-colored fumes come out of every opening of the house
ALL
(laughing and cheering)
RALPH
Look at'm run.
JAIME
That'll learn'em.
DELIA
That'sa way.

DAVE
Bout time.
WILMA
Give it to'em, Zeus.
ED
(giving high fives)
What'd you guys throw in there, tear gas?
JONES
No, something more appropriate. Flea bombs. Guaranteed to exterminate repulsive home pests and obnoxious troublemakers, all compliments of Jones Hardware.
After the fumes stop coming out of the crack house, more than twenty people leave their apartments, houses and businesses and bring ladders, paint and brushes to start giving the house a first coat.
TOM and DELIA join the on-lookers.
DELIA
(to Jones)
How about donating one more thing today, Jones? New locks for those doors.
JONES
(teasing)
Anything for you, little honey.
    CUT TO:
EXT.--MANILA STREET--DAY
PEDRO is followed down the street away from the church by ten grade schoolers. He is walking between Nate and Susanne, holding their hands.
ZEUS is approaching the church and walks over to MARLEEN who is watching.
ZEUS
What's weeth zee Pie Piper, or eet's something likes that. They follows heem like zee sheep follow zee ram. Thees ees only zee second time I've seen heem out of zee church.
MARLEEN
I set up a field trip with Bob to the Builders Home Center for one of our after-school tutoring groups, then faked a bad ankle, so the kids begged Pedro to take them, and I just looked at him and shrugged. He was trapped, but I'm pretty sure he caught on to what I was up to.
    CUT TO:
EXT.--MANILA STREET--NIGHT
BERT sits in his squad car.

ZEUS, holding a large white paper sack, is standing outside talking to him.
BERT
(looking suspiciously at the bag)
What? You want to, uh, ride with me tonight? Yeah, I'll take you straight to, uh, jail.
ZEUS
No, I means eet. You gots a tough, dangerous, thankless job 'ere. I'd likes to keeps you companies tonight while you're covering your beats.
Zeus's honest, innocent and humble tone takes Bert by surprise.
BERT
Well, uh, I don't know. The watch commander is supposed to approve, uh, stuff like this. By the way, what's in the, uh, bag?
ZEUS
I thoughts we'd likes some coffee and donuts while we're driving around.
BERT
Oh, jump in. I'll call the, uh, sergeant later.
BERT starts the car and begins patrolling slowly down Manila Street. Bert uses a spotlight to see into dark corners around the buildings.
I'm looking at each place of, uh, business to make sure lights that are supposed to be on are, uh, on and those that aren't, uh, aren't.
Bert slows down, uses his light, then moves on.
BERT (CONT.)
Ya know, Zeus, uh, I was going to try to run you out of, uh, Kimmel a few weeks back.
ZEUS
(Laughing)
I had a teeny, weeny feelin' that you were outs to get me.
BERT
Well, I, uh, figured you didn't have, uh, a green card and all, and you'd be noth'n but, uh, trouble around here. But, uh, just the opposite was true.
ZEUS
Thees ees a great neighborhood. Everybodies helps everybody.
BERT
That wasn't always, uh, true, and I don't care anymore if you don't have, uh, a green card. All those times I began to, uh, stop you, I just couldn't, cause I, uh, knew what you were really doing. In fact -- I'd get fired if this, uh, got out -- Jack tried to, uh, bribe me to run you out of

Kimmel. The next day, when I, uh, thought about how, uh, stupid that was, I gave the money to the, uh, Red Cross.

BERT and ZEUS each take a coffee and donut. They leisurely ride while they eat their donuts and drink their coffee.

BERT screeches to a halt and throws the door open. Coffee and donuts fly.

BERT (CONT.)
(speaking rapidly)
Someone just came out of the back door of Jones Hardware carrying a sack. Stay here.

BERT runs down the alley where he saw the burglar.

ZEUS gets out and runs around the corner to Plum Street where the cross alley meets the side street.

BERT (CONT.)
(to burglar)
Stop right there!

BERT runs to where the alleys cross, then turns right toward Plum Street.

The BURGLAR comes out of the alley and turns toward Manila, assuming Bert won't expect him to go to a main street.

As the burglar runs out onto the sidewalk, ZEUS steps over in front of him and just gives him a big body hug and lifts his legs, putting all his weight on the burglar. The burglar takes a couple more stumbling steps and falls, and the sack flies into the gutter.

BERT runs up and immediately cuffs the man.

BERT (CONT.)
Jack? What're you, uh, doing coming out of, uh, Jones's?

JACK
(indicating Zeus)
What's he doing here?

ZEUS
(picking up the sack)
Eet looks like he was making a weethdrawal, a beeg weethdrawal. There's about a thousand dollars 'ere. Deedn't you ever 'ears about zee jackass that ates too much clover? Thees ees just like that.

JACK
I can explain, Bert.

BERT
Shut up, Jack. Anything you say may be, uh, used against you . . .

JACK
You can't take me to jail. I'll tell them about the bribe . . .

BERT
So you admit to, uh, bribing an officer. Now I understand where those bills, uh, came from after you stuck your head into my, uh, car a couple of weeks ago. You heard him, Zeus, he tried to, uh, bribe an officer of the law.
ZEUS
I sure deed!
        CUT TO:
INT.--CHURCH
The pews are full of all the business people from the neighborhood and so are the folding chairs. Zeus is at the pulpit.
ZEUS
Hey, amigos, thees ees a meeting, I theenks. What's eet you wants to do thees week.
TOM fakes as if he's going to stand up and say something and Delia is ready.
DELIA
(to Tom)
Sit . . .
Tom grins and everybody laughs at his trick.
DELIA (CONT.)
(to audience)
Let's have a parade. Our street looks great, now. Let's show it off.
JONES
Yeah, it'll bring in some new faces to see what a nice neighborhood we have. Give the hardware some new business, too.
JAIME
(sitting and holding hands with Lyla)
Good idea. Since we bought the pizza parlor . . . well, the bank owns most of it . . . anyway, since we've expanded, I could stand some good advertising. The parade would bring customers.
ZEUS
Who's going to be een charge of zee parade?
DELIA
All in favor of Zeus as grand marshal of the parade say aye.
TOM
(jumping up)
AYE!
Delia and the audience laughs because Tom has fooled her twice.
ALL
(mostly together)

Aye.
ED
What will be in the parade?
NOELA
How about the junior high band?
DAVE
I just had my garbage truck painted jet black with silver lettering. I'll be there.
CARL
(to Dave)
Yeh, and I'll follow you. I'll fix up my dilivery van with a new paint job and lettering like yours.
BERT
I'll lead the parade with my siren going.
LYLA
Jaime and I will make a float that looks like a pizza on edge and put it in the back of our delivery truck. Right, dear?
Jaime smiles and nods.
KAREN
Mom, Ralph and I can get a Chinese dragon costume about twenty-five feet long.
PEDRO
(smiling at Karen)
That's a great idea.
JEFFERSON
I'll call the mayor's office to see if we can get some politicians to be in the parade.
ZEUS
Good ideas. Let's sets zee date.
    CUT TO:
INT.--PIZZA PARLOR
LYLA
(snuggling up to Jaime)
OK, Jaime, when are we going to get married?

Chapter 22. Two Cups of Coffee

    Naomi left her room, walked to Mark's bedroom door and knocked. She often thought about spending a night in his sanctuary.

    "I can't sleep. I saw your light on and heard you shuffling papers. Do you want to sit and have a cup of coffee? De café?"

    "Sure. I need a break from the script."

They walked down to the kitchen and Naomi started a pot of coffee, then she sat down at the table across from Mark. She intentionally let the flaps of her robe slip off her tan, smooth, shapely legs.

"What is heaven, Naomi?"

"You don't believe in chitchat do you?"

"Oh, sorry."

"That's ok. Anyway, I don't think it's streets of gold or pearly gates. That's just the way to describe it for poor people, people who struggle for existence all their lives," said Naomi, crossing her left knee over her right. She wanted Mark to notice, to scoot closer, to untie the robe, to slip his hands in and behind the robe, to move them up and under her night shirt to her bare back, to softly kiss just below her ear and then move down to the crook of her neck. She started to close her eyes as she thought...

"Wouldn't like a heaven where we knew everything." Mark, believing the robe had accidently dropped open and uncovered her legs, took the two flaps and gently lapped them back over her knees. He finished the procedure with a pat on her left knee. "What would be the purpose of living? It's probably why God gave us free will and infinite outer space for us to explore forever."

"Hard to imagine."

"And inner space must be infinite. Talk about something hard to imagine, but, when you think of the earth or even our solar system, it must seem microscopic from the stars that we can see only through telescopes."

"We must be wafted around in the universe like some dust being blown off a table. You'd think we'd feel it or see things move past us."

"It makes me wonder if God is omniscient. We have free will. Is God omniscient or do we give him surprises with our freedom? How boring to know how mankind will behave."

"Yeah. People pray to God to heal them, when if he knew they were going to get ill and didn't' want them to be ill, he wouldn't have let them get ill in the first place. Does that make sense?"

"I always wondered about those kinds of prayers too. What fascinates me is the attitude of the Greek gods and goddesses. The Greek gods were the only immortals. They envied the mortals because they only had one life. The gods wanted to feel the passion involved in living each day, since each day was so precious, could be the last, and the days were limited. It's like only having five days for a vacation.

You're all excited and crazy for the vacation to start and get depressed when you only have one day left."

"I know what you mean," commented Naomi.

"I think those who don't deeply believe in life after death are more frantic to reproduce themselves so that something of them remains after they're gone."

"You're probably right. What else do they have? Life without hope is no life at all."

"I like thinking about God as watching us and billions of other beings on thousands of worlds with hope, pride and sorrow. I like to think of God as giving us the means to think, question and find enough truth to live by and get along. God's given humans enough hints, but when I watch the news, I wonder if anyone is listening. As I read the *Koran, The Tao-te-Ching , Upanishads, Bible, Sutras, Bhagavad Gita* and other religious texts, the message is obvious—love and live in peace. Then religious leaders get ahold of the message and make it proprietary to their religion, and use it as power over insecure peoples. I just hope God doesn't give up on us. I was reading Barbara Kingsolver's Flight Behavior, and one of the characters says, "What was the use of saving a world that had no soul left in it."

"Wow. You ought to be a preacher."

"Funny."

"Noel told me in the airport as we were waiting to leave that prayer by others makes a big difference in Shirley and his mission. He says it's not like Saul of Tarsus' experience on the road to Damascus, but more like somebody pulling a few strings behind the scenes so that you have to really think hard about a past incident to see God's or an angel's handiwork."

Mark added, "I know prayer has worked in my life. Did you know tht Kae is an avid believer in God's intervention through prayer? She says she lives her life day by the day, not by the week or month. She seldom plans ahead but prays each day for help in everything she needs. She says prayers have found her a place to stay in a city during a holiday, a stranger to fix her flat tire, healing for her friends and strength to continue working at a mission long after her own strength had waned. Do you think there's a hell or angels?"

"It's too late to start in on another perplexing concept."

"My dad always said that hell was having to live with yourself. He's gone now, and I never asked whether he meant living with his own conscience or living with someone just like himself for eternity. I know lots of people who complain about the behavior of people who behave just like them. Ironic, hey? Ambrose Bierce defined a bore as 'A person who talks when you wish them to listen.' That kind of encapsulates the concept."

They finished their coffee, went upstairs, said goodnight and went to their separate rooms. Naomi crawled in bed and read further in *The Heart Is a Lonely Hunter*, which she had read twice before, and Mark sat down and continued writing and editing *Hey, Zeus*.

******

JAIME
Well, uh . . . I, was uh . . . going to ask you but I never got around to it.
LYLA
Don't I know it. Well?
JAIME
You mean I got to set a date now? There's two more pizzas to be made . . . Now?
LYLA
You better or you're going to have to get a new partner in this business, cause I won't be here.
JAIME
Now we don't have to get angry. Let's be sensible about this, dear. Uh . . . how about two months after the parade. That'll give us time to . . .
LYLA
How about two hours before the parade and we drive through the parade on our way to the honeymoon.
JAIME
Well, uh . . . OK . . . uh, but who's going to drive our float?
LYLA
I already asked Pedro, and he said how could he refuse if we were on our honeymoon.
JAIME
Why you sneak'n, conniv'n . . .
JAIME and LYLA hug and spin in the middle of the dining area, laughing and tickling each other. They stop when they remember that people at the tables are watching, and they hurry over and start making pizzas.
    CUT TO:
INT.--CHURCH
PEDRO is surrounded by 15 students who are listening to him read *The Hounds of the Baskervilles*.
MARLEEN is sitting in the background smiling like a contented teacher.

PEDRO
(reading)
"That we should have heard his screams -- my, those screams! -- and yet have been unable to save him! Where is this brute of a hound which drove him to his death? It may be lurking among these rocks at this instant. And Stapleton, where is he? He shall answer for this deed."
The kids are so completely engrossed in Pedro's smooth and suspenseful reading that when he stops it's as if they just awakened from a dream.
PEDRO (CONT.)
Well, we'd better stop there for today.
NATE
No, Mr. Pedro, please read just a little more. What happens to Mr. Stapleton?
ALL
Yeah!
PEDRO
I'm sorry, but I promised all your parents we would quit in time for supper, especially tonight since most of you and your families are working on projects for the parade.
(to Marleen)
Since you hurt your ankle, I'll just walk Susanne home, OK?
Marleen gives him a knowing smile and nods.
PEDRO (CONT.)
I'll pick up some Chinese food for dinner, too.
MARLEEN
(teasing)
I thought you didn't like Chinese. Abe's deli is on your way back. Pick up some . . .
PEDRO
(frowning)
You know I love Chinese. Let's go, Susanne.
    CUT TO:
INT.--LUNG'S RESTAURANT
KAREN is working the cash register.
RALPH is in the kitchen looking through the service window.
PEDRO
Hi, Karen. Here's Susanne, safe and sound. Bye, Susanne.
SUSANNE
(flirting)

Bye, Ped-ro.
KAREN
(to Ralph)
Ralph, will you watch the register for a moment.
(to Pedro)
Come sit down a minute. There's something I want to ask you.
PEDRO and KAREN move to the farthest corner of the restaurant and sit down across from each other at an empty table.
SUSANNE comes over and gives Pedro an iced tea and a big smile.
PEDRO
What did you want to ask me?
KAREN
I wondered if you'd help Ralph and me move the dragon through the street during the parade? Ralph wants to be the head and Susanne can take the tail, but we need you to help me in the middle.
SUSANNE comes over again and brings Pedro a fortune cookie and an another big smile.
KAREN gives her a dirty look and moves to the other side of the table, taking the chair next to him, basically pinning Pedro in and blocking Susanne.
PEDRO
I . . . can't. Sorry. But I got to drive the L & J's Pizza truck. Sorry.
KAREN
(showing disappointment
Oh, that's Ok. We'll try to find someone else.
PEDRO
But . . . I know I haven't known you long, but with me turtoring Susanne and . . . well . . . what I mean is . . . but we've been eating Chinese food from here for so long . . . and . . . well . . . I've got something I want to ask you too . . . would you go to the dance after the parade with me?
Karen takes his hand and smiles and nods.
PEDRO (CONT.)
Oh, I almost forgot. I need an order of pork fried rice and a dozen egg rolls to go.
KAREN gives Pedro a kiss on the cheek and goes to the opening to the kitchen.
KAREN
Ralph, we need one large number 14 and a dozen egg rolls to go.
KAREN hurries back to talk to Pedro.

SUSANNE has beaten her and is in her seat, forcing Karen to sit across from them.
SUSANNE
And Tuesday, Pedro, I think we should begin reading Robinson Crusoe. I just love the way you read. Your voice is soooooo deep and strong . . .
Pedro is smiling at this, but Karen is not. Pedro breaks open his fortune cookie.
KAREN
Read it.
PEDRO
(reading)
"Love is in your future."
KAREN
Susanne, you slipped that . . .
Karen starts to expose Susanne's trick, but decides not to. Susanne smiles again at Pedro as she leans against him. Karen's expression is unchanged.
   CUT TO:
INT.--DIFFERENT CHURCH ON MANILA STREET
The whole CONGREGATION STANDS with the playing of the WEDDING MARCH.
LYLA, in a beautiful white wedding gown, slowly walks down the aisle to JAIME and the PREACHER.
   PAN TO:
ZEUS is standing at the altar as the best man and MARLEEN, looking surprisingly nice, is maid of honor.
   CUT TO:
INT.--FELLOWSHIP HALL OF CHURCH
People are lined up for the RECEPTION in the church. The cake is beautiful and, of course, there is lots of pizza being served on fine, rented China. TOM, DELIA, and JONES are ahead of PEDRO coming through the reception line.
TOM
(hugging Lyla)
Best . . .
DELIA
. . . wishes, you two. Prettiest wedding Manila street has ever seen. And, Lyla, you're the prettiest bride I've ever seen. You look okay, too, Jaime. Now you two go off and have a romantic honeymoon, cause Tom here will keep an eye on the store for you, won't you, Tom?

TOM
(shakes hands with Jaime)
I sure . . .
DELIA
. . . sure will. Don't worry your pretty little heads about anything. You only have one first honeymoon, so make the most of it.
LYLA
Thank you, Tom and Delia. We'll try.
LYLA squeezes Jaime's hand.
JONES
(to Jaime)
Listen, when you get back from your honeymoon, you come into the hardware and you'll have a hundred dollar gift certificate for anything you want.
JAIME
Thanks a lot, Mr. Jones.
PEDRO
You are beautiful, Lyla. If Jaime hadn't married you, I guess that I'd have had to. I wish you all the happiness in the world.
PEDRO kisses Lyla, and they hug and laugh.
LYLA
Just don't wreck our truck, Pedro.
PEDRO laughs then shakes hands with Jaime.
PEDRO
You take good care of my step-sister, now.
JAIME
I will, Pedro.
MARLEEN hugs Lyla, then straightens Lyla's dress as if she has messed it up.
MARLEEN
You look just gorgeous, Lyla. Prettiest bride I've ever seen. You look nice, too, Jaime.
LYLA
You're the prettiest stepmother I've ever seen, too.
MARLEEN and LYLA hug again and laugh.
Next ZEUS hugs Lyla and shakes Jaime's hand at the same time.
ZEUS
Now you two remembers about what zee nanny goat and zee he goat do when they 'urries out to pastures, don't you?

Lyla and Jaime nod quickly, because they are embarrassed and hope to head off one of Zeus's animal stories.
ZEUS
Well, I tells you anyway. They gets zee bestest grass, that ees what.
Lyla and Jaime don't know which way to take his story, so they just smile.
NOELA and JEFFERSON with NATE come through the line and hug and shake hands.
    CUT TO:
EXT.--MANILA STREET--DAY
BERT is in his car with lights flashing and siren blowing. He's waving as he begins down the street.
The BAND follows him and is playing "The Battle Hymn of the Republic."
The FIRE TRUCKS come through with sirens and lights flashing.
PEDRO drives by with the J & L Pizza float and he throws out discount coupons.
RALPH, KIM, BLAKE and KAREN snake through with a paper dragon.
BOB drives the Building Center truck with Marleen and a bunch of kids in the back waving and throwing candy.
THE MAYOR is next in a beautiful stretch convertible. The mayor sits up on the back rest of the back seat waving.
DAVE's shinny black garbage truck with silver lettering and pin striping follows the mayor.
CARL'S delivery van follows Dave's truck and has the same paintjob.
ZEUS is riding on the back of Dave's truck, throwing out candy that looks like plastic trash receptacles, except these have candy inside.
ED drives through with a city dump truck. The amber light on top of the cab is flashing.
    CUT TO:
INT.--MAYOR'S CAR--DAY
The mayor, Jimmy Calhoun, is talking to his assistant, Mike Hazelton, who drives.
MAYOR
(smiling and speaking through his teeth)
Who in the devil is this Hey Zeus guy on the back of a garbage truck that everyone is yelling to?
MIKE
Yeah. More people are waving at him than they are you. Oh, sorry, sir. I'll check in to it, Jimmy . . .

CALHOUN gives him a dirty look.
MIKE (CONT.)
. . . I mean . . . Mayor Calhoun.
      CUT TO:
EXT.--END OF PARADE ON MANILA STREET--DAY
JAIME and LYLA drive by in a nice rental car (sticker right on the bumper) that is covered with streamers, writing and has cans clanking behind on a string.
EVERYONE WAVES and throws rice.
      CUT TO:
INT.--THE CHURCH
The floor is clear for the DANCE, crepe paper strips decorate the walls, Chinese lanterns cover the lights, and JONES is acting as D.J.
The song is just ending and couples are leaving the floor.
JONES
Now that last song, "Electric Slide," was for all you line dancers. We can get everybody on the dance floor for the next song, "Remember Me this Way."

      ******

    Mark's mind wandered to the night at Antler Inn. He wasn't a great line dancer, but he enjoyed the slow dances with Naomi. He couldn't figure out why he hadn't asked Miss Ardnas to dance. He hadn't even danced with her in high school. They had just been the best of friends and nothing more. He thought about what good friends he and Naomi were. They had so much fun riding their velomobiles around town and causing comment. Mark was sure everyone thought they were weirdoes. He wanted to be a weirdo in some ways, because he didn't like the lifestyle of the typical Christian.

    He was nearing the end of the script and it made him work faster.

      ******

PEDRO and KAREN are the first ones back on the floor. They know and execute the steps perfectly and with energy.
DELIA and TOM take the floor next, and their dancing looks more like a congenial wrestling match because Delia wants to lead and Tom refuses to follow. They are, none the less, having a good time and smile broadly.
ABE and KIM somehow dance a beat slower that the others, but their smiles show that they are having fun.
WILMA and ZEUS take the floor tentatively, although Zeus dares to put his arm around Wilma's waist in a cozy manner. Wilma still carries her purse and it swings and hits Zeus.

ZEUS
What's that you gots een your purse, Wilma? Eet bout knocked me over.
WILMA
It's a rock, stupid, to crack the skulls of any men who get fresh when they dance.
ZEUS
That's a beeg rock.
WILMA
Thirty-two caliber.
ZEUS moves his left hand from her waist and up onto the saftey of her shoulder.
Jefferson and Noela and Dave and his wife join the others on the dance floor.
Carl and a girlfriend come out in matching shirts, pants and cowboy boots.
Ed and his wife have a table close to the dance floor and can be seen behind the dancers enjoying the festivities.
LYLA and JAIME, in casual dress now, enter and take the floor just as the song ends.
PEDRO
(surprised)
Lyla, what are you and Jaime doing here?
JAIME
You can't believe how boring those rich folks downtown are. We tried to get some fun started in the hotel lounge, but they only had a piano player. Felt out of place.
LYLA
And the piano player didn't know any of our favorites, so we decided to come down here for a couple of hours of fun with our friends, then head back for a romantic spell in the hot tub in our suite.
PEDRO
(eyebrows lifted)
Whoooa!
    CUT TO:
INT.--MAYOR'S OFFICE
MIKE
(looking at the contents of a folder)
You, know, you asked me to check on that guy named Hey Zeus.
MAYOR
Yes?

MIKE
Well, he illegally entered the country at New Laredo. He has no green card, no job, no property, and no money, so he is a vagrant, besides the other laws he's violated, like trespassing. The least they'll do is deport him.

MAYOR
Yes, but that doesn't tell us why he's so popular. Is he a drug dealer, besides? He might be hiding or laundering his drug money. In that part of this town drug . . .

MIKE
No, that's the strange thing. He's been living in an abandoned church with an ex-prostitute, an 18-year-old boy and a bag lady.

MAYOR
Sounds perverted to me.

MIKE
Now wait . . .

MAYOR
Why wasn't he arrested a long time ago? Who's precinct is that, anyway? I'll give them a call right now and get down to the bottom of this . . .

MIKE
Wait a minute, Mayor Calhoun. I'm not done yet. That church is now a tutoring center for at-risk students, and it's become a sorta town hall for the neighborhood. My sources say that's where they organized the parade.

MAYOR
You gotta be kidding. That's a nice neighborhood. And not a bad parade for the per capita income of that area of town. Streets were clean and the houses maintained and painted.

MIKE
Not before Hey Zeus. Somehow he is the center of all of those improvements.

MAYOR
How?

MIKE
I don't know. He even helped a policeman, Robert Akers, who goes by Bert, to catch a burglar. Guess he open field tackled him right on the street and everything.

MAYOR

Who in heavens is this guy, super social worker? What do we do with a guy like that, put him in jail, give him a medal or put him on my payroll?

The mayor paces the floor, then goes to his desk and shuffles papers as if he means to take care of business.

MAYOR (CONT.)
He's the best thing I've seen in this town since I was elected. I need some neighborhood before-and-after stories for my speeches in the upcoming election campaign, and Manila Street will be perfect. Is there any way we can get him papers and let him stay.

MIKE
No, I'm afraid not. He's probably been picked up and is on his way back to New Laredo by now. At least I don't think he'll get any jail time.

CUT TO:

INT.--OLD CHURCH--NIGHT

Marleen, Lyla, Pedro, Jaime and Zeus are sitting around eating Mexican food.

PEDRO
(takes a big bite out of a taco)
Well, Zeus, I got a job today.

ZEUS
My 'earing ain't so good sometimes, Pedro. Repeats that again, please.

PEDRO
You heard me fine the first time. I'm working at Carl's, helping him deliver furniture and riding with Ed on the days he hits the wealthy neighborhoods.

MARLEEN
Listen to this, Zeus. He made Carl agree to let him work from 7:30 to 3:30 so that he can be back here by around 4:00 to help me tutor.

ZEUS
(his mouth full)
Now, who ees thees that we're talking about?

LYLA
Now quit teasing my little brother, Zeus.

ZEUS
No, I am proud of Pedro most of zee time. I knew he would amounts to sometheen' one days. My only problem ees that he broughts home Tex-Mex food for deenner tonight. I don't knows where I failed heem about good food.

JAIME

Obviously, Lyla and I think you should stick to Italian food.
ZEUS
(smiling)
Yes, I hears there ees a very good place over on Washington Street.
LYLA
We'd better never catch you over there.
Everyone laughs and continues eating.
> CUT TO:

EXT.--BERT'S SQUAD CAR--MORNING
ZEUS walks out of the church toward the car just as BERT starts to open the door to go into the church to get him. Zeus just goes over to the squad car and gets into the front seat, just as if it had been a taxi he had called for.
> CUT TO:

INT.--BERT'S SQUAD CAR
BERT and ZEUS are driving along in the front seat.
BERT
(puzzled)
How did you, uh, know that I was coming to get you?
ZEUS
Thees I do not know.
BERT
(frowning)
Well, anyway, uh, I'm sorry 'bout this, Zeus. The only thing I could, uh, do is keep you from doing some, uh, jail time and then take you back to, uh, Mexico myself. Government officials called most the, uh, shots on this one.
ZEUS
(laughing)
'Sa'wright, Bert. Zee officiales sometimes don't knows what they ees doing.
BERT
Well, we'll miss you, uh, around here. You especially gave me a, uh, few things to think back on and to, uh, laugh about, and you helped a lot of people on, uh, Manila Street. I really, uh, feel bad about this.
ZEUS
Don't you worries, Bert. Eet weell be good for me to see zee old bunch back home. I meess those goats and donkey's. Anyway, I'll be backs een bout three week, depending on zee border guards. I knows Gene and Bill pretty well. I weell find a way.
BERT

Well, I, uh, believe you, Zeus. You're one of a kind. The, uh, neighborhood wouldn't be the same, uh, without you.
>CUT TO:

INT.--CHURCH

Most of the neighborhood is sitting sadly talking about Zeus's deportation.

BERT is standing near the pulpit. As he raises both arms the crowd gets quiet.

BERT

I had to, uh, send Zeus back. Those were their, uh, orders not mine. But I, uh, made it easy on him. He didn't go to, uh, jail, and I drove him back to, uh, New Laredo myself. I'm, uh, sorry. I had to.

TOM starts to stand up and speak, but Delia puts her hand on his shoulder and pushes to stand up, which pushes him back into his seat. Tom smiles through all of this.

DELIA

Now, I've got something to say. We understand, Bert. We're just upset. Don't take none of our feelings personal, now. We know you did right.

BERT

Well, if this, uh, helps . . . he said he'd be back in, uh, three weeks . . . . And, uh, knowing what he was able to, uh, do around here, I wouldn't put it, uh, past him.

JONES walks up and takes the place of Bert and takes control of the meeting.

JONES

OK, guys and gals, I've got a plan for a "Hey Zeus homecoming." We've probably got less than three weeks to pull this off, so let's get organized. First of all we'll need . . .
>FADE OUT:
>FADE IN:

EXT.--BORDER CROSSING--DAY

There are two lanes of traffic going across the border.

ZEUS is hanging, spread eagle, on the far side of a cattle truck that is in the lane furthest from the guard house.

Zeus is obviously in cahoots with the driver and passenger of the truck because they can be seen giving Zeus hand signals.

BILL comes over to the truck driver's window.

ZEUS crawls along the side and onto the back gate.

BILL moves toward the back.

ZEUS is forced to spider his way to the other side of the truck.

The DRIVER signals Zeus that Bill is circling the truck.

BILL walks around the back and starts for the front.
ZEUS climbs over the hood with his face smashed against the windshield to get to his original position on the driver's side of the truck.
BILL hands the papers through the truck's passenger window and gets ready to wave them on. Bill glances toward a passenger car going toward Mexico.
>PAN TO:
EXT.--PASSENGER CAR--DAY
Bill sees that the children in the car are laughing and pointing at the truck.
>CUT TO:
EXT.--TRUCK--DAY
BILL
Gene, let that car go through and come over here. Walk around the back of this truck and I'll meet you at the driver's window.
GENE
OK.
GENE and BILL round their corners of the truck.
ZEUS pulls his body in tight against the truck, pulls his head down toward his body like a turtle, closes his eyes and holds perfectly still as if they might not see him.
BILL
(laughing)
Well, if it ain't ol' Zeus. Long time no see, aye-me-go.
GENE
Alright, Hey Zeus, get off the truck and start heading home.
>PAN TO:
ZEUS walking dejectedly away mumbling.
ZEUS
What's all thees talk about land of zee free and home of American friendliness? My old goats and donkeys treats me better . . .
>CUT TO:
EXT.--BORDER CROSSING--DAY
ZEUS is in a padre's suit and black hat, and he is slowly merging with a large group of nuns in habits and fathers in black who are walking back across into the United States from their annual visit to Mexico. Gene and Bill are on duty again.
GENE
Did you have a good time this year, sister? Well, good . . . Do you have anything to declare?

Some of the group members shake their heads to indicate they have nothing to declare.
GENE (CONT.)
Hold up your I. D., please . . .
Some members of the group do and some don't. It just seems a yearly formality for both Gene and Bill and the nuns and priests.
GENE (CONT.)
Thank you . . . OK, you can move along. Anything to declare? OK . . . See you next year, Father Alberto, Sister Elaine.
ALBERTO
I hope so, my son.
GENE (CONT.)
. . Nice day, huh? Anything to declare? OK.
There is more shaking of heads, and the group moves off with Zeus in the middle.
    CUT TO:
EXT.--GAS STATION--DAY
ZEUS, still in costume, is talking to an old couple driving a station wagon.
ZEUS
OK, then. You won't minds taking me to Kimmel then?
LADY PASSENGER
No, we don't mind, padre.
    CUT TO:
EXT.--MANILA STREET--DAY
It's Sunday.
ZEUS is walking north on the street toward the church. All the stores are closed, even the deli, and no one is anywhere on the streets.
He finally gets to the block where the church is but he walks on by. After he is about twenty steps beyond the spot, he turns and sees the church, not the church he remembers, but a new-looking church.
The bricks have been cleaned, the joints between the bricks have been pointed with mortar, and there is grass growing in the yard. New walks have been poured. The steeple has bells in it.
All the windows and doors are painted and the glass has been replaced. There's a low white fence bordering the yard.
The final embellishment is a new white sign with big black letters: Manila Urban Street-Improvement Committee.
In script under that: "We Make M.U.S.I.C."
In smaller print: Open 24 Hours, 7 Days a Week. In print below that: Established in 1996.

Beneath that is: Founder: JESUS CRISTIANO DELGADO GARCIA.
Then: Building donated by the Maranatha Assembly.
And finally, Keeper of the Faith -- Marleen E. Longstreet, B.A., M.A.
Zeus is dumbfounded and stands and just looks or reads for several minutes. Finally he hears talking coming from inside. When he opens the door the crowd is listening to Jones discuss plans for an upcoming block party and street dance.

CUT TO:

INT.--CHURCH

JONES

Now, we'll have to get permission to close the blocks between Grape and Apple streets. Then we'll get barrels and paint them . . . Hey, Zeus. I almost didn't recognize you in that priest's outfit. How ya doing, friend?

CUT TO:

ZEUS enters and walks toward the pulpit.
The entire crowd stands to get a better look as he walks by. Then they applaud.

ALL

SURPRISE!!

NOELA

Speech, speech.

LYLA

Yeah, Zeus, give a speech.

Others chime in with encouragement, and TOM and DELIA make him take the pulpit next to Jones.

ZEUS

Deed you guys ever 'ear the parable about zee donkey and zee goat? Well, zee donkey said to zee goat, I don't eats burlap do I. Why not, zee goat asked. See, that's zee problem, was hees reply. Thees ees the same things here. Then there's zee one about zee jackass and the sheep . . .

Everyone is laughing because his stories never seem to make sense and the laughing interrupts Zeus's story.

JONES pats Zeus kindly on the back and moves back into the pulpit.
ZEUS stands behind him a few seconds then walks down through the crowd, people reaching to shake his hand and pat him on the back.
He takes a seat in the rear of the church where he is hugged by Karen and Pedro.

JONES

Now, where was I? Oh, yeah, we'll paint the barrels festive colors and place them at each end of the blocked streets. Maybe put a few cement blocks in them to make them hard to move . . . uh, let's have a volunteer to head up the barrel subcommittee.
 CUT TO:
DELIA raises Tom's hand and he smiles and nods his head to indicate he will do it.
 CUT TO:
JONES (CONT.)
Someone else needs to be in charge of chairs and . . .
 CUT TO:
ZEUS is smiling through this and quietly gets up and steps out the back door.
 CUT TO:
EXT.--GAS STATION--DAY
ZEUS talks to a SEMI DRIVER.
ZEUS
So eet's OK eef I rides weeth you, huh?
DRIVER
(looking him over and laughing)
Sure, father. I'm not very religious, but I'll take you as far as I go. Hop in.
 FADE OUT:
THE END

    Chapter 23. Fortunate Tragedy

 Miss Ardnas appeared so happy at the meeting because of recent events. She had received a call from Cali, one of Franklin's former secretaries and lovers, who said, "Look at the newspaper." That was the total conversation.

 Before she even bent over to pick up the paper on the porch, she saw that Franklin was above the fold on the front page. She sat down on the steps and shook her head. After refocusing, she could see that Franklin was bare-chested and barefooted sitting on a similar step of a strange house. An EMT was checking his blood pressure and a policeman was standing behind watching.

 Looking closer she could see a little red streak below Franklin's lip, and he was holding his left arm with his right hand. The headline read: "Domestic Fight Disturbs Deer Forest." The body of the article didn't name names, but related that the owner of the house in Deer Forest came home at 2 am and found an intruder attacking his wife.

Miss Ardnas looked at the injured man again and was positive it was Franklin.

A few hours after she had finished the news article, her lawyer, Jeremy Kim, called and said that he had gotten a call from Franklin's lawyer and that Franklin had dropped the custody suit. Miss Ardnas felt her eyes tearing up. She choked out a "Thank you, Jeremy," and hung up. Then she did a little solo salsa dancing in the middle of the kitchen.

Jenni called with the rest of the story. As it turned out, Franklin had made a midnight visit to one of his insurance agency female staff members and was caught "bare butt in the act." Jenni chuckled. Miss Ardnas was horrified. Jenni said the husband grabbed Franklin by the arm, dislocated it at the shoulder, and then gave him a straight left jab to the mouth, knocking out a tooth, followed by a right cross to the eye. Franklin ran out of the house, but the husband caught him by the neck and called 911.

The police arrived and called the EMTs. Since Franklin had more things to worry about than his clothes, he was caught on the porch pantless. "That's why Franklin has an ambulance blanket over his lap in the newspaper photo. Caught literally with his pants down," giggled Jenni, as she said goodbye and hung up.

Miss Ardnas rolled the newspaper up and burned it in the fireplace. She didn't want Cam and April to see their dad like that. Then the phone rang again. It was Jeremy.

"I knew you were upset so I didn't go into detail. Have you seen the newspaper?"

"Yes, and a friend called to fill in between the lines. It's awful," said Miss Ardnas.

"Well, the kicker was that Franklin spent most of the night in the emergency ward and then at the police station explaining why he was in this couple's house. When he was finally released around 10 the next morning, he went to his house and found the CASA waiting. Mr. Dorsey had made an appointment to ask follow-up questions from a previous interview. He was standing on the steps ready to knock when Franklin pulled into the driveway. Of course, there was Franklin, dressed in borrowed pink scrubs from the ER, prison sandals, arm in a sling, hair looking a little like a woodpecker's, purple rings around his left eye and a black gap where his tooth had been. I would guess he had an epiphany at that moment about his chances of winning a custody suit."

"That's terrible, but I'm glad I learned the whole story before I meet my friends. I'm sorry for Franklin. He's such a mess and I don't see that he will ever learn."

"Well, congratulations, Miss Ardnas. I hope this takes a big load off your mind."

"Thanks again for all your help, Jeremy."

Chapter 24. Shit

"You're going to do what?" questioned Naomi. She was on her way from the home office of the dental supply company she worked for in Cincinnati to Wyandotte for the weekend. She had pulled over to answer her cell phone.

"Alaska. I called the church where I turned down the pastorate, they still wanted me. So I told them I was coming for sure this time."

"I don't know what to say, Mark. I know you've been upset but this is a big move. Kind of sudden, isn't it?"

"The only thing is that I will miss you so much. I wish you didn't have a job here, then you could come with me."

Naomi wondered if Mark was finally going to propose. "What do you mean, come with you?" she explored.

"You could be my assistant or something."

"Your assistant!"

"Yes, I suppose I will need a secretary, assistant pastor, music director, or something."

"You jerk. I wouldn't go across the street with you."

"Naomi! What's wrong?"

"What's wrong? What's not wrong! Goodbye."

"Wait. Don't hang up. I don't understand."

"No shit! We've been dating for months, I moved down to Wyandotte to be near you and you treat me like a baby sister or secretary."

"What do you, uh, well, uh, I'm sorry that…"

"You're a 35 year old with a 15-year-old's crush on a former high school friend, who you haven't even told."

"I…I…I"

"You have unreal ambitions about religion, life and love. Grow up, Mark. Bye."

"Wait, wait, wait…."

"What?"

"I don't know what to say."

"So what's new," responded Naomi as she ended the call.

Mark tried to call back, but she wouldn't answer. His head was spinning like the propellers on a beanie cap from the forties. So many things at once were too much to handle. He knew he could turn over the production of *Hey, Zeus* to the Bible study members, he was putting his velomobile up for sale, he'd given two-weeks' notice at Two Dollar Buys, he was working out the logistics of moving to Alaska, he was preparing for ministering to a new congregation and now he was trying to decipher this thing with Naomi.

Mark paced back and forth across his room, stopping only to rearrange some books in his bookcase, straighten his pillows and bedspread, check to see if his wastebasket needed emptying, scoot his dress shoes farther under the bed and glance blankly out the window. He wasn't having any luck sorting things out but his desk was neater after stacking and restacking papers and folders.

He decided to call Jerry. Jerry's secretary said he was in all-day meetings. Mark didn't leave a message. He heard Mrs. Grassley yelling at him. Although she was partially deaf, he had probably stomped too hard or straightened the desk chair too many times.

"Sorry," he yelled down through his doorway that he had just opened.

"What are you doing up there. Laws' I thought I heard thunder."

Mark came down the stairs and paced in front of Mrs. Grassley.

"Sit down and relax. Laws' you're as antsy as a flea on a sleeping dog lying in the hot sun."

"Sorry."

"What is it?"

"I took the pastorate position in Alaska. Remember, the one I turned down months ago?"

"Well, I'll miss you. We'll all hate to see you go, but I guess that's good news for you."

"Only Naomi got angry when I explained the situation to her."

"Explained what situation?"

"That I was going and I wished she didn't have a job and could come along as my secretary or something."

"Laws' you said that? Now I get why you have that squashed drip on your tennis shoes."

"Why is she mad?"

"How old are you! And I thought I was the only one around here that was mostly blind and deaf. She loves you."

"Wow. It kind of sounded like that. Where did that come from?"

The conversation continued in that vein until Mark was interrupted by his phone. He was thinking, *thank God, Naomi is calling.*

"Hello, Naomi. I'm sorry that…"

"Naomi? This is Jerry. Hey, pal. What'd you call about? My secretary said you sounded frantic."

"It's Naomi. I told her I was leaving and…"

"What do you mean leaving?"

"I decided to call back to the church in Alaska and accept the position."

"Well, congratulations."

"… and she called me a jerk."

"I've known that since our days rooming at seminary. That sounds like something I would call you but it doesn't sound like her. She called you a jerk?"

"Yes, she did. I said I would miss her and wished she could come with me as my secretary or something. Her aunt, you heard me talk about her, Mrs. Grassley, says Naomi is in love with me. How could that be? We've just been good friends, like siblings."

"Good friends? Mark, I've learned more facts about Naomi from you than I know about my own wife. You've shown me a million photos on your cell phone of Naomi, or you and Naomi. Remember when you put all of those pictures of Miss Ardnas on our dorm room wall back in seminary and were surprised when I knew you had a crush on her?"

"How could I forget? I had no idea everyone knew I was in love."

"Well, old pal, that wasn't love, that was a crush. Now you're in love. You're the only one who doesn't realize it."

"You're kidding!"

"I know how old you are, pal, but your social development age must be about 12."

"This isn't a joking matter, Jerry."

"Who's joking? You're in love, good buddy. Take a couple of hours, lock yourself in your room and think about the last few months with Naomi."

"That's silly."

"Do it. Do it now. Do it for yourself. Do it for Naomi. I hate to talk to you like a naughty child but I will: MARK, GO TO YOUR ROOM. Bye."

Mark tried to call Naomi again. She didn't answer. He decided to take Jerry's advice.

Chapter 25. The Deal

Sam, Jake, Duke and Jenni met at Sam's cell phone store. They were all good friends because of their relationship with Mark as their former pastor or their current Bible study leader. This was mostly a business meeting despite their taking some time to socialize.

"Hear about Mark?" asked Jenni.

"Yes, going to Alaska after all. Think we can talk him out of it again?" asked Sam.

"No. From what I've heard losing his job as pastor, being told not to attend the Followers Church and the rest of the gossip about his religious beliefs and their supposedly negative impact on the community, he's fairly discouraged and ready to move on," answered Jenni.

Duke put in, "I hate to see him go that way. The guy loves people, helps everybody, and promotes social inclusion and the end of religious bigotry. What the hell's wrong with that! Figuring out human nature is harder than solving one of my friend's blind puzzles." Duke actually had a puzzle up to his ear, and Sam could hear the steel ball bearing bouncing around inside.

"Well, too many people want black-and-white answers in a color-wheel world," said Jenni. "It's all about pretending to have the truth so that religious institutions can increase their membership, raise money, build fancy churches and pay big salaries to a lot of people—power and money."

"Yes, there are lots of people who believe their opinion is truth," added Duke.

"Well, I wish Mark the best," said Jake. "He's changed our lives for the better. Got us to dream again, kept us thinking and searching for some real meaning in a shallow, cosmetic, fast food, plastic and soulless world."

Everyone nodded in agreement to Jake's comment. Then the group got down to business. Duke and Jenni negotiated a deal with Sam to buy his cell phone business on a land contract, and the number of years and payment schedule was agreed on. Sam told Jake he would turn the monthly payments over to Jake for shares in his transit company.

Jake had already sold pd's and had mortgaged his house to buy four busses that looked like trolleys. He called his company Traksi. He planned to buy two more when he had the funds. One bus ran through the center of town east to west and one went north and south, each making a pass on the strip at the edge of town that contained most of the stores, restaurants and factories. The other two busses were almost like taxis. They took calls and zigzagged through town picking up and delivering riders as needed.

The taxi/trolley took more time to arrive at individual destinations, but not having to drive a car and find parking were things that convinced people to ride. He was also getting a boost in ridership from interviews conducted for the evening news, the newspaper and radio stations. He couldn't afford ads.

Summer school students especially liked riding the Traksis with their friends in the morning and after school, because they thought riding a cheese wagon was juvenile. The price of a soft drink at most restaurants was the fare. Factory workers did some "carpooling" with the Traksis.

Jake hoped as the system became more popular that some stores would decide to improve business by handing out free Traksi rides to paying customers. Then the businesses would settle up with Jake at the end of the month. Traksis cut down on traffic, air pollution, auto accidents and was a savings to most car owners. He painted the Traksis a symbolic grass green with white pinstripes. Lettered on the side was the slogan: "The Real Green.".

Jake said, "Before you all go, I want to read a letter Mark wanted me to make copies of and give to everyone in the Bible study:

Dear Beloved Bible Study,

Well, I'm going to take the job in Alaska. I hope it's the right move. It may seem like running away, and maybe it is, but I want to be running towards something too. I'll be disappointed if they want me to tell them the truth about God as I learned it in one seminary, or to give them my personal interpretation of the translation of the single Bible I choose to read, or agree without questioning my views. You know I can't do that and am wary of anyone who says he has the truth and all the other believers and religions don't. I'm not God, holder of the truth.

When I read and reread the red verses in a red-letter Bible, I am thunderstruck. What a wonderful example! Then I look at the 2000-year history of the church, with its greed, vanity, power struggles, exclusiveness, wealth, hatred, violence, translations and interpretations --I'm depressed. Somehow man has turned religion into a team sport or a political party with people taking sides and saying they're the best. Jesus was perfect love made flesh, and since him we have had only a few bright spots—Sister Theresa, Saint Francis of Assisi, Gandhi, Dalai Lama, Schweitzer, Mandela and King. Pitiful! We will never solve the problem of Robert Burn's concept of 'man's inhumanity to man' until we conquer what Tennessee Williams called 'man's inhumanity to God.' I'm ashamed.

It should be obvious to everyone by now that God is not planning to bring about world peace. I've ended my prayers during every Sunday and Wednesday Bible study with a plea for love and harmony between nations. I'm sure thousands of ministers and millions of parishioners have done the same thousands of times for thousands of years. God sent Love (Jesus) into the world and now, I think, it's up to us to follow him.

We can't just keep praying. It's like praying for healing but not going to the doctor for help. The quickest way to stop feeling guilty about the lack of world peace is to feel that you've put it into God's hands with prayer. Ask someone who is leaving church after a sermon concerning peace what they're planning for the rest of the day. They'll say, 'Go out to eat.' 'Watch the football game and take a nap.' 'Go to a movie,' 'Get together to play cards with some friends.'

They don't say I'm going to read the one- and two-paragraph stories in the Sunday newspaper about nations they've never heard of, find a book talking about other religions and cultures, donate money to the International Red Cross, loan some money through Kiva, sign up to volunteer with Habitat for Humanity or find someone in another country to Skype with.

How about volunteering to take in a foreign exchange student from a third-world country, providing partial support for the education of a girl in Central Asia, planning to go on a mission trip to pass out HIV-AIDS information to people in poor countries and the list goes on?

It's not too late for them to Google or Bing to see what they can do out there. We're supposed to be God's eyes, hands, and feet. They can be bright spots in the world. I wonder why so many counties in the Middle East are so susceptible to being taken over by dictators. Their histories go back thousands of years—they were way ahead of Europe in mathematics, astronomy, architecture, philosophy--yet tribalism is still strong and keeps them divided politically and religiously—easy prey, I guess. I hope someone figures out how to deal with this global problem. It's our or the next generation's challenge.

I love you guys and I know you will continue to make a difference in Wyandotte and the world. I can't wait to see Hey, Zeus when you finish the video. Thank you for all your past support. Please pray for my ministry in Alaska.—Mark, a servant of Jesus

The night Mark finished his rambling letter, he slept poorly. In his nightmare he had just taken off in a jumbo jet when the seats and fuselage vanished and he found himself caught—midair--in one of the contrails of the engines. These swirling cloud streaks coalesced into a dark fog that became a tornado, and he was flung out of it into a rain storm. Before he awoke, he was perched on the side of a mountain looking at a precipitous drop into a murky canyon.

Chapter 26: Well Fitting

"We fit together so well...it's like pieces of a puzzle, the way my hand fits the curve of your hip and the way your head rests on my shoulder, the way our hands just melt into one, and the way I feel complete when I'm with you...like the picture's finally completed and I'll never have to wonder what I'm missing," appeared as a message on Madison's email page with a note saying it was sent by a mobile device.

The computer beeped and then appeared: "I didn't write that and it's not great poetry like I usually read to you, but it says how I feel. I'm on my way over. Please, let's set a date."

Madison ran to the closet, pulled on a windbreaker, slipped on some sneakers, grabbed her purse and ran to the door. She hadn't known it was raining, so by the time she reached her car she was soaked. When she pulled her car out of the apartment parking lot, she turned toward the library. She entered the building and went to the farthest, most concealed booth to use a computer. In her head she had been writing another critique of the school system, so she decided to enter it on the computer and then send it to her home computer.

Delayed Education

Before children go to school they learn to walk, go to the bathroom by themselves, speak, do chores, avoid things that are dangerous, and get along in social units. All this happens because the children want or have to learn these skills.

Many preschoolers also learn such things as how to read, cook a little, change their siblings' diapers, and run video equipment. Another reason that preschoolers learn so quickly is that they are surrounded by older people–parents, siblings, neighbors. They're not part of an age-related independent subgroup.

Once upon a time, children wanted to become adults. Now they have trouble because adults want to be children. The attire of children of yesteryear was sneakers, T-shirts and short pants. Kids couldn't wait to own and wear long pants. Now short pants are the attire of everyone from cradle to grave, sometimes even in colder climes or months.

Research shows that boys often don't permanently leave home until they are about 29 years old. Kids used to play with toys that were miniatures of tools used by adults during work. Childhood has been extended and children now live in an independent subculture, with their own clothing styles, language, behavior and electronic toys that adults don't understand. Their toys now are often violent, sexy, reckless or silly video games that have nothing to do with productive adult life.

They don't want to leave this culture and become adults, because then they'd have to be independent and pay their own way. Now teens have independence–their own cars, TV's, mobile phones, computers, rooms, games–provided by parents.

Kids don't have to or want to learn to be adults any sooner than they have to. Financial responsibility is delayed, sexual responsibility is delayed, marriage is delayed, and, not surprisingly, education is delayed.

Madison felt that she was writing about herself.

"Gotcha, honey. I didn't receive a response from you by email, so I knew you were out," exclaimed William as he put both hands on Madison's shoulders.

Fighting off the electric sensations that normally coursed through her body when he massaged her shoulders or feet or gave her a big hug, she responded: "How did you know I was at the library?"

"Your car is in the back row. Couldn't miss it when I started cruising the places you like to go."

"Well, here I am. Why did you email me?"

"It's time, Madison. You need to make a decision about us. Let's go someplace and talk. Coffee shop, wine bar or ice cream sundae parlor?"

"I don't feel like any of those."

"What's wrong? Am I pushing too hard?"

"To be honest, for me, yes. I don't think we're going to work."

"But you love me and said you would marry me."

"True."

"Well, I sent you an email. You didn't get it but it went something like this." William pulled a chair up next to her: "'We fit together like pieces of a puzzle, the way my hand fits the curve of your hip and the way your head rests on my shoulder, the way our hands melt into one, and the way I feel complete when I'm with you.' Isn't that the way you feel?"

"How do I say it? I love you but I also love my independence. I don't want to be known as somebody's wife, Mrs. William Marshall. I would love to make you happy by fulfilling your dream, but that's not going to play well if I don't fulfill my dream. It's like the directions during an ocean liner drill, 'Put on your life preserver and then help someone put on theirs.' In other words you don't have to drown yourself to save someone else. You both can survive."

"So what does that mean for us? Do we just date until we're 85, no children or grandchildren, and then still have separate accommodations when they put us in a nursing home?"

"Good question. Sometimes I want to have children, but then at times I know I need to grow up. The wick of my maternity candle is growing short, but if I don't feel ready, then I don't feel ready."

"Do you still want to date?"

"I don't want to get in your way of finding the perfect wife and having a home, children and grandchildren. I think you need to move on, get over me, find someone who fits you like the puzzle you're talking about."

"I don't like this conversation. I thought we did fit."

In frustration, William kissed her on the forehead and walked out of the library. She put her head on her arm and felt the tears soak through her windbreaker.

Chapter 27: The End

Mark had to quickly wrap up business in Wyandotte, because he had promised that he wouldn't keep his new congregation in suspense. Previously, the Alaskan congregation had been so excited waiting for Mark that they had decorated the little church and baked the community's favorite desserts for the welcoming ceremony. But then he had called and said he'd changed his mind. He couldn't keep them waiting long, because he was sure they were fearful of *deja vu*.

The two weeks while Mark was finishing at Two Dollar Buys and packing his clothes and books, Naomi purposely delayed returning to Wyandotte. She had scheduled all of her clients in the southern part of the state, staying in motels, and even remaining on the road during weekends. She wouldn't answer Mark's calls and wouldn't call Mark, even when her friends begged her to do so. He even called her using Duke's phone, but as soon as she heard his voice she hung up.

All their friends knew both Naomi and Mark were miserable, but there seemed no way to resolve their differences. The Bible study had a subdued farewell dinner at Denny's Restaurant, and then he was gone.

When Naomi found out Mark had moved out, she finished up her business calls that week and finally came home. Mrs. Grassley was sitting on the sofa when Naomi walked heavily through the doorway pulling her suitcase. The wrinkles and sunken areas below Mrs. Grassley's eyes had grown and deepened. Naomi looked even worse, with dark circles around her bloodshot eyes and atypical creases at the corners of her mouth. Naomi walked over, bent down and gave her aunt a kiss on the cheek. Mrs. Grassley was visually weeping for Naomi and unable to choke out a hello.

Mrs. Grassley took a deep breath, removed the contents of an envelope, and said, "These are yours, honey."

The aunt dropped two items into Naomi's hand. Naomi looked down at her palm to see a diamond ring and an airline ticket.

The End

About the Author

Joel Robbins is a retired high school English and journalism teacher and a retired journalist. He grew up in the Midwest, living in Ohio, Indiana and Kentucky. He served two terms, a total of two-and-a-half years, in Azerbaijan in the Peace Corps, where he taught English as a foreign language and instructional methodology at Şəki Pedagogical College and Khazar University.

He is married and has two children and four grandchildren. He loves to read, hike, volunteer at a Florida state park, and travel. He has visited more than 40 countries.

Welsh Pears is Robbins' first novel. *Ursa Caucasia* and *Appalachian Tales* are his other works of fiction. He also self-published a previous book, *InGear: Peace Corps & Beyond*.

He lives in Florida with his wife, Sara, and cat, Sugar.